PENGUIN BOOKS

REJECTION: A SUMATRAN ODYSSEY

Ashadi Siregar first came to public attention as a writer in Indonesia in the early 1970s for his humorous novels about campus life, which were bestsellers and are still in print. Many were turned into film. Ashadi was born in North Sumatra in 1945, the year that Indonesia declared its independence from Dutch colonial rule at the end of World War II, and spent his childhood there. Upon graduation from high school in 1964, he moved to Yogyakarta in Java, where he completed his university studies in political science at Gadjah Mada University, and has lived there ever since.

Apart from his literary work, Ashadi Siregar has had a stellar academic career. Until his retirement in 2010, he was a faculty member at his alma mater in the Department of Political Studies and the Department of Communications, as well as teaching in the Postgraduate Centre for Performance Studies. From 1992–2014 he was director of the Institute for Research, Education and Publishing (LP3Y), a non-government institute in Yogyakarta that focuses on the development of journalism and journalistic training.

Ashadi lives in Yogyakarta.

Jennifer Lindsay is an award-winning writer, translator, researcher and cultural ambassador whose breadth of work reflects her deeply lived understanding of Indonesia. She studied in New Zealand, the United States and Australia.

Jennifer has translated many literary works from Indonesian into English. Her translations include four anthologies of essays by Goenawan Mohamad; Leila S Chudori's novel *Nadira*; Hersri Setiawan's *Buru Island: A Prison Memoir*; Linus Suryadi's poetic work *Pariyem's Confession*; and short stories by various writers.

Jennifer has edited, translated and contributed essays to many academic volumes, writing on cultural policy, cultural history, performance, media, and language. She also directed a documentary film about Indonesia's cultural missions during the Soekarno period.

An Honorary Associate Professor in the School of Culture, History and Language at the Australian National University, she now focuses on translation and divides her time between Indonesia and Australia.

Rejection: A Sumatran Odyssey

Ashadi Siregar

Translated by
Jennifer Lindsay

PENGUIN BOOKS

An imprint of Penguin Random House

PENGUIN BOOKS

USA | Canada | UK | Ireland | Australia
New Zealand | India | South Africa | China | Southeast Asia

Penguin Books is part of the Penguin Random House group of companies
whose addresses can be found at global.penguinrandomhouse.com

Published by Penguin Random House SEA Pte Ltd
9, Changi South Street 3, Level 08-01,
Singapore 486361

First published in Penguin Books by Penguin Random House SEA 2022

Copyright of original work, *Menolak Ayah* © Ashadi Siregar 2018
English Translation Copyright © Jennifer Lindsay 2022

ISBN 9789815017069

Typeset in Caslon by MAP Systems, Bangalore, India

www.penguin.sg

This translation was generously supported by
Tony and Helen Reid
Alan Feinstein
Rosalia Sciortino

Contents

PART ONE: Marga

Chapter 1   3

Chapter 2   25

Chapter 3   43

PART TWO: Begu

Chapter 4   63

Chapter 5   75

Chapter 6   91

Chapter 7   107

PART THREE: Inang

Chapter 8   125

Chapter 9   139

Chapter 10   149

Chapter 11   157

PART FOUR: War

Chapter 12   171

Chapter 13   187

Chapter 14   205

PART FIVE: Amang

Chapter 15   233

Chapter 16   243

Chapter 17   257

Chapter 18   267

Chapter 19   281

Chapter 20   295

List of main characters   313

Timeline of historical events   319

Glossary   323

PART ONE

MARGA

Chapter 1

From the slope of the hill, the view opened wide below. The lake surface was a blue mirror reflecting clumps of white cotton. The breeze did not stir the calm surface of the lake. It was like a painting of moving clouds. A road wound along the edge of the lake, and from a distance you could hear the sound of the bugle horns on the bus that travelled between Medan and Tapanuli and as far as Central Sumatra. This had to be the Sibualbuali bus. The breeze creeping to the foothills carried the musical sound of the bugle horns. So melancholy. It felt like the distant past. So nostalgic. How he longed to be inside that bus.

It felt like no time at all since he had been dangling off the back of a bus, nimble as a monkey. He had been a bus conductor on the Medan-Bukittinggi route. It took a lot of skill to climb on top of the bus using the ladder at the back to arrange the passengers' luggage on the roof. Then, when everything was neatly ordered and covered with a tarpaulin, he would clamber down and get back into the bus through the back window. At every town, the bus would stop at the terminal, and he would have to climb back up to the roof again and hand the luggage to the passengers getting off. And of course he had to check the post. On the roof of the bus was a special postal box for transporting the post between districts.

3

How he missed that red bus that travelled from town to town. How he missed the smell of burning diesel. How he missed the shrill peal of the bugle horns and the chatter of the passengers. And yes, he missed the passengers who came and went, some of whose faces he had forgotten, but others who remained vivid in his memory.

He was not a bus conductor now. Here he was with a group of armed soldiers. It was wartime. The central government of the Republic of Indonesia in Jakarta called it a rebellion. Some called it a regional revolt—a few disgruntled army leaders in the regions expressing their dissatisfaction with the government of President Sukarno.

Morning roll call was over. The commander had given a speech. Every morning it was the same. Speeches, speeches, speeches, and never any fighting. Long speeches about the fight, about regional development, about the central government, and he understood none of it, or how any of it related to what he was ordered to do here and now. Even though it was holding up buses. Check the post, round up the passengers. Take anyone who turns out to be a government civil servant, especially army or police. Today he had not joined the ones who had gone below. He and a few others were keeping watch from a distance. They were checking that the passengers put up no armed resistance, but the chances of that were slim. Now that there were armed rebels in the Tapanuli interior, the police never rode public buses. And if any did, you could be sure that on their identity papers in the column for occupation was written 'trader' or 'staff of a private company'.

From the slope of the hill where he lay with his fellow fighters, he could only gaze at buses in the distance. The grass was covered with pine needles. An aroma of fermentation rose from the brown, drying needles. But he imagined he could also smell the bitter diesel fumes from the shoe-box sized bus in the distance below. That lilting sound of the bugle horns at the bends. His place on the back seat of the bus. That throb of the engine that seemed to creep over his skin. That hard seat. Ah, travelling in the dead of night, with the shake of the roaring engine as it gasped along the pot-holed, steep and winding roads.

The long-distance buses that connected Sumatra's towns were usually assembled locally. Only a few engine and chassis parts were originals from European factories. The body of the bus was made of wood, beautifully crafted. Most of the workshops for building bus and truck chassis were in the Lubuk Pakam area. The bus company owners gave their companies names like Sibualbuali, Lubukraya, Dolok Martimbang, Sibayak or names of mountains in the Tapanuli and Karo areas. There were also names of rivers, like Batang Gadis. Usually, the bus-company owners were Batak. Every bus was painted in bright colours and fitted out with bugle horns, and passengers often chose which bus to ride depending on the driver's skill at playing melodies on them.

Those tunes blasted on the bugle horns were like the sole local entertainment. As the buses passed by, people would stop whatever they were doing to listen to the melodious call. Sibualbuali drivers were renowned. Their buses had covered the Medan to Bukittinggi route for ages and their drivers were known as the star performers of the road. The buses were an integral part of the lives of inter-town travellers. Men drinking rice wine at the roadstalls along the route would learn clever riffs on their guitars imitating the bugle horn tunes. These tunes would evolve into drunken song, with the original composers forgotten. Oh yes, the Sibualbuali buses became legend all along the roads of East Sumatra, Tapanuli and Central Sumatra. And even though he was just a Sibualbuali bus conductor, he shared the pride of being part of it. But he had to leave it all behind.

Should he regret it? Would his life's path have stopped there? Bus conductor, moving up to driver or workshop chief, with the pinnacle maybe becoming head of some town office, like Siantar, Tarutung, or Bukittinggi? Would that have been his life? There was his grandfather, a man of great spiritual powers called a *datu bolon*. There was his father, a big shot in Jakarta. And him? Would he have just been swallowed up on the Medan-Bukittinggi route?

And now, here he was, among these soldiers most of whom he had not known before, or at least they had not known him. He had come across some of them in Medan or Siantar. He remembered them, but they did not remember him.

Yes, here they were. One squad. And who were these people? Among them was an ex-policeman who once took the registration papers of his bus. His style was to find reasons to strictly implement the law. After the driver handed over his licence, the policeman bellowed, 'papers!'

Spot checks. Indicator light not working. One brake light dead. Windscreen wipers not working. Too much exhaust. Anything at all according to the letter of the law. If necessary, even the bugle horns could become a serious issue. The dangerous time was after the 15th of the month, with pay day still two weeks away. The policeman would scan for misdemeanours, eyes moving according to the needs of his pocket. Tondi remembered that policeman's face well, because he was the one Tondi had to meet behind the mahogany trees. He couldn't remember how many times. Always to pay a bribe to get the papers back. The bus inspection was just for a bigger pay-off. Police were the inter-city bus thieves.

Then there was the soldier with a red insignia on his arm who had once beaten him.

'You dare fight a soldier, huh?'

It had been over something trivial. He had elbowed some member of the soldier's family—younger brother, nephew or some such—in a queue. It was at the Rex cinema and the queue was for scalped tickets Tondi was selling. It was no big deal. He had not elbowed him deliberately. When people are pushing in a crowd, this is normal, after all. He gave it no more thought. But that soldier had hunted him down to the Padang restaurant in the market and beaten him black and blue. One army hothead against a civilian. Well, we'd see if he was so tough now when he was a rebel and had to fight against the national army.

Or take that civil servant over there, the man who usually wandered around the street stalls booming, 'Taxes . . . taxes . . . taxes . . .'

That was why people called the local markets 'Taxes'. To market sellers, any dealing with the government meant taxes. Selling inside or outside the market would incur duty—whether the goods were sold or not. And if you did not have money to pay duties, then even your fried bananas would be seized. Needless to say, those oil-soaked fried bananas would never find their way into the cash registers of Sukarno's government over in Jakarta. Yep, government officials were the small stall-holders' extortioners.

And there were many others. The war had brought him together with them in one squad. They certainly did not know or remember him, because he was just some youth who did not even count in their world, the world of people with power in the town of Siantar. He and his friends might hang around the cinema and scalp tickets. Youth like this were called 'louts', and once labelled it was no wonder they became targets of the police and low-ranking soldiers. Not to maintain order, but because of competition. When the cinema showed American films, the police and soldiers would also hunt down tickets to scalp to subsidize their income. And though they might be small fry in the power scale of things, they could still use their power to grab small-scale economies by oppressing small-scale competition.

Tondi was fed up with power. He was just the son of a fried-banana seller in the town. They were just low-level, small-town bureaucrats, but in that town, they thought they were big shots. The only authority he respected was the police wearing white helmets emblazoned PM, the military police, because when they turned up, the local police or soldiers on ticket-scalping duty scarpered.

Uniforms—police, army or public servant—can turn someone into a creature that enjoys power. But here he was now in a soldier's uniform and he did not get even a whiff of that power. Maybe because they were in the forest? How can you show off your power to monkeys, apes, snakes and jungle animals?

It had been some months since he left Siantar. Longing for the town seethed within him. Siantar, officially Pematangsiantar, was a drive-through town for traffic from Medan to areas in the south;

the plains of Toba, Angkola, Sipirok and Mandailing, down to the lowlands of Minang and Riau. But now, here in this Toba interior, he was together with people who once oppressed him, in utterly different conditions. If it were not for this fight against the central government, he would never be on the same level as them.

His name was Tondinihuta, but his mother, grandfather and neighbours all called him Tondi. He was cleaning his knapsack and rifle. And just take a look at this rifle—what use would it be if he had to face a battalion in convoy? When he got those few days of training along with other volunteers, the sergeant had told them that every company had weapons, from handguns to rifles and machine guns. And artillery. But during the entire training he never once learned how to use all those weapons. Sure, he got to look at them and others besides. Just look, mind, when the instructor showed them. The rest of the time was spent learning how to march, lying prone, and listening to lectures. The training was only a few days in the forest on the shores of Lake Toba, and most of it was endless lecturing that bored him stiff.

'We're fighting for our region's development!'

Yeah, yeah, sure! Tondi nodded at every utterance even though none of this meant anything to him. Then he received his weapon. Was it possible to win battles with training like this? Especially when he got to know some of the other soldiers. The only thing those army, police and public servants had done until now was keep alert for chances to make money. Come on—what kind of 'development' were they fighting for?

The majority of members of Tondi's squad were ex- army and police. Among the public servants were some who had also fought in the war for Indonesia's independence. Of course, they did not need extra training in fighting. They were given ranks according to the ones they had before, during the independence war. They looked imposing enough in their uniforms, but when they had to run or climb hills, they soon got out of breath. Most of them were middle aged, or at least over thirty. Only Tondi and five others were young, and because of their youth they had never experienced battle.

When Tondi joined, he had already dropped out of school of his own choice, but the other five had been tempted away from their high school desks.

So far, he had not been involved in any fighting. Their main activity was to hold up buses, check the passengers and the post, then retreat into the forest. Tondi had no idea what these hold-ups were about. Maybe it was just to show that there were still bands of rebels controlling this area beside Lake Toba. But lately, the hold-ups had slowed because the buses travelled in convoys with protection from the feared Siliwangi division of the national army. You would never hold up buses travelling in a convoy like that.

Tondi's squad was part of the army group that had retreated from Medan with Colonel Simbolon. He had joined them from the beginning, as part of Pardapdap's platoon. Pardapdap had been a sergeant major in the military police, and was one of the soldiers who had left his national army post to join the rebels in the forest. He was also Tondi's neighbour and lived in one of a row of simple bamboo houses in the neighbourhood of Pematang near the Bah Bolon river.

Pardapdap lived there with his wife. It was just the two of them as their children had married and gone to live in other towns far from Siantar. Pardapdap seemed to be lonely at home. When he returned in the evening from guard duty, he would often ask Tondi to join him at the coffee stall. They would chat and play chess. Usually, Pardapdap would talk about his experiences during the independence war days. Tondi would complain about his fate as a bus conductor. He wanted to be like his father who, after the independence war, had gone on to bigger things in Jakarta. Pardapdap knew Tondi's father from the Japanese occupation time, when he had been his commander in Sibolga. He could sympathize with Tondi. He knew that Tondi's father was now someone important in Jakarta, but he also knew that here in Siantar, Tondi was just a boy raised by his mother who sold fried bananas. A boy who had to leave school because his mother could not afford the fees.

Could he offer the boy a change in destiny? He remembered that after the war for independence, young fighters of school age were given opportunities to study on a government-bond scheme. Maybe there were opportunities like that now. But then, right around that time, the regional struggle had begun. Now the enemy was not the Dutch. As Pardapdap saw it, this war could be the gateway to a different life. Before independence, he had been a truck driver. During the Japanese occupation, he had become a soldier and when the independence war was over, he had received army education until he joined the military police.

That night in December, Christmas was still in the air. Pardapdap brought his official white jeep home. Two other military policemen were in the jeep with him. He knocked on Tondi's door.

'We're leaving,' he said.

Tondi grabbed the three sets of clothes he owned and bundled them into a sarong. Then he said goodbye to his mother. He had already told her what he was going to do. She could only stare as he left. All those years ago, her husband had left to fight like this. And now, her son. It felt as though a lump of iron was pressing on her chest. But there were no tears.

The jeep headlights were not very bright, only a dim yellow beam cut the black of the night. Pardapdap was driving like the devil.

'We have to rush,' he said. 'Captain Pohan telephoned me earlier. He was my commander during the war.' He seemed to be directing this explanation at Tondi. 'Colonel Simbolon's subordinate, Lieutenant Colonel Wahab Makmur has betrayed him. Colonel Simbolon has left Medan and is now moving towards Tapanuli. Wahab Makmur has given orders for his arrest. We have to get there first. What will the world say of a subordinate arresting his own commander?'

This was all too murky for Tondi. He had never understood the ins and outs of military affairs. Until now, his neighbour, Sergeant Major Pardapdap, Military Police, was the most senior ranked army officer he had met. Those other fellows, Lieutenant Colonel Wahab Makmur, the commander of the army regiment based in Siantar, and Colonel Simbolon, the regimental commander based in Medan, were in a power stratosphere far too high for him.

The town of Siantar was now well behind them. At the village of Sinaksak, the soldiers who had been ordered to block Colonel Simbolon's entourage lay in wait. Pardapdap turned on the jeep's flashing red light and siren as he approached the soldiers behind the barricade. He knew the soldier in command. It wasn't clear what they said. Tondi could only vaguely hear Pardapdap's words:

'The important thing is that you've carried out your orders. But it must not come to bloodshed between us.'

'Yes, *Tulang*,' the commander answered. His military rank was higher than Pardapdap's, but kinship surpassed that hierarchy. In Batak custom, tulang is a male relative on the maternal side, and must be highly revered.

When Colonel Simbolon's group arrived, the motor convoy stopped. Colonel Simbolon got out of his car and greeted the commander of the barricade. This was the first time Tondi had set eyes on the army commander who was the talk of the coffee stalls. Pardapdap greeted Captain Pohan and explained the situation in Siantar.

'Many do not agree with Wahab Makmur's actions. They're standing by to give you safe passage to Tapanuli, Sir,' he said to the captain.

So it was that Pardapdap's jeep led the way, avoiding the centre of the town where barricades had been set up. The convoy followed the small roads, leaving dust behind them in the cover of night lit only by a thin moon. Pardapdap knew this area like the back of his hand. It was where he had been a guerrilla fighter during the war for independence. They travelled southwards towards Prapat, a small town on the edge of Lake Toba. And this was the beginning of Tondi's long journey, a journey that commenced towards dawn at the end of 1956.

* * *

A year had gone by. Pardapdap was now leading rebel soldiers who were supposed to be a platoon. That was why he was a lieutenant, according to the rank he had before during the years of Indonesia's fight for independence. Tondi was a member of this platoon made up of ex-soldiers, police, and civilians, who had just wanted to sign up. They called themselves freedom fighters, which was the term used during the independence-struggle days. But the central government in Jakarta called these raggle-taggle troops a rebel army.

At the beginning, their base had been in Balige. But air force planes often flew low overhead in that small town, probably looking for the rebel headquarters to bomb. So they left. They went into the jungle, westwards of Lake Toba, around places like Dolok Sanggul and Oman Ganjang. Some went to the east, to the area of Parsoburan and Huta Garoga. If you drew a straight line from these places to Rantau Prapat in Labuhan Batu, all you would find is untamed jungle. It was a huge area under their control. The central army had control only of the towns connected by paved provincial roads from Dutch times. But the small settlements along the tracks in the jungle had been virtually unchanged for centuries. They were still isolated and had escaped government attention both in colonial times and now in the era of independence.

Tondi was part of the group of rebel soldiers based around Lintong Nihuta, between Balige and Dolok Sanggul. Attacks by the Jakarta government army had become increasingly fierce here. The news was that Colonel Simbolon had gone to Padang to join the central command under Lieutenant Colonel Ahmad Husein. Communications between the forces still in the Toba area and their central command were now cut.

Tondi was beginning to be bored with jungle life. Then, one day, he was ordered to carry a letter to Bukittinggi. He did not know why he had been chosen for this task. Out of the blue, his platoon commander, Pardapdap, had taken him to meet the battalion commander.

'He's been to Bukittinggi often,' said Pardapdap, by way of introduction. The battalion commander, before entering the jungle, had the rank of lieutenant in the Indonesian national army. During the years of fighting for Indonesian independence he had risen to the rank of captain, and this was his rank again now. So his rank rose and fell according to his fate as defender of the republic. He looked Tondi up and down.

'Recently I ordered him to accompany a communications officer to fix our platoon radio,' Pardapdap added.

Still the battalion commander did not react. Tondi thought about that mission when he had accompanied the communications sergeant, just to crank the pedals of the dynamo that provided electricity for the radio. He had watched the sergeant turn the dial looking for the short wave, but the radio was mostly used to find western music. There in the jungle, the songs broadcast by Radio Malaya or Radio Australia provided them with some entertainment.

'He's the grandson of Ompu Silangit,' Pardapdap added. Now Tondi caught a flash in the eyes of the battalion commander.

'But he's too young,' the battalion commander said. 'How old are you?' he asked Tondi, addressing him in the Batak language.

'Seventeen, going on eighteen,' Tondi replied, also in Batak.

'Hmm,' the commander exchanged glances with Pardapdap.

'He can visit his grandfather first, to ask him the best way to go,' Pardapdap said.

'Very well. You are to take this letter to Bukittinggi. You do not need to know the contents. In short, this is an important letter from the commander of our forces to our top command in Central Sumatra. Whatever happens, you must not get caught by the central army. If you are caught, you must first destroy this letter. How you do that is up to you. What is important is to get to Bukittinggi as fast as you can.'

When he said 'our command', this meant it was higher than the battalion commander. Was this the commander of a regiment, a division, or what? Tondi did not want to know. He was just a soldier without any rank so there was no need to bother about military hierarchy. All he felt was a pang of joy that he was going to leave that place.

* * *

Tondi was now separated from his squad. Alone on the ancient path. First, he stole into his grandfather's small hamlet, set on a hill between Laguboti and Balige. The hamlet, fenced with dense thorny bamboo thicket, consisted of only about ten houses and was not on any paved road. The hill was far from the main road, at least five kilometres away. There was only a dirt road. From the hill, you could see straight to Lake Toba. His grandfather was a newcomer who had ended up there. He came from a distant village, at the foot of Pusuk Buhit mountain beside Lake Toba.

This was his grandfather, Ompu Silangit. He was known all over the Toba area. No one knew his exact age, and he himself never talked about his birth or his past. Only the old people in the hamlet talked about when Ompu Silangit was young and how he had joined the war between King Singamangaraja XII and the Dutch. The Batak War. He had left his own village at Pusuk Buhit and joined the king's guards at Bakkara, the centre of the Singamangaraja kingdom. When King Singamangaraja XII died, the Dutch captured Ompu Silangit and imprisoned him for a long time. He still followed the ancient religion that worshipped *Debata Mulajadi na Bolon*, the Supreme Source of All Life, and he venerated nature and good spirits. This was the Batak religion more commonly called *Ugomo Malim*, which the Batak people followed long before the coming of Islam or Christianity.

Ompu Silangit lived in a house at the top of the hill, set apart from the other houses on the slope and outside the bamboo thicket fence that encircled them. From below, his house with its protective trees seemed enveloped in magic. It stood beneath a dense, shady banyan tree beside the local graveyard. This was the only place that local authorities could find for Ompu Silangit when the Dutch had asked them to give him land.

Tondi knew this place well. During the Japanese occupation and the years of struggle for Indonesia's independence that followed, this is where he had stayed and first gone to school. It was not a traditional style North Sumatran house people call *ruma bolon*, with a huge, curved roof and elaborate carvings, but just a plain house with wooden walls and floors, and a tin roof. The floor was raised about one and a half metres from the ground. The space underneath was clean, and this was where his grandmother used to do her weaving.

During the day the house was quiet. People rarely came to visit. Initially, this was because the house was a place to avoid. In the Dutch times, after Ompu Silangit was released from prison he was forbidden to return to his own ancestral village, or *huta*. As a kind of exile, he was given land on the western side of the lake, far from his home. This is where he built his simple house. He was only a freeloader on other people's land. This is why he did not have a traditional style house. You can only build a house like that in your own huta.

In the beginning, Ompu Silangit had been an outcast. His raised house under the ancient banyan tree was not just a residence but a place of exile. If people did visit, they would come secretly at night so that local security officials would not see. Once, someone reported a visitor who was then called in to the district office where the police tortured him. But over time people came visiting more openly, after the district head, a Batak, often came to visit.

After the Dutch fled Indonesia, Ompu Silangit was actually free to return to his own land. He had the right to repair his traditional house and live there to continue the position of his father, his father's father and all those before him who became *raja bius* or traditional leader. But Ompu Silangit did not return to his ancestral land at the foot of the Pusuk Buhit mountain. The traditional house destroyed in Dutch times was gone now. It was not that he was breaking with the past, but he felt it was not fitting for him to build and live in such a house.

So now he lived here. And even though it was simple, the house still had an aura. Neighbours would not visit just to pass the time of day. Usually, people would come because they wanted to ask for healing or for advice in solving some family problem. The atmosphere in the house was always calm. The neighbours' pigs would snort and roam around the whole hamlet, but they never set foot in Ompu Silangit's yard. Ompu Silangit himself did not keep pigs, not even chickens. As Tondi remembered, when he stayed there, he only ever ate meat if the neighbours brought it. His grandmother would cook it, but especially for him. His grandparents only ate vegetables and fish from the river or the lake.

* * *

As Tondi began to climb the hill, night fell. It was so dark he could not even see his hand. A sliver of light shining through a crack in the wall was his magnet. He entered the yard of the house, feeling like an insect seeking warmth. He walked up the wooden steps. The sound of his shoes made a soft thud. For a moment he stopped stock-still before the door. He could hear his grandfather inside, clearing his throat.

'*Masuk ma daompung,*' his grandfather said in Batak from behind the door, inviting him in. 'Enter, my grandson.' The tone was even. As though he had been waiting for some time.

Tondi took off his shoes, all the time wondering whether his grandfather knew that he was coming. Then again, his grandfather could address anyone as 'grandson'. He pushed open the door. The light from the lamp blinded his eyes. He sat on the floor on a woven mat and leant against the wall. Ompu Silangit looked directly at him. Tondi approached and greeted him, then sat facing his grandfather, took off his knapsack and placed it on the floor.

Nothing had changed in that room. It was as though time had stopped in the whole house. Since he was small, as far back as he could remember, his grandfather's shoulder-length hair had been silver. When his grandfather went outside the house, he usually wrapped his head with a white cloth like the turbans that Muslims who have been on the *haj* wear. The walls were still dull, with stains here and there from his grandmother's betel nut, streaks of black from lamp soot, and charcoal scratchings that Tondi had made when he was a child. Everything was recorded in that space.

His grandfather was never one for small talk. So Tondi had to get to the point. That he was now part of the rebel army that was in the jungle. That his mother was still in Siantar. That when he left her, she was still selling fried bananas by the railway bridge. That since the time he met his father when his grandmother died, he had had no further contact with him. His father never sent any news. No letters at all. Tondi said all this calmly, while suppressing a pressure like sharp stones crawling in his chest, crawling up to his eyelids, hurting his eyes.

Ompu Silangit merely took a deep breath while keeping his gaze fixed on Tondi.

'So now you want to fight,' he said slowly, as though to himself.

Their conversation had been in the Batak language. In this house Tondi never spoke Indonesian, or Malay as his grandfather called it. Nor did anyone who came to visit. But Tondi knew that his grandfather could speak Malay because he had heard him speak it once in Siantar. As far as Tondi knew, that was the only time his grandfather ever went to Siantar. It was when he had just finished junior high school and was going to start high school. His grandmother, though, had come to visit a few times.

'No, I don't want to fight. I just wanted to leave Siantar. I didn't know what else to do when I had to stop school. It was Commander Pardapdap who ordered me to see you, Grandfather. He said he had been here once,' Tondi said.

'Yes, I know who he is,' Ompu Silangit said. 'He used to be under your father when he joined the Japanese army in Sibolga. Yes, he has been here.'

'He said you could show me the way to Bukittinggi.'

'Show you the way. Oh yes, the way. But will you get to your destination? Come, eat now.'

His grandfather rose and walked slowly to a room at the back, which was used for keeping food. It was near the steps at the back of the house above the kitchen. The kitchen hearth for cooking was made of three river stones, each the size of a coconut.

Tondi followed his grandfather. Since his wife's death, Ompu Silangit spent every night alone in the house. The room above the kitchen was lit by a single small oil lamp. Rice, vegetables and grilled fish were already set out. As though prepared for a guest.

Tondi descended the wooden steps, lit the fire in the hearth that was already stacked with dry wood, and heated water in the kettle on the hearth. Soundlessly. There was only the hiss of steam and the crackle of fire. Since he was a boy, Tondi had become used to his grandfather's soundless movement, without talking. Only his grandmother would humour him by listening to his stories of playing in the fields, and she would tell him stories about the spirits of the lake. But now silence had blanketed the house. His grandmother was no more.

The kettle boiled. Tondi put out the fire by scattering the embers. He lifted the kettle, black with soot. Without saying a word, he poured water into the porcelain cup with coffee. It looked as though everything had been prepared since evening. His grandfather must have known he was coming.

Ompu Silangit never ate at night. Usually, his food was brought to him in the front room, where there was a place to eat. All matters of the stomach had to be finished before twilight. The front room was always clean before sunset.

So here was Tondi eating in silence in the back room. His grandfather hugged the hot mug with his two hands. His eyes shone softly beneath his white eyebrows. Tondi continued with his head bowed, engrossed in his food, but his thoughts were flying everywhere.

What would the path shown to him be like? A path is a line made from one point to another. From one place to the next. But it also might not go anywhere, because a long path can still only go around and around in one place. Every person follows his path. There are times when a father shows the path for his child to follow. There are those who prepare that path, smooth the way, so the child can step forward without tripping. So to find a path in this life is good fortune. But Tondi had not yet come across this good fortune.

He finished eating. His grandfather stood and moved to the front room. You could not hear his steps. Unlike Tondi, who made the floorboards creak. His grandfather pointed to the corner where he usually slept. This was the sign that there was to be no more conversation that night. Tondi went to another corner. The night was on the threshold of dawn. The wind carried the cold from the lake, creeping through the cracks in the wooden walls. There was little time left for sleep.

The next morning, they followed the path along the ridge of the hills. His grandfather pulled up the fish net he had set in the stream the previous night. The stream was perfectly clear, flowing from the mountains surrounding Siborong-borong, towards Lake Toba. You could see fish swimming in the stream. His grandfather had put fragrant grass in the fish trap to attract the fish.

'*Goarmu, Tondinihuta. Ahu do na manggoarimu,*' his grandfather said to him, speaking Batak. 'Your name is Tondinihuta. It was I who gave you that name.'

Tondi remained silent.

'You were born in Siantar. When were you born?'

'In 1940,' Tondi replied. 'Eighteen years ago,' he added, when he realized that to his grandfather his birth had no connection to the modern calendar. He had his own calendar.

'As the first-born grandchild, from the moment you were born, your name should have been used by anyone to address your *amang*, your father. He should be called *Amani Tondi*, Father of Tondi. And the same goes for me. As your grandfather, your *ompung*, I should be called *Ompuni Tondi*, Grandfather of Tondi. But it did not turn out that way. Your name did not stick to your amang and ompung.

Tondi remained bowed in silence before his grandfather.

'When you were born, your father was still very young. Your father wanted to give you a name from the book of his religion, the Christian religion he learnt at his Dutch school. But I named you Tondinihuta. You need to know what it means. And why I gave you that name . . .

'*Tondi* means spirit, soul, the spirit of life. Huta has more than the common meaning of village. Remember this. It means the residence that becomes the source of life, the source that unites children and grandchildren of a community. So your name means the spirit of a community's land.

'No matter where a Batak roams, their home is their huta. But where is your huta? You were born in a time of confusion. The place where you lived was not your huta. And our clan or *marga* does not have its huta here, either. Because I was stranded here, you do not have a huta. The path you must travel is still long, and I cannot be with you along the way,' his ompung said softly.

Tondi was taken aback. His mind swirled with memories. When he was small, his ompung had taken him to the village at the foot of Pusuk Buhit a few times. Another time, he had gone with him to the summit of the mountain, a young man carrying him. He had gone there again when he was in junior high school, walking himself this time. His ompung often made them stop to rest on the slopes, unlike the previous time. Age was clearly creeping up on his grandfather's worn body. But the view of the lake and the natural wall of the Barisan hills quickly redeemed all exhaustion from the climb. From the summit of Pusuk Buhit he could see the surface of the lake stretched below, and the land around it. Steep walls rose on almost all sides of the lake. Lake Toba was like a giant crevice, its water reflecting the white clouds and blue sky. The walls formed by the hills seemed carved. There were rocky outcrops that looked like people with long hanging hair, or dangling dogs, or horses poised to leap.

They were not on the summit of Pusuk Buhit now. Ompu Silangit gazed without blinking. His white hair and eyebrows shone in the sun.

'Your father left you, and never cared for you. Even so, it is up to you to continue the name of your father's marga, my marga, the marga of our ancestors. You also must know our marga's history. In days past, we used to be the *ulubalang*, or warriors, for the Batak king, Raja Si Singamangaraja. Some of us were even appointed *parbaringin*, or priests. This was handed down in our marga from generation to generation. We always guarded our king and wagered our souls for his safety.'

Tondi had had conversations like this with his grandfather before. But he had not really understood them, being too young.

This time it was different, sitting there in his green army uniform beside Ompu Silangit on the bank of the stream.

'Now, my grandson, whether you want it or not, whether you like it or not, you are in the middle of a war. And what kind of war is it? In the past, people fought over land. But actually, that was not war. It was just quarrelling because of human greed. Let me tell you about real war. First, there was the Padri War that destroyed Toba lands. I do not know what kind of war that was. Later, there was another war, when the Dutch attacked us, setting all the huta ablaze, destroying Bakkara and assaulting our king. The Batak people, and especially our marga, joined that war. We had to protect our king. And why did we risk our lives for our king? Actually, it was not the person of the king we were guarding. We were guarding our religion. Our religion is our Batak customary law, our *adat*. If a king is distant from this, he is no longer king. The king is living embodiment of the law of Mulajadi na Bolon, the Supreme Source of All Life, which has been handed down in human form to our world.'

They pulled up the net. A few fish flapped around. The fish, a bit larger than an outstretched hand, glinted silver in the morning sun.

'I, you, anyone, we are all human. We are not incarnations of the Mulajadi na Bolon from heaven. As humans, we can only carry out custom. It is the king who is the incarnation of Mulajadi na Bolon law.'

Tondi remained silent. He removed the fish from the net, as his grandfather continued, talking in an even tone.

'In this war going on now, you might come face to face with your father. He is in the national army, and lives in Java. He might have to join the war against all of you here in Batak lands because that is his job, to fight. But what kind of war is it when it comes to Batak killing one another? This is no longer a conflict over water or rice fields or agricultural land. You might come face to face with your father, and what then? Will you fight him? When people fight, local law should restore peace. But now this law means nothing. People follow it for ceremonial occasions but is has nothing to do with their daily lives. Take you, for instance. What need will you have for Batak law in this war?

Tondi was speechless. But it seemed his grandfather expected no answer. He did not even move his head but busied himself skewing the fish through the gills with reeds.

Adat. Oh yes, he had often heard about that. Those complicated customs related to marga regulated all relationships between Batak. Every Batak was tied to a position according to marriage connections.

They returned to the house at the top of the hill, along the way picking leaves from the cassava planted in rows between the beans and clumps of greens beside the path.

Back in the house a girl was waiting. She was about thirteen or fourteen.

'This is Lasmia, Luhut's daughter,' Ompu Silangit said. 'She comes here before school to help with the cooking. She goes to the afternoon session.'

'What class are you in?' Tondi asked, to be polite. He didn't really need to know, but he remembered her father, Luhut.

'First year of junior high school, *Amangboru*,' she replied shyly, using one of the Batak words for uncle. She took the fish and cassava leaves from him.

In the front room there was hot coffee in a porcelain pot. A few cups were set upside down on a mat. It had been like that for as long as Tondi could remember. The house was always set as if ready to serve guests coffee. Ompu Silangit never bought coffee himself. Usually, visitors brought him freshly ground coffee along with palm sugar, salt and other daily necessities.

Lasmia took a tube of bamboo the length of a small child's arm and blew through it to fan the fire in the hearth. You could hear her breaths rustling the flames. Every now and then she would look up. She could not see the people in the front room upstairs. The main house had only two rooms, one big room at the front, and one behind it. When Tondi was small, that front room had felt huge to him. When he ran from one wall to another, it felt like a long way. He once counted that it took him fifty steps to cross the floor. In the back room, things like rice, dried fish and sugar were stored. The front room was used for sleeping and receiving guests.

Usually, Ompu Silangit slept in the eastern corner. His grandmother used to sleep in the southern corner. And when Tondi was small he could choose which corner he wanted to sleep. Sometimes he would sleep with his grandmother, sometimes alone, and sometimes with a guest who stayed overnight.

Lasmia continued to blow on the fire through the bamboo tube. The vegetables bubbled away. Her curiosity about that man in the green uniform also bubbled within her. She half remembered him. Ompu Silangit had not introduced him earlier. But that was normal, she thought. Male guests were never introduced to girls. If Ompu Silangit had introduced him, it would not have been for her sake, but because he knew her father.

As she stirred the vegetables that skittered around in the pan, she tuned her ear to the room above. She hoped that Ompu Silangit might mention the young man's name.

'When the war is over, you must return here, Tondi,' Ompu Silangit said. The porcelain clinked as spoon met cup.

'Oh, his name is Tondi. That's right, Tondi,' Lasmia remembered. She used to address him as Amangboru back when he was still a boy. As a Batak, you must always observe the rules of family relationships.

Tondi could feel a splinter in his chest. He could hardly bear to look his grandfather in the eye. Those eyes looked so tired. Tondi had never seen his grandfather's eyes tired like this.

His grandfather lived all alone here. The locals showed him respect, but still, he was living outside of his own huta. The people around here were from his wife's marga, the marga that had bestowed upon him the blessing of his wife. But he was living in the house on land from his wife's side, as though living off them.

'Why did you not return to our own huta, Grandfather?' Tondi asked.

Ompu Silangit looked at him piercingly.

'Our ancestral home was burnt down during the Batak War. Then destroyed during the Japanese time. Let our lands in our village be run by others. I have no right to live in the ancestral home. I am a defeated man.'

Tondi was startled. He heard the bitterness in his grandfather's voice.

'If you guard your king at a time of war, you must be prepared to die before him.' Tondi could hardly hear his grandfather's voice. 'The reason you are fighting is to protect him.'

Tondi had often heard stories about the last battle in the village of Onom Hudu when King Singamangaraja XII died in a rain of bullets from the Dutch soldiers. The Batak king died because it was his ill-fated day. Ompu Silangit had been there.

That is the story Tondi heard told at the rice-wine stalls, but not directly from his grandfather. Ompu Silangit had also been shot, but it was not his ill-fated day. He was only unconscious, and then captured by the Dutch. An army doctor treated him. The story went that he had been shot at and that cannon shot had also fallen near him, yet there was not a single pellet in his body. Whether fact or fiction, Tondi had never searched for the answer.

'I am a defeated man and witnessed only destruction in Batak lands. You can see how barren is our land, how poor our people, probably as a result of that long war. And to this day I do not understand what those attackers were defending. The Paderi and the Dutch, what was so important for them to defend that they destroyed the lives of people in a distant place? Had the Batak ever taken land belonging to them? Never. Yet they destroyed our lands.'

Tondi sipped his coffee. It seemed to stick in his throat. For the first time he noticed the lines around his grandfather's eyes. He had not noticed those lines before. Was it because he had never been this close to his face?

Yes. Nothing had been repaired even from the more recent wars, and now everything was once again in chaos. The only thing war leaves behind is destruction, Tondi thought to himself as he rubbed his foot. Sitting cross-legged had given him pins and needles.

'And now you are going to fight. So what are you defending?' Ompu Silangit's voice echoed.

Lasmia stepped silently on the wooden floor. She set the food down before Ompu Silangit and Tondi.

Chapter 2

Actually, Lasmia should have recognized the young man. Tondi had lived in this house as a boy. That was about six or seven years ago. Every morning he would run down the hill to go to the only primary school in the village. Lasmia would often play in the yard of the house.

They were related through Tondi's grandmother. She was the cousin of Lasmia's father's grandmother. It meant that Lasmia had to call Tondi Amangboru, one of the words for uncle, and call Ompu Silangit's wife *Inangboru*, one of the words for aunt. It was extremely important to observe these complicated levels and terms of address.

Lasmia had heard that her inangboru was Ompu Silangit's second wife. Just who his first wife was, and what happened to her, she did not know. She did know that his first wife did not come from these parts, but from the western shores of Lake Toba. She had heard only snippets of stories from the women talking. The women would chat all day long as they did their work, moving from one chore to the next. They did almost all their work together, from taking a bath and doing the laundry at the well, to planting rice, picking vegetables in the fields, pounding rice, bargaining at the market and organizing ceremonies. Every huta was fenced with dense, tall, spiky bamboo. Whenever the women exited the huta, they would always be in a group. It was extremely rare for a woman to walk alone. This was probably for security, for warfare had been constant since the time of the ancestors.

Stories about Ompu Silangit and his family were also the stuff of conversations in the coffee stalls. It was like the legends about the origins of the Batak marga. But in this case, the stories of this particular family were real because people knew the characters. People loved to retell Ompu Silangit stories, like when he used his special martial art 'tiger move' against the Dutch. People said he was invulnerable, and even though he had been shot, had not died. And that he had two sons who to the villagers were as legendary as martial arts champions.

And the stories went even further back. It was said that Ompu Silangit's father had been a raja bius heading several huta in the Pusuk Buhit area. In those terrible times when the Dutch were putting increasing pressure on King Singamangaraja XII during the Batak War, he had ordered his son Rajabondar—for that was Ompu Silangit's childhood name—to join the king. Rajabondar was his only son. But to serve his king, he sent his only son to fight. His marga was duty-bound to protect the king and provide brides to the royal family.

Rajabondar was not even twenty back when he became a royal warrior. He was already married. His parents were worried that he might die before having an heir, so they arranged a marriage. As Rajabondar left for the Batak War, he was prepared for death.

That is how Ompu Silangit came to have two wives back in the time of the Batak War. The storytellers in the rice-wine stalls would tell it like this:

'Rajabondar departed for battle, leaving his wife behind in his village in the foothills of Pusuk Buhit. And during that war, his wife gave birth to a son who was named Silangit. She died when her son was one year old. She was buried in the village, and people forgot about her. Nobody remembered her name. Her grave is lost. For who tended graves in a time of war? People barely had a chance to bury the war dead. Her husband never returned home, and her son never searched for him.'

The storyteller would become more excited, seeing his listeners' unblinking gaze. No matter how many times the story was told, it was always exciting. The story would go like this:

'During the war, Rajabondar stayed by his king's side. In today's language, we would call him an adjutant. That is why he witnessed the moment when the Dutch soldiers rained King Singamangaraja with bullets on the banks of Sibulbulon river in the vicinity of Onomhudon.'

A pause for a sip of rice wine, and the storyteller would go on.

'Of course, you all know, if the king had not been betrayed by one of our own, he would never have been shot dead. Captain Kristopel, a Pale Eyed One, received a message from a Batak who was on their side saying not to shoot the king, but to shoot the guard beside him. You see, if our king is touched by blood, he loses his invulnerability. Now I ask you, how would any Pale Eyed One have known that? Again and again our king was encircled and shot at, and always escaped. But eventually his day of ill fortune came. So it was. There is always a traitor. The Dutch rewarded that traitor by making him a local official, and his children could attend Dutch schools.

'Not long after the war, Rajabondar's father died. As a loyal follower of King Singamangaraja, the death of the king by Dutch bullets affected him deeply. Many a raja bius like him became ill after the war. Not only because they no longer received tribute, but because their sons had died in the war. Some of them lost all their sons, which meant the end of their marga.

'Rajabondar, who became known as Amani Silangit, or Father of Silangit, was lucky to live past the war. Lucky, you ask? Yes, he lost his freedom. He had to live in prison in Tarutung for years. People often saw him with his legs shackled when he worked on the roads, or when he had to clean the yards or houses of the colonial officials. While he worked, there would be soldiers watching him. They had been ordered to keep close watch, but not to stand too close to him. He was dangerous.

'That's right! Dangerous. He had magic. Anyone who dared look him in the eye would fall under his spell.'

The storyteller would look around dramatically, as though he had personally witnessed this magic power. Another sip of rice wine. The storyteller would continue:

'Actually, he could be free if he wanted. All he had to do was agree to the Dutch offer to become a local official. But he refused. To him, working for the Pale Eyed Ones was no different to betraying his sacred ancestors. Because of his obstinacy, he was considered a dangerous rebel. Later, he was allowed to leave prison on the condition that he lived on the other side of the lake, far from his village. Even so, he was watched. These days we would call it house arrest. The military went to fetch his son from Pusuk Buhit, to be raised by his father.

'So Tondi actually had an *amangtua*, an uncle on his father's side, named Silangit, his grandfather's first child. According to Batak custom, once a man has a grandson, he should be named *ompu* with that grandson's name. As Tondi was the first grandson (as far as he knew), his grandfather should be called Ompuni Tondi. But people had known Rajabondar as Amani Silangit, or Father of Silangit for a long time, and as a sign of respect they addressed him with the honorific title Ompu, and so it was that he became known as Ompu Silangit. He had that name before Tondi's birth, and it stuck.

'And where, you might ask, is that first son, Silangit? Well, some say he went off travelling as a young man. One of that type that goes away and never returns,' the storytellers would snarl.

* * *

Tondi never knew where he had gone. He only heard the tales told at the rice-wine stalls. Some said he had gone to become a royal guard in one of the small Malay kingdoms on the eastern coast. But this was all just from stories he heard. His ompung had never said a single word to him about this son of his. His face would go blank and cold as though he had not heard when Tondi would ask whether the stories he heard were true. Tondi realized that his ompung did not like to talk about it, and so he never brought up the subject.

Old people who had known the boy Silangit said that he was very clever. He never attended school because the Dutch would only admit children whose parents had become Christian. Even so, he could read and write in roman script. It was astonishing. Traditionally, Batak did not have schools. Every descendant of a local ruler would learn to read and write Batak language and script from their father. Being able to write Batak was nothing unusual, so the boy Silangit would have learnt this from his father.

But what people did not know was that Ompu Silangit himself could also write in roman script because he had learnt from a guard during his time in prison. People said that Silangit could also write in Arabic script because he learnt from a goldsmith in Balige. This was not so. They did not know that his father Ompu Silangit could also read Malay written in Arabic script. During the Batak War, the sultan of Aceh had sent military advisors to assist King Singamangaraja in his fight against the Dutch, giving training in the use of weapons and war tactics. They had taught Ompu Silangit to read Arabic script. He had to learn it because one of his duties was to read the correspondence from neighbouring Islamic lands. He kept his ability to read Arabic script secret because he did not want to raise the suspicion of the Dutch. Ompu Silangit's son later had to study all these things at night from his father.

Ompu Silangit was actually far more skilled than any raja bius or datu around. Was this because he had escaped death during the war? Perhaps. What was clear was that he could read the old palm-leaf manuscripts called *pustaha* that held Batak knowledge about medicine, prediction and vanquishing evil spirits. He could also read Malay manuscripts written in Arabic script which the officers from Aceh had given him. There he found mantras to conquer spirits and genies. The Dutch had burnt all these manuscripts, but he had stored them in his memory, and later, he rewrote some that he knew by heart.

Ompu Silangit had wanted to pass on all this knowledge to his son Silangit as fast as he could. He felt hounded by time. He was a datu bolon—a man of great spiritual powers—but he was also a widower.

His son, without supervision, began to frequent rice-wine stalls. He would leave home, where he had to study with his disciplinarian father every night under a torch flame, as though leaving house arrest. He had to sit up straight and read the texts lined up in front of him. If he slackened or dozed, his father would tie him upright to force him to sit up straight. Only when his eyes could no longer decipher the marks on the thin sheaves of bamboo, very late at night, would his father allow him to lie down. Every night it was the same. He preferred practising martial arts to sitting around reading and copying Batak texts that gave him a headache. Especially when he had to listen to lessons about the old Batak religion that made little sense to him. His father followed the ancestral religion, but Batak people could not pass on this religion because the Dutch forbade it.

So if there was a buffalo cart going to Balige or even as far as Siborong-borong, Silangit hitched a ride, facing backwards as he sat at the back of the cart, looking at the place he had just left. It really was exciting to see the road recede into the distance. And, when he wanted to return, he would wait for a buffalo cart going in the other direction. He would get back home before dusk. Everyone knew he was the son of Ompu Silangit, so if he was hungry, there were always people to give him food. But he spent most of his time at the house of the goldsmith, a Malay from Balige. It was probably this Malay man's stories about the lands beyond Batak lands that inspired him to leave his village. Or maybe it was because he did not want to be the son of Ompu Silangit. The attraction of distant lands coupled with his disciplinarian father at home seem to have pushed him to leave. Or perhaps that Malay goldsmith also introduced him to Islam?

So, when he was fifteen or sixteen, Silangit left his father. His farewell was almost inaudible.

'I'm leaving.'

It had been no leave-taking. A cold separation. His father had only looked up for a moment, then turned his gaze to the lake. The house on the hill went silent.

Children should of course leave their parents' house. A daughter is taken by her father to the house of her husband with a loving farewell.

A son goes away to distant lands. But a separation of mutual hate? Silangit left and went off with that Malay goldsmith to the eastern coast. All that knowledge he had received from his grandfather— what use would it be over there? And from the time he left, he never sent news and never returned to visit his father. Some people said they had met him on the eastern coast, and that he no longer used his marga name. He called himself a Malay.

'Now, cutting the link with your ancestors is the most cursed act a Batak can do,' the storyteller would explode in anger. His face would become tense, and he would thump the table, making the listeners around him jump.

And the storytellers had every right to be angry. How could the son of a datu bolon just erase his marga? But now he was no longer the son of a datu bolon. He was a guard in a Malay kingdom. Maybe he had become like that because the Dutch considered his father dangerous and had placed him under their surveillance, whereas most of the small kingdoms in East Sumatra had submitted to the Dutch colonial government.

After Indonesia's independence, the Malay kingdoms on the east coast of Sumatra came to an end. Some were destroyed when people attacked the palaces and aristocrats. No one ever heard any trace of Ompu Silangit's son, and no one knew if he was still alive. Maybe he had become a success, but if so, clearly not as a Batak. A Batak is known by his marga that he receives from his ancestors.

No one knew Ompu Silangit's feelings. He never spoke of that son with his neighbours. After his son left, Ompu Silangit married a young woman from the village where he was living in exile. He did not take a wife from the marga in the Samosir area that should provide wives to his marga, because he was not permitted to leave the place where he was under house arrest. The Dutch considered the Samosir area and the western shores of the lake, including Ompu Silangit's own village as potential rebel bases. Ompu Silangit was forbidden to go there. He was only able to return after the Japanese defeated the Dutch, but he chose not to.

Ompu Silangit had another son with his second wife. His age must have been quite advanced by this time. This son too became the talk of the neighbourhood. His name was Pardomutua. When he was a young man, he joined the Japanese occupation forces near Sibolga as a volunteer. After Indonesia's independence, he went to Java. People said he became a big shot, an officer in the Indonesian national army, and then married a Javanese woman of noble birth, the daughter of some aristocrat from Solo or Yogyakarta. Not clear which. What was clear was that the marriage happened during the independence war, when the republican government was based in Yogyakarta and Pardomutua was fighting somewhere in the area. Maybe at the time he said that he was unmarried. And now, they say, he has a few children.

Pardomutua was Tondi's father, but he had left Tondi and his mother when Tondi was only two years old. Tondi's mother never divorced his father. As a deserted wife, she was, as the saying goes, 'wedged without support, tethered without a rope.' Even so, she never thought of getting a divorce. Such a thing would not occur to a Batak woman. That was why, when Tondi was young, he was sent to live with his grandfather Ompu Silangit, so that the tie with his marga, his ancestral line of descent, would not be broken. Even though Tondi's parents had lived together as husband and wife for only three years, Tondi's mother felt she was fully within her husband's marga. Her life was consumed with the struggle for survival and her wish to raise her son to further that marga line.

Her husband had left just a few months after the Japanese arrived in 1942. He had taken his wife and toddler to his father's house and then continued on to Sibolga. For a soldier to leave his wife and child with his parents when he went away to fight was normal. He made no promises of return. No one could imagine the future. What lay ahead was war. Who could guarantee a return? As he was the descendant of a line of royal warriors, maybe it was the fighting blood in his veins that led him to sign up. Who knew where he got the news that the Japanese needed soldiers.

Initially, Pardomutua joined a Japanese language course run by the government of occupation. Then he was given work as translator, helping the Japanese authorities. Later he joined the Japanese navy and took part in battles in various seas in Indonesia. Why the navy? Perhaps the view of the vast Lake Toba that he had enjoyed every day had been tugging at him? Anyway, he did not stay with the navy. After independence and the formation of the Indonesian republic, he joined the Indonesian army and his career took off.

Pardomutua never sent news to his father, let alone his wife. She had to forge her own way during those long years of war, from the Japanese occupation through the war for independence. She had to bring up her son while staying at the house of her father-in-law, Ompu Silangit. And this was no place for taking it easy. Food was scarce. People could not work their fields because their village was in a battle area. Ompu Silangit had to forage for food in the forest. During the war for independence, Tondi's mother would sneak into areas occupied by the Dutch forces to get salt and other necessities you could not find in the forest near the village. Since time immemorial, salt had always been brought in from the coast. Lake Toba was as wide as an ocean, but you could not make salt from its water. In the forest, people used to burn palm fronds or rattan and use the ash as a salt substitute, but the taste was not the same.

When the war for independence finally ended, Tondi's mother left her son at Ompu Silangit's house. She knew that she could not depend on Ompu Silangit's fields, which did not get enough rain. In that village there was no productive land. The locals only just managed to make ends meet.

That was separation number one. There was no sadness. Tondi felt closer to his grandmother, his *ompungboru*. It was his mother who felt twisted with sorrow, especially when she saw that her son did not cry to see her go. Oh poverty, poverty separated her from her only child. She went to Siantar, a town she already knew. She had visited this town a few times in the Dutch days when she was first married and lived in a plantation before the Japanese came.

In Siantar, she found work as a cook in a government hospital. At the recommendation of the head of the hospital, a doctor who had once worked in the plantation where she had lived before, she was promoted to become a member of hospital staff.

But then his mother's life had to change. The new Republic began to rationalize all government systems until even hospitals had to rationalize their staff. She lost her position because she did not have the necessary qualifications.

So it was that Tondi's mother was thrown into her present work. After the hospital, she ended up with a small fried-banana stall under the railway bridge close to the bamboo house she could afford to rent. It was a lean-to built against the concrete bridge support, with trains passing overhead. There was only one hearth in the stall, but her fried bananas were famous in the town.

Tondi stayed on with his grandfather until the end of primary school, but there was no junior high school there. Like other students, he would have had to go to school in the nearby town. He could not have lived alone in the town, so he went to live with his mother in Siantar. It was a pleasant town, cooled by the mahogany, tamarind and almond trees planted along the roads. The town centre was pretty, the one Dutch colonial legacy that remained.

It was around this time, maybe his second year of junior high school, that for the first time Tondi was shaken to the sinews, to the marrow of his bones, to the arteries of his heart.

Ompu Silangit had sent someone—oh yes, yes that's right, it was *Lae* Luhut, Lasmia's father—to meet him. The man addressed Tondi's mother as inangboru, the term used for female relatives of your father. He took Tondi back with him to Toba. Tondi's mother did not join them. She had to look after her food stall, or maybe she just did not want to go. She probably had her own reasons, which Tondi did not yet understand.

Ompungboru, his grandmother, had died. Tondi was in shock. His chest felt constricted, under constant attack from the never-ending wailing. The women took turns at lamenting over Ompungboru's body. Their laments told of her goodness and the beautiful memory of her when she was alive. The mourning went on for days. Funeral pennants soared to the sky. Ceremonial drums sounded unceasingly.

Followers of the Batak religion and King Singamangaraja, who had never appeared before because of pressure from the Dutch, all came. People came from the villages, not only nearby, but from far distant places in the interior. You could not begin to count those who came from the towns along the main road. Some brought their animals so there would be a good supply of buffalo and pigs to slaughter for feeding all the guests. The din combined with the sadness.

And that meeting happened. Tondi would remember it forever. He was sitting at the feet of his grandmother whose body was covered in layer upon layer of traditional woven *ulos* cloth, in the midst of all the wailing women.

Ompu Silangit called him over.

'This is your father,' he said calmly, indicating a tall, well-built man with pale, rosy skin.

And he met that man, at the age of thirteen. Tondi said not a word. The man was silent too. Had they embraced, Tondi would only have come up to the man's chest. Between the two of them was a space of about a metre. It felt so far. Or, more precisely, like a distance of thousands of kilometres.

'This is your son, Tondi,' Ompu Silangit said deliberately.

The drumming in the yard throbbed in Tondi's ears. All he could do was look at that man, his body, yes, his body, not his face. And not even his body, but his army uniform that wrapped around that large body.

So this is the man I have dreamed about all this time. The man who was just a name. The man I wanted to meet. But what kind of meeting was this? There was Ompungboru's body covered with ulos cloth, laid out in the middle of the room. And there was the man in his green uniform upright with his big body so that if Tondi had wanted to look him in the face, he would have had to look up. Tondi did not want to meet him. All he wanted was to be with his grandmother who used to cook him the meat the neighbours brought. Food she made especially for him.

Ompu Silangit went down from the house together with the man, to greet guests who had just arrived. From the window frame,

Tondi could see the top of the man's head, with his shiny hair.
On his shoulder were three stars on a black background, showing
his rank. Tondi did not understand that it meant his father was a
colonel. All he took in was the uniform. He did not even remember
the man's face. From a brief glance he just thought that the man
looked like his grandfather.

He remembered how annoying some of the old women were.
They talked drivel, competing with their silly comments. 'Oh, doesn't
Tondi look just like his father.' He felt his breathing become shallow.
When people said that he looked exactly like his grandfather, he was
proud. But with this man he had to call father, his chest tightened.

His grandmother was buried beneath the banyan tree not far from
the house. All the days of mourning the women had been covering
her with cloth and wailing their laments. But did any of them wail
for her son who never came to visit her when she was alive? Her one
and only son who might be a big shot in that place far away but was
lost to his own parents? Was it because now he followed the new
religion that he wanted to distance himself from his father who still
followed the religion of his ancestors? Does religion have to divide
father and son, divide people? Tondi did not know. He did not hear
those laments, nor could he understand all the poetry the women
sang. But Ompungboru's burial had awaited the arrival of her son.
He was the one most anticipated, while the women wailed and the
drums sounded and people kept on coming as though they would
never stop and food was cooked incessantly.

After his grandmother had been buried, there was a conversation
that Tondi did not fully understand. He was sleepy, because for days
there had been little time for sleep. That man was there in the room,
the man he had to call amang, father, along with his grandfather
and some other old men who he used to call ompung, amangtua
or tulang, all terms for uncle depending on seniority and whether
they were on his mother's or his father's side. They were the only
men inside. Outside, sitting in the yard, were the men from his
grandmother's side, men he had to call amangboru. They had no

right to take part in this discussion. As for the women, they all sat in the back room.

Someone, Tondi did not remember exactly who, opened the conversation:

'Amani Tondi, Father of Tondi, are you going to take Tondi to Jakarta?' It was said like a question, but because it came from a senior of the marga that had bestowed Tondi's father with his wife, it was like an order.

Pardomutua, Tondi's father, was nervous.

'Yes,' someone joined in. 'You should give him a good education over there in Jakarta.'

Pardomutua did not reply. He looked at his father, but Ompu Silangit turned his gaze to the window.

'Hey, Tondi, you should get ready to go with your father and become a Jakarta boy,' someone added.

Tondi remembered only his reply, which was half a shriek. 'No. No. No. I want to stay with my mother!'

Some men came up to him, coaxed him. But Tondi paid no heed to the swarm of their words. He stamped the wooden floor. It was a loud thump. Some of the men approached him, still trying to persuade him.

'I don't want to go!' Tondi yelled.

Ompu Silangit gave a sign for everyone to sit back down. It seemed that Tondi's screams had closed the meeting that was to pressure Pardomutua to take his son back with him to Java. The man took a deep breath and shrugged his shoulders while looking at his father and all the men beside him sitting on the floor and leaning against the walls. Tondi, seething with anger, looked at the man. He did not fully understand, but could see the half-hidden relief in his face. Oh, he would never forget that expression of relief. Ompu Silangit just took a deep breath, stroked Tondi's head and muttered, as though to himself:

'That's enough. There's no need to go on with this. His mother is not here now. She must be asked whether she wants her son to be taken to Java. For she is the one who has raised this boy all this time. She is the one who nursed him, who fed him as a baby, who has worked to find food so this boy could grow to who he is now.

The men exchanged glances.

'But . . .' someone wanted to speak. But Ompu Silangit had decided.

'It is not up to all of you to determine the path of his life. Even though you are the marga of my son's wife, our *hula-hula*. You cannot force him. His mother might not agree. This boy is the only thing she has in the world. So do not force things.'

The men were quiet. There followed a rumble of muttering. Expressions of anger and dissatisfaction beamed from some of the men. But no one dared speak up.

'Every person has his own path,' Ompu Silangit went on. He stroked Tondi's temples. Then he turned to Pardomutua and said calmly: 'When you go, take with you my staff, Tunggal Panaluan. I hope that you will get a son over there in Java.'

Ompu Silangit ordered Tondi to get the staff that was leaning against the wall on the western side. It was made of dark, black wood, about two metres long and carved all over with figures of humans, lizards and other animals. This sacred staff was used as part of rituals for calling the spirits. Ompu Silangit made a sign for Tondi to fetch the staff, which was bigger than Tondi, and give it to his father. To Tondi, the staff was just a long wooden rod. This is why he casually handed it over with the tip pointing towards his father. The sound of the shocked reaction of those gathered was like hundreds of bees buzzing in the room. He should have handled the staff with the appropriate respect.

Pardomutua was speechless. He looked at his father. So he had ordered this boy, this boy here, to hand him the sacred staff, Tunggal Panaluan. He did not want to hand it to him directly himself. What was the hidden meaning here?

He knew that his father still followed the old religion, still worshipped Debata di Banua Ginjang, the Lord of the World Above, and that he venerated the spirit of Si Raja Batak the first human and source of life of everyone known in Batak religion and legend. Pardomutua was taken aback.

In Jakarta, he had a happy family. A beautiful, educated wife, clever in social situations. She was a graduate from a high school for girls, the daughter of an aristocrat who used to be a civil servant in Dutch times. He had three children at home, all girls who took after their parents with their good looks. Even with all these blessings, he still secretly longed for a son. But he brushed aside this longing when he saw his wife's smile, his daughters' gaiety and the everyday joy in his large house. After all, as a modern man, are not daughters and sons equal?

And now, here, the Tunggal Panaluan, a son. The Tunggal Panaluan, a son. Here was a son he did not know at all, and who did not know him. Pardomutua remained lost for words, and did not dare look at his father.

When Pardomutua prepared to leave the house, people went looking for Tondi. But he had gone to play in the fields with some boys herding the buffalo. There were still five buffalo that had not been slaughtered for the funeral ceremonies. They would now be the collective property of the village, along with a few pigs, because Ompu Silangit never slaughtered animals.

Ompu Silangit did not send anyone to fetch Tondi. He and his son, Pardomutua, left the house and walked down the hill. They parted at the foot of the hill where the cars were parked. Pardomutua had only a brief moment to say goodbye to his father. He was in a hurry. He had to go back with some government officials from Tarutung who had come to pick him up. He busied himself chatting to those people in their army uniforms, and with the civil officials. There was an army commander, a regent, a judge and who-knows-what else. Pardomutua merely shook his father's hand, and then immediately greeted the people waiting there. He got into one car, the others got into the other cars to make a convoy to accompany him, and they took off, leaving just a cloud of dust at the foot of the hill.

He was a big shot from Jakarta. Everyone knew he was close to President Sukarno. The villagers had once seen his photo in the newspaper, standing next to the leader of the nation. That photo had been the talk of the town for a long time. So it was understandable that the local government officials showed him great respect.

Tondi did not care that his father had left. He was enjoying playing with his friends herding the buffalo. And if he got bored playing with them, it was because he wanted to go back to his mother. Then his mother arrived. Ompu Silangit had been sitting at the foot of the hill since earlier, and said only a few words to his daughter-in-law, without looking directly at her.

'Over there, under the banyan tree.'

He could be referring to her son, Tondi, but it might also be her mother-in-law, her inangboru. She merely gave a respectful nod, also avoiding looking at him. According to tradition, it was taboo for a father-in-law to speak directly to his daughter-in-law. If there was something to be conveyed, it had to be done through a third party. Ompu Silangit remained sitting on a large stone under the shady tree where people took a rest on their walk. He remained staring at the end of the road. Perhaps he was remembering the cloud of dust made by the cars that took his son, Pardomutua. A man who had left his father and his son, the generation before him and the generation after him, with no sadness whatsoever. Ah, a bitter parting.

Tondi's mother almost ran up the hill. Her panting mixed with her sobs. Tondi was with a few women who had been at the grave for some time. Her sobbing erupted. She howled her laments as she hugged the grave, laments blocked by the damp earth. Her wailing brought Tondi to tears. The graveyard was under an old banyan tree that provided shade. It was a sacred tree. The village children did not dare to play near the graveyard, but Tondi often swung from the roots like a monkey, or like Tarzan in the comics. Not this time, though. He did not want to play. There was no telling how much time had passed. There was no sound of the birds that usually chirped busily as they hunted for spiders. Just the wind rustling the leaves that fell on Tondi and his mother. The earth was damp, chilling the soles of his feet. His mother sobbed laments at the grave for a long time. The damp earth dirtied her face. And still she hugged Tondi with her left arm and her mother-in-law's grave with her right. And her laments pierced the stillness.

'Inang, Inang, Inang. Who do I have now to protect me? Who do I have now to ask for blessings? O Inangboru, how should I raise your grandson?'

Oh, wise wife. She had purposely come late to the funeral so she would cause no problems in the village for her husband. She had thought that Pardomutua would come with his new wife and children. It turned out he came alone. Even so, it would have been a problem if she, as daughter-in-law, had been there at the same time as he was. All these years and he had never formally divorced her. He had left her, just like that. People from her marga would accuse her husband and demand that he take responsibility. If the bride's marga accused the groom's marga in this way, then all the blessings they had bestowed on the groom's family would be lost. Their life would be empty. She did not want any interference in the respect shown to her mother-in-law. Her problems were her own affair.

So Tondi returned to Siantar with his mother. He went back to school. He returned to his mother's food stall in the centre of town. Days passed, and sometimes he longed for his grandmother to visit once again as she used to do, bringing rice harvested from their fields. Of course, this wish vanished when he remembered her grave. Then, he longed for the house on the top of the hill. He longed for his grandfather. Now, if his grandfather ordered him to study all those old books, he would do it. Not like before when he would make excuses not to study them at night, especially when he had school homework to do.

The extent of his world was the space between the tiny plot in Siantar and the house on the top of the hill on the shore of lake Toba. All his longing was grounded in poverty, poverty in the town and the poverty of his marga. But at least it stopped him from thinking about his father. Tondi never met that man again. He was just a vague shadow. He could never envisage his father clearly. Every now and then he wanted to recall his face, but there was nothing mapped except a green uniform and the mark of his rank against a black background.

Faces are for remembering. But if he had been able to remember it, would it not have added to his pain? For what always returned was the desire to wipe memories. He did not know his father's face clearly because he had never stroked that face or plucked his whiskers as young children do with their fathers. He wanted to erase that shadow. But how could he do this when every time he looked in the mirror he would see his own face, his grandfather's face, and the face of that man? Especially when he reached his teens.

Chapter 3

A chiselled face. A square jaw. One of those Batak who have pale, pinkish skin. Tondinihuta's father and grandfather were both like that. Tall in stature and big-boned. Tondi, turning eighteen years of age, was over 180 cm tall. Like his grandfather. He was going to have his grandfather's build. It was only lately that Ompu Silangit's shoulders had started to sag. He was not as erect as Tondi remembered him, even though his body was not yet bent. People in the village said he was a hundred years old. But probably, because of his white hair, they were exaggerating just to fuel the stories told at the rice-wine stalls. He was probably in his eighties. Climbing up and down that hill though, seemed to have kept him in good health. When he sat cross-legged on the floor, his back was completely straight.

And on this morning, he was sitting leaning against the wall, where he always sat facing the front yard. Tondi therefore took his place to the side, facing the door leading to the back room. Ompu Silangit took out from a wooden chest beside him some dark brown sheaves of bamboo and bark, etched with Batak script.

'When you were small, you always found some reason to complain if I told you to read these manuscripts,' Ompu Silangit said. His voice was level, showing no anger or regret.

But Tondi bent his head with a pressing sense of remorse. At his village school he had learnt to read Batak script. He could only recognize the letters and write a few simple words on the slate. When the lesson changed, the slate was wiped clean, so the students quickly forgot them. Most likely even the teachers could not read the old texts.

However, Tondi's lessons did not stop with school. At home, his grandfather would order him to read the etched writing. It made him sleepy. It was always old mantras for healing, summoning good spirits and exorcising bad ones, almanacs to know good days and bad days, rules of Batak custom, or examples of how to live well. Someone in his grandfather's position had to master such knowledge in order to lead sacred ceremonies and give advice in ceremonial gatherings.

Tondi studied the texts because he loved his grandfather. And Ompu Silangit was gentle in his supervision, no longer the iron disciplinarian. When Tondi was tired, he would lie down and fall asleep right there on the floor. His grandfather would just sigh and cover him with a blanket. Sometimes Tondi would rest his head on Ompu Silangit's thigh, something impossible back when Ompu taught his own son. A grandfather is the source of love, but a father is a strict teacher's cane. And is it not a blessing to have your loving grandfather care for you? Even though his grandfather did not go by the name Ompuni Tondi. The tie of love is not only from a name. His grandfather taught the pustaha not with discipline, but with an outpouring of kindness.

Or perhaps he had made peace with the times and was resigned to the fact that the knowledge of his ancestors would disappear. All this knowledge that was the foundation of the Batak religion. If people now followed new religions, if the young generation left the ancestral religion, then what use would they have for these ancient texts? They were reminders of the past, whereas people now were interested only in the present and the future. All that was needed nowadays was knowledge that could be used to work in offices and factories, or activities that produced money. People had no need to ask when was the right time to plant rice or to fell trees in the forest.

But Ompu Silangit knew that even though Tondi was lazy at studying the old texts, he could understand their contents. There was a kind of magnet in his eyes that drew in the etched letters so they stuck in his brain. Maybe it was natural talent, or maybe it came from his childhood suffering as a boy deserted by his father. He had a father, but he had never known him. Nature—the earth, the stones, the tree trunks, the wind—had raised him. He was like white cotton that absorbed all the holy water of the teachings in those pustaha. Like his name, it was not his brain that absorbed the contents, but his tondi, his life spirit. Nature gave him sensitivity, so his spirit was beside him as he faced those texts.

'Do you still remember the contents?' Ompu Silangit asked, breaking the silence.

'Yes, I remember everything. But I don't know the use of it,' Tondi replied.

Ompu Silangit sighed. So his grandson would not be staying in these Batak lands in the interior. It was impossible that he would become a datu or a raja bius, let alone a priest of the Batak religion. His old eyes stared at the letters etched on the bamboo.

'Yes, the times are different now. I cannot give you provisions for your life journey. These days, you get provisions from school. Your father completed the Dutch junior high school because a local official sponsored his school fees. But this good fortune bore him along the path to a dark world. Even though I deliberately named him Pardomutua. I gave him that name at a time when I could not control my hatred of the Pale Eyed Ones. I thought his name would keep him from being close to the Dutch. But I was wrong. Because that name turned out to make him distant from me.'

Ompu Silangit had named his son Pardomutua. The word *Pardomu* means 'meet', but no Batak would give that name in that form to his son. The usual form was '*Pardomuan*' meaning 'meeting'. Batak liked to give names that had good meanings like '*pardamean*' for 'peace'; *sintong*, 'true'; *sahata*, 'harmony'; *sahala*, 'supernatural fortune'; *togar*, 'hale and hearty'; *ruhut*, 'good principle'; *hasian*, 'love'; and so forth. Pardomutua's name, though, recalled Ompu Silangit's

time in prison, because all he heard there was the soldiers and
Dutch staff hurling curses at the locals: '*godverdomme*'. But to his
ears, this sounded like '*pardome*'. Using that curse word for his son's
name was a reminder of how the Dutch had treated the locals, and
with the addition of *tua* meaning 'supernatural power', expressed the
wish that Batak knowledge would make his son superior to them.
He had hoped that his son would return to their ancestral lands and
become the local ruler there.

But Pardomutua did not want to become what his father
wanted. His life changed when a local official acknowledged him as
his adopted son so he could go to a Dutch school. This was another
story that came about through Ompu Silangit's friendship with a
public servant of the Dutch colonial government.

Ompu Silangit had once helped that official. The story was
that someone who wanted the official's position had targeted him
with black magic. The official was from Sipirok, a Batak from the
south who had received a Dutch education and become Christian,
unlike the rest of his family who were predominantly Muslim.
The Dutch colonial government promoted him to the local
government position in the Toba region. They probably chose
him because they trusted him in this region formerly ruled by King
Singamangaraja. There were other educated Christian Toba Batak
who came from the north who qualified for the position, but the
Dutch posted them elsewhere. Consequently, the outsider found
himself the target of black magic and poison, something the colonial
government's world did not understand. Such things were often
used as weapons in competition.

So it was that the official became ill, and his stomach swelled so
much that he looked like a heavily pregnant woman. In indescribable
pain, he was taken to the hospital in Sibolga. The Dutch doctors were
unable to make a diagnosis or cure him. The army commander at the
prison arranged for the prisoner Ompu Silangit to go to the hospital.
As Ompu Silangit massaged the patient's swollen stomach, the
doctors circled the bed, scrutinising every move of this man with the
white headcloth and wearing a coarsely woven sarong. Ompu Silangit

called for some coconut oil and clean water. He rubbed coconut oil on the patient's stomach and then massaged him, keeping his eyes closed. Then he gave him water to drink. The patient vomited a huge amount of fluid mixed with black blood. There was a rotten stench. Soon after, his stomach compressed. Miraculous. The Dutch doctors just looked at one another, shrugged their shoulders and left.

The official believed that Ompu Silangit had saved his life. Ompu Silangit gave him a special charm to wear around his waist when working in the area. So although the official was Christian, he still needed the protection that came from the traditional healer.

Soon after, Ompu Silangit was released from prison but forbidden from returning to his huta. That was when he was sent to live on the hill and given an allowance for his daily needs from the government. Later, when he married a local girl, he was given land to cultivate. The hill became a kind of place of exile. The government forbade the locals to have any contact with him. If he wanted to leave, he had to ask for permission, but he never did. The furthest he ever went was to the bottom of the hill. During the day, he would till his fields, and at night he would write down all the ancient texts he stored in his head. He would make pustaha to replace the treasures lost during the war.

Things improved when the official who he had healed got a new position in the district that governed the villages in the area. He often visited the house on the hill. He was interested in the pustaha that Ompu Silangit was writing. He himself had begun to collect old texts from various villages and had sent many boxes to Leiden University and museum in Holland, and given some to Ompu Silangit.

Now the locals did not have to visit Ompu Silangit in secret. And then Pardomutua was born. The official decided he wanted to educate the boy. For this, he would have to adopt him. So it was that Pardomutua later went to live with the official and became Christian. Ompu Silangit was merely informed. He himself never set foot in a church.

'So it was,' Ompu Silangit went on, 'that your father could go to school back in Dutch times. At school, he did not use the name

Pardomutua, but his Christian name. As for you, you also have a
Christian name. Back in the days of the Pale Eyed Ones, to become
Christian was to gain entrance to Dutch schools. But you were not
so lucky. You were born just before the Dutch collapsed. Everyone
was now free to go to school. But for us, it was a different problem.
I did not have the money to pay for your schooling. I had no wealth to
live in the town. My only wealth was the knowledge in the pustaha.
This was the only thing I could give you.'

A shiver of pain crept into Tondi's chest. His grandfather's
croaky and even-toned voice stirred up regret he could not ward off.

'I know that times have changed. It is not possible for you to live
in our huta. I know that raja bius are not needed any more, let alone
priests of our Batak religion. You have been baptized Christian. I do
not know if you are allowed to store the knowledge of our ancestors
in your head. The Christian priests say our old teachings must be
wiped out.'

Tondi could only look down at the mat on the floor. Ever since
he was a little boy, he had wanted to please his grandfather. He had
managed to graduate from junior high school in Siantar. At vacation
time, he had returned full of joy to his grandfather's house. But what
did that joy mean to his grandfather? His vacations had seemed so
short, but still he spent every day and night, opening the pustaha
and devouring the contents. Whenever he came across something
difficult, his grandfather, who always sat leaning against the wall,
would explain. Tondi had no wish to go and play in the fields with
friends of his age as he had done before. His friends did not live in
the village any more anyway, as they went to school in Siborong-
borong or Tarutung. But that was not the reason he focused on
reading all the texts. It was a kind of passion that came from he knew
not where, driving him to quench his thirst.

Actually, when he finished primary school, he had wanted to
go to the special junior high school for training teachers. After
graduating from the four-year course there, you were guaranteed a
job teaching at a primary school. But he was not accepted, based on
his school reports. Only those with the highest marks were chosen

to enter that special junior high school. Becoming a teacher was no small thing. His marks were good enough, though, for him to enter the general junior high school.

While he was at that school, he studied hard to get good marks each year. In his final year, his marks were good enough to get entry into the senior high school for teachers. His mother did all she could, borrowing money to buy the appropriate clothing. Now he had to wear long trousers and a long-sleeved shirt. There were books to buy, and the required textbooks were not available in Siantar. You had to buy them at a book shop in Medan.

He worked hard in his first year of that high school, trying to get good enough marks for a scholarship. Bonded scholarships started in the second year and were then assessed annually. Students who did not make the grade lost their scholarship. Those who graduated from the school without losing their scholarships were given immediate employment as government teachers, without even having to apply. Their time on the scholarship was counted as time already served in the public service for determining their salaries. You started work with a big salary. Every student wanted a government scholarship.

But it seemed Tondi's brain was not brilliant enough, or maybe he was exhausted from searching every night for bananas, sweet potato and other things for his mother's stall. While working at the stall, he would have his books open. But his school marks continued to fall, and he did not make the grade for a scholarship. He felt he was a failure. It was his own decision to leave school and help his mother pay back her debts. This was how he jumped into the whirling wheels of travel from town to town and worked as a bus conductor.

His grandfather continued, 'Before the Dutch came, the knowledge held in these pustaha was extremely valuable. Every raja bius had to study this knowledge. Your amangtua studied but did not like it. Hated it in fact. Your father did not study it at all. He used the knowledge he got from his Dutch school and has now become an important person. Yes, important . . .'

Ompu Silangit's face clouded over and the breeze coming through the door ruffled the strands of his white hair. Tondi was moved. Ompu Silangit continued slowly:

'My father was raja bius in our huta for his entire life. Among his brothers there were some who became parbaringan before the Dutch government banned the priesthood of our religion. Then I was exiled here. I do not have any male relatives. My sisters had died long before the Dutch left, and none had married. So I have no nephews from my sisters. I have two sons, but they have both gone far away. I have no one to carry on all this knowledge. I might as well have no children. Will all this Batak knowledge be buried when I die?'

Tondi had never before heard his grandfather's voice like this, as though buried under a pile of earth. Reverberating and soft.

'You are my grandson. I should be bequeathing an ancestral house to you. But I cannot. The Dutch soldiers burnt down our ancestral home during the Batak War. This house here is built on land that does not belong to our marga. I am an exile and a pauper. I have nothing to leave to you. The only thing I have to pass on is the knowledge in these pustaha.'

Tondi looked around. The rooms were exactly as he knew them from his childhood. Without decoration. The walls had never been painted and actually did not need paint. The wooden boards were made from trees hewn in the forest, chosen by Ompu Silangit himself. He and some villagers had felled the trees and together dragged them to the foot of the hill. There they had cut them into planks and carried them, a few at a time, to the top of the hill.

'Your uncle was born in our marga ancestral lands at the foot of Pusuk Buhit. He was fortunate that his umbilical cord was buried in our huta. Your father was born here, and the spirits guarding his umbilical cord are here. As for you, you were born in foreign lands, not in Batak lands. More distant still from your ancestral home,' Ompu Silangit said.

His father was born here. Pardomutua was born in this village. So his umbilical cord was buried in the yard of this house, under the banyan tree. This was where one of his tondi lived. According to the old beliefs, every person has a few spirits. There is the *tondi sigomgom*, the spirit within you as your soul; there is the *tondi sijungjung* which is outside of you and is your guardian; and there is the *tondi sanggapati* which stays where your umbilical cord is buried. If cared for well, you can make contact with this spirit, and it will always protect you and warn your other spirits when danger threatens.

Tondi remembered some years ago his grandmother coming to see him, carrying a message from his grandfather telling him to visit the house where his parents had once lived on the plantation in Dolok Merangir, when they were newly married. He went there with his mother and grandmother. They took the train from Siantar, then a rickety old bus. The house had long gone. His mother could only point out where, more or less, his umbilical cord was buried. At the time, he was tired and uninterested because he was too young to understand the importance of this place where his tondi sanggapati resided. He fidgeted. It was only when his mother and grandmother scolded him that he sat and stared at the earth. His mother said some Christian prayers and his grandmother sprinkled some water from a bottle that her husband had given her, and then mumbled some words. And that turned out to be the last time he saw his grandmother. She died just a few months after she returned home. Tondi felt a stabbing in his chest. His tondi was disturbed. Now he could not possibly return to the place where his tondi sanggapati resided far beyond Batak lands.

So, Tondi thought, my father Pardomutua's umbilical cord is here, and yet he does not respect its tondi. He does not need its protection. He is a Christian with modern ideas. He never returned home to visit his father. Tondi felt his father was incredibly distant. He had only heard stories about him from the old people in the village. There would usually be some old man who would invite him to a coffee stall and then ramble on about all kinds of things, from the ghosts of the lake to his father's childhood.

Back when Tondi was a boy and lived at his grandfather's house, it was as though the village cared for him, so he never felt the loss of his father. Every adult male in the village was like his father. He called them by the various names for father and uncle, amangtua, amanguda, amangboru. The word amang is what you call your father, but it can also be used as a term of endearment for a boy. There were many men he could call amang in the village, and they all showed him love. On top of that there were many men who were relatives on his mother's side, whom he called tulang. The love poured upon him from these maternal relatives was more protective. You could say he was spoilt in the village. At least, he never missed his own father.

His father was now a high-ranking government man. How high? Tondi wondered. The last time he met him, at his grandmother's funeral, he had the rank of colonel in the national army. Probably his rank had risen since then. But what did that mean? What does a father mean to his son? Maybe a father would also ask what a son means to him. Ompu Silangit had once said that a father has the duty to show the path his son will follow. Just show. There is no single path he can choose. A father merely shows the path he considers to be best according to his experience. But there is no guarantee that his path will take his child to reach his destination. Maybe the child will find his own path.

'I never showed your father a path,' Ompu Silangit said. 'He went to the Dutch school. That school showed him the path to follow. And I do not understand what he studied. He studied at a Dutch school, got guidance from Dutch people and then he fought against the Dutch. I never studied that Dutch alphabet. I only know Batak script. I can also read Arabic letters because I had an Acehnese friend. I never had any Dutch person showing me a path. So, if I had fought the Dutch, I would not have been fighting my own teachers.'

Tondi watched Lasmia replace the coffee pot on the tray with a new one full of hot coffee. Outside, the sun shone hot and bright, but the sunlight did not reach the inside of the tin-roofed house. The wind passed over huge stones the size of buffalo, clumps of bamboo and the shady leaves of the banyan tree before finally entering the house through the door and the window shutters open wide.

The breeze cooled the room. The birds were chirping noisily in the shade of the banyan tree, as they busily pecked at the fruit.

Ompu Silangit went on. 'When I was a boy there were no schools. It was only the old people who taught the children to read the pustaha. Yes, only a few people could read, but any person who could read would be teacher to his children. All parents could show the path. There might have been no schools, but people could find their paths.

Ompu Silangit looked over at Lasmia who was sitting respectfully, her legs dangling on the steps that went down to the kitchen, awaiting any order from him. Actually, it is not proper for girls to sit in a doorway. But this was the door at the back, and usually only women would pass there. Men would go up and down to the house through the front door.

'Take Lasmia here,' Ompu Silangit said. Lasmia was startled. 'She is lucky that now there is a junior high school near this village. She can go to school. Maybe she will go on to senior high school after that, who knows. Maybe her schoolteachers will give her lots of guidance. The longer she studies, the higher the school, the more people who will give her guidance. Maybe her own parents will no longer be able to give her guidance about paths for her to follow. Then she will marry. And do they teach Batak custom at school? What about her children later on? Will there even be any Batak people if they do not know our custom?'

Tondi looked over for a moment. The girl was embarrassed. Being discovered eavesdropping or peeping was enough to make a Batak girl skedaddle. But her curiosity overcame her embarrassment. Or perhaps she was not the shy type. She quickly recovered. Her direct gaze returned with her curiosity, making her dark eyes sharp and clear.

Ompu Silangit gazed absentmindedly out the door. The white belibis birds were flying above the clump of bamboo. Crows were cawing in the distance. Someone was shouting, chasing the birds in the dry rice fields.

'More and more parents are no longer parents. They do not carry out their duty of showing the path. So you, Tondi, should not feel disheartened even though your father never showed you the path. His other children who live with him in Java are probably the same. He will certainly surrender them to school so teachers can show the way. But what do teachers know about life paths?'

Tondi did not react. Only Lasmia, sitting on the floor near the kitchen, was startled. Indeed, do teachers give guidance for the journey of life? All they did was give out homework. Algebra, English, biology, history, geography of Indonesia and the world. What was all this for, and when would she use it?

'Remember what I am saying to you today, Tondi. Not all parents give guidance to enable their children to choose their own paths. Some feel that because they are rich, this will pave a way for their children. By giving them wealth, they think their children will travel easily through this life. That is no guarantee. All the wealth in the world will not necessarily become the path to your destination. That very path might actually destroy the child.'

Tondi looked carefully at his ompung. He was following only some of what he said. Not to mention Lasmia, who could overhear only parts of the conversation.

Ompu Silangit rummaged around in his wooden chest. He pulled out something wrapped in red cloth and placed it on the floor.

'Tonight, you can leave this place. Yes, tonight. Sleeping in the forest is no problem. It is true what Pardapdap told you. I will show you the path to take. This is a path no Dutchman has ever traversed. In former times, yes, long ago in the days of old when many Batak had to move south, they would travel along this path. During the Batak War the path was often used again. I am going to tell you the marks of that path in the forest. But no one unclean can pass.

In the heat of the day, Ompu Silangit made scratches in the earth, showing the path in the forest. Tondi had to remember huge old trees, shapes of hilltops, large stones, depths of rivers, and bends in the forest. The path was under the tree canopy in Batak land running north to south. It did not pass through Sibolga, as the main road for public transport did, but went direct to Sipirok. From there, another path skirted Sidempuan, going through the forest towards Kotanopan. Another path went from there through the forest around Muarasipongi and Rao, villages on the border of North Sumatra and Central Sumatra. The path then went on to Bonjol. Ompu Silangit explained the path to that point. He himself had never been further on the path, from Bonjol to Bukittingi.

The long secret path Tondi would travel would not go through any town he knew. The names of places were unknown to him from his geography lessons at school. They were just names of features of nature. His grandfather also explained to him where to find food in the forest, from honey to fruit.

'So,' Ompu Silangit said. 'I travelled this path many times when I was young. I think it will not have changed much. We cannot say that of the future. When there are more people, and when people are greedier, maybe they will fell this forest. If that happens, we will no longer have the forest path. But then maybe people will not be so busy fighting. They will be busy thinking about getting rich.'

Tondi studied the marks drawn in the earth. Ompu Silangit opened the package in his hand.

'I cannot give you anything at all. But take this with you,' he said, sliding over a kind of dagger with a wooden sheath.

'This dagger stayed with me for decades. Compared to weapons of today, it has no value. But it is not a weapon. And it is not for cutting food. It is a friend. A relative. It holds magic power.'

The hilt of the dagger was made from black wood in the shape of an elephant's tusk. The wooden sheath was finely carved. Tondi had never before seen this dagger from his grandfather's chest. There was nothing special about it. Then he drew it out of its sheath. The sun struck the blade with blinding light. There were markings on it like a map of a river's path. Maybe because of the sun, the dagger felt warmer in Tondi's hand. The blade was black iron, and completely unlike the shining steel blades that Tondi knew. The army bayonet he was carrying also had a blackish blade, but not pitch black like this. Waves of warmth radiated from his hand right up his arm and seemed to flow over his whole body.

Tondi replaced the dagger in its sheath.

'Now I have no more burden. There is nothing more for me to keep. Your father already took the Tunggal Panaluan. This dagger is for you. The pustaha are all that remain. I do not know who I will give them to. I only had two children. Your amangtua whom you never knew, and your father. Had your amangtua returned, he should have kept these pustaha. But he went away when he was only fifteen never to return. I hoped he would want to become a raja bius and return to our huta, our ancestral land. Unlike your father, he never went to a Dutch school. He studied only from these pustaha. But so be it. He left. He never returned. Every child must leave, and not all of them return,' Ompu Silangit said as he stared into the horizon.

'I will return,' said Tondi, softly.

Ompu Silangit put his arm around Tondi's shoulder and pulled him close, all the while staring towards the west, towards the lake.

'At least I am relieved because I have a descendant. The marga will not end with me. I will not be the one to cause the line to be severed,' he said.

Tondi was silent. Not a word. To be in the embrace of his tall, strong ompung always used to make him feel calm. But this time he was troubled.

'If you do come home, I might no longer be here,' Ompu Silangit said.

Tondi was startled. He looked at his ompung, but Ompu Silangit continued to stare in the direction of the lake. Tondi's anxiety churned into sorrow. His ompung's soft, calm voice seemed to pounce on him and rip apart every layer of his chest.

'I have to visit someone who needs medicine. You just leave later, there is no need to wait for me. Just leave the house as usual.'

Yes, as usual, there was no need for anyone to watch the house. Tondi and his grandfather looked at each other. Tondi's blood rushed. The eyes that met his looked dejected. Since when had his grandfather been so old? Had he not noticed his face before? But just last night those eyes had shone so piercingly.

So it was, a leave-taking, although without sadness. Just an exchanged glance. Ompu Silangit merely held his grandson's head for a moment, then turned to go down the hill. An ache swelled in Tondi's chest. His eyes stung from a creeping heat. The wind billowed Ompu Silangit's loose shirt, and wisps of his long white hair that dangled from his headdress waved with it. The silver of his hair reflected the sun. He moved further away towards the foot of this hill.

The sun was now directly overhead. Lasmia appeared from behind the house and said awkwardly, 'I have to go home, Amangboru. It is time for me to go to school.'

Tondi did not react. The girl ran down the hill, following Ompu Silangit who was already distant. She turned back a few times. But Tondi did not notice because his eyes were staring at his ompung's back, his shirt and white headdress, and his steady step through the boulders sprawled on the slope of the hill. A few buffalo were resting in the shade of the trees. Grasses covered the ground at the base of the hill. Between the boulders and the grasses was a track where the buffalo carts passed.

He turned his gaze and his eyes fell on the brown wooden planks of the house walls, the upright poles standing on stone foundations, supporting the house, and the earthen-floored space beneath the house, dry and clean. This was where his grandmother used to weave. Her loom was still stacked there. How Tondi longed to go back to his childhood and live here with his ompung and ompungboru. Even with the poverty and limitations, it had been truly joyful. But who can ever go back to the past? He must leave now, but before that, he had to visit his grandmother where she lay under the banyan tree. Only chirping birds kept watch at her grave. And falling leaves. Tondi cleaned the grave. It looked as though it was often cleaned, because there were no weeds or moss. This was Ompungboru's final resting place.

The journey on which he was about to embark was unlike any he had made before. He had often crossed the Toba plains when he worked on the bus on the Medan-Bukittinggi route. But he had never stayed anywhere along the way. The bus made only short stops at Balige or Siborong-borong, and a longer stop in Tarutung. Ompu Silangit's house was inland. From the route the bus took, the hill in the distance looked like just a hump of earth, the houses hidden by underbrush. Passengers probably thought the hill was a graveyard, because many hills in that area were cemeteries.

Now he would not be taking the usual roads. And during this time of rebellion, the roads were quiet. The buses from Medan or Siantar travelled in a convoy with army protection. Only rarely would one or two buses dare to drive without escorts.

Tondi left. He walked with the setting sun behind him. He took a shortcut towards the Bonandolok forest, leaving the inhabited area and the main road further and further behind him.

He had to head south. During the Batak War, King Singamangaraja's forces had waged war here, but they went in the opposite direction, moving north, infiltrating the Dairi area. Way back then, Acehnese who lived in the north had also entered the forests around here and joined the Batak army fighting the Dutch. They would help any group opposing the Dutch, with weapons or manpower.

But this time it was different. The Acehnese were busy with their own war, over religion. There was still fighting in Aceh against those who wanted to establish Darul Islam, an Islamic state. Batak, with their different religion, would of course not participate in such a war. Before the regional troubles, the national army had even sent many of the Batak soldiers now in the forests in the Toba area to put down the Darul Islam rebellion in Aceh. Who knows how many bullets they had fired at the Acehnese. The long history of friendship in the past, fostered during the fight against the Dutch, seemed to have vanished without trace in the life of the new republic, Indonesia. You could even say that the national quelling of rebellion was even more cruel, because the Indonesian soldiers sent on missions were often chosen deliberately because they were of a different religion.

Now, the fighting was no longer in the north but in the south, in Central Sumatra. The line of rebellion against the central government ran through all the forests linking Tapanuli with Minangkabau. Friend and foe could change in this war. And Tondi had to go on a long journey, probably without being aware that he was becoming part of the rope connecting Batak with Minangkabau.

PART TWO

BEGU

Chapter 4

The first birdsong came with the dawn that uncoiled the crimson sky. Long, golden shafts thrust down to earth, piercing the branches and leaves. The sun sent its warmth creeping over the dew on the leaves. The forest began to come to life. Slowly and surely the sun replaced the cold of the night.

A small crack split the forest, a path rarely traversed. This path had never been sealed. Here and there, shafts of light were more plentiful, revealing the brown earth. Huge trees protected this place. The earth was damp. The age of the trees was reflected in their huge trunks and the wrinkled, blackened bark. Storytellers say that back in the times of the Batak ancestors, marga groups withdrawing from the centre of Batak lands passed through this very forest.

According to the old stories, the Batak used to live in the area around the mountain called Pusuk Buhit on the west of Lake Toba. In the middle of the lake is an island, commonly called Samosir. Actually, it is not an island, but land that stretches from the foot of the mountain to the middle of the lake. The land in the centre of the lake is not separated from the land on the shore. It was in recent times that a channel was widened so that boats could pass and Samosir seemed to be separated from the land around, especially the foot of Pusuk Buhit. The area around Pusuk Buhit became the ancestral heartland of all Batak people. The mountain and the plains at its foot are considered sacred. The origin of all Batak people on the face of the earth is here. Every one. They are the descendants of the first human called Si Raja Batak who came down from the sky. He had two sons, Buru Tateabulan and Raja Isumboan, and from them others were born, and it is from the grandchildren of Si Raja Batak that all the Batak marga began.

It is said that the land around Pusuk Buhit could no longer accommodate all the descendants of Si Raja Batak, so some of them spread to the plains away from the lake. The area around the lake became too crowded, and there was conflict between families. Whereas Cain murdered Abel because of their competition for God's love, the descendants of Si Raja Batak fought over the real-life problems they faced. Fighting over land erupted easily. Usually, various marga allied to combat others. Inevitably, in such quarrels one party has to give way. So it was that the groups that left the centre and the lands around the lake moved ever more southward. Tondi had heard these stories often when he was a boy.

'This is how it is. The Batak who live on the lowlands beyond the island are always envious of those who still live in the ancestral heartland, and are the most highly respected of all,' the storyteller would say, wiping the spittle from his mouth, perhaps from talking so much, or perhaps from the rice wine.

Once, Tondi interrupted, 'But King Singamangaraja himself came from the plains beyond the ancestral heartland.'

'Ha, ha. Yes, you are right. Well done, Amang. But you surely know that King Singamangaraja had to pay his respects to those at the Heart. Usually, one of his wives came from the marga there, around Pusuk Buhit. And so he had to be respected, you see!'

The storytellers always had reasons to back up their stories.

'Do you know the very first marga to come out of the ancestral heartland?' Before Tondi had a chance to answer, the storyteller would answer himself because indeed the question was merely intended to get the interest of the audience in the rice-wine stall.

'The Siregar marga. Among Si Raja Batak's grandchildren, Siregar was one of the youngest. But this marga was also fond of a fight. While still residing in the ancestral heartland, Siregar and his children took the harvest belonging to their relatives who were passing by on a boat on the lake. This made everyone angry. In the end, Siregar and all his kin were cast out, and they left the ancestral heartland. Even though, if you think about it, what they did was perfectly acceptable.'

'What do you mean, acceptable?' one of the drinkers would sneer, 'just because your hula-hula marga is Siregar, you say "take" not "steal". What's acceptable about that?'

'Wait a moment,' the storyteller would become more excited as he had their attention now, 'the descendants of Si Raja Batak had multiplied by then, even though the land had not increased. Remember, the Siregar marga was the youngest. Maybe they received a smaller share of land. It's not clear whether the older marga wanted to share land with the Siregar group. Am I right? Am I right?'

There was a splatter of spittle.

The listeners nodded eagerly.

'So it was acceptable for him to take the produce of his uncles. Think about it. What could people do if they didn't have land? Taking that produce was just like paying taxes today,' the storyteller retorted.

'Taxman or thug?' someone heckled.

'Now, now,' the storyteller merely chuckled. He paid no mind and continued. 'So after the Siregar marga was exiled, the little land that they had was divided among their uncles. There was no recompense. If you think about it, those older marga who stayed in the ancestral heartland are in the Siregar marga's debt to this very day.' Another chuckle as he looked around. His audience understood the sign, and someone refilled his cup with rice wine. And he went on.

'So the youngest, Siregar, with his children, had to find land to cultivate in the Toba plains, south of Pusuk Buhit, in the area we now know as Muara. And he was forbidden to set foot in the Heart. All he could do from his new huta every day was to gaze back at the ancestral heartland.'

This was when the storyteller would pick up his two-stringed lute, the *hasapi*, and begin to tune the strings. When he found the right note, he would begin to hum, and other drinkers would join in with their guitars. It was common for drinkers to sing. Sometimes it would be a funny, satirical song they had composed. Or it might be a song about daily life, especially the lives of palm-wine drinkers. But the storyteller would most often sing songs about history, and this time he sang of the fate of the Siregar marga.

Over time, the Batak who remained in the ancestral heartland began to feel their island was too small. The population had increased and there was not enough land, so some of them left the island and went to live on the Toba plains. There was a huge influx of population there. Batak people prided themselves on having a large number of children and grandchildren. The prayer at every wedding was the hope for dozens of children. Intermarriage between marga was intended to get as many children as possible to carry on the male line marga.

'When the population increased around Lake Toba, the Siregar marga suffered once again,' the storyteller went on. 'The other marga now on the Toba plain, once again allied against the Siregar, taking their land with the excuse that the Siregar had no right to live there. Eventually, some of the Siregar marga were forced to leave Muara. They went south. This was a difficult journey because the group included women, children, and the animals they had managed to save. I think there were no buffalo carts back then, or even if there were, they could not go through the forest. So the group walked through the forest. Their suffering was extraordinary. Some fell, unable to go on, and had to be left behind. And this is why, among the Batak, it is the Siregar marga that is most widely dispersed over Tapanuli. They are in north, central and south Tapanuli. They walked from the Toba plains all the way to the place that came to be called Sipirok. There they stayed, probably because they could go no further. What is clear is that this group had proved its physical strength and spirit. Who knows how long that journey took? Perhaps decades. So it is not surprising that the survivors of that journey built a kingdom. Only the strongest men, women and children made it to the end of the journey. The others died along the way,' and the storyteller looked around, satisfied.

'That's why the Siregars in Sipirok are different to Siregars in other places,' he went on.

'How so?' someone asked.

'Well as I said, those who made it to Sipirok were the strongest physically and spiritually. Whereas the Siregars who could remain in the Toba plains were those who the other marga did not consider dangerous. And those who live between the Toba plain and Sipirok are descendants of the ones who were not strong enough to go on. So the marga that was exiled and tested by the ancient forest is the Siregar marga that built a kingdom larger and wealthier than those people in the Toba area or in the ancestral heartland. The kingdom in Sipirok had a real king, a real palace, power and land, unlike King Singamangaraja in the Toba lands, who was more like a customary and spiritual king to the Batak. The people of the Siregar marga in Sipirok also usually consider themselves to be smarter. Basically, they feel they are superior to other Batak. They did not even want to acknowledge the power of King Singamangaraja in Toba,' the storyteller would say.

The rice-wine stall stories could range over thousands of years. The listeners actually already knew all these tales. But they still loved to follow the storytellers' journey to the past. It was the rise and fall of the story, interspersed with musical interludes here and there that they loved. As a boy, Tondi would sit quietly, listening attentively to the storytellers who never seemed to run out of stories. Especially after gulping down their rice-wine and burping to their heart's content, they could go on for hours until they were frothing at the mouth.

* * *

Tondi had been longing to visit Sipirok for a long time, but he had never had a chance. Back in the days when he was a bus conductor, he worked on the Tarutung-Sibolga route, not the Tarutung-Sipirok route. The road to Sipirok was notoriously bad. It had not been repaired since Japanese times. The road between Tarutung and Sibolga was winding and followed the hills. There were some places where vehicles coming in the opposite direction could not pass. This was why the buses and trucks on this route were fitted with bugle horns. The drivers would play them like a musical instrument, making melancholy melody. You could hear them from miles away. Certain melodies were associated with particular places. When passengers heard them, they would immediately know where the bus was passing through. For instance, if the bus was passing the town of Siborong-borong, there was a song associated with that place. Whenever a driver heard the horn of a bus coming from the other direction, he would try to find a place to pull in where the two buses could pass. Without this camaraderie and mutual respect, all traffic would come to a standstill, unable to move forward or back. The only way out was to slide into the ravine on the side of the road, dozens of metres deep, and be smashed to smithereens.

From Sibolga, the bus went on to Padang Sidempuan. It stopped here for the night, and then early in the morning continued to Bukittinggi. Usually there were some passengers who got off at Padang Sidempuan, and others who got on. In his bus-conductor days, Tondi knew this town only from these night stopovers in both directions. The other towns he passed he only ever saw from the bus. Even if the bus stopped, the conductor was responsible for the security of the passengers' luggage that was carried on the roof. He had to check the tarpaulin covering the luggage and make sure it was tight so that the rain could not get in, and no luggage would be lost. Especially the post, which was the most valuable cargo carried in a wooden box on the bus roof. He could not leave the bus until it arrived in Bukittinggi, which was where the bus stopped for a full day and night.

At this moment, though, Tondi was not in any town. He was in the belly of the jungle that the Siregar marga had traversed when they searched for their land of hope hundreds or thousands of years ago. Their journey from the Toba plains to Sipirok. Who led the exiled marga like Moses had led his people on the long journey to find land? No one knows. New generations replaced those who journeyed. All that stayed were the mountains, rivers and huge rocks.

Tondi was surrounded by ancient trees. For centuries, people had wisely protected this forest. They would only fell trees according to need, and for immediate use. No one ever thought of felling trees for profit or wealth. A tree was felled because it was needed to build a house, whether a new one for newlyweds, or to repair an old one. And before any tree was felled, first you had to ask the spirit inhabiting it whether it agreed for the tree to move to a human residence. The trunk to be felled is the body of the tree, and every tree has its spirit. And this was the case not only with trees, but with any object to be taken from nature, be it fish in the lake, stones in the river, birds in the forest, or rice in the fields, they must all be courted, just as in human life a young woman must be courted and coaxed so that her spirit is willing to move, to leave her father's marga and join her husband's. When the betrothal ceremony takes place, the dowry that is paid is actually not to purchase a bride, but to ask for the willingness of all parties on the woman's side to relinquish her. It is not only her body that moves to the house of her husband. Her spirit must also be sincere and willing to move. So too must the spirit of a tree be courted, because after it becomes a house, it will become part of the life of a family. No one wants to live in a house where the wood comes from a tree whose spirit was not willing to leave the forest. That house will be hot, like hell for its inhabitants. This is why no one wants to live in a house built of wood that has been stolen. Felling a forest tree without getting the consent of the tree and other spirits in the forest is the same as stealing. Cutting down forests just for worldly wealth is plunder.

The path that crept in the gaps of the forest trees was truly a man-made wonder. According to those who own the story, the path the Siregar marga forged thousands of years ago was used again as a secret route during the Padri war in the south and during the Singamangaraja war in the north. During the Dutch times and the Japanese occupation, no army or government people ever traversed this path.

The creation of this path followed completely different principles to the roads built by Dutch engineers. They chose routes on the plains and along ridges of hills based on principles of efficiency and technological know-how. Using their theodolites, the engineers would select the closest distance, and use stones and asphalt in the most efficient way. If necessary, they would blow up the hill. The path in the forest, however, used the principle of efficiency for self-preservation. The ancestors who pioneered the path chose bends and curves in the mountains as places to hide.

The Dutch built the sealed roads. In places, they burrowed through mountains, building tunnels as shortcuts. From Medan to Kotaraja in the north, to Bukittinggi in the south, the road crossed hundreds of rivers and swamps. Hundreds of bridges had to be built. Even though the sealed road was now in poor condition, it was a legacy of the Dutch that was of immense value to independent Indonesia.

And now, that sealed road was carrying rumbling convoys of army troops. The trucks and armoured cars roared as they climbed the steep slopes. If the Dutch had not built those roads, could there even be a war? The war Tondi was in now, fighting the central government, seemed to repeat the past. Out there the national army was on the roads, while their enemy snuck around on the ancient path in the forest forged by their ancestors.

The birds had left their nesting trees. The winding road far below looked no larger than a belt. The roar of the engines went on. Tondi was amazed every time he looked at that road so far beneath his feet. The huge boulders scattered here and there looked like black dots. The villages fenced with thick bamboo on the plains below seemed no more than small clumps of bushes. He felt the cold of the forest in his bones. The spirits of this place had surely been with him thus far. Maybe also the spirits of those people who had fallen on their forest journey.

Was it the bird song that had woken him or the roar of the army convoy? He drew a deep breath into his sour mouth. He opened his knapsack and looked for food. There was only palm sugar. He bit off a small chunk. There was his pistol, and the cloth he had slept on last night, still damp from the dew. The dagger his grandfather had given him was still there.

He still had a long way to go. He thought about his stealthy journey thus far. If I am captured, he wondered, will I admit that I am Tondi or my full name Tondinihuta as on my identity papers? And who will acknowledge papers signed by the commander of a battalion that has joined the rebel army, anyway? Will I mention my marga? Who will capture me? Will it be someone of the same marga as me, or from my hula-hula marga? Or a Karo soldier? Or a Javanese soldier with no tie to Batak kinship customs? Which soldiers are in control around here? And does Batak kinship have any meaning at all in this war?

Tondi scrutinized the road below. Soldiers from the central army had made the locals slash and burn the growth beside the road. Probably this was so they could easily spot any rebels blocking the road, but in fact what it did was make the road stand out clearly like a curved black snake flanked by a brown line on either side. Actually, close battles rarely occurred. The central army and the rebel army merely exchanged mortar fire. The central army, headquartered in the towns, would fire shells in the direction of the rebels' hideouts in the forest. The rebels would retaliate by firing their bullets around the outskirts of the towns. Booming at night meant a battle was going on. But the chances of the rebels actually firing shells on the central army headquarters were slim, because the headquarters were situated in residential areas. The rebels might have family living there. Shooting between troops happened in short bursts, because the soldiers from the forest only wanted to cause a night disturbance for the town-dwellers. Sometimes they would come down, block the passing traffic and fire at it before going back to the hills.

The convoy was a long way off now, hidden behind the mountain. The forest was silent once more. Tondi plunged through the undergrowth, parting bushes that rustled at his touch. He was heading for a landmark between two huge wild fig trees in the south with tree trunks the width of the embrace of two men. Even from there, the Toba plains would still be a long way. The next landmark was a hill shaped like a sleeping buffalo.

This was his seventh day. Walking in the forest alone, he had to be prepared for the sounds of the jungle. The grating of insects, the

yelping of gibbons, the screeching of birds. The forest provided food
to be shared with monkeys and birds.

The further he went, the more the forest enveloped him in
intimacy. It felt as though he was walking somewhere he already
knew. Every bend, every stone that emerged in the earth seemed
familiar. Sometimes he would come across an old village, and
suddenly he did not feel strange in that place. Could he have lived
here in a previous life? He had the same feeling he had back when
he wandered in the undergrowth behind his grandfather's house.
Everything felt familiar to him. It no longer startled him to hear
the gibbon's sudden yelp. Step by step he moved on, following every
object that outlined the path.

He had been separated from his fellow soldiers only a few days,
but how very distant this forest felt to the rebellion going on. Time
did not seem to move here. There was just the rising sun, the setting
sun. Sky clear or cloudy. Rain or dry. No need for any almanac.

Battles were the sign that there was a rebellion going on.
But walking in the forest, Tondi was not involved in any fighting.
Back in his training he had learnt to take weapons apart and
reassemble them, and to fire with rifles and pistols. They said that
he had special aptitude because he managed to shoot on, or near, the
target. As far as he recalled, he had fired only twelve rifle bullets and
fourteen pistol shots the whole time. That was it. Then, together
with the rest of the group, he was sworn in at the lakeside, and
pledged the oath of loyalty to the cause. And what was that cause?

There were three areas in Indonesia that demanded to be heard:
North Sumatra, Central Sumatra and North Sulawesi. The people
in these regions had asked the central government to pay attention
to development in the regions. Since independence, very little of
what the regions produced was returned for their development.
Military commanders formed regional councils, which local figures
joined, and they made demands to the central government. Some
areas no longer wanted the central government telling them what to
do, and so they kept their own resources to use for their development
projects. Tension between the central government and the regions

heated up, and exploded when the central government fired the army officers involved with the councils. Having no other choice, the regions turned. The Indonesian republic was like an invalid. Its body was feverish, but its head way over in Jakarta did not want to know. Sukarno who ruled at the head ordered the army to fight the army at the body.

Tondi felt all this political stuff had nothing to do with him. What was important to him was that someone had given him the chance to leave his job on the intercity buses. When Pardapdap had invited him along, all he had to do was sign a form. Fill in his name, date of birth, education and so on. Then he was given a uniform and a pistol. Some others got rifles. He had no idea why, and he didn't care.

Chapter 5

Battles, wars and rebellions were far away in other forests. In this jungle, the problem to be faced here and now was to walk from one landmark to the next. Cross rivers and swamps. At particular times, look for food and a place to spend the night.

And then this day came. Tondi could see lace of smoke above the trees. The sky was clear, the sun hot, but the temperature comfortable. There had been no storm. This meant the smoke was not from a tree struck by lightning. It must be human made. The smoke was in the direction he was moving. A valley at the foot of a mountain.

He had been travelling for days eating only fruit and yams, and drinking honey, as his grandfather had advised him. He had not killed any animal, even though he had often come across deer, mouse deer and wild boar.

'Do not eat flesh, do not eat food with blood. Most of all, do not eat wild boar. This is the dirtiest animal. It is a scavenger. Make sure you keep your body clean. If you are in a state of cleanliness, then you can meet the protectors of the forest. They will help you,' Ompu Silangit had told him.

But Tondi was bored with his daily diet of fruit and roasted yam. If he came across other people, then perhaps he would get some variety in his menu. But were these people from the national army? He did not think so because those soldiers would never penetrate so deep into the jungle.

The valley was close now. Tondi peeped from behind some trees. There was a wooden shelter, a raised house. The floor was about two metres above ground level. A log with carved notches for climbing formed steps. Smoke billowed from a hearth in the yard. There was an aroma of freshly cooked rice. It was quiet. But the clay cooking-pot, with its contents bubbling away on the fire, meant the person doing the cooking was nearby. Tondi surveyed every corner. Under the house, an old woman was weaving.

From another side, emerging from a gap in the undergrowth came an old man. He was carrying a catch of fish strung through the gills with a reed. The old woman came out from beneath the house to take the fish. It looked as though they were an elderly couple.

Tondi walked slowly, but surely, deliberately stepping on dry leaves and twigs. The couple looked up. Strangely though, they registered no surprise. They just looked at him, and if there was a glint in their eyes, it was an expression of sincerity and friendship.

'*Horas Amang, Inang,* greetings Father, Mother,' Tondi addressed them politely.

'*Horas,*' they chorused. They continued studying him, from top to toe. They did not seem to be interested in the pistol hanging at his hip. Nor was there any hint of suspicion.

'Come over here,' the old man said to Tondi, speaking Batak. Then he addressed his wife. 'Cook the fish, Inang, so we can partake of it together.'

The accent and intonation of the man's Batak language was a little strange to Tondi's ears. It seemed to be a mixture of Samosir and Mandailing. From his bus-conductor days, Tondi was used to hearing variants of the Batak language from people of different regions. But he had never heard this particular one.

The old man made a sign to Tondi.

'Come, enter the house,' and he went up the stairs first. Tondi followed. At the threshold he sat, took off his shoes and let them fall to the ground.

The house had only one room. The floor was wooden and covered with pandanus mats.

'I am Ompu Bulung,' the old man said. 'I live here alone with my wife.'

Tondi introduced himself. The room was clean. The mats had an aroma of fresh dry leaves. That was strange. They were also of fine weaving, edged in black and chequered in the middle. They were clearly woven at home, because Tondi had earlier noticed drying strips of pandanus leaf. This kind of decorated mat was usually used in houses of highly respected people who often had visitors. But here, in this shelter in the middle of the forest, who would visit? Tondi sat on the mat with its colours still bright and shiny.

Ompu Bulung folded some betel leaf.

'There's no tobacco here,' he said.

'I also do not smoke,' Tondi said.

Ompu Bulung did not react. He merely cast his clear gaze at Tondi, looking him in the eye.

'I'm going to Bukittinggi.'

Ompu Bulung's brow furrowed for a moment.

'Bukittinggi,' he muttered, 'that's a long way.'

'Yes, I don't know how long it will take me to get there.'

'So you are going via Sipirok?'

Tondi nodded.

'Sipirok, if you don't lose your way, is about three days from here,' Ompu Bulung said. 'Do you know the path?'

Tondi nodded again.

'Oh yes, yes, if you've made it here, you must know the way,' Ompu Bulung said. 'If not, like most people you would go round and round in circles at the edge of the forest over there.'

Ompu Bulung's wife came up carrying the steaming rice. The smell of the grilled fish made Tondi hungry.

'Let's eat now,' Ompu Bulung said.

Ompu Bulung's wife's face was smooth, with few wrinkles. Tondi found her clear skin surprising, given that she was here in the middle of the jungle. And her clothes, although coarsely woven, were clean. She was not like Batak women he knew, who loved to talk.

Her voice was soft, and she spoke sparingly, inviting Tondi to take some food and add more rice. This must be dry rice, not wet paddy rice. It was crispy, soft and slightly perfumed. They ate almost soundlessly. Ompu Bulung, too, was not like the usual, talkative Batak men. He was silent while he ate. He seemed even respectful before the rice in his plate. He reminded Tondi of his grandfather.

The food set before them was rice, grilled fish and boiled vegetables sprinkled with andaliman seeds, which were bitter on the tongue and spicy in the mouth and stimulated the appetite. The grilled fish did not taste bland. Where had the salt come from? They all ate as though it were a sacred ceremony. The plates were made of clay and wood. All the tools in the house were made of things found in the forest. There was no glass or tin.

The ceremonial meal was over. Nothing was left. Ompu Bulung's wife carried the empty dishes downstairs. Ompu Bulung picked up some grains of rice that had spilled on to the mat and placed them on a coconut placemat. Tondi did the same. The mat was now clean.

'If you've come from the Toba plains, and you already know the path, this means you have been walking in the forest for seven days,' said Ompu Bulung.

'Yes,' Tondi replied.

'Who told you the way?'

'My ompung.'

'He has been through here?'

Tondi nodded. Ompu Bulung looked Tondi sharply in the eye. It made the hairs on his neck stand on end. The old man's pupils were like deep holes, hypnotic, so that although Tondi wanted to look away, he could not do so, but remained captured by those eyes.

'You had no difficulty finding the path here?' Ompu Bulung's voice released Tondi from the capturing gaze.

Tondi took a breath.

'No. I felt as though I had been here before. None of the landmarks that my ompung gave me were difficult to find.'

Ompu Bulung nodded. Who knows what that meant. His nodding seemed to hold mystery.

Outside, it was getting dark. Strange. Even though it was not yet evening. Perhaps it was clouds? But the weather was fine. And the sun was indeed setting, although it was still the middle of the day. Could it be that time moved more swiftly here?

Tondi looked outside, confused. He had planned to use what was left of the daylight to continue on his way, so he could reach the foot of the mountain before nightfall. It was impossible to walk in the dark.

'You can sleep here for the night,' said Ompu Bulung, noticing Tondi's confusion.

'But . . . but . . .' Tondi looked at his watch. He did not trust his watch because it was just some cheap thing that he had bought at a street stall in Medan.

'We have not had any guests for a long time,' Ompu Bulung said. Tondi hoped the old man was going to tell stories about his life. But no. Ompu Bulung looked away, glancing at the pistol Tondi had unbelted and laid on the floor when he entered the house.

'You have joined the fighting?'

'Yes, but I have not seen any real fighting so far,' Tondi said.

'So you have not yet killed a man?'

'No.'

'War is always about killing.'

'I don't know if I could kill someone if I was in a real fight.'

'But isn't the war you are in now about killing? Who is fighting whom?'

'I don't know,' Tondi said, his voice flat.

Our fighting is to put pressure on Sukarno. That is what those lecturers always said to the volunteers. But would Sukarno really give in to the pressure of a few demands? The proof was that his government had sent in troops, and war had broken out. At the beginning, fighting between Sukarno's troops and the rebels in the forest had been half-hearted. There were ties between them. Many had fought side by side during the war for independence, and some had family ties. They were careful with their mortar fire to not cause any casualties. The noise of gunfire was just like the bamboo fireworks during the Muslim fasting month.

But recently, the fighting had become no longer a game of hide-and-seek with mortar fire. It was the real thing. Sukarno's government had mobilized and sent in new troops whose soldiers were of a different ethnicity to the rebels, so family was no longer a consideration when firing bullets. The government soldiers thought nothing of using long-range mortar fire, with widespread destruction. Worse still, the government now deliberately exploited differences between Batak groups. The rebels who went into the forest were mostly Toba Batak, like Colonel Simbolon himself. Now, to confront them, Sukarno sent in troops who were mostly Karo Batak, a group that historically had always been in conflict with the Toba Batak.

So if Tondi was being asked who was fighting whom, and who was the real enemy, he could not answer. His father lived in Java and was not part of the rebellion. He was loyal to Sukarno. So was his father his enemy? He had heard that Sukarno had sent in troops from West Java, parachuted in by plane from Medan, and they were busy occupying the towns on the Toba plains. Other troops from central and east Java had come by ship and landed in Padang. The rebels had been forced to retreat further into the forest.

And now, he must get to Bukittinggi, carrying a letter that had to reach the rebel headquarters there. The question was, would he even be able to reach that town?

* * *

The curtain of night had fallen over the forest. The birds had returned to their nests and ceased their chirping. Or maybe Tondi could no longer hear them. After days of sleeping with a blanket of only mist and dew, the room felt warm. The light of the coconut-oil lamp flickered. Perhaps because he was in a warm room, Tondi felt his eyelids grow heavy with tiredness. He was pleased when Ompu Bulung invited him to sleep. He stretched out in the corner of the room and in only a few seconds, was in a deep sleep.

The night was silent. All the animals of the jungle, even the insects, seemed to have fallen into a deep sleep as well. Even the wind barely moved. There was not even the sound of rustling in the leaves.

Suddenly Tondi felt the house rocking. An earthquake? He tried to open his heavy eyelids. The room was completely dark. He groped around on the floor where he was sleeping. He could feel himself being rocked. Was he dreaming? He felt the house moving. When he finally managed to open his eyes, he found he was in a space much smaller than Ompu Bulung's house. And he was puzzled. Ompu Bulung and his wife were sitting respectfully before him. They had changed their clothes, and around their shoulders they each wore an ulos cloth with glittering thread. It was not like the ulos back home that Tondi was familiar with, which were made from red, white and black thread.

'*Hu boan hamuna tu raja nami*; I am taking you to meet our king,' Ompu Bulung said calmly.

Tondi sat up awkwardly. Where was this king's place they were taking him to? The room jerked forward. Outside, he could see many oil lamps lighting the path. It reminded him of when the buses he used to ride would go through Muslim villages in South Tapanuli and Central Sumatra after the holy seventeenth day of the fasting month. Oil lamps were set in front of every house. The neatly placed torches would flicker and flare in the wind, moving like a yellow wave. And now here he was in a village, the road lined with houses. There were rows of lamps burning brightly. And as for this moving house, it turned out that he was on a cart that was larger than usual. The floor was lined not with a mat, but with thick carpet.

Tondi's mouth was locked tight. The cart kept rolling forward on the smooth road, drawn by two buffalo. Then they went through a large gateway. The cart stopped. The buffalo stood stock-still. Ompu Bulung made a sign to Tondi to follow. Tondi rose and got down from the cart.

In front of him stood a Batak traditional house, extremely large. Black, white and red carving covered the pillars and the walls, luminous in the light of the flame torches. The brown wood looked old, but strong. A buffalo head crowned the top of the roof, the distance between its horns, from point to point, measured about two metres.

When they entered the house, they were in a large room. Tondi's gaze met the eyes of an old man, his white hair hanging from a white headcloth. He had an ulos cloth around his shoulders and he sat on the floor, hard up against the wall. To his left and right, men sat leaning against the wall. Only men, and all of them in white headdresses like the one his grandfather Ompu Silangit wore. Every man had a glittering ulos cloth around his shoulders.

'*Horas*,' the old man said in greeting.

'*Horas*,' Tondi and Ompu Bulung replied. They sat before the old man. So this is their king, Tondi thought. He looks no different to Ompu Bulung in his dress and the way he acts. Ompu Bolung sat and gave no gesture of respect, did nothing special other than answer the king's greeting.

'So where is the dagger?' The old man suddenly asked, speaking in Batak with an accent like Ompu Bolung's that sounded strange to Tondi's ears.

Tondi was shocked. How could he know? The dagger was inside his knapsack. He pulled it out slowly and placed it in front of him.

'That dagger came from here, from our kingdom here,' the old man said. 'It has been used many times in human combat. It has licked much human blood. Do you still need it? Remember, this dagger cannot be used just for cutting animal meat. The spirits of the humans whose blood it has licked will weep.'

Tondi became more nervous.

'I do not know,' he said, hesitantly. My grandfather just told me to carry it.'

'What for?'

'I do not know,' Tondi said.

The old man and Ompu Bulung exchanged glances.

'Ompu Bulung, you live on the border of our kingdom, and your house is close to living beings. Does this dagger still have use in these times?'

'For war, no longer, my king,' Ompu Bulung said.

'Yes, living beings today use guns,' the king said.

'But if the spirit of this young man still needs the power from his ancestors, then the dagger is still useful,' Ompu Bulung said. 'As for war, it has no use, especially because he doesn't even know who he is fighting. And it is not useful as a mere decoration. The blood of humans that has dried on the blade is not for decoration.'

'Who do you most hate in your life right now?' Tondi heard the sudden question ring in his ears.

'Do you have enemies?' the old man went on.

An image of his father flashed across Tondi's mind. But he could not utter his hate because there also appeared the protecting image of his grandfather whom he loved and honoured. Oh, how those two faces resembled each other. How could he hate someone who looked so much like his grandfather?

Tondi felt pressure in his chest. Sharp stones were stabbing deep in his heart.

'If you are not fighting, you do not need weapons. If you are fighting, then you must know who your enemy is. You must be serious about killing. War is for killing. We who live in this kingdom never fight. But we often see humans fighting each other, over beyond. Humans always choose war as the way to control other humans. The war you have joined now must also have one party that wants to control and one that does not want to be controlled. Both sides want to win. In every battle, only one side can win. Or they will both be destroyed. It can never happen that they both win. Fighting half-heartedly, fighting without spirit, is pointless. War is done in battle, and every battle has killing.' The old man's eyes shone in the lamplight.

Between the rebels and Sukarno's government, who wants to control and who resists being controlled, Tondi wondered.

'If you still want this dagger, take it,' the old man said. 'But use it as it should be used in war.'

Tondi did not move. The face of the old man sitting before him reminded him of his grandfather's face. But his skin was reddish and clearer. The shining thread of the ulos cloth around his shoulders glittered.

'This war you are part of will not last long. Not like the ones before it. And you will be unharmed in this war. The real war you have to face is not this one,' the old man said, bringing the conversation to a close.

He gave a sign to Ompu Bulung who touched Tondi on the arm, asking him to move forward. As he rose, Tondi picked up his dagger and put it inside his knapsack.

'*Horas*,' he said while making the respectful gesture raising his hands, palms together to shoulder height to the old man called 'our king', and to the men in the room.

'*Horas*,' came the reply in chorus.

Tondi accompanied Ompu Bulung out of the room and walked away from the house.

Ompu Bulung said, 'So now you have met our king and all the kings under him in the kingdom.'

As they walked, Tondi was lost in thought.

'Only those who are clean in body and mind because they have purified themselves can meet us,' Ompu Bulung continued.

Tondi was still thoughtful. He remembered his grandfather's words, telling him not to kill any jungle animal and not to eat meat while in the forest. All along the way, he had only eaten fruit, yams and honey. He had followed his grandfather's words. He would observe everything he said. The parting he had found so wrenching seemed to push him out of the protective cocoon he had been in all this time. He decided then and there to become Ompu Silangit's successor.

Ompu Bulung invited Tondi to one of the houses.

'Rest here a while. Tomorrow there is something I want to show you,' he said.

The house they entered was an ordinary Batak house, made of wood with a palm-fibre roof. From a distance, the house's shape looked like a ship. The support poles formed a row of giant trunks. The walls of the house were carved. Tondi and Ompu Bulung entered a room with the floor covered in finely woven mats. A flaming torch was in the centre.

Towards dawn, Tondi awoke. Ompu Bulung was sitting beside him.

'Drink some coffee,' he said.

Tondi sat up. His knapsack and pistol were still lying on the floor. The coffee was served in a clay cup. The aroma was delicious. He had never smelled such an aroma before. The bitterness of the coffee mixed with the sweetness of the palm sugar felt sticky on his tongue.

Through the doorway, they could see the yard. Girls were pounding the rice. The dawn's sun sent shafts of light through gaps in the foliage. The rice pounding thudded, accompanied by the young girls' singing. Although it sounded like Batak songs, it was unfamiliar to Tondi. And it was strange, too, that people here did their rice pounding at dawn.

The sun rose further. Ompu Bulung invited Tondi to go down from the house. They walked past the girls.

'If you wanted a wife, which of them would you choose?' Ompu Bulung suddenly asked.

Tondi was confused. He stole a look at the girls. They were beautiful. They wore brightly coloured blouses.

'I do not want to marry yet,' Tondi said. He had a flash of his mother. This then changed to the face of a young woman. That gentle face had been mapped long ago, but the expression seemed to call him. An oblong face, soft, bright eyes with long, black lashes. A woman over there. She seemed to be calling Tondi's name. They spent only one night together, but the memory was eternally knotted inside him. Nothing could untie it. Now that knot seemed to be pulling him out of the calmness of this place.

'You can stay here, if you wish. The king likes you. You can be his son-in-law,' Ompu Bulung said.

Tondi was startled. The face of his mother again flashed through his mind. And the face of his father. He gnashed his teeth.

'I do not wish to stay here. I still have a long way to go. I have to prove I can live,' he said.

'What's the difference? You can also live right here. Look at this girl in the yellow blouse. She is the daughter of our king,'

Ompu Burung said teasingly. This was the first time Tondi had seen any expression in the old man's face, unlike his impenetrable face earlier.

Tondi turned. He looked at the girls pounding the rice. They were all wearing bright blouses. Their clean, rosy faces shone in the dawn light. Their red lips moved as they sang, their breathing attuned to the rise and fall of the pestles in the wooden trough and their song rhythmically punctuated by the pounding.

'There will come a time I will have to cross the sea, to Java,' Tondi said, almost mumbling.

'What for?'

Indeed, what for? Tondi was taken aback. Was it for himself, to prove to his father that he was now a man? But what kind of man was that? Crawling around in poverty.

'What is it that you want from life?' Ompu Bulung's question ambushed him.

'To get rich,' Tondi almost replied.

But he didn't say it.

It was true he wanted to escape the pit of poverty. But was getting rich the right answer? It was true that if he were rich his mother would not have to be stuck in her little food stall. But was that it? Did he want his father's acceptance? Was that really important? Meanwhile his mother would still be a woman with a food stall with no husband beside her, whether officially divorced or not. No, it was not wealth, and it was not just a case of his father's acceptance. He wanted that man called Pardomutua, that man who was called his father, to bow low at his mother's feet.

Tondi looked at the girl in the yellow blouse. His mother's face flashed again across his mind. He welcomed it. Her face disappeared, but then he saw the image of his father. The man who had abandoned him and his mother all those years ago.

Ompu Bulung continued studying Tondi.

'Stay here for a few days,' he said.

'Thank you, but I should leave this very day.'

'Don't do that. You are here in our kingdom, so you must be our guest for a few days. That is the custom of our kingdom. Surely you will not refuse. You can use the time to study our knowledge. Much of the knowledge in your pustaha comes from us.'

Tondi looked around. The houses stood neatly in a row. There were no animals roaming around. The yards were clean.

'Has anyone taught you the art of combat?' Ompu Bulung asked.

'When I was small, my ompung taught me tiger-move martial arts,' Tondi said.

Ompu Bulung nodded.

'And what's the use of that knowledge today? You and your enemy have guns. You will fight with guns,' he said.

Tondi was silent. Ompu Bulung asked him to show some of the combat moves he had learnt. The old man nodded.

'Sharpen your eyes,' he said. Then he put his palm on Tondi's brow. Just a few moments. Tondi felt a cool current from the hand flowing into the crown of his head, turn in the cavity of his skull and flow right through his body. First it penetrated his eyes, nose and ears, then forced through the pores of his skin. When he opened his eyes, he was face to face with Ompu Bulung, but he did not mind those hypnotic eyes that drew him in as they had earlier. All he could see was clear eyes.

'We gave knowledge to your ompung when he was your age. Actually, he wanted to stay here, but when your country was struck by war, he went home. He never returned. If you want to receive knowledge from us, you must understand that this knowledge cannot win wars in your time now. Today's knowledge is different. Our knowledge is powerless in confronting the knowledge about battles of the Pale Eyed Ones.'

Tondi raised his head and looked around. Things felt strange. Sounds were much sharper in his ears. He could see the bees crawling on the branches, and even the grains in tree bark many metres away. He could smell what was cooking in the distant hearth. The acuteness of his senses confused him—the combination of what his eyes could see, his nose could smell, his ears could hear, his salivating tongue and even the breeze softly blowing on the pores of his skin. Confusion, dizziness, and then he swayed. Ompu Bulung took him by the shoulders to stop his fall. Tondi tried to stand up straight.

He questioned with his eyes.

'Don't worry. This is normal,' Ompu Bulung said. 'We have opened all the senses in your body. From now on, we accept you as one of our marga. You may come here any time. Even if a time comes and our kingdom vanishes, when humans in great numbers enter this territory, we will not vanish. You can meet us whenever you wish, wherever you are.'

That day, Tondi ate at the feast. Drums sounded. The villagers beat the *gondang* drums for their annual cleansing of life ceremony. Ompu Bulung asked Tondi to join the gondang group and play the gong. People began to dance. Some among them moved like the tiger-move martial art Ompu Silangit had taught him. Tondi was enthralled with the dance, all the while listening carefully for the cues to play the gong. It felt as though his hand hitting the gong was being moved by some external force. As he followed the sound of the drums, his senses became more focused on everything audible, visible and sensed in any way. Every time he struck the gong it was on the correct beat. His breathing felt attuned to the resonance of the gong, regulating his pulse. Gradually the clumps of colours, the buzzing sounds, the aroma of herbs and spices, the rush of the wind and the flood of saliva all subsided, and he felt a profound calmness in the midst of the resonance of the gong that echoed from far away. His whole body felt enveloped in comfort, from his skin to his veins, something he had never experienced before.

The ceremony went on for seven days. At night, the village was quiet, as though there were no inhabitants. Only the flaming torches brightened the yard where the ceremony took place. But there was not a single person around.

On the third day, early in the morning, Tondi took his leave.

'Very well then, if you do not wish to stay here any longer,' said Ompu Bulung. 'I have nothing to give you that has any value in your land. So take this.' He held out a bamboo flute. It was black, as thick as a thumb, as long as a forearm and with five holes. Tondi weighed it in his hands a few moments, then put it in his knapsack.

The old man accompanied Tondi to his cart drawn by two buffalo. The sun was rapidly climbing in the sky. The sounds of the ceremony faded behind them. Strangely, in this jungle there was a smooth path for a buffalo cart. With the rocking of the cart as it moved in the shade of the trees, Tondi felt sleepy. He tried to keep himself awake. But he had never felt his eyelids as heavy as this. He slept.

He awoke with the dew dripping on his face. He wiped the moisture from his face as he opened his eyes. The sun was reddening the eastern horizon. Did I dream last night? he wondered. When Ompu Bulung took me out, the sun in the sky was at the height of a punting pole, so it was around seven in the morning. Now it is dawn. The mist in the forest was beginning to part. He twisted himself up.

He had slept under a sugar-palm tree. The dew that had gathered on the fronds was dripping. It tasted sweet when it flowed into his mouth. So it was not dew. Where bunches of sugar-palm fruit had been cut, the sap dripped. Some of it had dampened his shirt. He had certainly slept well last night.

When the fronds of the sugar-palm trees dry and turn yellow, but there are still blossoms to produce sugar, the fronds are cut. Tondi saw there were no containers set to collect the sap. He looked around him. There was no Ompu Bulung. There was no house and no buffalo cart. There were only huge trees. And the shoes on his feet felt damp. Ah, dreams. The mystery of the ancient forest embraced him. He had slept the night on a thick, dry mattress of palm fibre.

It turned out that he was on the other side of the valley, at the place that was his next landmark. He looked below, back towards the plain in the distance that he had left behind. He thought he could see an orchid on a banana-tree trunk and hear the chirping of baby birds. He was unsure of his sight and hearing. Could his eyes and ears really see and hear that far away?

Chapter 6

Tondinihuta twisted, stretched his muscles and straightened his bones. How could he have slept so well last night, with only sugar-palm roots for a pillow? Thick palm fibres covered the earth, making a sleeping mat. The tree that the fibres were from was very old. Some leaves were dry, and the fronds pointed to the sky.

In the old stories, sugar-palm trees were said to be favourite haunts for spirits. This was because these trees were not just plants, but transformations of a beautiful and wise princess. She had many suitors. They were prepared to fight and kill each other to win her as a bride. Finally, to stop this futile fighting, she chose to turn herself into a sugar-palm tree. As a sugar palm, she said, she could be of use to all humanity. Her clothing became the outer skin; her black hair, the fibre; her arms, fronds; her slim fingers, reeds; her breast milk, sap. Open her protective clothing, and you find her essence, the white flesh that can be turned into sago, a food to sustain life. And so it was that her entire being was devoted to humans for eternity. Palm fibre roofs cool a house. Men are bonded in friendship when they drink liquor made from the palm sap. Sitting under a fibre roof drinking palm wine is like nursing at the princess's breast.

Last night he had slept in the princess's lap. He had never before been so careless about going to sleep in the forest. Normally, he would prepare the place to spend the night, creating a makeshift shelter with the raincoat he carried in his knapsack, and building a fire to keep wild animals away. How was it that he had slept here without any preparation? Well, the princess must have protected him, because he had not experienced any danger.

The sun was slanting from the east. The sky was still crimson. Those experiences over the last few nights, were they real, or had he dreamt them? Tondi stood and took a good look around him. This was not the place where he had ended up yesterday. And he could not remember the path he had taken to get here. Had these recent memories been wiped by his deep sleep? He had never experienced anything like this before.

He was on the slope of a mountain. A sharp smell hovered. Wind from the summit brought sulphur vapour. Close by were traces of settlement. It looked as though people used to live here. There were remains of large hearths that looked as though they had been used for an iron forge. There were bits of rifle barrels and muzzleloader cannons strewn around. Probably, this had been a hideout during the Batak War. Tondi had seen blacksmiths' forges before, where they made knives, blades and hoes, but this hearth was huge in comparison. So it seemed Batak used to make guns and cannons. Why was this skill not passed down?

Piles of sulphur here and there on the yellow-brown earth. Remains of ammunition and an iron forge. A weapons workshop in the middle of the jungle. Tondi looked carefully at these traces of an earlier generation. Pieces of rusted weapons and pots protruded from the ground. There was some Arabic script on a large rock, facing west. Tondi had learnt to read some Arabic script at high school and he could read: *Allahu Akbar—Muhammad Rasulullah*, Allah is great—Muhammad is His Prophet. So this must have been written by the Acehnese troops who joined the Batak War. Below, etched in Batak script was *Ahu si Singamangamara*, the sign of His Majesty, Singamangaraja.

Seeing these traces of the past made Tondi reflect. Perhaps it was only in his head, but he could just hear the alternating beats of pounding iron. Sighs of the bellows in the hearth. Sounds of hooves. Whinnying horses. Commands shouted in Batak. Cries of *Allahu Akbar*. Explosion, explosion, explosion. He not only heard it. He saw it. This hiding place under attack from Dutch soldiers. Fighting. No time to reload rifles with ammunition. Fighting with Acehnese short swords now. Acehnese and Batak holding ground. Ambonese, Javanese and Dutch attacking. Falling on both sides. The attackers coming on like a torrent. The entire Batak and Aceh side dead. And the fighting stops.

Then, only the sound of the tramp of soldiers' boots as they walk around collecting their dead and treating the wounded. The bodies of the Acehnese and Batak picked up one by one and thrown into the ravine on the side of the mountain. The soldiers depart, carrying their dead on their shoulders and bearing the wounded in stretchers. Tondi saw it all as though it was right in front of him, and he could smell ammunition and blood. Who knows how long that battle lasted in the past, but it all went by in a flash before his eyes.

Now it was quiet. He could hear calling from deep in the ravine. He looked below. His view was blocked by thick underbrush. But he felt as though far down he could see a pile of bones stacked together as one, Batak of their ancestral religion and Muslim Acehnese. Allied in death. Now they had all become spirits, *begu*, calling to Tondi in one voice, he did not know what language it was, but he understood it. Tondi called back a greeting, imagining a 'horas' for the spirits of the Batak and 'assalamualaikum' for the spirits of the Acehnese. Then he turned and left that place. His feet felt as though they were fettered with cannon balls, his tread was heavy, but his chest felt free.

The Batak had long cultivated ties with the Acehnese in the north, who brought in weapons, from rifles to cannons. Aceh was a rich kingdom, able to buy modern weaponry, matching the Dutch colonial army. In the Aceh War, while fighting the Dutch, the sultan of Aceh had also brought in weapons for King Singamangaraja's troops. A close working alliance had developed between the Acehnese and the Batak.

The sultan of Aceh had sent in military support to King Singamangaraja, so the Dutch had to face two territories of battle at once, in Aceh and Batak lands. The Batak lands, located in the interior, relied on relations with the Acehnese sultanate via the land route crossing the jungle from Karo, Gayo, through to the Aceh centre at Kutaraja. This aid was cut when the Acehnese sultanate finally fell and the Dutch occupied Aceh. Many Acehnese fighters then voluntarily came to Batak territory to join the Batak fight against the Dutch.

This was also when Acehnese skills were greatly valued. Apart from advice on warfare, some Acehnese had skills in repairing broken weaponry. They could also make ammunition, even though their raw material was volcanic sulphur. Needless to say, the quality of this ammunition did not equal that of the Dutch, but there was no choice. As time went on, the Batak soldiers had no logistical support. They had to fight at close range, and meanwhile Dutch weaponry was becoming ever more sophisticated. The Dutch were now using machine guns that did not have to be reloaded with ammunition one bullet at a time.

The Batak lost the Batak War, falling like fireflies before the machine guns. The Dutch launched a strategy different to the one they used in other regions when they sent in troop expeditions with high mobility. Probably, they were advised by Batak traitors to King Singamangaraja. Only Batak knew the secrets of nature in Batak lands. So it was that the Dutch troops were able to blockade the Toba plains, and the locals were unable to trade their produce and buy war supplies. The Dutch placed soldiers with machine-guns at every road so that King Singamangaraja's followers were blockaded. Now the Dutch had only to wait for the Batak soldiers to give up and carry out suicide attacks. And so it was that King Singamangaraja fell after months of blockade.

The Dutch won the twenty-nine-year war through this final blockade. It was certainly effective, because from time immemorial Batak had chosen places to reside in isolated locations. These isolated areas were the most powerful places of defence. But in the Batak War, they were the cause for their defeat.

The home of the Batak ancestors is around Lake Toba. The lake is a gigantic caldera formed after a volcanic eruption, an eruption so terrible that it hurled away the top half of the mountain, leaving only a huge lake in what remained. The location the ancestors chose was protected by steep mountain slopes, with entry through only a few passes. For eons, this isolation was fortunate, because there was little chance of warfare with other groups.

Usually, war was only between marga groups, and fought over land or family honour. Each marga then protected itself with an enclosure fence of barbed bamboo. Wars between them involved only sharp weapons and, if they had a powerful spiritual leader joining their side in the fight, magic would be employed too. So there were usually two methods of war: during the day the people would fight with spears and knives, while the nights would be marked by explosions and flashes of fire. This kind of war did not last long. Once it reached the ears of King Singamangaraja, he would send the raja bius in charge of those fighting to make peace. There would be negotiation to resolve the conflict by handing over to each side what was rightfully theirs, or honour would be restored by an apology from the wrongful party. Then, there would be a cleansing ceremony with the blessing of King Singamangaraja, carried out by the raja bius as his representative maintaining harmony in custom and religion, and bringing justice to restore the essential truth of Batak life. Order was protected by Batak custom and religion through the customary kings and the highest priest, King Singamangaraja.

But great wars had destroyed these connections. The first war with an outside force was when the Muslim reformers called Padri accompanied by southern Batak, assaulted the Toba lands. The Batak from the south who were part of the Padri force had converted to Islam, but from childhood they had heard stories about their marga and ancestral land in Pusuk Buhit and around Lake Toba. When the Padri pushed north, they were familiar with the lie of the land and knew all the paths. They were able to launch lightning attacks from the mountain passes, piercing right to the centre of King Singmangaraja's power.

The Padri and southern Batak devastated the Toba lands. Their attacks were swift, but they destroyed villages and infrastructure, and carried off Toba Batak men and women as prisoners of war. They sold them as slaves in a few small towns on the western coast of Sumatra. As a result, thousands of Batak lost their marga. Slavery was abolished only when the Dutch colonial government was effective in Sumatra. However the children and grandchildren of these former slaves did not want to identify as Toba Batak, and became absorbed into the local population. Some took the marga of Mandailing but steadfastly refused to acknowledge any origin in Batak territory. Others identified as Minangkabau or coastal Malay.

Unlike the Padri War that destroyed villages and enslaved people, the Batak War that followed did not destroy Batak life. It ended the power of King Singamangaraja, the sovereign of Batak custom and religion, but it coincided with the Dutch implementation of their new policy that allowed natives access to western education. Schools were established, and many Batak children, especially those whose parents wanted to leave the old ways and convert to Christianity, were able to go to school. Batak people leapt ahead into western civilization, riding the vehicle of higher education.

The remaining followers of King Singamangaraja who continued to follow traditional custom and the Batak religion, now carried on their beliefs and practices in secret. They were the only ones able to care for the tondi and safeguard relations with the ancestors and spirits inhabiting sacred places and the forest. Christianity and Islam cut these connections. Sacred places were destroyed, the ancient virgin forest lost. The spirit inhabitants, the begu, had to move to fairy-story land. Begu were disappearing from life. But how can you cut all conversation with the ancestors when the marga is still part of you, and stories of the ancestors are passed down from generation to generation? How can Batak people live without tondi?

Eliminating begu meant denying tondi. Begu are spirits of people who are dead but still in the world before going on to *banua ginjang*, the world above. Tondi are spirits of the living, as the force that starts life when in the womb, exists in consciousness, and leaves after death. Every tondi will become a begu—be that a good begu, residing in a sacred place to give protection to its descendants, or a bad one, to be employed by black magic for evil purposes. The disappearance of the Batak religion helped sever connections with the begu world, which meant loss of the guardianship to ensure that your tondi becomes a spirit for human good. Could this be why the southern Batak were so cruel in their raids and abductions during the Padri war? What kind of spirit would drive Batak people of the same ancestral origin to kill and sell into slavery their own kin?

Tondi took another look around him. He had travelled far into the belly of the interior. This journey had turned out to be more a pilgrimage. All those traces of earlier generations: dislodged stones; paths made by groups passing through, or by soldiers; all of this was proof of the never-ending struggle for life, from one generation to the next. Could this be his own personal pilgrimage from the northern Batak lands to Bonjol in the south?

Pilgrimage or war, or whatever you wanted to call it, he still had a long way to go. But he felt his body was warmer than on previous days. His blood seemed be flowing faster in his veins. He had no pain in his muscles as he had on the other days when he awoke in the morning in the open air. And he did not feel hungry.

If all that happened last night was just a dream, if indeed Ompu Bulung and his wife who gave him food were not real, then this meant he had not eaten since midday yesterday. But why, then, was he not at all hungry now? Maybe that dripping sugar palm sap had given him energy.

He felt stronger than on previous days. The morning breeze felt warm. Tondi took a deep breath and held it. When he breathed out, his breath blew away the breeze blowing on his face. He did this a few times, and each time he warded off the breeze coming from the south.

Without having to repack his knapsack, Tondi left this place. He should be able to tell the direction from the sunlight through the trees, but he pulled out the compass that his commander had given him, to be doubly sure. Strangely, the needle of the compass spun wildly. This had never happened before. He had been using the compass on his journey, together with the landmarks his grandfather had given him without any problems so far. The compass had worked well. Why was the needle going crazy now?

As he walked, he kept glancing at the compass needle. Maybe it has broken, he thought. He put it in his knapsack pocket. Better just to follow the landmarks. During the day, he could tell direction from the position of the sun, and at night, if the sky was clear, from the stars. His grandfather had also taught him about using the stars as guides. On his journey, every night before going to sleep, he would look at the sky, and he got to know the stars. But until now he had never walked at night.

This morning he felt extremely fit. He had been walking for days alone, in the middle of the jungle, but his body was not as tired as yesterday. Was this because of his dream last night? But it all felt so real. He could see the face of Ompu Bulung, his wife and the others at the traditional house, and felt that he would immediately recognize them if he saw them again. Usually, when you wake you cannot remember the faces of people in your dreams. Except for people you already know. But the faces of the people he met last night were mapped clearly in his mind. Were they from the world of dreams?

The jungle closed in. Sounds of birds, monkeys and insects seemed to be reminding Tondi that he was the one and only human here. He suddenly felt a rush of longing to meet another person, and this made him catch his breath. On previous days, he had never had such a feeling. This was a vague longing, not a longing for his mother, but a new kind of longing entirely.

Longing for humans? Who? What was he longing for, actually? He was walking alone in the middle of the jungle. If he were still a bus conductor, he would have people around him. He remembered the bus driver and his performances on the bugle horn, playing all those songs. He remembered the Chinese restaurant with its burning aroma of fried garlic. The Padang restaurant with its plates of food in the window. People pushing in the queue for tickets at the cinema.

The rice wine that warmed the body. And he remembered the bus passengers—the complaining ones, the friendly ones, the women. Yes, he remembered the women. A woman. How long ago was that?

* * *

It was on the road from Medan to Bukittinggi. The young woman got on at Lubuk Pakam and was going as far as Padang Sidempuan. Her seat was right at the back of the bus, on the long bench running from one side of the bus to the other. It was the most uncomfortable place to sit because you felt all the bumps. If she was going to sit there for the whole trip, her bones would be shattered. It was also where Tondi sat. When the bus was completely full, he would vacate this seat and sit on a low wooden stool that he put near the door. On this particular day, only the young woman was sitting there, so there was room for Tondi on the passenger seat. The young woman sat close against the window on the right-hand side. Tondi sat on the left. Because of the distance between them, they did not greet each other. But in a journey through to Sidempuan lasting at least twelve hours, would you really keep quiet?

The woman was about thirty. Tondi was always respectful to women he met on his travels, including the passengers. He always thought of his mother whenever he dealt with women, especially if they were older. This woman leant her head against the window. The wind was messing her hair under her headscarf. The scarf often slipped down and every now and then she would reorganize it. But again, the wind would ruffle her hair, which was loose under the scarf.

The woman from Lubuk Pakam. A pale, pinkish face and a profile like someone from India. Thick eyebrows and curved eyelashes.

The bus had been on the road for more than half the day. The town of Prapat was long behind. But you could still see the surface of Lake Toba now and then from behind the hills as the bus climbed to the heights. As the bus moved, Tondi dozed on and off, especially during the heat of the day. The minute the bus slowed, he would wake up and, before the bus stopped, he would be ready in the doorway.

At Siborong-borong the bus stopped. The woman bought some steaming sticky-rice cakes from someone selling them through the window. The woman offered one to Tondi.

'Please, have some,' she said.

'Thank you,' Tondi said. On these long journeys, it was common for passengers to share food with others in adjacent seats and with the bus conductor and driver.

'How long have you worked on buses?'

'Two years this year,' Tondi replied, chewing the hot rice cake.

'I notice you know lots of the passengers.'

'There are a few regulars.'

The woman glanced sideways at Tondi. A hard face, with a typical Batak protruding jaw, but still young. Over the trip, she had noticed his agility, and how firm he was with the staff at the terminals when they stacked the luggage on top of the bus. Seeing how skilful the conductor was made the passengers feel their luggage was safe through to their destination.

Tondi was drawing his own conclusions. From his experience mixing with so many bus passengers, he knew this woman was not Batak. She was probably a Deli Malay or Minang who had lived in East Sumatra a long time. Her nose was slightly pointed. Her mouth was small, and red without lipstick. Maybe her pale skin made them look red. But her skin was not pale like a Chinese person's. And her hands were smooth, so obviously she did not work with her hands.

'Do you live in Sidempuan, *Kak*?' Tondi asked, using the Malay term of address for sister.

'I used to live in Lubuk Paham. A friend of my husband asked him to open a business in Sidempuan. He went on ahead six months ago.'

'What kind of business?'

'Construction. My husband supervises the builders.'

'Why didn't you go there together?'

'He had to get his work organized first, find a house, all those things. I also had to take care of the house in Lubuk Paham and look after the children.'

'How many children do you have?'

'Three. Still small. The oldest has just turned five. I've left them with their grandmother.'

'Why didn't you bring them?'

'When things improve, I'll get them. This is nothing new. It's the third time we've moved. We lived in Kisaran, then in Binjai . . .' she said.

'Sidempuan is a lot further,' Tondi said.

'Oh well. My husband never manages to stay long in one place. He always wants a change of job.'

'Has he always worked in construction?'

'No . . . he's done all kinds of things . . .' her voice was rising now but she did not seem to be aware of it. Then it went back down.

'My husband is from Padang. During the revolution he was in the army. But after 1950, he was, what did they call it, "rationalized". He was terminated from the army. Since then he has kept changing jobs.'

For some time, there was only the sound of the engine and the whistle of the wind. The bus was following a winding road, and sure enough, the back bench was hell. The woman was tossed around. And as Tondi predicted, she got carsick. It was not only her, with her slim body. Even strong men would often vomit when they sat up the back. Tondi rushed to help her. He grabbed the bucket used for water for the radiator to catch the vomit.

Her face was deathly pale as outside the dusk sky turned red. They seemed to creep along the road from Tarutung to Sibolga, and the hairpin bends made the bus rock from left to right. The woman was not carrying any eucalyptus oil with her, so Tondi borrowed some from a passenger up the front. He rubbed some on the nape of her neck. The smell of the oil also lessened the stink of the vomit in the bucket under the seat. Tondi thought of his mother as he rubbed the woman's neck with the oil. He often did this to his mother, massaging the nape of her neck to lessen her stiffness after hours of frying food. And he found himself becoming anxious as he recalled his mother in her stuffy stall.

Sunset had shifted into night. As they approached Sibolga, the woman slumped. She was exhausted from all her vomiting. The bus stopped for a while here. The stop was at a restaurant, and all the passengers got down to eat and stretch.

'You're not getting off, Kak?' Tondi asked as he removed the vomit container.

She shook her head weakly.

'Well, you just wait here, then. I'll get you something to drink. Do you want anything to eat?'

'No,' she rasped, 'but something to drink, if you could.'

Tondi went off with the bucket to wash it. The woman was staring out the window.

Tondi was gentle. Not like when he yelled signals to the driver reversing the bus, or when he cursed and joked with the bus company staff when arranging the luggage. His voice was strident when he was on the roof of the bus, but soft when he spoke with the passengers.

He came over and put two empty cups, a porcelain coffee pot and some dry biscuits on a chair. He filled the two cups and said:

'Kak, you must eat a little. If your stomach is empty, you'll get worse.'

'I still feel sick,' she said.

'Do it like this. Dip a biscuit in the coffee. If you eat a bit, it will lessen the nausea.'

Tondi showed her how to dip the biscuit in the coffee. Then he slurped the wet, hot biscuit. The woman followed his example. After a few bites of biscuit, her face slowly began to regain colour.

'You see, it helps a bit, doesn't it?'

She smiled, answering Tondi's smile. And her nausea slowly subsided. It seemed she had never tasted such delicious coffee.

Tondi went over to the restaurant and ordered two plates of the basic rice menu. The woman got off the bus, and they took turns to wash their hands at the tap. Then they ate inside the bus.

'I hear people call you Tondi,' she said. 'Wherever we stop, people know you.'

Tondi just smiled.

'My name is Habibah.'

So it's Kak Bibah, then?

Habibah giggled.

'I'm sorry I caused you all that trouble earlier,' she said.

'Ah, that's normal.'

'Actually, the staff at the bus terminal told me that the only seat left was right at the back. But I was determined. I just could not wait another day. But I never thought it would be so painful sitting here.'

They had finished eating. They got off and washed their hands again. As before, Tondi turned on the tap for Habibah to wash her hands, but she pulled Tondi's hands to wash under the tap at the same time.

'The way ahead is not as bad as the way we've just come,' Tondi said. 'From here to Sidempuan there are still bends in the road, but not as many. But it will be very cold. And the wind is strong. If it stays like this tonight, to keep out the cold I usually drink a little toddy.'

'Toddy? What's that?'

'A drink. Some people call it Chinese wine. It's made in Medan.'

'It's alcoholic?'

'Just a little. I keep some ready,' Tondi said as he brought out a bottle from the store box under the seat. He poured a little into his cup that still had some coffee.

Habibah sniffed it.

'You mustn't have too much,' Tondi said. 'If you have too much, it makes you sleep. Usually, I have just a glass. It warms me up.'

Habibah watched Tondi as he swallowed small sips.

'Just take a little, Kak,' Tondi said. 'The wind on the road later on will be really cold. Straight off the sea.'

Indeed, the bus did not have windows that closed. There were only window frames with a piece of canvas above that you unrolled to keep out the wind and rain. The bus was old, but the engine still ran well. The body and the floor were made from thick planks of wood that had been replaced many times.

Tondi poured some of the drink into Habibah's cup. It mixed with the coffee. She took a small sip. Warmth flowed into her chest, then to her stomach. And it seemed to calm the nausea that had stuck in her stomach. She took another sip. Warmer still. She smacked her tongue and licked her lips. It tasted sweet. The glass was empty.

'That's better, isn't it?' Tondi said. 'As long as you do not have too much, it can take away the nausea.'

Habibah nodded. Her body that had felt weak and cold now felt warm. And her heavy head was now light. In fact, she had never felt this warm and light. She looked at Tondi with an expression of thanks.

The other passengers were getting back on the bus. Tondi got off to return the plates and cups.

'Please ask how much I owe,' Habibah said.

'Don't worry about it,' Tondi said, switching to Malay dialect. 'Drivers and bus conductors and their families never pay here. That's normal.'

'So whose family am I then?'

'Mine,' Tondi replied, with thick Malay intonation.

Habibah laughed. Tondi checked the luggage on the roof. Then, while still on the roof he gave a sign to the driver to start. As the bus began to move, he slipped down the side and entered the bus through the window.

The cold wind penetrated the bus, bringing a cold sea mist. This was wind from the Indian Ocean, via the Tapaian na Uli bay, coming right through the window. The bay opened to the wild Indian Ocean, but the small islands facing the bay gave some protection so the sea in the bay was calm, reflecting the moonlight. The bus followed the road along the coast.

Habibah was relaxed and reclining. Her body that had so ached earlier now felt refreshed. She felt happy. Was this what made drinkers sing? Warmth spread to every part of her body, from her stomach up to her chest, and down, to her secret hollow.

The bus cut through the darkness. The sides of the road were lined with sago palms and thorned pandanus. Coconut palms stood erect in lines. Their trunks appeared in obscure shadow, some going straight up, some leaning sideways. A swampy smell came through the windows and spread through the bus. The sago palms held tight together at the edge of the sea. Once in a while a pandanus plant would reflect the bus headlights. The throb of the bus engine filled the cold night. The passengers had fallen silent. They all preferred to fall into the embrace of sleep. Tondi himself, as was his normal practice, was half asleep and half awake.

Habibah glanced sideways. Tondi was sleepy. Habibah felt happy and free. Everyone was asleep. But she was not sleepy. The sense of happiness tickling her chest made her want to fool around. Who with? Tondi was sleepy. Was it this warmth that dared her on, or a new intimacy? Habibah stretched out along the back seat and lay her head in Tondi's lap.

Tondi woke. In the dark, he was shocked to find a head in his lap. Habibah was lying on the back bench. Tondi stroked her hair. Habibah took his hand and put it on her cheek, then held it on her chin. Confused, Tondi stroked the wisps of her hair on her cheek and chin that had escaped from her headscarf.

The bus sped on, headed for Sidempuan. This was where her husband was waiting for her after six months of separation. All the other passengers were asleep.

Her hand took Tondi's sweating palm and led it to infiltrate her blouse. Creeping between layers of cloth. Hills pliantly overcome. Nipples forcing through fingers.

Part of Tondi's body stretched. He was sure she could hear the beating of his heart. Was it his palm that was wet, or was it sweat from the skin on her taut breast? Her hand continued to direct his, while she gasped softly. Her slim body, its tiny mounts. Tondi's hand was like the sky enveloping mountains. The mountains squirmed as they yielded. The mountains were wet. Every now and then the bus rocked and leaned into the bends in the road. She stroked Tondi's face. Her hair was fragrant, with a rose perfume. Tondi could even smell her talcum powder.

Her skin was incredibly smooth. He had never before known a woman in this way. Mountains. Warm lips. The toddy tasted sweet. Sweetness lay on these willing lips. A bus speeding along a road and this was where he discovered woman. He discovered mountains and valleys on the seat right at the back of the bus that continued to move. Only the driver at the front was still awake. All the passengers were sound asleep in the cold night wind.

Hidden in the dark of the bus. Stifling moans. She was no longer carsick, but was making Tondi carsick. She placed Tondi on his back on the seat and lay on top of him. Then, under the cover of a batik cloth, the two bodies twisted and turned. Tondi's body convulsed in the darkness of the roaring bus that cut through the black of the night. This was where his masculinity first gushed forth. Something lost or something found, as he turned sixteen?

Chapter 7

The forest seemed endless. Annoyance, anger, exasperation, fury, whatever you call it, it dogged Tondi's every step. Traversing the forest meant confronting sharp thorns, tumbling logs, rivers to ford on slippery stones. No other person. No women. Oh, the body of that first woman. How he longed for the whistle of the cold wind and the throb of the bus all the way from Sibolga to Sidempuan. For the slippery sweat on the skin, the willing lips, the twisting tongue, the sweet toddy-perfumed breath. And the mountain in the palm of his hand.

Was she still in Sidempuan? A woman he got to know on a journey, but who had given him such an unforgettable experience. An eighteen-hour journey, and in the last few hours of it she taught him about being a man. Before leaving, she had given him her address, but Tondi had never had a chance to look for it. And even if he had, would he have visited her? He remembered how someone was waiting for her at the bus stop.

Habibah was her name. A long, loose blouse covering her slim body, elegant. A calm face, but at night her sighs held boiling lava. A volcano beneath the surface of a calm sea. Her lips like leeches, sucking with force from a vacuum that drained his all.

In the distance the mountains soared. Tondi was now in the area of Sarulla, the border between North and South Tapanuli. He was closer to Sipirok. He still had to cross the high country but was entering land that had been cleared. He could smell the aroma of roasting coffee beans. He sniffed, searching for the direction the smell was coming from. He crossed the area of cleared forest. Whoever had cleared this land must have been living here for a long time.

He came to a coffee plantation, with leafy coffee trees growing between a few forest trees that had been left for shade. The plantation was cool. Green and red coffee berries clustered on the branches. Bees crawled among the berries. The fruit was ripe for harvest. Tondi crept deep into the plantation.

There were hoofprints of horses on the earth. Tondi had had enough of walking through the forest. Seeing the hoofprints, he thought how nice it would be if he did not have to keep walking. He followed the hoofprints along a footpath and came to a raised house in the middle of the coffee plantation. The space under the house was around two metres high, as is common with plantation houses. The roof was thatched with *alang-alang* grass.

Tondi observed for a while. Was this a house like Ompu Bulung's, the one he had been to, whether in reality or in a dream, a few days ago? Tondi saw an old man with white hair. Then another man, younger, aged thirty or so. His age was difficult to tell from his blank expression. They were obviously the farmers who had made this plantation. Beneath the house, a horse was tethered. Dogs barked and approached. They seemed to have smelled Tondi's presence.

The old man turned. He reached for his musket hanging under the house, and alert, turned to face Tondi. Tondi walked slowly, as the dogs kept up their barking.

'*Horas*,' Tondi said.

The old man returned his greeting. The younger man merely glanced for a moment and went back to his work. The old man did not let down his guard. He asked Tondi to sit in the yard lined with rattan mats, all the while holding his musket. It was an old muzzle-loader. Probably from the Batak War days.

Tondi introduced himself, starting with where he had come from and where he was going. But he did not mention his squad. He was still trying to work out which side the two men were on. The muzzle-loader the old man was holding had to be loaded from the barrel and reloaded after every shot. Villagers who still had these old weapons used them for hunting pigs.

'My name is Sibalok,' the old man said, in a southern Batak accent. 'This is my son-in-law, Sibalatuk. We have worked his land here for five years now.'

Then they got into discussion about their marga in the common opening conversation to work out their connections and relationship. It turned out they were not from the same marga, as far as the ancestral line went, but the man's wife came from the same marga as Tondi's mother. This meant the man was equal in level to Tondi.

'This is the inang,' Sibalok said, introducing his wife.

'*Horas, Inang,*' Tondi greeted her.

'*Horas, Amang,*' she replied warmly. '*Sian dia do ho?*' she asked in Batak—'where are you from, Son?'

'He's from Laguboti,' her husband replied.

Tondi looked around.

'It's only the four of us who live here. My daughter and son-in-law have no children,' Sibalok went on.

There was a younger woman, with dark skin worn from hard work in the forest. Her hair was wrapped in a crumpled piece of cloth. She did not smile. Her face looked dirty. Absentmindedly, she fanned the fire in the hearth until the water in the kettle boiled. Then she poured it over some coffee.

'So you are headed for Sipirok?' Sibalok asked.

'Yes, *Amanguda.*'

'To walk here from Humbang is quite a distance. Compared to where you have come from, the distance ahead is not so far. But I have heard there is fighting going on around Sipirok. I don't know any more than that. I heard that news three months ago when I went down to the market.

'Which soldiers are in Sipirok?' Tondi asked.

'How would I know things like that? Please, have some coffee.'

'How far is it from here to the nearest village?'

Well, on horseback carrying a load, usually half a day.'

'Are there soldiers there?'

'How could there be soldiers in villages in the interior? The army is only in the towns, in Tarutung, or every now and then they go through Onan-Hasang or Sarulla. At least that's what people say. I don't know for sure. I've not been there for ages. They say that these days, if you want to leave your village, you have to carry a letter from the assistant district head. That makes things very difficult for us. Our fields are in North Tapanuli. Our village, too. But Sipirok is closer for us, and it is in South Tapanuli. We actually come from Sipirok. So it is really difficult organizing official letters.'

The man's daughter served some boiled yam while her husband went on with his work making bamboo strips. Then, without a word, without a glance, he got up, carrying the strips.

'Where's he going?' Tondi asked.

'Sibalatuk? To the plantation. There are many wild boar there. He has to protect the plants.'

'What's the bamboo for?'

'To fix broken fences,' Sibalok replied. He seemed to have understood Tondi's suspicion. He glanced at the pistol the young man had at his hip.

'Don't worry about him. My son-in-law, poor man, is not quite right in the head,' Sibalok said.

The daughter, busy with pots at the hearth, gave a little cough. A sign, perhaps, for her father to change the subject.

'Yes, that's how it is. He had a fever for five years. When he recovered, he was confused like this,' Sibalok ignored his daughter's sign to desist the commentary on her husband.

Tondi felt reassured.

'If I may, I would like to spend the night here,' Tondi said. 'I could sleep here, below.'

'Yes, yes, of course,' Sibalok hastily replied.

Sibalok saw that his visitor was still young. In their initial conversation they had established their inter-family connections. But the light in the young man's eye made Sibalok reluctant to look at him directly. His protruding brow made his eyes look black and dark, penetrating, as though ready to shoot anyone who crossed his will. And what did an old muzzle-loader mean when compared to the automatic pistol at his hip?

It was evening now. Sibalok invited Tondi to bathe at the hot spring. While bathing, they continued their conversation. It seemed that the old man had not chatted with anyone for a long time. Batak men rarely talk to their wives and children, and especially not to their children-in-law. Particularly if their son-in-law is mentally ill. Batak men usually feel free to chat with their nephews, or children of their male relatives. Sibalok was also eager to hear about what was going on in the towns, so distant from his current world.

The hot spring water flowing from the belly of the ancient volcano massaged their skin and blood. Sibalok was the first to get out.

'Don't stay too late, Amang. After bathing, we will eat,' he said as he set off.

Tondi continued to enjoy the flow of the hot water, letting every pore of his skin open. His body had hardened during his jungle journey. And there in the pounding water, again he recalled Habibah. His fingertips exploring the secret parts of her body. The sighing lips as his locked hers. The seething blood. The body in an all-enveloping spasm.

Tondi got out of the hot spring. Back at the house, Sibalok was waiting. Steaming red rice had been set out.

'Where is Sibalatuk?' Tondi asked.

'Usually, he takes his food to the plantation. He keeps guard at the shelter on the western corner. That low-lying area is where the boar often enter,' Sibalok said in a flat tone.

'Longgom, bring the meat up here,' Sibalok's wife called out.

'Yes, Inang,' Longgom replied from below.

The daughter served the spicy venison stew. There was also dried meat cooked in chilli sauces. She and her mother did not join them eating. This was common Batak custom, for the women to eat apart from the men.

Earlier, the daughter had been dressed in men's clothes, probably her husband's or father's hand-me-downs, threadbare and ragged. Now she was dressed in a woman's long, loose blouse which, although rough, made her look neater. She had taken off the crumpled cloth that covered her hair which now hung loose. It was dark black and shone in the light of the flame. She had probably also bathed in the hot spring, because her dark skin no longer looked so rough. It must have been the dust. She seemed much older earlier, but now it was clear she was around thirty. Around the same age as Habibah. But her skin was dark brown like salak fruit seeds, not like Habibah's pale skin. Strands of hair dangled at her temples, rocking with her every movement. She did not smile even once, but that jiggling hair gave her a friendly expression. It looked as though she was younger than Habibah. But would her lips be as sweet?

Tondi devoured the food set before him. The stew was soft, the venison melting into the sauce. The hot, spicy aroma whetted his appetite that he had stifled throughout his trek. He was supposed to keep away from meat and spicy food. But could he now end that fast? Was it now the time to end the self-restraint his grandfather had imposed on him? He would forget, and not think about his tondi turning wild. He would forget that this wild spirit is no different to the begu.

The horse was tethered to a pole under the house. A rattan mat was laid on the ground. Tondi stretched out. Night moved in. The people above in the house were soon asleep. There was no more sound of talking. Tondi made a pillow out of his knapsack. Although the house was quiet, Tondi could not sleep. The crickets on the ground and the tree insects were calling each other. The moon in the west cast yellow light, silhouetting the trees and leaves.

The door of the house opened. Longgom came down bearing a flaming torch. She called the guard dog, but the dog was out wandering in the plantation. She had to set off alone. Every night she kept her husband company guarding the plantation.

Tondi's heart skipped a beat. The woman's body went further from the house, and the flame of the coconut-oil torch licked the darkness. Her body was outlined in the light of the torch and the moon.

Now. Tondi got up. No shoes. Like a wild animal chasing its prey, he hid among the tree trunks and coffee bushes. He was driven entirely by his animal instinct, hunting the woman. And his hard step on a twig startled her. Her scream was stifled, her voice lost in the man's attack. They fell together rolling on the ground. The torch went out.

'Don't . . .' she shouted. But a hand stopped her mouth. Her body was pinned down, her breathing fast. She struggled to resist. She fought like a deer trying to free itself from a tiger's grip. The wrestling of wild animals, without sound. The deer was in the grip of the animal with the force of a savage tiger.

'Be quiet,' the man hissed. This was not the voice of the young man she had seen earlier, but the growl of a wild animal ready to rip its prey apart. In the moonlight, the man's eyes glared, piercing to her heart.

The grip of his hands on her throat hurt her. The more she struggled, the more it hurt. She stopped struggling. Sore, frightened, confused, uncertain and overcome with other undetermined feelings, she faced this strange man who lay on top of her. He pressed his face hard against her cheek. She hardly dared to breathe. But the man's mouth was exploring her face, spreading heat. And if she did not struggle to fight back, she felt that heat even more.

The man's sweat dripped on to her face. Male smell from skin pores convulsed with lust. The smell of passion she had never known. The woman's hair perfumed with candlenut oil. Dark black hair, some covering her forehead. Writhing bodies, heating every vein. Sweat from resistance. Sweat streaming now from glands steaming hot. Glands making spasms in the crevice in her body, ready to receive a ready man.

A yellow moon. An ancient breeze, gently blowing. Coffee leaves slightly swaying. Longgom's struggles no longer refusal, tightening muscles no longer rejection. Skin taut, restraining hot passion. Primeval passion, imprisoned for years. Writhing and sobbing at the same time. Pain and enjoyment both. Full yellow moon glowing on her face. A single teardrop welling in the corner of her eye. She kissed the man's face, his mouth, like a wanderer lost in the desert finding water. Cricks of crickets. Hoots of owls. Screeches of civets looking for ripe coffee beans. Sounds of the forest in tempo with the woman's moans and sighs.

The earth was shaking. This was Boraspati, the dragon god and guardian of the earth's belly, who gives fertility to the earth but can wipe out the world with his quakes. Tondinihuta—would he become Boraspati to give fertility to this woman or would he destroy her world?

For Tondi, this was the primeval passion he had been carrying for days. In his dreams. In his solitude. In his longing. Thrusting all of this into this woman's body. His legs tramping the earth, as though climbing steep mountains. Gasping, climbing mountain slopes bearing his body that moved one step at a time, nature that must be mounted to reach the summit.

Primeval instincts meeting in the middle of the jungle. The jungle-walker's muscles relaxed. They lay on their backs looking at the moon. The breeze dried the sweat on their limp bodies. Their breathing began to calm down. Songs of the forest returned to fill the silence. And the rustle of a step. Tondi sat up, alert.

The woman's husband was walking, mumbling some incomprehensible song. He passed beside them, stopping for a moment. Tondi got up. But Longgom gently tugged his hand. Sibalatuk walked on, still singing his song. He left those swamp boar right there, his wife with another man, a boar he could have killed then and there.

'Let him be. That's how he is. Every night he walks around and sings like that.'

'But . . .' Tondi said.

The woman pulled Tondi towards her, and said flatly: 'He doesn't understand what he saw.'

Tondi was shocked.

'What do you mean?'

'He has never performed his duty as a husband,' she said.

'So . . . ?'

Her eyes shone, piercing him to his heart.

'Yes, this was my first time.'

Tondi was bewildered. The woman explained.

'He fell ill the day after our wedding. People said someone had cast a spell on him. Before I married him, somebody else had asked for my hand but I refused him. He was offended, so he sent a spell. The datu said that actually the spell was meant for me. But Sibalatuk was weaker than me, and so the spell affected him. On our first night he got a fever. He was screaming and climbed the wall. He climbed a sheer flat wall. The datu could only heal the fever. He has been like this ever since. We have never done anything . . .'

'All this time . . . ?'

'Five years. Not once,' Longgom said, pulling closer to ward off the cold forest wind.

'Inang is very disappointed, and especially Amang, because my husband is his nephew, his sister's son, who he hoped would give him grandchildren. He is my cousin. Amang did not want to stay in the village, so he brought us here to clear the land.'

'You don't have a brother?

'No. And that is also something that causes Amang constant disappointment in this life.'

The wind was biting. Her naked body shivered. They stood, erect and facing each other as they put on their clothes, each looking at the other's body in the moonlight.

'I want to have a baby, and if I get one, I will look after it well,' she said haltingly.

Tondi caught his breath.

They walked arm in arm. She had never experienced this, walking in the full moon. The fragrance of the coffee flowers followed them.

'I am sure I will have a child from you,' she said. 'You will leave tomorrow. Tonight, I do not want to sleep. Let's not sleep,'

Longgom said softly. The moon struck her face, which was shining now, completely, unlike earlier in the day. Her clear eyes did not blink as she awaited the answer.

'Yes, let's not sleep,' Tondi said.

And now Longgom led Tondi to a protected place. Alang-alang leaves carpeted the earth. They made love all night long. The wedding night she had been awaiting five years. Until dawn. And the two bodies finally fell asleep in the dew that blanketed the valley.

The sun brought the wedding night to an end. It had been short, but it was as though a span of years had been compressed into one night. When Tondi awoke, Longgom was not beside him. He stood and headed for the house.

Sibalok greeted him: 'It seems that you preferred to sleep in the plantation. Did you not trust us, Amang?'

'It's not like that,' Tondi said.

'Come and have some coffee,' Sibalok said.

Tondi sat before him. Longgom came down from the house. Apart from her shining face, there was no difference in her. She served the coffee and rice porridge. Little escapee curls of hair played at her forehead. Every now and then she stole a glance.

'If I may, I would like to buy your horse,' Tondi suddenly said.

'What? I only have that one horse. Without it I cannot take the coffee to the village,' Sibalok replied.

Tondi opened his knapsack and pulled out some money. The commander of his battalion had given him some legal tender, and he had not used any of it up to now.

'I really need a horse. I have to get south as fast as I can.'

Sibalok raised his head and looked at the young man. His look was pleading. Sibalok stroked the horse's mane.

'Let him take it, Amang,' Longgom said.

'But . . . but . . . how will we carry the coffee?'

'Let him, Amang. He still has a long way to go. He needs a horse,' she urged. She threw Tondi a furtive glance, and from his eyes she received a soft glow of thanks.

'I don't know the price of horses here, but I hope this money is enough to buy a replacement,' Tondi said, putting down a bundle of the highest denomination notes.

Sibalok looked carefully at the young man, and then at Longgom. It was not usual for his daughter to involve herself in his affairs.

'Very well, Amang,' he said. Then he stood and got the horse ready, putting on the thick burlap saddle.

'Thank you Amanguda,' Tondi said, respectfully taking his leave while leading the horse away from the house. Then he mounted the horse, which began to walk slowly.

The dog chased him and would not get out of the way. It did not want a stranger riding the horse. The horse stopped.

'I'll go and call the dog,' Longgom said and walked towards the horse. Tondi dismounted. They walked side by side away from the house.

Sibalok was still looking at the wad of money, confused. His wife came down from the house.

'Whose money is that?' she asked.

'It's from the young man,' Sibalok said. 'He bought our horse.'

'Where is that man really from?' his wife asked.

Sibalok shrugged his shoulders.

He looked in the direction Tondi had gone, but he was out of sight. Tondi and Longgom were walking in single file along the path. At the foot of the hill, they stopped.

'I'm thankful we met,' she said, 'even though we will probably never meet again. But I am sure that I will have a son from you.'

Feminine instinct probably always holds prediction. Transcends space. Moves in the certainty of life yet to come.

'Do you have anything I can give your future child?' Longgom asked.

Tondi was confused. He looked her in the eye. Her eyes were clear, sincere and loving. It had only been a single night, but she had given herself to him. Forever.

Tondi thought hard.

'Well, this,' he said, taking off a medallion he had around his neck. When he had joined his rebel squad, he had been given a medallion engraved with the symbol of the Barisan hills. Before leaving Balige, he had asked an engraver to write his name and date of birth on it. He remembered that when he had been at Ompu Bulung's house playing the gondang drums, the young woman in the yellow blouse had been very interested in this medallion. She sat close to him, and had asked him for it, but he did not give it to her. Was that all a dream?

But right now was real. He gave Longgom the medallion.

She took it and kissed it. Tondi mounted the horse. She tethered the dog.

'I'm off,' Tondi said.

'Yes,' she said softly. With all her heart, she felt as though she was bidding her husband farewell. And with all her heart, she was prepared for her husband to never return.

Tondi nudged the horse and began to move on. The tethered dog tugged against the rope and barked incessantly. And in Longgom's heart a sense of loss tugged at her too. Her damp eyes followed him, the furrower who had cast his seed. The damp seed planted deep, exciting her every sinew. She would tend this seed and make it grow, showered by rain and warmed by the sun. The mountains around Sarulla would continue to stand and from them hot water would spring. The swooping mountain winds and the moon in the sky had witnessed the primal marriage. Her fertile field, five years fallow, would grow this seed. It would blossom in the Sarulla plain. Would it become the generation to open the future?

The horse followed the path. As it descended the hills, it walked one step at a time. When the ground was flat, it trotted. Its hoofs skimmed the wet earth. This Batak pony was not like a big Arab horse. If Tondi let his long legs dangle, they almost touched the ground. But the pony was strong, its legs short but as strong as iron as it trod the ground.

The horse's brown flanks shone after the rain. Its mane was wet. Every now and then it would whinny as it clattered its hooves on the reddish, sticky clay soil.

The rain had just stopped. He had been riding all day in the pouring rain. The sun came out again. Tondi's clothes and the saddle were drenched from the downpour. Now the sun started to warm him. He was further away from the coffee plantation. Further from Longgom, the woman who had given her whole body to him, who had received the sacrament of marriage bestowed by the full moon and the open sky.

This was the day of Tondi's birth. His birth as a man about to face battle. She had baptized him amongst the seedlings, so that when he entered the field of battle, he would be a man.

It was a woman, his mother, who taught him as a boy to take risks in life. It was a woman, Habibah, who introduced him to the life of a man. And now another woman, Longgom, had made him wrestle with life itself. His mother, Habibah, Longgom: three women on this earth who not only introduced him to life, but also complicated it with questions about the meaning of the presence of men. Three women with three men they called husbands.

His mother's husband, the man he had to call amang, was in Java, which might as well be the other end of the earth. That man who had humiliated his mother, deserted her, because he did not find her good enough for his new life. Can a husband discard his wife just because she is exhausted, dishevelled and uneducated? Who had made her like that, having to spend all day in front of a fire, frying food in her stall?

She had insisted that Tondi remain at school. She had been bitterly disappointed when he decided to leave school. She vented her anger for days. Maybe she had not realized that the world of education was beyond reach of a seller of fried bananas. Nor was it the world for the grandson of a datu who only received gifts from people he helped in the village. Anyway, schooling should not have been his mother or grandfather's responsibility. But his grandfather never wrote to his father to tell him to support his son. Nor did his mother, who did not once utter a single word requesting help. As a result, they crawled around in poverty in Siantar and the Toba plains.

Tondi's head rocked as the horse ran, heading into the wind. It was wind from the south, from the mountains. He was now in

South Tapanuli. Sipirok was still a full day's journey away. If possible, even though his commander had told him not to enter the town, he wanted to slip into Padang Sidempuan. He wanted to see Habibah.

Would she still remember him? They had parted at the bus stop. Her husband, a man in his late thirties or so, had been waiting there late at night. Habibah had introduced them. Tondi had felt awkward as he shook the man's hand. Was it right to extend his hand with the palm still smelling of Habibah? But the man offered his sincere thanks, for Habibah told him how Tondi had helped her when she was carsick during the trip from Tarutung to Sibolga. He knew, he said, those terrible bends in the road. Habibah also looked at him with sincerity. The sincerity of each, though, had a different meaning, making Tondi confused. Oh, Habibah with her slim fingers, who had stroked his face and drawn it to her lips. Her scent was on his hands. Her husband was of small build, with a long face, lined from his life's journey. Was he really as old as he looked? And what was the meaning of 'husband' to Habibah, when she spent the last part of her journey home to meet him seducing another?

The Sarulla plain was further behind. Longgom too. The woman who said she would raise his child. Tondi choked in the cold wind. Would a child really be born up there in that lonely place? If it happened, and if that child was a boy, would it not be Tondi's son to carry on his marga? How would the conversation about kinship connections go in the future? But Longgom, a wife who wanted a child, did not want a husband who would give his marga to his son. Longgom already had a husband. A man with a vacant gaze, who stood watching his wife roll around with a strange man under the coffee trees. Would Longgom raise that child with her husband?

Wife and husband are the fusion of two lives in one world to bring life. His mother and her husband had brought life to him. Habibah and her husband had brought life to their three children. But what of Longgom and her husband, would Longgom bring forth a son? And what for? The woman nurtures the seed in her womb, protects it until it becomes life, and then raises it. What is all that for? His mother had to suffer the degradation of poverty day upon day. Habibah entrusted her children to others so that she could be with her husband. And Longgom, if she had a child, how could she make that child the marga of her husband?

What is the meaning of 'husband' to a woman? The tie of husband and wife can make the woman part of the husband's life. But is that tie still necessary when the husband deserts her? Or, even if he does not desert her, can a woman turn to another man?

There were things Tondi did not understand. Was all of this called a wife's loyalty, commitment or such like? Back when Tondi was still living in the village with Ompu Silangit, his grandmother had once taken him to visit his mother who was working as kitchen staff at an army hospital in Siantar. His mother was struggling, crushed between young passion and loyalty. But loyalty to whom?

PART THREE

INANG

Chapter 8

Here, she uses her own name. Not *Ina ni si Tondi*, Mother of Tondi, but Halia. That was her name before she had a child.

Halia, a woman not yet thirty, spent her days supervising the preparation of food at the government hospital. Back in the Dutch times she had gone to primary school up to the second class, which was the last class of the three-year school. The language of instruction was Batak. Students learnt arithmetic and to read and write in both the Batak and roman alphabets. This education was sufficient for her to supervise administration in the hospital kitchen. She could write what kinds of dishes were required based on the needs of the patients and staff, and prepare all the ingredients.

She performed her duties well. But who takes any notice of those who work in a hospital kitchen? People know only the doctors, administrators and nurses. Those working in the kitchen are constantly overwhelmed with huge pots and open fires preparing meals three times a day, with the heat of the kitchen draining every drop of sweat.

Halia was in charge of kitchen administration. However, if there was a cook off work she would help out with the cooking herself. She and her kitchen co-workers had been employed not through any official government process. The hospital was a relic of Dutch times. The occupying Japanese army had taken it over and carried off much of the equipment, who knows where. During the fight for independence, the hospital had continued as best it could, often with no medicines. After the Round Table Agreement of 1949 and Dutch recognition of Indonesia's sovereignty, the Dutch kingdom had given some aid in the form of medical equipment, medicines and even doctors. Halia got work at the hospital because she knew the hospital manager, a doctor of the Partogi marga who happened to come from her village in the Toba plains. Other cooks and staff had similarly got their positions because they knew someone who worked at the hospital. It was all done unofficially, with no letters of application with attached copy of school certificate. There were even some blind people working in the hospital kitchen.

One morning, Halia was called to see Dr Herman. He was a Dutchman, aged around fifty, and a specialist sent by the Dutch government. In the colonial days, he had spent a long time in the Indies working in various government hospitals. During the war for independence, he had been in Holland. After the recognition of Indonesia's sovereignty, he had submitted a request to the Dutch government to join the aid program for Indonesia. He wanted to spend his old age there.

He lived in a house the government had provided in the hospital grounds. It was a sturdy house, but the gardens were run down. You could still see the effects of the war there. The Indonesian government had no money for the upkeep of government buildings. Dr Herman had to accept things as they were. He had no household staff, only a cleaner in the morning. His meals came from the hospital kitchen.

Halia met him in the doctors' room. She knew who he was, but had never talked to him.

'I'm the kitchen manager,' she said, standing before his desk.

'Please take a seat, Kitchen Manager,' and then, when she was seated, 'I'm wondering whether you would be able to help out cooking for a party tonight at the house.'

'My name is Halia.'

'So Halia, can you help?'

'For how many people?'

'Around thirty.'

'Yes of course. I'll bring a cook.'

The doctor thanked her and asked her to work out what she would need.

'What sort of food do you want to serve?' she asked him.

'The usual *rijsttafel* for parties.'

Together they listed the dishes for what the Dutch called 'rijsttafel', steamed rice with a large variety of dishes. While Halia calculated the cost, the doctor observed her writing diligently at the desk. She had an aura of maturity and tenacity. Her skin was dark, shining. Long, thick eyelashes protected her black eyes. Her hands were strong, and her body plump and firm. This was the body of a Batak woman who works hard, he thought. He had once worked in Tapanuli. He often saw Batak women working in the fields and carrying water from the springs hundreds of metres back to their village homes. He was always impressed to see them walking up and down the hills with the two-metre-long bamboo slung across their shoulders.

'This is the cost, doctor,' Halia said, passing him the calculation.

Dr Herman observed her hand. The palm was reddish, the fingers slim but strong. Her writing was neat. Then he handed her money for shopping.

And he did not forget those strong fingers. The black eyes. The thick eyebrows. The firm voice with its thick Batak accent.

Dr Herman was holding a party for some Dutch people who had just arrived from Holland. Most of them had been born and spent their childhood in the Indies. Some had been in Japanese internment camps. After World War II and the Japanese surrender to the allied forces, they had been taken to Holland but longed to return to the Indies. But the long war of independence kept them in the land of their ancestors. Some, who were not from wealthy families who could support them, had to live in government transit camps. This was a huge contrast to their former life in the Indies, when they were plantation lords, and their every need was met.

They were used to the tropical sun. Now having to live in a cold country, they constantly longed for the land of their birth. But the fighting did not stop, because after Indonesia declared its independence, the Dutch government sent in its army on the pretext that they were carrying out a police action to restore order. As far as Holland was concerned, Indonesia was still the Dutch East Indies. In its propaganda, the Dutch government referred to its 'police actions', but ordinary Dutch civilians saw it for what it was—war. Government politics most infuriated those in the transit camps, because life in Holland was far from normal. The Dutch were living on aid from the American Marshall Plan, which gave funds for the rehabilitation of Europe after the Second World War. It really was too much. Here in Holland, people were being neglected, while the Dutch government was spending its aid from foreign countries to fund war.

Independence for Indonesia. Why not? The country would still need professionals to work in the plantations. Professionals could work anywhere, for any company. Many worked in South Africa. The plantations and oil wells in Indonesia were all properties of Dutch, British and American companies. To a company, what difference was there between the Dutch government and the Indonesian government? What was the point of fighting? Only the army wanted war. Had these warmongers not learnt their lesson from the bitterness of life during World War II?

Now, here they were, back in this warm heaven. The food they had missed, first-class wine out of crystal glasses, all this restored their spirits. This is what made them different from the Batak. When Batak people endure something that disturbs or defeats their spirit, there will be a ceremony to heal that spirit which is held with a feast or *horja*. It is a long, complicated ceremony and has links with the ancestors. To the Batak, it is not the food that is important, because the ceremonial food cooked is actually not even that delicious. The ceremony and feast mark the gathering of kin linked in the Batak kinship system with the spirits of their ancestors. This is where the tondi is healed. To the Dutch, however, it is enough to have delicious food and wine to restore their spirits.

The party was enjoyable. Most of the guests were Dutch people returning to work on the plantations that had been left neglected throughout the fight for independence. Other guests included Dr Partogi, the managers of the hospital and other Indonesian doctors. All, except for Dr Herman, came with their wives. Everyone was happy.

It was only a year since the fighting for Indonesian independence had ended. And now, here were Indonesians and Dutch gathering as friends. Needless to say, the cause of the fighting had been the army. These Dutch people had spent more of their lives in Indonesia than in Holland. They were happy that the fighting was over and that now relations could be built between the two countries. They could go back to their old jobs as professionals, managing the palm, rubber, tea or tobacco plantations around Siantar. They were happy to speak Indonesian again, which they called Malay. Now they could eat Indonesian food and enjoy lamb curry, chilli sauce and prawn crackers.

Particularly the food served at the party. The guests praised the food, and as usual asked to meet the cook. Dr Herman called Halia and the cook. Halia stood shyly before the guests as he introduced her.

'Thank you, thank you. Amazing! The food Madam Halia made was absolutely delicious. We have not eaten food like this for such a long time. Thank you, thank you,' came the chorus. Men and women. Sincere gratitude.

They greeted Halia. The women embraced her and kissed her cheeks. They were all middle-aged. Some looked old. But perhaps they had aged in the Japanese internment camps? When the women embraced her, Halia remembered another time in her past, when she was a new bride. Where were they all now? Where was Mevrouw Capellen who had been like a mother to her?

A Dutch man was playing the piano. It was out of tune and had not been played for a long time. But who cared? Someone sang.

It was a snippet of a remembered Batak song, most of it wrong. People laughed. Wine made them happy.

People urged Dr Partogi and his wife to sing. Give any Batak man a glass of palm wine and he will get up and sing. This was champagne, but he sang two songs anyway.

'Sing us a song, Halia,' he said.

'No, I can't sing,' Halia replied.

'Oh, come now, don't be shy.'

'Yes, sing for us, Halia, to make this wonderful evening complete,' Dr Partogi's wife said, leading Halia to the piano.

So, hesitantly at first, Halia began to sing a Batak song that had been popular in her youth, and it turned out the piano player knew it. Dr Herman's house—usually so gloomy and quiet—was merry that night. The doctor had been cooped up in this big old house for weeks. Now, the lights shining brightly, the piano tinkling away, Halia's soprano voice joined by the alto voice of the piano player and the laughter of the guests changed the mood both of the house and Dr Herman, who seemed to be going through a metamorphosis.

He was sitting, relaxed. He felt content. His daily meals from the hospital kitchen might not be identical to the patients' meals, but they still felt like war rations. Whenever he wanted a change he would go to the Chinese restaurant, but it was not like eating at home. Tonight, he had enjoyed the food cooked with spices according to his taste. After decades of living here, his taste had changed. His appetite for western food had gone.

He leaned back in his chair and watched Halia sing. Clouds of cigar smoke occasionally obscured his view. She was not very tall, was wearing a simple dress, and had dark, smooth skin. Her shiny black hair was pulled back in a simple bun.

A full stomach, delicious wine, cigars of the best Deli tobacco, and the Batak song Halia was singing. Dr Herman drew a deep breath. He felt coolness in his chest, like menthol. He knew this song well.

It was back when he worked at Tarutung. In the evenings he used to hear young men play guitar on the street. More often than not, they were out serenading at the house where the unmarried young women lived together. It was a large, two-storeyed, traditional wooden house. The young men would sit outside on the steps. No one ever visited alone. On their way there and when returning home, they would sing. You could hear the voices soaring from way off, piercing the still night.

Tarutung was a cool town, situated between Prapat on the shores of Lake Toba and the western shore of Sibolga, facing the Indian Ocean. It was surrounded by hills and valleys. The majority of houses were made of wood with tin roofs. The Dutch lived in brick houses in a beautiful complex with palm trees lining the streets. Every house had a garden. Their Javanese gardeners were probably brought over from East Sumatra, where they had formerly worked as plantation coolies. They were excellent gardeners. The cool climate meant you could grow roses all year round. Dr Herman had felt it was one long honeymoon, living there with his wife. The Dutch residents would often gather at night at their club or at one another's houses. When they tired of the town atmosphere, they would go on holiday to Prapat or Sibolga, soaking their feet in Lake Toba or the sea. How enjoyable it was. He and his wife had no children, so it felt as though the honeymoon was never-ending. Tarutung, the town of mountains and mists. Heaven beneath the ever-warm sun.

World War II had ruined everything. Dr Herman and his wife did not evacuate to Australia in time along with many other Dutch. When they got to Medan, the ship had already left. They were detained in separate Japanese prisoner-of-war camps. Dr Herman was sent to Java, and his wife to Malaya. From heaven to man-made hell, such is the wheel of destiny.

For more than three years, the Japanese truly created hell. When the war ended, the allied forces liberated all the detainees. They left the camps. Dr Herman met his wife again, but the camp had destroyed her, body and soul. This was the result of that hell of war. Dr Herman stayed with his wife and did his best to restore her health. But while medicine might be able to heal the outside, it was unable to touch the inside that had been so crushed. She had no will to live. The Batak would say she had lost her tondi, and it had to be called back. But Dr Herman had not lived long in Batak lands. How would he know about that? What was clear, and what his wife knew, was that the honeymoon was over. Dr Herman cared for her, but she died two years after their return to Holland.

And now, here he was, back in the land his country had once colonized. It made no difference to him. National borders are thin. Nationality should not divide people. To a doctor, there are only sick people and healthy people. Dr Herman blew his cigar smoke. Halia's song had long ended. He could hear the faint clink of glasses.

The party was over. The house would be gloomy once more. That lulling chorus of young male voices in Tarutung, Halia's clear voice, when would he hear it again? He would go back to living alone in this big house. Thoughts of wartime suffering returned, and he remembered his wife, destroyed at war's end.

* * *

Halia's singing at Dr Herman's party sprang from her past. Her childhood beside the lake. Going with other girls to fetch water from the well at the base of the hill. During the day, they would sing. The bamboo tubes they carried across their shoulders would rattle as they walked. But in the early morning, they would walk quickly. The sound of the clanging bamboo would wake up the little children still asleep curled up in their sarongs. The cold morning air blowing in from the lake would pierce the skin. After she finished her three years of primary school, she spent every day of her life between the spring and the kitchen. Or with the older girls, weaving under the houses.

This cycle of life ended when she was married off to Pardomutua. It was a marriage that seemed inevitable. Because of Ompu Silangit's marriage in the village, her marga became the hula-hula marga to Ompu Silangit's. So she had to marry Ompu Silangit's son. Married off, because she was never asked about the matter, it was all arranged by the parents. And what did marriage mean to her?

No point in mentioning love. She knew only the law of custom, adat. Her family received gifts to respect them as the bride-giving marga. The wedding made her a wife, and then a mother.

All she knew was that Ompu Silangit had called for Pardomutua, his son who worked in Siantar. He was a graduate of the Dutch junior high school and worked as a clerk for a Dutch company in Dolok Merangir. She herself did not know him, other than his name and his family. Their villages were far apart. Until now, any young male visitors were from villages nearby. But none of them made any impression on her. It was just the usual fun, a group of young men visiting a group of girls at one of their homes. A time filled with singing, joking and teasing. The girls would sit inside, and the boys outside on the steps. They would not look at each other. Only the voices would go through the door. This is why, before marriage, partners never knew each other well. All each knew of the other was that so-and-so was a son or daughter of family X. No more than that.

And the proposal came. Acceptance or rejection had nothing to do with her. And there were no reasons for rejection. The reason for acceptance was clear. Their marga as hula-hula to the family of Ompu Silangit.

Halia was sixteen. She was taken to Balige to meet the Christian pastor. She was married in a church, and the traditional feast afterwards was held in her village, with all her Christian relatives and wider family in attendance. Then she left the village. Before this, the furthest she had ever travelled was to Tarutung. Now she was taken off to a rubber plantation run by a Dutch company, and it felt like the end of the earth. It was in Dolok Merangir, in the Simalungun area. For the first time, she saw a town that was busier than Tarutung. People in the plantation usually shopped in Siantar, but it was a long way, over an hour by car. The settlement was made up of houses arranged along sandy roads paved with broken coconut shells. When you trod or drove on them, there would be a cracking noise, crunching under the car. The newly-weds lived in a brick house in the complex. Plantation workers lived in wooden barracks, set at a distance from the complex and had their own life there. Company staff mixed only among themselves. Pardomutua, as a clerk, was included in the Dutch circle.

Halia began to be immersed in this world she had never known. Before this, she had only ever known of the Dutch, the Pale Eyed Ones, as evil creatures who had ruined Batak lands, or the opposite, as pastors who taught love, kindness and religion. But now she had to mix with Dutch people, even though she was often stranded at the margins. Most conversations were in Dutch. She had only attended primary school, which was taught in the Batak language with a smattering of Malay. No Dutch. She had only begun to speak Malay after a few months in Dolok Merangir. So mostly she kept to herself while her husband chatted in Dutch at parties. Or she went to the kitchen and helped the hostess prepare the food. She learnt many things about kitchens, but not about manners in Dutch social gatherings. The Dutch ladies liked her, and knew her as a young, diligent and helpful Batak woman. But her husband was offended.

'Don't be some Dutch person's cook,' he said.

'I'm not a cook.'

'Working in a Dutch kitchen, that's a cook,' he snapped.

'But I'm learning. The Dutch ladies are teaching me cooking.'

'Well stop it. We're respectable people. We're not like those Batak sold as slaves. We're descendants of the royal line. It's not right for you to work in some Dutchman's kitchen.'

'All I'm doing is helping the hostess. And learning at the same time.'

'When you don't mix with the guests, that already affects my status. It's even worse when you work in the kitchen.'

'But you know I can't speak Dutch. How can I mix with them? In the kitchen, the ladies speak Malay with me. Some of them can speak Batak, like Mevrouw Capellen who used to live in Batangtoru.'

'You're right. You can't speak Dutch. So learn!'

'I've tried, but I can't.'

'Well, if you can't help raise my status, the least you can do is not lose it!' Pardomutua snarled. His sharp glare shut her up.

Batak men were always like that. In Halia's experience, Batak men always snapped when they spoke with their wives. Her father was like that. Everyone in her village was like that.

Her husband, Pardomutua, had brought her to this foreign place. There were one or two Batak people on the plantation, but the language commonly spoken was Malay. Within the complex, people mostly spoke Dutch. She was wrong whatever she did. Never mind Dutch, she still had to think first if she tried to speak Malay. And all her husband did was snarl. He never helped her face this foreign world. He was always impatient.

The only time he did not scold her was when he wanted her body. He would have her as much as he liked. When he had had enough, he would lie on his back and look at the ceiling, as though nothing had happened. Do Batak men need only their wives' bodies, and not the whole of them? The whole, including ignorance, worry and confusion when confronting an unfamiliar world?

Whatever Halia's question, Pardomutua's answer was only complaint. It seemed she would have to find answers herself. Or his reply would be another question, making her feel she was facing a school examination. There were never any satisfying answers. But when did he ever satisfy her? Maybe once or twice in bed, when he was thrusting away. But most often he led her only halfway along the road. Then just left her there.

Lying beside him on the bed, Halia looked at this man sleeping so soundly. She studied his face. A chiselled jaw, a pale, reddish face, a hairy chest. They were a young couple. When they married, Pardomutua was aged nineteen. Maybe because he had worked and socialized with people much older than him where he worked, he looked more adult than the young men in her village who still lived at home with their parents. Or maybe it was because he was big and tall like a Dutchman.

She wanted to be able to like him. She was the only person close to him here, in this place so far from home. Every night they would lie together on one bed. She felt his sweat sticking to her, even when she was out of the house. She wanted to like him, to like his body, his sweat, his nose, his mouth. But how? He would come up to her, take off her sarong, and if she did not undo her clothes he would tug at them, as a sign for her to do so. Then he would thrust in his planting stick, even though the soil was dry and unprepared. Every night it hurt, although sometimes less than others, when Halia could climb with him. But that was rare. Probably it was because the soil was moist in the days before she menstruated. So she could never be sure of what she was feeling, and wondered whether this was some kind of climax or just getting her period. How could she enjoy it?

Most often, after thrusting away and releasing all his tension, he would collapse for a moment, then lie on his back, let his breathing settle, and sleep. His daily routine had to end with this release in bed. Every day. When they were newly married, Halia would cry and refuse because she was menstruating. Maybe he did not know that every woman has times when a man should leave her alone. The way he saw it, the woman he had married should be like a field ready for planting at any time. When does a field refuse the planter?

Batak boys are different to girls. Girls are used to being together with women, at the spring when they do the laundry or fetch water, or under the house when they weave. Girls are used to hearing older women talking. And they might talk about anything. Girls talk about the most private things with their mother's younger sisters.

Boys, on the other hand, are usually together only with other boys of their own age out in the fields. They play all day long, and only go home to eat. They never chat in a friendly way with their fathers. If they chat with an older male, it is with their amanguda, their father's younger brothers, and they never discuss women. Pardomutua had no amanguda at home. He knew only his father, who was old, and he had never known his grandfather. Then he had gone to school in Siborong-borong, far from his father's house, and had boarded at the house of a government official and later continued his schooling in Tarutung. He had spent most of his life living in the town, boarding at someone else's house. Probably all he knew about women were things he had overheard from men comparing notes in the coffee stalls. Unmarried adult men often boast about their relations with women. Maybe all this coffee-stall gossip had given Pardomutua wrong ideas.

When Halia was in her early teens, she still had a lot to learn about life, but then she was married and considered to be adult. Particularly when, in the Batak marriage ceremony, witnessed by all her friends, she was handed over to her husband's marga. From then on, she was no longer part of her own marga. She was completely released from it. The advice in the marriage ceremony for the bride has nothing to do with the husband's obligations to support his wife. It is all about the wish to have children soon, lots of children, boys and girls. What kind of advice is that? It must be what makes Batak men want their wives to lie on their backs ready for the planting stick.

Somehow, a seed grew in her womb. Her first child, growing from the seed planted by the man with the planting stick. Now that she was pregnant, she was no longer confused when there were parties at the company houses. She could stay at home. Sometimes the Dutch women would visit her and teach her to knit or embroider. The Dutch women liked her, her innocence, her diligence and her politeness when she asked about things she did not understand.

When the time came for the birth of her first child, her husband's mother came from the village. For just one month. But this was a happy time. Her inangboru cared for her, slept in the same room as her, and protected her.

Pardomutua slept in a different room. Their first child was a boy. What better joy than that? All her feelings of loneliness, alienation and worthlessness vanished. And her inangboru brought a message from Ompu Silangit. It seems that the old man knew in advance that the baby was a boy. He gave him the name Tondinihuta. There was no argument about that. So Pardomutua had to forget about all the names he was considering, including Dutch names he had read in books, like Willem and Karel, and names from the Bible like Jakobus, Matius, Mikael, Petrus and so on. The Dutch ladies loved to look at the baby with its pale, reddish skin. Only its hair made it different from a Dutch baby. They took turns to visit, and their

visits were not because of Pardomutua the clerk in their office, but
to entertain Halia, the young Batak woman, so hardworking, *eerlijk*,
innocent and sincere. The woman who had become a young mother,
at just seventeen.

And the Dutch pastor who led the Batak church in Siantar came
to the house to offer, well, not really to offer but to force, a name.
Maybe he thought that by giving a Biblical name, this Batak child
would become Christian like the Dutch. Pardomutua was happy
to accept this name from the pastor, and so it was that this name
from Holland got stuck on too, and the baby's birth certificate read
Immanuel Tondinihuta. But the baby's parents never used that
foreign name, Immanuel. A beautiful name meaning God is with
us. No, the boy was coddled as Tondi. Tondi, Tondi, the name more
familiar to Ompu Silangit. God is far away in heaven, but tondi is
inside every Batak.

Chapter 9

The fertile field took the seed, nurtured it and brought the seedling to the face of the earth. The seed planted not through love. Love was a word too foreign to Halia who grew up in the Toba interior. The seed grew because it happened to fall on fertile soil that had been prepared by Batak custom for just this purpose. It was a guarantee that the marga would continue. But to Halia herself the value of this child far exceeded anything that custom said. The child was a wall that safeguarded her. The baby's crying that so annoyed Pardomutua was her protection after her mother-in-law returned home. With the excuse of holding Tondi, she could escape and leave the room. She would spend long periods of time cuddling her baby in the large central room.

The baby became her shield to avoid her husband. True, there was no comparison between the pain of childbirth and her nightly suffering. But the pain of childbirth, the pain that had tested every bit of her strength and endurance and taken her to the threshold of life and death, now brought her joy, because she could avoid the pains of night. She could escape, but for how long? There would come a time when the baby would be bigger, and not cuddled constantly.

Over these past weeks, her entire life had centred on the baby. It was as though nature had led her to becoming a mother.

And because she had only ever been the field for his seed, she was unaware that her husband was furious in his bed alone, waiting to have that body again. Now there was only a gaping gulf between her and her husband.

Pardomutua, at around twenty years of age, was a stallion champing at the bit. But what did Halia know about passion? She was used to her husband's anger and shouting. What was any different about his fits of anger now?

The angry young stallion got even angrier whenever he looked at his wife's defiant face. Her breasts swelled with milk. Her nipples popped out of the baby's mouth. Her hips looked more shapely. Everything about her taunted him. It was time to plant the field.

Halia was unperturbed. While the house was so calm for her, it had become a screeching hell for Pardomutua. The baby's shrill cries attacked his eardrums, making his brow throb. All the hormones in his body clumped in his head, pulsating from within his skull, giving him an endless headache.

Then there were times Pardomutua did not come home. It started with him playing pool at the staff recreation hall. Halia preferred this to him yelling at her to stop the baby crying which only made the baby cry even more. Healthy babies anywhere have a strong cry. The Dutch ladies said that the stronger the cry, the healthier the baby. How is it possible to stop a baby crying just because its father is home? And shouldn't a baby's cries bring its parents joy?

Anak do hamoraon hu. Sons are my glory, as the old Batak saying goes. It is not gold, not land and not big houses that are your wealth in life. For Batak, the greatest suffering is the cutting of your marga during your lifetime. Life is the continuation of the genealogy that goes back thousands of years. Life is to nurture the humanity that descended from the skies through Si Raja Batak. Mankind that descended from the skies is the manifestation in this world of the supreme source of all life. Sons continue the marga. Unfortunate indeed is the person unable to continue the chain of life bequeathed by Si Raja Batak. Cursed is he who does not value the chain of humanity that must be nurtured from one generation to the next.

So why was it that Pardomutua seemed to not love his son? After all, Pardomutua was the son of Ompu Silangit, a datu who had a deep knowledge of Batak manuscripts. As son of a datu, he should be precisely the one to appreciate the value of this boy. With his pink skin, with his hearty cries, was the baby not truly the descendant of Ompu Silangit, the famous warrior of the Batak War?

To Halia, children were everything. She had been raised in the Toba interior, and followed the instincts passed down from the ancestors without a second thought. She did not know her husband's real world. Who was Pardomutua? He had left his village when he was young, only eight years old, and returned home only in school holidays. Had his father Ompu Silangit really managed to teach him the contents of the old manuscripts? In town, Pardomutua read stories by Dutch writers that were taught at school. After he went to Tarutung, his town life was stronger still. He was more familiar with the American films they showed in the cinema. And of course, his friends from school.

Pardomutua's school experiences never left him, affecting the way he treated his wife. Back when he was a teenager at junior high school, he had a crush on a girl in his class, a girl with pale golden skin. He would never forget her and her hair pulled back in a ponytail. The whole class would play basketball, boys and girls together. It was great fun. During a game, he bumped into the girl, and for the first time his hand accidentally touched her breast. She blushed bright red and ran away. Pardomutua was excited. His hand felt as though it had an electric shock.

After that, the girl often glanced at him, a strong young man almost as tall as the Dutch schoolmasters. His skin was rather pale, and he had fine hair above his top lip, on his chin, and under his ears, a sure sign he would be hairy later on. That brief collision had left the trace of his sweat. His hand, deliberately or not, had touched her full breast. And the nerves in her breast tingled. This seemed to be something that differed between the town girls and the girls in the village. Maybe their close contact with boys stimulated hormones that pumped to their sensitive parts.

And Pardomutua found himself wanting to look at her all the time. From the point of view of marga, she came from South Tapanuli, and she was Muslim. She was in Tarutung because her father worked there as a judge. She was distant from him in every way. He was at school because the government official paid his school fees, but he was still just the son of a datu from the Toba interior. Anything more different from the girl's family was difficult to imagine. As a judge, the girl's father was part of the most respected group in town. He mixed with Dutch people. He played tennis on the court restricted for the Dutch. The girl also mixed with Dutch people, even though at school Pardomutua was much better than her at Dutch. The teacher often asked him to give examples in class of Dutch conversation. And in algebra, she had problems with her homework. Dutch and algebra, this is what raised Pardomutua's standing among the children at school, both the Dutch students and the locals.

Yes, you could say the girl was not smart at school. Or maybe she was lazy. Maybe studying with the cleverest in the class would improve her marks. So after the basketball incident, she deliberately dawdled after school. As class monitor, Pardomutua was always the last to leave.

'You're still here, Nuriah?' he asked, while tidying the desks.

'Yes. You know that homework, I can't do it.'

Pardomutua looked at her exercise book. Then he showed her some things. She began to work on it, and clapped her hands when she worked it out.

'That wasn't so hard after all,' she said. 'What about this one?'

Pardomutua solved the problems one by one. Each time, she cheered. Every now and then her red lips would break into a smile.

They started walking together. The hot sun stroked them. They walked slowly along the side of the road in the shade of large palm trees. Tarutung was a hill town. Usually there were cool breezes. But on this day, there was not a breath of wind. The sun beat down like piercing needles, but they did not feel any of this as they walked in single file. Pardomutua looked at the nape of her neck. Smooth, golden skin, with drops of sweat, her neck and nape shining. Such a cute neck.

That evening he went to visit her. Nuriah introduced him to her parents as a friend from school who was helping her with her schoolwork in preparation for the final examinations. It was their last year of school. She needed tutoring to complete her homework.

So it was that Pardomutua entered an entirely new social circle. Nuriah's family was very Dutch in their habits. When she said goodbye to her parents, Nuriah would kiss them on the cheeks. Lunch was complete with table manners. They used knives, forks and spoons. When they used spoons, you could hardly hear any sound at all. This was utterly unlike the way people ate in Pardomutua's village. But that was not the important thing.

Longing, passion and the excitement of the touch of skin were moments that made him feel like a man. A young woman who seemed to come from another world had entered his life. She often watched American films. She knew about western ways of love; the way girls could kiss boys on the mouth. To Pardomutua, she became the world of dreams come true.

But this dream-come-true did not have much time left at school. After examinations were over and as the vacation approached, a school group went for a picnic at Sibolga beach. This was where Pardomutua realized how short their time together was.

'What do you plan to do after you pass your exams?' Nuriah asked. They were walking on white sand under the shade of coconut palms.

'Work. Some of my family have asked me to work in East Sumatra.'

The breeze was playing with Nuriah's hair. They were walking apart from the rest of the group, at the water's edge, the waves licking every now and then.

'And you?' Pardomutua asked.

She did not answer. She took a deep breath, inhaling the sea air.

'Will you continue your schooling in Java?' Pardomutua persevered.

Nuriah shook her head.

'So, what . . . ?'

'I don't know. My mother told me I have to marry my cousin, my father's brother's son. My parents both agree about that.'

'Oh,' Pardomutua mumbled. 'Where does he live?'

'Batavia. He'll graduate as a doctor next year.'

Pardomutua felt his throat tighten. In the distance, fishing boats were skimming the waves. The sea breeze struck his eyes. Stung. They continued walking, leaving a long track in the sand.

So that's how it was. He might recall his teenage years, but the memory that bit the strongest was the sand splintering under his feet as he walked along that beach. Pardomutua felt defeated there on the shore. How could he, graduating from a junior high school in Tarutung, ever compare with a graduate from medical school in Batavia? Tongues of sea licked his feet, as though trying to cool the hot coals burning his temples. And to top it all, it was the ideal match, her cousin on her father's side!

Sibolga no longer seemed beautiful. The waves that crept sighing to the shore seemed to be saying, you're a defeated man. The rainbow over the sea seemed to be taunting, are you brave enough to conquer this wide sea as far as Batavia, way over there?

* * *

Halia was engrossed with her baby. One day, Mevrouw Capellen, the assistant manager's wife, came to see her. Cautiously, she asked some questions, speaking in Batak.

'Halia, how are your relations with your husband these days?'

'Relations?' Halia looked at the Dutch woman in front of her. The lines around her eyes seemed to deepen as she looked at Halia. It was as though her green eyes wanted to open Halia's chest.

'Are you looking after him well?'

'Of course. I prepare his meals and wash his clothes whenever he's at home. But these days he's rarely at home.'

'Ah, precisely,' Mevrouw Capellen looked deeply at Halia. 'Looking after your husband is not just a matter of giving him food and clean clothes.'

Halia frowned. Her questioning look made Mevrouw Capellen shake her head and go on.

'Have you ever asked yourself where he goes when he doesn't come home?'

'Why should I ask him? Aren't men free to go anywhere they want?' Halia replied, her voice level.

The Dutch woman glanced at the baby Halia was cuddling. A young mother who had suffered the pains of childbirth. The older woman drew a deep breath and sighed. She herself had never given birth. She was confused about how to say in Batak the words she wanted to say.

'Are you caring for him in bed?'

Halia tilted her head, watching the older woman pace back and forth.

'Now how can I do that? I have to care for the baby. He gets mad when he hears the baby cry. So I sleep with the baby in a separate room,' Halia replied innocently.

Mevrouw Capellen shook her head.

'Your baby is six months old now. It is time for you to sleep with your husband.'

'How can I? Who will sleep with the baby?'

'Find a Javanese woman to help. There are usually coolie widows looking for work. You can ask her to come to the house in the day to help you in the kitchen, and at night to watch your child.'

'I don't want anyone else to watch my child.'

'It is for the sake of you and your husband.'

Halia stared at her, amazed.

'And also for the peace for us living here in the plantation,' Mevrouw Capellen went on. This made Halia even more confused.

'It's like this, Halia,' Mevrouw said, impatient now. 'You ask that husband of yours where he goes when he doesn't come home, and who he goes out with.'

'I don't dare ask that. A Batak woman does not ask her husband such things,' Halia replied weakly.

Mevrouw Capellen shook her head.

'I notice when the two of you are out walking, you always walk behind your husband. That might be how things are in Batak country, where people walk in single file. But you are not living there now. The Dutch way is for husbands and wives to link arms.'

'No matter where I am, I will always be a Batak,' Halia said.

'But your husband, Pardomutua, is not a Batak here in this company.'

Halia was speechless. She tried to digest Mevrouw Capellen's words. Tondi's cries distracted her. And then she forgot the conversation.

One afternoon, Mevrouw and Meneer Capellen brought Pardomutua home. His shirt was torn and his face scratched. Halia was confused. Pardomutua said nothing. He went directly to the bathroom and cleaned himself up. Then, without a word, he went straight to the bedroom. The slamming door startled the baby, who started to cry.

Halia looked Mevrouw Capellen in the eye for answers. The older woman took a deep breath.

'Meneer Steenberg is in hospital,' she said.

And so it was that the scandal that was the talk of the Dutch in the plantation finally hit Halia.

Who knows how long it had been going on, maybe since Meneer Steenberg, the plantation assistant, had gone to Batavia on work duty four months ago, but Pardomutua had been having an affair with Mevrouw Steenberg. She was aged somewhere between thirty and forty. Halia knew her, but the two women were not particularly friendly. Mevrouw Steenberg was tall and slim and had a slightly stooped back. People said she was shaped like a prawn. She had golden hair and her skin was reddish, like a boiled prawn.

Evidently, Mevrouw Steenberg and Pardomutua had gone together to the resort in Brestagi, a favourite hill-station recreation place for the Dutch. It certainly was brazen of them to carry on at hotels there.

And the stories spread sure enough. It had been the talk for quite some time, until it reached the ears of Meneer Steenberg. When he found out what was going on, his wife reacted with indifference.

'How is this any different to our usual custom of exchanging door keys?' she said.

Among the Dutch, at the end of parties married couples often played something they called 'exchanging keys'. By exchanging house keys, they exchanged partners.

But Meneer Steenberg had never imagined exchanging keys with the Pardomutua couple.

'He is a native, an *inlander!*' he roared.

'But he's better than any other man I've known,' Mevrouw Steenberg replied nonchalantly. 'Other men don't satisfy me. Pardomutua is different. He's strong.'

Her gaze seemed taunting. Meneer Steenberg felt himself counted among those 'other men'.

He almost hit her there and then. But he remembered that he was a civilized man, and a gentleman should never hit a woman. Then he rushed off on his Norton motor bike, its muffler roaring, looking for Pardomutua.

The challenge was without weapons. They met in the middle of a field under the shade of some palm-oil trees. The earth beneath the trees was scattered by these men defending their honour. And it came to pass that Meneer Steenberg, who was over forty, was beaten black and blue and surrendered. He was taken to hospital.

So this film-scenario story became the talk of the plantation for quite some time. Dutch ladies gossiping together would giggle, but were also envious of Mevrouw Steenberg who dared get what she wanted. What other entertainment was there in the isolated plantation other than satisfaction in bed? Oh, how lucky Mevrouw Steenberg had been.

Halia, however, never asked questions. The incident passed as though it had nothing to do with her. The stories that fuelled the Dutch ladies' gossip did not interfere with her enjoyment with the baby. But she did follow Mevrouw Capellen's advice to 'care' for her husband Pardomutua. The older Dutch woman was like a mother to Halia, even though she would never understand her.

The conjugal bed held no attraction to Halia. She lay on her back as a duty because Pardomutua needed her body to satisfy his seething hormones. But she was always on the alert to escape the moment Tondi cried. As for what Pardomutua might be feeling, she could not care less. How could she understand that to him, bed had become fun. His experience with Mevrouw Steenberg, the filly with the blonde mane who had made love to every inch of his body, had shown him how women could be active partners. From below, above, the side, it was all wrestling to perfect the union of their bodies. How boring now the flatness of his wife, lying still and passive on her back, like a cold, banana-tree trunk.

Chapter 10

Siantar was now like a dead town for the Dutch. Maybe all towns were like that. Since Indonesian independence, there were no more social clubs for Dutch civil servants. Back in the colonial days, the *sosietet* building in Siantar had been the centre of social life for the Dutch working on the plantations, at nights and on holidays. If they had enough of dancing, there were always billiards or card games. Every now and then there were American films shown at the club before cinema release. It was a facility for the colonials, and a place where Dutch civil servants, company employees and colonial army people met.

Before World War II, every town had a club like this. In front of the building was a sign: *Verboden voor Honden en Inlanders*, Dogs and Natives Forbidden. The warning about dogs was to stop the Dutch bringing their pets into the building, but the sign was offensive in equating natives with dogs. During the fight for independence, this sign was often mentioned to ignite rebellion against the colonial army.

But at the same time, the clubs did provide a service for 'natives'. Dance bands were employed there to accompany the dancing. It was because of the clubs that local Indonesians could play western music on instruments like violin, clarinet and saxophone. Before the clubs existed, most locals played only traditional instruments.

As the number of local musicians who could play western music increased, so did the number of Dutch musicians decrease, because it was expensive to bring musicians out from Holland.

Locals working at the clubs were either entertainers accompanying the dancing, or waiters serving the Dutch their food and drink. It was entertainment colonial-style. But all this vanished in an instant when the Japanese army arrived. Then, with Indonesia's independence, the Dutch lost their colony.

Now the climate of war was over. After the 1949 Round Table Agreement, relations between Holland and Indonesia were established and Dutch companies could operate again in rubber, tea or tobacco. Dutch people began to return, including those who worked in the plantations around Siantar. There was not much entertainment now. They compensated with dinner parties, moving from house to house.

But Dr Herman felt awkward at these parties after a while. It was always couples there, and he particularly disliked the revival of the decadent practice from the colonial time of 'house-key swapping'. If the old clubs were still around, he would not feel so lonely. He could play billiards or cards. You did not have to be a couple for that, unlike the dinner parties. Dr Herman's world was different to that of the Dutch from the plantation. They were wealthy. He worked at a hospital on a small salary as part of the Dutch aid program for Indonesia. He had no private practice. He began to go to dinner parties less frequently and spent his spare time listening to classical music on his gramophone. He would sit alone in a dimly lit room smoking a cigar and let the smoke swirl around his head.

He was getting on in years. Here in this distant land, he was feeling increasingly alone. All his family were in Holland. His mother was in her late seventies now. He had some cousins over there, but would they visit her? Before leaving Holland, he had placed his mother in an old-people's home and given all the money he had received as prisoner-of-war compensation to pay the costs of her care. She would be well cared for. But would she be happy? An old-people's home could not alleviate the loneliness of old age.

Like he was feeling now. Happiness cannot be found in loneliness when you have no family near. His mother had no husband and children near her. Her husband had died in the war and her only child was in a country far away. Dr Herman could understand that pain, for he had been alone since his wife died, and they had no children.

To be alone in old age is a dark and bitter future. Dr Herman had thought that by leaving Holland he could escape the feeling of being closed in, and forget the death of his wife. When he was back in Holland, he had to experience winter again, at a time when the government had not yet repaired basic services. The gas supply was often cut off. The electricity was often disconnected, and the heating did not work. He found himself longing for the warm tropical sun in Indonesia. He could not stay in Holland with his mother in an old apartment building that had been only partially repaired after the war. Facilities at old-people's homes were better because the government prioritized services for old people and children. After his mother was settled in a home, he was alone in the old apartment. Every time the heating in the apartment broke down, he longed for the sun that warmed his skin and made his blood flow.

But it turned out that the warmth of the Indonesian sun was not enough to dispel his loneliness. His house felt cold. Mould was spreading on the walls, making them look as though the plasterwork was incomplete. He spent more time at the hospital, and when he was at home he listened to music. Classical music, which sometimes only increased the feeling of emptiness in the house. Violins, wind instruments, the beat of the timpani, providing quiet solemnity that alternated with biting pain. Loneliness could not be fended off with sound, it seemed.

So, during the day when he had no patients, he found himself often passing the room beside the hospital kitchen. Halia would be writing. Or if the desk was empty, she would be in the kitchen. Or they might run into each other in the corridor. She would smile. The day would be bright. All she had said was good morning, but her clear voice reminded Dr Herman of the time she sang. That sentimental song young Batak people used to sing.

Their conversation would be about food. He would look over the ingredients for the day. Piles of vegetables in big woks. Seeing the ingredients would spike his interest.

One day, he summoned up courage:

'I used to like cooking. When my wife was alive, I was the one who cooked because she did not like being in the kitchen,' he said.

'Really. And now?' Halia asked.

'No opportunity. Or, to be more precise, I don't have the right equipment at home.'

'If you like, Doctor, I could get it for you.'

'Really?'

'Of course. There are some things in the storeroom that you could use in your house.'

'Thank you. I could cook on Sundays if I am not on duty,' Dr Herman said.

Sunday came and Halia helped him prepare the ingredients. She brought along a cook from the hospital. The doctor was skilled at chopping and preparing, from the main course to dessert. This was the first time in her life that Halia had ever seen a man cooking in the kitchen. Where she lived, the only time men cooked was for ceremonial feasts, and even then, they only did the heavy work like stirring the huge earthenware pots or keeping the fire alight. The women did all the chopping and preparing, and anyway, the menu was limited.

Halia was impressed when the meal was served. There were four kinds of dishes, meat and fish. The dessert was tempting. Dr Herman beamed with pride. Halia had never seen him so happy. Maybe it was the heat in the kitchen, maybe it was his happiness, but his usually pale skin glowed.

The three of them sat at the table. Halia and the cook were uneasy at first, sitting at the same table as the doctor. Halia sat across from him. But her unease slowly dissipated as she saw him so happy. They ate and joked.

So it was that the Sunday lunches became a regular event. Every Saturday, Dr Herman would say whether or not he had to work the next day. After church, Halia would invite one of the hospital cooks to go with her to help Dr Herman in his kitchen. Sometimes they would deliberately cook more than they needed and send the extra to the head of the hospital and the other doctors. Dr Herman seemed to particularly enjoy doing this. When he received a note of thanks with some funny comment he would laugh aloud. His spirits seemed to be restored, rekindled by his Sundays in the kitchen.

The kitchen was large, with white-tiled walls. Since the start of the Sunday lunches, the walls had been cleaned regularly, and now shone. Dr Herman lined up his ingredients on the bench and looked them over.

'Last night I decided to cook Dutch-style food. I want to try a new sauce recipe,' he said.

Halia tidied the pots and pans. Dr Herman looked again at the ingredients on the table. His brow furrowed. He was totally absorbed, as though facing a patient on the operating table. Beef. Prawns. Fish. Eggs. Shallots. Onions. Garlic. Celery. Asparagus. Carrots. Cucumber. Paprika. Chillies. Tomatoes. Hmmmm. He began to put aside what had to be sliced or chopped. Usually, Halia and the cook would do the peeling, but this time it was just Halia. Dr Herman did not notice. He was slicing away, cutting everything evenly and neat. As he worked, he talked about what he was going to make.

The smell of frying food filled the air. The kitchen resounded with the crackle of deep frying and the hiss of the flame. There were three kinds of dishes. As usual, each dish had a name that Halia found difficult to remember. She would just say a kind of stir fry, but his fancy name had a nasal sound to it.

He turned down the flame, then took off his apron and washed his hands. Halia laid the food out on the table. It was only the two of them. Dr Herman realized that only then, when he saw the settings at the table.

'Where's the other one?' he asked, confused.

Halia could not help but laugh. The doctor really was absentminded. They had been together, just the two of them, for hours and he had not noticed. Dr Herman was startled. He was not absentminded now as he looked at her laughing so freely. Her white teeth flashed. He had never seen her laugh like this.

'Well, well . . . so I see. It's just the two of us,' he said, brushing off his astonishment.

Then they became awkward. Just the two of them eating together in the large room. Soft music on the gramophone. When it was three of them, they would joke while eating, but now it was quiet. Halia felt self-conscious as she used her spoon. Eating alone with a man. A strange feeling twisted inside her.

But what was strange? Being together over the past weeks had brought them close. Chatting, joking, laughing, had made this man no longer strange to her. But now she felt clumsy. It was not only Halia. He felt the same. They finished their meal faster than usual. It was delicious, but when swallowing the food seemed to stick in the throat.

Usually, after the meal it was Halia and the cook who would do the cleaning up. But this time Dr Herman brought the empty plates to the kitchen and put them in the sink. He washed the dishes. A Batak man never washes dishes. The kitchen is the woman's realm. Women would even scold their sons standing in the doorway and tell them to get out. Probably that is why Batak men feel uncomfortable in the kitchen. But here was this Dutch doctor, perfectly happy in the kitchen washing dishes. Did all Dutch men help their wives in the kitchen? Halia wondered. She cleared the rest of the food and tidied the dinner table. All the while glancing back at the kitchen.

She went to help dry the dishes. Without a word. But every now and then she would steal a glance and see his red face. The wrinkles at the corner of his eyes and the grey in his eyebrows were sure signs of his age. But when he cooked, the light in his eyes was like a boy playing with toys. Maybe this was the only time he was happy. Why, she wondered, do people in the village call Europeans 'Pale Eyed Ones', when actually their eyes were green or blue? Halia looked at his eyes, blue and clear like the surface of Lake Toba.

They went into the sitting room. Halia's awkwardness just would not go away. She fiddled with the pages of a Dutch magazine.

She did not understand the words but there were pictures of beautiful scenery. Dr Herman changed the record that had a picture of a dog facing a loudspeaker. Classical music filled the room. He lit a cigar.

'Do you like this kind of music?' Dr Herman suddenly asked.

Halia got a shock. She listened carefully for a moment.

'I prefer our Batak music,' she said, laughing.

'Oh yes,' he replied, laughing too. 'But unfortunately, there are no recordings of it.'

'Yes, that's a pity,' Halia said.

'Perhaps you would sing a song like you did at the party? I will accompany you on the piano.'

Halia nodded.

'Right,' Dr Herman said, taking her hand and drawing her over to the piano.

Halia nodded, but she was suddenly embarrassed when she remembered the song she sang before.

Ende ni Silangkitang
Di bulan tula ditumbahon
Palias na marimbang
Taganan tu na ubanon

The song Silangkitang
Sung when the moon is full
Rather than courting the young
Better a grey-haired old fool

It was a song young people sang as a joke amongst themselves. But now, here she was facing an old man with grey eyebrows.

Her hand felt hot in his. She wanted to pull it away. But the heat of his hand seemed to glue their skin together. They stood facing each other. When she looked up, Halia found a clear blue lake that reflected the soft light. Her chest was beating fast. She did not dare look. She tried to release her hand. But he held on to it tightly.

When she managed to wriggle her hand free, their fingers ended up entwined. Every nerve in her body tingled.

The only sound was the music from the gramophone. And the beating of her heart. Her heart had never fluttered like this before. Even when she was young. The warmth of his hand was like embers that burned deep, flowing through her veins, heating her skin, heating her flesh. She had never experienced her heart going so crazy, making it hard to breathe.

His eyes beamed softness. Heat was slowly piercing her chest, and yet she shivered. Her body went limp and she fell as he embraced her.

Her whole body quivered when the skin of her face touched his. Never before had a rush of blood made every layer of her skin tremble, and her body burn. She felt she was steaming and shivering at the same time. And then she went even more limp as his mouth touched her lips.

Chapter 11

Never had her heart beat like this. On her first night with her husband she had trembled, but with fear. His big crushing body left her almost unable to breathe. Her entire body had gone cold, her breathing shallow. And as she shivered, he kept thrusting away. She shivered with cold.

Pardomutua never warmed his wife's blood. His experience with Mevrouw Steenberg had not taught him how to treat a woman. Quite the opposite, all he knew was how he wanted a woman to treat a man. He had surrendered his body entirely to his Dutch lover, letting his skin accept her roving fingers, her lips and her tongue. He never once regretted that experience, in fact he longed for it. He had hoped in vain for his wife to act like that. And he had not known how to teach her.

Halia had spent years in a marriage full of worry and fear of her husband, and then more than ten years alone. Her body had passed youth without experiencing normal youthful feelings: desire and passion. She was a Batak village girl who had been stranded in a foreign environment at a young age. It was a life she could not understand, with values unknown in her family circles. In the Batak world, the only values were those concerning social relations between marga. The very idea of knowledge that taught wives how to relate to their husbands in bed was unknown. Traditional custom was no better. The old manuscripts held nothing about women making themselves seductive to their husbands. The sacred knowledge was all about calling ancestral spirits. To Batak, knowledge was magic, and had nothing to do with physical enjoyment. There was black magic to make others sick, but no magic for love.

Now, nearly thirty, she was a woman in her prime. And it was only now that she felt the confusion of heat flushing over her body for the first time. It was gentleness that had conquered all her skin, every nook and cranny of it. To this man, it was not the thrusts of lovemaking that were important, but caresses, the brush of lips on cheeks, eyes, ears, necks, breasts, chests; roving, inquisitive tongues; soft touches that made veins pump hot blood, making the body damp with sweat.

From one day to the next, she wanted this man. It was not the desire of the earth for the plough, but the cold earth that has for years yearned for the soft sun to warm it. Day after day, it was the longing of a grown woman, who kept her relationship with this man tightly hidden. She felt as though she was intoxicated while treading a secret path. Worry mixed with desire. Looks and caresses had intoxicated her.

Then the moment came. That evening, Halia was in her small, rented house outside the hospital complex. Dr Herman arrived, in a hurry. His term at the hospital was going to end. He was to be moved to a hospital at Kutaraja, at the far north of Aceh.

'Come with me,' he said.

Halia was dumbstruck. Confused.

'Halia, will you marry me? Let's marry,' Dr Herman's voice seemed to be slapping her.

Marry? Become his wife? She was speechless. The word that had not troubled her for so long suddenly cast her down to the ground. The word that reminded her she was a wife. She had never divorced Pardomutua.

But this man's cool gaze gently overcame her. The calm, lake-blue shining from his eyes looked ready to cure her fever for evermore.

'Become my wife. You told me you have a child. Let him become my child,' he said, haltingly.

Halia remained dumbstruck. Dr Herman took her hand, spreading his warmth through her palm.

'When my time is up here in Indonesia, we can go to Holland. Your son can go to school there.'

Halia did not react. And still she could not utter a word when the doctor left the house.

Become the wife of Dr Herman, the Dutch man? All those previous months that had so intoxicated her, suddenly felt like a time of chaos, stabbing and slander. Until now, all she had wanted was to enjoy the softness and passion that flowed through her body. She had never once thought about marriage with this man. And if now she was being confronted with marriage, then what about her husband? All these years she had done nothing about divorce. Was now the time to ask for one?

Divorce. This dreadful word had never crossed her mind. As long as she was not divorced, she remained in the circle of Pardomutua's marga. Her son, Tondinihuta, was cared for as part of that marga.

Worry made her spin. She wanted to be together with this Dutch man, the man who had taken her, so gently, on an exploration of every corner of her body. But how can a wife leave her husband's marga after her family has received the bridal dowry? How could she take Tondi to become the child of a Dutchman? How could a child possibly be cut out of the chain of descendants of Si Raja Batak, the source of all Batak marga?

She was filled with uncertainty. Dr Herman gave her time to think about it. To think about yes or no, that sounded so easy, but it dragged her into a whirlwind that made it hard to breathe. The passing days pressed in on her.

She was standing on the edge of a ravine. Far, far below lay a blue lake. From far away, Tondi was running towards her. He was calling to her with his clear, bell-like laugh. Then he slipped on the steep path. She ran after him, trying to reach him, but failed. He slipped and slid down into the lake.

The lake looked so small way down there. She felt as though she was on the summit of a tall mountain. She was standing so high she felt she could reach the clouds. The water in the lake rose, reached her feet and kept rising, soaking her whole body. The lake water was warm, making her blood flow quicker. She was drowning in warm blue water, all of her skin felt as though it was being stroked gently, by a man's creeping lips and tongue. But the water kept on rising, reaching the sun. Then the sun changed, it was Pardomutua's face. It exploded. Shattered. Threw her. And all the lake water at the foot of the mountain was shaking her. The holy creature, Boru Saniang Naga, at the bottom of the lake was shaking, making the water seethe. Halia was dragged down. And still Boru Saniang Naga was not satisfied, tossing her against the steep banks at the lake's edge.

Oh, what terrible dreams! Dreams that came one after another making her wake in a sweat, gasping for breath. Her own sweat disgusted her. It seemed to carry filth from behind her pores, soiling her body. All the passion she had known became hellfire that was burning her up. She felt as though she was covered with filth, wrapped in dirt that had to be washed with a whole lake's worth of water.

Thoughts of divorce, images of marriage, brought constant nightmares. Strange, these thoughts did not make her imagine freedom to love, with no more need to hide. Secrecy came with tension. Wouldn't becoming husband and wife mean the bliss she had enjoyed would be there forever, and not something brief and furtive? Should she not be thankful that she had this chance of happiness at this time in her life? The urge to follow her yearning for physical intoxication would not subside. Yet her feet were overcome with vertigo as though standing on a high precipice, struck with fear looking at the chasm below.

Tomorrow she had to give Dr Herman an answer. He was going to leave the town. Before he left, he had to know whether Halia would be part of his life, his partner for the rest of his days.

Halia felt the house crowding in. The four walls seemed to be moving, threatening to crush her. Maybe she was having palpitations, making her short of breath.

She started. She could hear rushed footsteps outside. And shouting, a voice she knew:

'*Ina ni Tondi*, Mother of Tondi, open the door . . . !'

There was knocking at the door. When the door opened, her heart skipped a beat.

There at the door stood her son, Tondi, with her mother-in-law, Pardomutua's mother. Tondi dived to hug his mother's legs. Halia trembled under the gaze of her inangboru, with Tondi's small hands clutching her leg.

'He has had a fever for these last few days. He has been crying constantly. Ompu Silangit would not give him medicine but told me to bring him here to see you,' the old woman said.

Something stuck in Halia's throat. And the flood she had been holding back these past few days flowed like a torrent. She lifted Tondi and cradled him to her body, straining to carry this boy who had grown so heavy. She hardly noticed, because she was trying so hard to stop an explosion of sobs. But she could not quell them heaving in her chest.

'What's wrong?' her inangboru asked.

The broken dam of tears made her stagger with Tondi still in her arms. Her inangboru led her to sit on a chair. Tondi's head was wet from her sobs. It seemed that his fever was being sprinkled with cool lake water. His hot face cooled with his mother's tears.

'Your illness, my son, is because of me. Don't be sick now, my son . . .' Halia sobbed.

Halia's inangboru set about arranging the things she had brought with her. She was not like other Batak women who talk constantly. With Ompu Silangit, the two of them would spend their days with minimal conversation in a house that was always quiet. The only sound in the house on the hill was Tondi's shouts.

Halia stopped crying. Tondi's fever subsided. Her inangboru set out some cakes on a plate.

'Ompu Silangit told me to make you this cake. *Itak*. From the old days,' she said.

Halia raised her head. Oh Debata, dear Lord, did this old man in the interior know what had been happening over these past few weeks? Halia trembled as she looked at the cakes on the plate. *Itak gurgur*, rice-flour cakes made by rolling the mixture into little balls before steaming them. They melted in your mouth, and were sweetened with palm sugar. But it was not the sweetness that was important. And the cakes were made not just as a treat to eat. Usually a mother would make them, rolling them with her hands, and her fingerprints would be on every single one. The cake was eaten to restore spirits. A mother's fingerprints, a caring mother, gave power to the cakes so they could restore weak spirits.

Mangan ma itik on daining, her inangboru said in Batak, 'Come child, eat the *itak*.' She picked up one and popped it into Halia's mouth.

Halia held back the flow from her eyes. She swallowed the rice ball, feeling the sweetness gush in her mouth. The tears that escaped the dam of her eyes flowed to her chest and washed away the crumbs.

'Now you feed some to Tondi,' her inangboru said.

Her inangboru continued to feed her while she fed her son. One mouthful at a time. Tondi nestled in his mother's chest. It was as though with the rice cake and her tears, the crisis that had so enveloped her peaked. The black dust, soot, all was shed; fell, drifted away, vanished.

'This is a new ulos cloth I have woven. Use it as a blanket if you are cold,' her inangboru said softly.

Halia dared not raise her head. Her inangboru put it around her shoulders.

And the dam burst again. Halia slipped down from the chair and placed her hands on her inangboru's knees. Tondi rolled to the floor, then hugged his mother, confused. Halia's sobs broke on her inangboru's lap.

Oh inang, inang, inang. This is my mother, after my own mother died. Halia remembered her mother's funeral when she was still a small child. Her father had remarried her mother's younger sister. Her new mother was no stranger to her, but still, she was not her own mother.

All women need a mother. A place of support in a crisis. She does not have to talk about that crisis, but the love that flows from a mother can disentangle the knots inside. Only when a woman has grandchildren does she not need her mother, because now she is the cool wellspring for her daughters and daughters-in-law.

Halia's inangboru stroked her hair. She was just as confused as Tondi seeing Halia sob like this. She did not know why her husband had told her to visit their daughter-in-law, especially when Tondi had a fever. He had merely put a herbal compress on the boy's forehead, and told her to leave quickly.

'He will get better when he meets his mother,' was the only thing Ompu Silangit had said. And his wife was used to asking no questions, because there was much in her husband's world she could not understand.

During the long journey on a crowded bus, Tondi's fever had made her extremely worried. And now here she was, with all this crying going on. But when she felt Tondi's head, his fever had gone.

Halia's answer for Dr Herman was clear. Answering yes or no actually did not need consideration, for the more she weighed things up, the more she found herself sucked into a whirlwind where she could not breathe. Her choice was between her son and his Batak marga or to be with this Dutch man. She could not possibly take her child into the life of this foreigner, no matter how much she might want to be with him.

So Dr Herman left for Kutaraja alone. He would always remember the town of Siantar. Those months of Sundays had revived every organ and vein in his body, all his life spirit. And that would all disappear without trace.

Halia felt shards of sadness at the parting. But the time she spent with her son made the pangs of sadness more fleeting, and then pass.

Ah, Ompu Silangit way over there in Batak lands. Did he know everything going on under this sky? He had ordered his wife to bring Tondi to her and stay with her, to protect her from overwhelming sadness.

Tondi was still on holiday. This new place felt so different from his grandfather's village. His mother's house at the edge of the hospital complex was next to a zoo. He was free to play there, crawling inside between the broken fence palings, and the sound of his laughter rang out as he ran around under the pine trees.

When it was time to go back home to the village, Tondi took with him happy memories. The big hospital yard, the animal cages in the zoo, the pine trees with turtledove nests. The sound of the cooing of the turtledoves filled the large, quiet yard. And now he had to leave it behind.

Halia went on with her life with renewed strength. Parting with the Dutch man had turned out to be a blessing. She felt that being alone meant more to her now, because she knew that she still had ties to her Batak homeland and that her son would not become a lost person. For after all, wasn't that what you became if ties were severed with the ancestral heartland? She would ensure that her son kept those ties. What did going to school in Holland mean if he turned out like a kite whose string had been cut? What is the point of being in a beautiful place if you cannot return to your origins?

A mother's duty is to nurture the seed, give it birth, and give it to her husband's marga. She had fulfilled her duty. So was her pleasure in lovemaking with a man who was not her husband a sin? According to the pastors at church, there was absolutely no doubt—sin, sin, sin! It was all spelled out in one of the Ten Commandments. Sin, yes, sin. But was it wrong when she had never had any pleasure like this with her husband? And if it was wrong, then who had she betrayed, who had she wronged? Not Pardomutua, that's for sure. A son had been born, but he had neglected him. No one could blame her, because she had produced a son in this world to continue the marga.

The Dutch man had given his all, had invited her to explore fingertip by fingertip, hand by hand, arm by arm, taking her on discovery to every corner of her body, nerves that excited her in the pleasure of passion. All the years with her husband had brought her only anxiety and fear. But with this Dutch man, just a few months had imprinted experiences she would never forget.

Halia continued to work hard. One day, Dr Partogi, the head of
the hospital, called her into his office. He looked glum. Ah, this is
it, Halia thought. She had been told two months ago.

'I've done the best I can, Halia,' he said, speaking in Batak.

'Yes, I understand,' Halia replied slowly, also in Batak.

'I explained to the head of the office of the department of health
in Medan that your work here is excellent. You must know him, of
course. He visited this hospital. He understands, but the decision
has come from Jakarta.'

'Yes, I understand,' Halia mumbled.

'So what will you do now?' he asked, his voice breaking.

'I don't know.'

'If you like, you can work afternoons at my private practice.
I already have one nurse there, but that doesn't matter. I can have
two workers.'

'Thank you, I will think it over,' Halia said.

'Don't take too long. My wife will be happy if you work at my
practice. I mean, she'd be pleased if there was not just one nurse
working with me, and a young one at that,' he said.

Halia smiled. She knew what the head of the hospital meant.
She was close to Dr Partogi and his wife, who were both Batak.
They often asked Halia to help with the cooking when they had dinner
parties. Recently, there had been some gossip about the doctor taking
his nurse to Prapat, on the shores of Lake Toba. Siantar was a small
town that could make you feel stifled because there was nothing to
do. Especially if you were a doctor worn down by the heavy workload
at the hospital and your private practice. He needed a break, but the
town was too small, and gossip spread easily.

Halia looked around her as she walked along the long corridor
of the hospital veranda. Wide, green lawns and rows of pine trees.
She would leave this place.

Her replacement was a young high-school graduate who had
taken a course in nutrition run by the department of health. That is
how it was now. As the wheels of government became increasingly
organized, the administrative rules became stricter. First it had

been any employees who were illiterate. Halia did not have the qualifications now required to work in the hospital. The emergency post-war period seemed to be over. She was out.

Anyway, she wanted to get away from everything that smelled of hospital. She had been breathing in the smell of disinfectant every day these past years. She wanted to get away from it. And so she turned down the offer to work at the private practice. She had had enough. No more.

* * *

Now, she spent her days in a lean-to food stall with a tin roof that sold fried bananas, cassava, sweet potatoes and yams, far from her rented rooms where she lived with her son, Tondi. Every day she walked to the food stall, carrying her provisions on her back. Tondi would come with her on his way to school and help by carrying the firewood. By the time he got to school, his shirt would be dirty and sweaty. The days were hard. The stall was beneath the railway bridge, and every now and then the place would roar and shake when a train passed overhead.

Frying with glowing charcoal, the smoke was endless. Ash and charcoal made the stall feel stifled and hot. Day after day Halia would go there, and without saying much she would fry food on the hot fire and occasionally smile at the customers. Hot oil would spurt, blackening her hands.

No one knew why she had opened this stall. With her skills, she could have worked at a large restaurant. There was such a restaurant in the town, frequented by Dutch company people. As a private business, it was not bound by government civil service regulations. The important thing was to serve delicious food quickly. There were many people around who would vouch for Halia's capabilities. Dr Partogi's wife did not understand why Halia had first turned down the offer to work at her husband's practice, and then did not want to work at that restaurant.

'I like my work,' was Halia's only reply.

'But it's too heavy for you,' Dr Partogi's wife said.

Halia merely smiled.

The bananas seemed to flutter as they sizzled in the hot oil. Halia's skin turned rough and dirty. She never wore nice clothes any more. Early in the morning she would go to the main market in Siantar to buy bananas directly from the first sellers or intercept them on their way to the market to buy the best ones. All day long she would be engrossed in her work in front of the fire. Every day she was enveloped with cold morning dew and hot smoke, but her sole ambition was to sell the best fried bananas in town, or at least in the area.

Was this some kind of deliberate self-torture? Only Halia knew. Other people only saw the smile of the woman they knew as *Ina ni si Tondi*, the woman with the stall under the Siantar railway bridge.

Then one day her tenacity was crushed. Tondi came to the stall. His mother had been waiting since morning to hear about his school report.

As soon as she saw him, she knew. His head was bowed in defeat. They avoided looking at each other.

'I can progress to the next class, Inang. But my marks are not good enough for a scholarship,' Tondi said weakly.

His mother nodded.

'Never mind. We'll work something out so you can still go to school,' she said.

It was all very well for the government to give scholarships to future teachers, but how does that help the likes of us roasting in this shack, she wondered.

Tondi understood. He saw his mother keep calm, but he knew exactly what their situation was. How could that fire in the lean-to food stall under the railway bridge possibly provide for his schooling? High-school students had to have clean white shirts and wear shoes, unlike junior high-school where there was no school uniform and no requirement to wear shoes. And quite apart from the clothes, there was no way a food-stall boy could manage to pay the school fees.

His mother was trying so hard. But trying was just a path, not the reality of the hoped-for destination.

PART FOUR

WAR

Chapter 12

You could hear gunfire in the distance. The pounding conversation of shells as they stabbed the earth. Explosions of rifles barking like firecrackers. The mountain slopes were dry. At the foothills, hot sulphuric spring water had etched trails of white lime. The hills were barren. He had arrived in Sipirok. A flock of sparrows chirped noisily as it flew north in convoy, probably scared off by shells falling in the dry rice fields. From the mountain slope the view was clear to the land below.

He had left the Sarulla highlands far behind. Now, which direction should he go? Fighting was raging, and one side was the enemy. It was hard to tell who was friend and who was foe at the best of times, but what was their position here in this place? The fighting was now outside of the town. The rebel forces were all holding out in the forest. The central government army was doing a clean-up operation in the forest around Sipirok, firing shells from the Sipirok-Bulupayung road towards where they thought the rebels were. He could see a convoy of trucks the size of match-box toys stretched along the Tarutung-Sipirok road. The shooting was aimed at the hills where the rebels were. You could hear the gunfire. 12.7 machine guns, they were. Showering who knows how many hundreds of bullets.

Sitting bolt upright on the hill with an open view to the valley below, Tondi held the reins of the horse he had ridden from Sarulla. The horse was sweating. The steep path he had climbed to the summit had been covered with scrub with white flowers moving in the wind. Now, Tondi sheltered behind a clump of balaka palms. The small green fruit of the balaka, endemic to this region, is bitter but quenches thirst. Tondi chewed some as he observed smoke rising from some treetops in the valley over to the west. From up here, in the hot, treeless plain, that shady grove of trees looked like an oasis.

Smoke billowed. Most likely the house had been hit by shells fired into the village. So, he thought, there are still many innocent victims, even though Colonel Simbolon had wanted to avoid a clash between armies. But see, bullets were flying everywhere, probably because the soldiers firing were outsiders, who did not choose targets carefully, and did not care about the locals. Most likely, the commander who ordered this attack did not care about the locals because he had no relatives in the area.

Soldiers who came from this area usually still observed local Batak custom, whether they were in the rebel army or the central army. At least they thought about locals as possible family. That was why Colonel Simbolon had chosen retreat from Medan. But now that was all in vain, because the army sent in to fight Simbolon's troops saw things differently. The war no longer paid any heed to family ties.

This seemed to be the government's deliberate strategy in wiping out the rebellion. They understood the Batak family system all right, but turned it against them. They would send in soldiers from the region, but from a different ethnicity. War strategy employed every tactic, including inter-ethnic rivalry, fanning hatred. President Sukarno and his army chief of staff in Jakarta, General Nasution, were well aware of this. Their agenda was clear: this ongoing rebellion was costing too much. They needed a quick victory.

* * *

Tondi's thoughts wandered. He remembered when his platoon commander, Pardapdap, had first invited him to join as a volunteer. Pardapdap had been frothing at the mouth, from anger or from the rice liquor he was drinking as they chatted at the kiosk in the corner of the Siantar market.

'Treachery . . .'

Tondi did not understand but kept quiet.

'They signed the pledge, but then reneged,' Pardapdap grumbled.

'What pledge?' Tondi asked

'The army commanders in this region pledged to remain unified in their demands. But then some subordinates carried out an order from Jakarta to arrest their own officer, Colonel Simbolon. Now we have war. But the enemy we face are our own friends. It's more difficult to fight people who used to be your friends.'

'Why did they do it?' Tondi asked.

Pardapdap shrugged his shoulders.

'Who knows? Solidarity means nothing. Army officers had just returned from a meeting in Jakarta where they conveyed the people's wishes to the government. When they got back to Medan they reported to their commander, Colonel Simbolon, and told him about an idea some senior officers in Jakarta had.'

'And?'

'Colonel Simbolon and some regional officers made a pledge based on that idea. Maybe it was a trap from the start. He trusted his subordinates too much,' Pardapdap's voice was bitter.

'What's a pledge, anyway? How can all this fighting now be just because of something called a pledge?' Tondi asked naively.

'Oh Tondi . . . A pledge is not a thing. It's loyalty to ideals. All those who signed agreed to fight for those ideals.'

'Ideals, you say. What ideals?'

'For a better life. To organize our own development. For the right to manage our own region. With all the natural resources we have here, we could speed up development. Maybe even help Java. Not like now. With all our resources we're still poor. We're like dead chickens in a granary. The central government siphons off all our wealth and uses it for people over in Java. This has to change.'

This political stuff went way over Tondi's head. Even the promised fighting was something he had never imagined. But he had felt fired up with enthusiasm and had wanted to be part of the fight right away. He was not like Pardapdap, whose bitterness was that of an older man sick of fighting. The Japanese. The Dutch. The Darul Islam rebels. It just never stopped. But what other choice was there for a soldier?

'We fought for independence. For what? For a better life. Our commanders wanted the central government to pay attention to us here. And this is the reply we get. We have to fight yet again,' Pardapdap's voice was hoarse.

Pardapdap had remained loyal to his commander. It was not just the loyalty of a subordinate; he believed his commander had noble ideals. Maybe this came from the revolutionary days. A commander became a leader to his men not just because of his rank or because the government appointed him. Loyalty was forged through the personal qualities of a leader as someone with shared ideals.

During the revolution, Pardapdap had fought alongside Captain Sinta Pohan, a battalion commander then based in Medan. It was the same Captain Sinta Pohan that Pardapdap had learnt was escorting Colonel Simbolon as he retreated to Tapanuli that December night in 1956. And so Pardapdap had joined them on that journey from Sinaksak in Siantar, a journey more intense than any during his guerrilla days. Being a guerrilla fighting against the Dutch army was a duty, but retreating from a city to avoid fighting your own soldiers was painful indeed.

Captain Sinta Pohan's battalion had set up its base in the interior. From there, they had recruited volunteers for battle training. On that fateful night of the journey from Siantar that Tondi had joined, Pardapdap had deserted his post to join Sinta Pohan's troops. He could not bear to serve under a commander he thought had betrayed the cause. A few others at his post had joined him. Meanwhile, some local figures coaxed a few unquestioning youth, like Tondi, to join as volunteers. Most had no idea what they were volunteering for. Some left home without telling their parents. When Tondi left, all he said to his mother was:

'I just can't go on working as a bus conductor, Inang. I want to join Colonel Simbolon's rebellion.'

Colonel Simbolon was like a father to the soldiers in this part of Sumatra. He had been based in Medan as regimental commander. When the fighting for independence had ended, the entire region had been destroyed. Roads had not been repaired. Bridges had not been rebuilt and the only way to cross rivers was by raft. Most large colonial buildings were in ruins.

Worst of all, soldiers were living hand to mouth. Negotiations between the Dutch and Indonesian governments that ended with the transfer of sovereignty in 1949 included stipulations about the Indonesian army. Indonesians who had been soldiers in the Dutch colonial army, including those who were part of the State of East Sumatra army in the Dutch-conceived United States of Indonesia, now had to be absorbed into the Indonesian army. So it was that the Indonesian army in North Sumatra was made up of three groups: the revolutionary soldiers, the former colonial army soldiers, and the East Sumatra army soldiers. Bringing them together as one regular Indonesian army was extremely difficult, because the revolutionary soldiers had spent years fighting the other two groups for Indonesia's independence. This difference in their backgrounds was the main spark of conflict. Now, the central government was exploiting this situation to fracture the army groups.

The situation was even more complex because during the war for independence, the Dutch army and soldiers from the state of East Sumatra were based in the towns, living in barracks the Dutch had built. After independence, they continued to live there. The revolutionary soldiers, though, had carried out guerrilla warfare and never had fixed places to stay. When they were called in from the interior after independence, the only barracks the new Indonesian government could provide for them were tin-roofed, wooden shacks in plantations. Formerly storage sheds, they had been abandoned during the war and parts of their walls and roofs were missing. The holes had to be plugged with thatching and bamboo before they could be used.

Most of these former guerrilla fighters were unmarried, but some were married. After years of separation, families were reunited but had to live in these makeshift barracks. Leaking when it rained. Flimsy bamboo partitions. Perhaps the unmarried men could cope with partitioned quarters, but not the married ones. Couples had to live in cramped communal quarters and had no privacy.

While having to live like this, soldiers were still sent on military missions against the Darul Islam rebels in Aceh. It is difficult to imagine how they felt having to leave their wives and children behind in leaky, makeshift barracks. What's more, even though the Darul Islam rebels wanted to establish an Islamic state, they were still former independence fighters who, just like them, were also dissatisfied with the decisions of the central government in Jakarta. Their rebellion sprang from poverty and the terrible conditions in Aceh.

The dissatisfaction that arose in Sumatra was understandable. Most of Indonesia's profitable former Dutch oil fields and plantations were in North Sumatra. All the oil and plantation produce was exported, but the profit from those exports flowed only to Jakarta. Foreign trade was under the control of the central government, and none of the profit was being fed back into development in the region where the resources came from.

Regional army commanders began to act on their own initiative, exporting plantation produce themselves and using the earnings for local development, especially for repairing army barracks and improving the lives of the families of soldiers sent away to fight. The revolutionary era black-market trade was revived. Back then, this kind of trade had funded war logistics, but now the central government considered such activity illegal. This added to tension between the central government and the army in the regions.

President Sukarno just would not listen. Some said this was because he was under the influence of the Communist Party that encouraged him to ignore the regional demands and to enforce a strong centralized government, ruling with an iron fist. He was becoming more of a dictator.

It turned out that the solidarity pledged by the army commanders was fragile. Jakarta ordered the second and third in command, who had signed the pledge, to arrest their superior, Colonel Simbolon. The two competed to carry out this order, and because of the lack of coordination, Colonel Simbolon was able to escape. This is the story of what Pardapdap called treachery.

Tondi had been dragged into it. He was not in the army. He had been a volunteer since his training days when Pardapdap asked him to join. His job had been to get food rations and make coffee and tea. He never knew anything about Colonel Simbolon's ideals. All he wanted was to fight. Fighting was a path. There were many paths to reach your destination. But the fast track was war. The ending was clear. Win or lose, both were clear endings in the journey of life. Loss in war was clearer, namely death—well, that was better than crawling around from day to day, defeated in poverty or meaninglessness in a time of peace. Or victory. Was that the end of the path this war might offer?

His father had become a big shot through war. So why not him too? If there had been no war, would his father have made it? True, he had Dutch high-school education. But would that alone have given him a position as high as the one he now held? The way Tondi saw it, only war could produce men of rank. Without the war right now, he would still be hidden away in the poverty of his mother's food stall. The boom of gunfire and shelling were sounds that would bring him to his destination, even though he did not know whether that direction was the right or the wrong one.

But there was reality that Tondi did not know. Not every battle becomes the path to victory for those involved. Did he realize that to be safe and alive at the end of a war you have won is no guarantee you will enjoy that victory? There are no fruits of victory. Independence was victory to a new nation at war. But not everyone who joined the fight enjoyed that victory. Look at Pardapdap who was still poor, living in makeshift barracks. And so many others who fought for independence and were then just cast aside. And if victory is no guarantee, then what about loss? Who knows, Tondi wondered, where the path he was following would end.

* * *

At last, the gunfire from the road died down. The army convoy moved on. From the slope of the hill, those matchbox trucks looked like snakes. The line of trucks followed the curves of the winding road. Once the booming ceased, the forest fell silent. There was only the rustle of the wind in the leaves. Slowly, Tondi walked down the hillside, leading his horse. The area where the shelling had been directed was to the west. There was smoke rising from a house or tree on fire. He went towards the smoke.

From a distance he could make out some ramshackle shelters made from bamboo and wood, like small sheds, under the trees. In the valley were a few wooden houses that must be owned by locals. The shots fired from the road had not hit those houses. It was only the trees and clumps of bamboo set at a distance from the houses that were burned. It looked as though the shelters were a rebel base. It was impossible that the central army would have a base like this in the forest. Their bases were always in the towns or, if outside the town, were set among local houses. And when there was fighting, they always used convoys, and never left their vehicles.

Tondi approached cautiously, one step at a time. Suddenly he was surrounded by a group of people from behind the bushes, pointing rifles. One of them took his knapsack and pistol.

'Walk!' said the man prodding his rifle into Tondi's back. He took Tondi to meet the commander.

And now, finally, Tondi met one of the groups of rebels that had retreated from Sidempuan, the company led by Bagio.

Bagio was of Javanese descent but born in Sumatra, in Deli. He was cheerful by nature, and short and stocky in stature. Standing, he only came up to Tondi's chest. He had been a soldier in the revolution, back when there were no stipulations for anything like height.

'There's no way you can continue to Bukittinggi,' he said, inspecting Tondi's document. He frowned.

'How long have you been travelling?'

'About twenty-five days,' Tondi answered.

'That can't be right . . .' Bagio estimated.

'Why?' Tondi answered, confused.

'Come now. Try and remember when you left the Toba area.'

'It was July 1957,' Tondi replied.

'Try hard to remember correctly.'

'I am remembering correctly.'

'Take your boots off,' Bagio ordered.

Confused, Tondi did as he was told. Bagio inspected the soles of his boots. Tondi had been given new boots before he left. The soles were worn, but the boot leather was still in good condition.

The commander shook his head.

'Do you know today's date?' he asked.

Tondi's brow furrowed at the question.

'The year is now 1959,' Bagio said.

'It can't be,' Tondi laughed.

'Do you think I'm joking? It is now February nineteen-fifty-nine!' Bagio spelled it out. 'We just celebrated the anniversary of the PRRI rebellion. If you left Toba territory in 1957, then you must explain where you have been this past one and a half years.'

'PRRI? What's that?' Tondi stuttered. When Pardapdap had taken him to the Toba interior, there had been no such thing as PRRI.

'The army councils in Padang and Medan established the Revolutionary Government of the Republic of Indonesia or PRRI in February 1958.'

Tondi was flabbergasted. His journey flashed before his eyes. He looked around him at these faces he did not know. Then he pulled out the notebook he had been given at the end of his military training. There was written his name, number and name of his company. He had also used the book to write notes about his journey. Every night before he went to sleep, he had written a diary entry in pencil, as he had been taught to do during training.

It was not even a month. He had been walking for seventeen days, then three days staying with Ompu Bulung, plus the journey to Sarulla and the night at the coffee plantation. It had been just that one night with Longgom. The journey from Sarulla to here had taken one day. Now they said it was 1959, so how had he been travelling one and a half years?

The commander in front of him turned Tondi's travel document over and over.

'Yes, this letter is dated July 1957. I know the commander of your battalion. What's his name?' he asked.

'Maruli,' Tondi replied.

'And your platoon commander?'

'Pardapdap.'

'Hmm. Pardapdap, eh? He's dead. Shot a year ago near Batangtoru.'

'What?' Tondi was shocked. He felt pressed by a huge stone. His head was heavy. Pardapdap's face seemed to suddenly appear in his head along with other images; Ompu Bulung, the chief raja and all the raja bius at the feast deep in the forest. The images flashed, alternating.

'Yes, Pardapdap took part in lots of battles against the Dutch and never suffered a single wound. And then he ended up killed by the bullet of a fellow Indonesian,' Bagio went on.

But Tondi was barely listening. Before his eyelids flickered Pardapdap's wife left behind in Siantar. A kind woman he usually addressed as *inangtua*. Would her children come to care for their mother?

'The letter you're carrying is useless now. It is a request for codes for communication between the field troops and the head command, and for you to be trained in code in Bukittinggi as a non-commissioned officer. But there's nothing now for you to learn. Our troops are separated and scattered all over the place. Contact between us and headquarters was lost a while ago and we cannot contact our government in Bukittinggi. Sukarno's army took over the town a long time ago. Communication has been cut off,' Bagio said.

Tondi was silent.

'So you've no idea where you've been all this time?' Bagio asked.

Tondi was as still as a statue. There were other questions, but he no longer heard them. There was rumbling deep in his head. It struck the walls of his skull from within, penetrating every cavity, making the veins in his temples throb. Sounds like rushing waves of wind. He remained sitting. Finally, the commander gave an order to one of the troops:

'Take him away to rest. Guard that he doesn't leave the room.'

The soldier led Tondi who walked like a blind man. His eyes were wide open, but he saw nothing. His body moved sluggishly, following the leader.

He lay on his back in a room locked from the outside. His eyes were open, dizzily staring in the direction of the thatched roof. Whenever guards entered the room, they found him in exactly the same position. Only the movement of his chest showed that he was breathing and still alive. Everything that had happened to him throughout his journey now revisited him. Boulders in the river. The bamboo house in the rice field. Ompu Bulung. The raised house made of wood and its roof of palm-leaf thatch. The girls in their long blouses. The *tortor* dance and the drumming. The dry leaves that seemed to swish against him. Longgom. The wonderful fragrance of coffee flowers. Longgom. The perfume of candlenut oil. The pleasure of the rush of his seed, followed by pain deep in his chest as he faced a woman's gaze. The gaze of eyes like a deep, black lake, with a hypnotic force that drew him in until his body lost balance and fell. Was all that real? Which encounters were in his dreams, and which when he was awake? Where and how could he find out what was dream and what was reality?

For two whole days and nights he lay flat, not waking, not eating, not sleeping. The commander went in and out of the room, but Tondi had not moved.

The long path lay behind him. The winding path. Ompu Bulung's village, clean and clear at night. The sound of the gondang drums with their incessant beat. Long lines of light cast by the coconut oil lamps on the wide yard. The traditional feast, merry and orderly. People dancing. Young women with clean faces. Sounds of laughter.

Then Longgom, the woman in the coffee plantation in the quiet Sarulla field. The woman who entwined herself around him, clenching him with her strong legs. Marriage under the moon, caressed by the wind, on the soft earth. Seed gushed forth.

Flashing images. Unceasing. Blazing colours, black, white, red. The swish of an ulos cloth covering him. It all hit him, shook him, overcame him.

That little house on top of the hill. His grandfather's simple house. Walls of hard wood. Roof of rusted tin. The sacred staff Tunggal Panaluan standing upright in a basket of rice for a ceremony to call spirits. His grandmother's grave in the low-lying ground. The sound of ceremonial drums playing incessantly. His grandfather's hoarse, flat voice. The manuscripts, all those opened pustaha that must be read, must be read. That dagger, that dagger, which Ompu Bulung said was their gift to Ompu Silangit.

Tondi awoke and knocked on the door, calling the guard. He asked to see the commander.

'I need some incense and rice wine,' he said.

The commander Bagio's jaw dropped, then he said:

'Incense and rice wine? You've gone two days without eating, and now instead of asking for food, you want incense?'

'I have to find out what happened to me. I want to *martonggo*,' Tondi said.

'*Martonggo*? What's that?'

Tondi did not reply. He went outside.

'Find some incense and rice wine. He wants to *martonggo*, if anyone knows what that means,' the commander ordered.

Someone ran off to one of the local houses to carry out the order. Among the soldiers was a Batak who tried to explain to the commander, but Bagio, of Java-Deli descent, did not fully understand.

'Well,' he said, 'it's probably best that we just wait until we have the incense.'

Tondi came out of the shack and went over to a large tree. As he walked, he asked for his knapsack. He sat beneath the tree together with the other soldiers who sat down around him. The incense and rice wine were set out. Very slowly, Tondi pulled out the dagger his grandfather had given him. Then he pulled out the folded ulos cloth. He startled. The bamboo flute that Ompu Bulung had given him fell out of the ulos as it unfolded. All this time on the journey, he had not fully unpacked his knapsack.

So. It was true that he had been in the jungle kingdom. So it was true that he had met Ompu Bulung and his king and all the raja bius of that kingdom. He weighed the flute and the dagger in his left and right hands. A bamboo flute, but it was as heavy as the dagger. Without saying a word, Tondi spread the ulos cloth on the ground and placed the dagger on it beside the rice wine in a cup. He made every move slowly, his hands felt as though weighed down by heavy stones. Then he began to burn the incense. Someone helped fan the flame.

He had never done this before. But when he was a boy, he had once seen his ompung call spirits this way. Back then it was with the full paraphernalia: the Tunggul Panaluan staff standing upright in a basket of rice; a black chicken beside the staff; and rice wine. Now all he had was incense. But his instinct was leading him. An ancient instinct that flowed through his veins and lumped in his chest. He blew the flute, high pitched. It felt as though that lump in his chest was being blown away, penetrating the dark night. The shrill sound of the black bamboo flute. It was no melody he knew. It was only shrill high-pitched notes that pierced the stillness and then sighed as they fell creeping on the cold earth. His flute playing stopped and his voice began to mumble in ancient Batak:

Hutonggo, hupio, hujou, hupangalului,
sumangaot ni ompunami,
sahala Daompung Pane na Bolon, Naga Padoha,
na marholiholihon batu,
na marsibukhon tano,

na marhosahon angin,
na marbatukhon ronggur,
na marijurhon udan . . .

I invoke, I call, I summon, I approach,
the spirits of our ancestors
O Grand Mother Pane, Naga Padoha
With bones of stone,
With body of earth,
With breath of wind,
With cough of thunder,
With spit of rain . . .

His mumbling echoed in the dark, punctuated every now and then by a slap on the earth. Tondi continued to utter the long mantra, the mantra he had once read in a pustaha. His thoughts were so clear that every letter of the ancient script he had ever read was mapped in his memory. Time passed, the incense smoke billowing up among the leaves. The thick, dark night under the tree was dimly pierced by a single burning torch. Its flames flickered with pitch black smoke. The aroma of incense hovered. The moonless night grew colder. The wind ceased. Leaves stopped their rustling, and even the crickets fell silent.

Suddenly, one of the soldiers seated there, a middle-aged man, fell backwards. Tondi took his head in his lap and made him take a sip of rice wine. After one sip, the man went rigid and started twitching.

'What's happening to Masrul . . . ?' the commander whispered. But no one replied. Everyone felt the air suddenly get colder, gripping, wrapping their bodies, making the hairs on the backs of the necks stand on end. The incense smoke gave off a strong aroma.

Tondi kept making the man sip the rice wine. The man kept on writhing, twitching like a slaughtered chicken. His eyes bulged. Then he went still, stiff. His eyes were open with a vacant stare.

'*Didia do au saleleng on?*' Tondi spoke to him in Batak, his voice deep, 'Where have I been all this time?'

'In the sacred kingdom, together with us who inhabit the jungle of all your forefathers,' came the answer from the man lying stiff on the ground.

The army commander was startled. The man had answered in Batak, yet he had been born and raised in the Minangkabau area and did not speak Batak. Bagio knew this for a fact. Incense smoke filled his nostrils. There was not a breath of wind, but the cold enveloped every pore of his skin. Tondi continued conversing with the Minang man.

One of the commander's staff who was Batak tried to translate the conversation. But he found this difficult because it was ancient language, rarely used. This kind of language existed only in the old texts, the pustaha, and was used for mantras and not for everyday conversation.

'How long did I stay with you?' Tondi's voice sounded over the gasps of the man panting on the ground.

'Three of our days, three of your seasons, our day, your dry season . . . our night, your rainy season . . . you ate our rice, you drank our water, we wanted you to stay with us.'

'Why should I stay in your kingdom?' Tondi asked.

'It is better for you to be with us. Outside you will find only blood. You will find only fire. You will find only thorns,' came the man's voice echoing among the tree roots.

Tondi fed him some more rice wine. Then he thanked him. He placed the man's head on the earth. The man lay limp now. Slowly, his bulging eyes closed. And he slept.

Tondi took a deep breath along with those around him. He and the commander looked each other in the eye.

'So. It seems that I have spent months in the home of the spirits in the jungle,' Tondi said calmly.

The commander was speechless. The night now returned to normal, and a cold wind reminded him that it was late.

'Take Masrul over to the shack,' the commander said.

'He's called Masrul?' Tondi asked. The commander nodded.

'I have to apologize to him when he becomes fully conscious. I caused him great trouble. I have no idea why he was the one the spirit entered to become the medium,' Tondi said. 'Is he Batak?'

Bagio shook his head.

'He is Minang and has been under my command since the revolution days,' he said.

There seemed to be some unseen thread between Tondi and the man. Earlier, in the dim light of the flaming torch, Tondi felt that he had met him before. He could not be sure. But where? As a bus conductor on the Medan-Bukittinggi route, there were too many faces for him to remember each one. The spirit of the sacred forest had chosen this man as his medium. Why him among all those present? The answer would remain hidden as a secret of nature. But indeed, it came to pass that Tondi seemed destined to spend long days with this man.

Chapter 13

All the time Tondi had been in the jungle, the war had been dragging on. He had started his journey in July 1957. Now it was February 1959. Seasons had passed, but for him it felt as though it had been only a few days. One clear day was one dry season, one cloudy day a rainy season. He had taken food and drink only a few times, but this had sustained him for three whole seasons. If short time can be meaningful, then what use is there in living season upon season in the hubbub of humanity? Life in the midst of the Toba jungle is short but long in its stretch of human time. That compressed life, why leave it behind? The secrets of the ancient forest were unfathomable. Especially life in the belly of the jungle, the sacred kingdom.

And was it his real self that had exploded in the coffee plantation in Sarulla? Which of his selves was it who seized the wife of a helpless man right there in the open air? He felt that it could not possibly have been him, Tondi, a young man who had not long since bade farewell to his mother. If he had been on his journey for three months when he met Longgom, then he had only just turned nineteen. Now he had to calculate the actual time that had passed, and not what he felt had passed. Whatever he felt now turned out to be illusion. But as for the reality, who could explain?

'Eat now,' the commander said, in his Javanese-Deli accent. He joined Tondi across the table.

'My name is Bagio,' he continued. 'In this current war, my rank is lieutenant. But actually, that's because that's what it was during the revolution. In 1950, after independence, there was what they called "rationalization" of soldiers' ranks. Mine was downgraded to sergeant. Many others lost any army rank they had, so I suppose I was lucky. But it wasn't fair. Many former Dutch colonial army soldiers entered the Indonesian national army with no change to their rank. Those of us with little education were not treated well. Later my rank rose, slowly. In the national army I was promoted to the military police and my last rank was sergeant major, based in Sidempuan.'

Just like Pardapdap's story, Tondi thought. But he merely nodded and continued eating. It was grilled venison, tough and rubbery, and took a lot of chewing.

'These soldiers here in my company were under my command before, during the revolution. Some had already left the army. When my former commander asked me to go to Medan, I called some of my earlier soldiers to join. That's how this company was formed.'

Tondi continued eating and did not speak.

'Hey. Where did you learn to call spirits?' Bagio asked, changing the subject.

'My grandfather was a datu,' Tondi replied, without expression.

'The hairs on my neck stood on end just then. In Java, old people often deal with spirits. They give them offerings on the eve of special days.'

Tondi did not react. He wanted an end to this conversation. Bagio waited a while. Tondi kept his head down and stirred the rice mixed with corn on his plate. Bagio went on.

'What did you do before the PRRI rebellion?'

'I was a bus conductor. But I went into the forest before there was any such thing as PRRI.'

'Yes, yes. The PRRI was officially declared only in 1958.'

'What is it, actually?' Tondi asked.

'It's a long story. Before it was declared I was still in the military police in Sidempuan. I only heard dribs and drabs. Army leaders in a few areas were not happy with the way the central government was developing the regions. But even I felt there were things that were unfair.'

Tondi studied the face of this man across from him. It was a round face, with greying temples. His body was stocky, darkened by the sun.

'Actually, this rebellion didn't have to happen, if only the central government had paid attention. If you listen to the radio broadcasts from Jakarta, they say we want to bring down the Republic of Indonesia. What rubbish. I myself, my fellow fighters in the struggle for independence, all of us, we gave our all for this republic. What more could we give? All we want is to make this republic better. We love this republic. How could we rebel? We're accused of wanting to seize President Sukarno's power. Now tell me, how could we do that from here? If others in Jakarta want to seize power, let them do it. Just wait. Sukarno will see for himself what it's like to be betrayed by people he trusts. Right now he's using General Nasution to smash us. But we'll see how Sukarno feels later on if Nasution takes over. Sukarno's treatment of us, who fought for independence, is deeply painful. I pray he will get his just deserts.'

Bagio's face was angry. His voice rose in pitch. The pain of one disappointed in love. He watched Tondi fiddling with his plate for a few moments. It was unclear whether Tondi had even heard Bagio's passionate speech. Anything to do with the revolutionary struggle for independence never seemed to move him.

'But the struggle of people in North Sumatra back then was nothing compared to what the people of Central Sumatra went through', Bagio said, his voice weaker now.

Oh yes, the Minang people were renowned for their commitment to the republic. Long before Indonesia's declaration of independence, smart intellectuals from this area had been opposed to the Dutch, and afterwards their spirit did not fade. During the revolution, when Dutch forces occupied Yogyakarta in Java and arrested some of the highest members of the republican government, the republic's centre of government moved to Bukittinggi. Civilians led the emergency government that controlled all of Sumatra. The Dutch kept bombing but did not succeed in destroying it.

The troops who held Central Sumatra at that time were the Banteng Division. When the war for independence ended, many soldiers were decommissioned, which is a polite word for 'fired'. But not all left because they were made to. Many left because their reason for fighting in the first place was to fight the Dutch, and when the Dutch left Indonesia, they resigned of their own accord. Some returned to working in business, others chose to continue their education in Java or overseas. Usually, the ones who resigned went on to lead successful lives as businessmen or intellectuals in Jakarta. The soldiers who were 'decommissioned' though, usually had low education or were chronically ill, and this caused problems. After years of fighting, these former soldiers could not find proper work. Many were abandoned to fend for themselves.

Community figures understood the difficulty the former fighters faced finding work. They realized that this was not only because of their low levels of education, but also because of the lack of any government-sponsored development in the region. No work opportunities were being created. After five years of war, there was no repair. Rivers had to be crossed by raft, factories were in ruins, gaping holes as large as buffalo in the roads. How could things be left like this? Development would create employment, the local figures said.

Some army officers of the Banteng Division who were still active together with former members who were now successful businessmen and intellectuals in Jakarta and elsewhere, called a meeting to discuss development and ways to help the lives of former soldiers in the region. Dissatisfaction was spreading.

In Central Sumatra there was a legendary figure from the revolution days, Lieutenant Colonel Ahmad Husein. He had charisma as a leader. Like many leaders who have risen from below, he felt himself to be father to his troops. Coming as he did from the

Minangkabau intellectual tradition he was also a sharp thinker and community conscious. He felt that he had moral responsibility for the lives of his former soldiers, and for the community he led.

'Do you know Sungai Dareh?' Bagio suddenly blurted out.

Tondi nodded.

'Never forget it!' Bagio went on. 'That's a historic place for people in the regions.'

Sungai Dareh was a village in Central Sumatra, but it had become an extremely important site when the emergency republican government of Indonesia was in Sumatra. Even though it was just a small village, Sungai Dareh became a symbol of the people's struggle in Sumatra.

'The only schooling I ever had was primary school in the Dutch time,' Bagio said, 'and that was only a non-government school, and I didn't even graduate. Have you heard of Taman Siswa? Well, that was where we got lessons about world history, a kind of lesson in politics. They didn't call it politics, though, to avoid getting into trouble with the Dutch government. I still remember my teacher, a Minang man we called *Uda* Caniago. He made us aware of the independence movement, and it was because of him that I could later compare the struggle of people in Sumatra with other places, Java in particular. I could see how they differed.'

Tondi raised his head. All this stuff about the fight for independence had never been anything he bothered about. When he was at school, history lessons consisted of memorizing years in the lives of great men, kingdoms and kings, and never made you think about earlier struggles. It was as though history was only about lives of the powerful. Nothing to do with the struggles of the people in those kingdoms.

'Do you know what the difference is?' Bagio persisted. Clearly, he did not expect any answer from Tondi, who had his mouth open—half from astonishment and half because of the hot chilli pepper he had eaten. Bagio went on.

'From way back in history, people in Sumatra have always built connections with the international world. In Dutch times, the people of Aceh and the people in west Sumatra cultivated relations with the Ottomans in Turkey. During the fight for Indonesia's independence, freedom fighters in Sumatra had relations with people in Malaya and even Siam. People in Java usually carried out guerrilla war, which meant moving further and further inland where they were more protected from attack. As a result, however, it was also difficult for them to establish connections with the outside world.'

'This is why, during the revolution, the vice president of the republic, Mohamad Hatta, before he and President Sukarno were arrested when the Dutch attacked Yogyakarta, made a mandate appointing leaders of the emergency government in Sumatra. And this emergency government based in Bukittinggi kept up links with the international world. Don't you ever forget that Mohammad Hatta is from Sumatra and that's why he was well aware of the need to always connect with the international world. Syahrir, the prime minister at the time and also one of us, was the same. He saw the need for international support for our struggle. They knew our fight for independence as a nation would mean nothing if we did not get international recognition.'

Tondi was not all that interested.

'During the emergency government time, connecting overseas was via the Dareh River,' Bagio went on.

Tondi raised his head slightly, but it was enough for Bagio to register that he was listening.

'That place must be remembered for its importance to Indonesia's history,' Bagio said. 'It's an inseparable part of the fight against the Dutch.'

The Dareh River is in Central Sumatra, and is a thoroughfare between the west and the east coasts. From there, the freedom fighters could cross to Singapore, dodging between the small islands scattered between Sumatra and Singapore. From Singapore, they would go on to India, or even America, usually assisted by Chinese labourers at the port and sailors on Australian ships at anchor. They were the foreign friends of the revolution. Indonesian fighters would bring with them produce like rubber and coffee to trade for weapons. There were many traders in Singapore who helped out.

After independence, when dissatisfaction with the government in Jakarta rose, the Dareh River came alive again. It was a meeting point for people in the region. It was at Sungai Dareh that the resolution was made to oppose the injustice of the Jakarta government. Connections with the outside world from the earlier independence time were revived.

'Do you understand what I am saying?' Bagio said.

'What?' Tondi raised his head.

'Ah, what's the use! Whether you understand or not, you're part of the fight now,' Bagio said.

* * *

So, Tondi thought, on this great journey of his, here he was stuck in some PRRI army hideout somewhere near Sipirok. There was no chance of going on to Bukittinggi now. On this first morning after being released from arrest, he went to chat with the man who had been his medium the night before. There was a path that crossed the scrub-covered hills. The sun beamed warmth, banishing the dew that dampened the bushes. Up here, the cool of morning had not yet gone.

Masrul was sitting on a tree trunk in front of his hut, hugging his legs, his sarong wound around his neck, gazing into the distance. He was warming himself in the sun. His thin body looked even smaller in this position, like a cold baby monkey. His skin was light in colour, like a Chinese, and his face was long with thin lips and a pointed chin. He had not shaved, but had only a few sparse, soft whiskers. His eyes looked sad, or perhaps it was exhaustion. When they shook hands, his small fingers were swallowed in Tondi's large, rough fist.

'Uda Masrul,' Tondi said, addressing him with the Minang term for brother, 'I'm sorry for causing you such trouble last night.' Tondi already knew from Bagio that Masrul had been in the army during the fight for independence. He had been in the same battalion as Bagio but had been decommissioned around 1950. Since then, he had changed jobs often. Before this fighting broke out, he had been in Sidempuan working as a builders' labourer. That was when Bagio had asked him to take up arms once again. And now here he was, stuck in some cold, damp hut.

Masrul smiled as he took Tondi's hand. The wrinkles around his eyes made his oblong face look older. He shifted on the tree trunk to make room for Tondi.

'Don't worry about it. I myself don't know what happened,' he said. 'Anyway, it's good that this worn-out body of mine had some use.'

The sun's rays shone through the gaps in the leaves. Birdsong was still filling the gold-tinged morning.

'I'd never before done a ceremony like the one last night,' Tondi said, 'so I didn't know beforehand who was going to be the medium.'

'You were amazing,' Masrul said. The expression in his eyes changed, teasing now. He looked directly at Tondi. Tondi saw a happy face, quite unlike that man sitting alone hugging his knees.

'I once saw my grandfather call on spirits when he was treating a sick person. But what he did was different. He released a black chicken. I just followed the sudden urges in my mind.'

'Why do you think I was the one the spirit entered?' Masrul said, as though asking himself. 'It seems I have a talent for mixing with spirits, ha ha.'

'Maybe you were empty at that moment,' Tondi replied.

'Empty?'

'Yes. We are actually like vessels. Usually we are filled with our own life force. The fuller we are, the stronger we are. If we're empty, it's easy for those of the unseen world to enter us.'

'Yes, that's probably right. Lately I've been feeling as though I'm not here in this place,' Masrul said slowly.

'What do you mean, Uda?' Tondi asked gently, again using the familiar Minang word.

'I don't know. I keep thinking about my children.'

'Where are they?'

'In Sidempuan. I don't know how they are. I've no idea how my wife is coping, They're still small. I married too late.'

'How many children do you have?'

'Three. Well, four now. When I left, my wife was pregnant, almost ready to give birth,' Masrul said in a voice halfway between laughter and pain.

'Haven't you had any news since the fighting began?' Tondi asked.

'I haven't even seen my youngest,' Masrul replied, vaguely.

'Is your wife from Sidempuan?' Tondi asked.

Masrul jolted, and Tondi asked again.

'No, she's a Malay,' Masrul replied. 'During the independence fighting, I joined Bagio's soldiers in East Sumatra. When the war ended, I lived in Lubuk Pakam and that's where we met. We moved around a lot, but finally returned to Lubuk Pakam. She followed me to Sidempuan, hoping that would be the place where we would stay. But I can never stay long in one place. And now, look, I've been dragged back into fighting.'

As Masrul spoke, Tondi was taken aback. He hardly heard anything after the words 'Lubuk Pakam'. All he could think of was Habibah. He focused his memory on that time at the bus stop in Sidempuan.

Yes, of course! This was the man who had waited for Habibah. He was Habibah's husband. Oh, God! This was the thin, earnest man who shook his hand and thanked him after Habibah explained how Tondi had helped her during the journey. But to Tondi, that thank you had stabbed his chest and unnerved him. He still had the smell of Habibah on his hand. Her oil, the sweat from her breasts, the soft mount in his palm, the rosebud lips, he could feel them all whenever he thought of her.

And now, this was her husband.

'Your wife, Uda, is she Kak Habibah?' Tondi asked hesitantly.

'Yes. How do you know? Do you know her?'

'I don't think you remember,' Tondi said. 'I was the conductor on the bus Kak Habibah took when she went to Sidempuan.'

Masrul narrowed his eyes to sharpen his vision. Or to force his memory.

'Oh yes, yes,' he said, but actually he was not sure. The dim dawn light at the bus stop had maybe clouded his memory.

Or maybe because his attention at the time was only on his wife. When he shook the conductor's hand it was just a passing gesture. But to Tondi, the entire journey of that night was stuck fast in his mind.

'It's been a long time,' Masrul finally said.

'It was a few months before I entered the forest,' Tondi said.

'Yes, two years ago, I think.'

'And since you left, all this time you've had no news of them?' Tondi asked.

Masrul nodded weakly.

'Four little mouths to feed,' he said, almost inaudibly.

Tondi did not dare imagine Habibah, so he looked at Masrul. The thin man sitting beside him looked so frail. His skin had once been light, but now time had left it wrinkled and dark. But when their eyes met fleetingly, Masrul blinked with amusement.

They spread out to the south, looking for areas not yet controlled by the central army. Every now and then they would attack army transport vehicles passing on the roads, and then immediately retreat out of the line of retaliating fire. This was where Tondi finally experienced the real whistle of bullets and smell of gun smoke, not like the pretend days of his training. The sound of bullets was so close to his ears that he was relieved when Commander Bagio ordered them to retreat. It turned out that fighting did not create a mood of heroism as in all those stories about the revolution he had heard. He put his pistol away. He had not yet fired a shot. The target was too far away, and why waste bullets? One or two shots fired from Bagio's men were answered with rounds of enemy automatic rifle fire followed by shelling. Bagio's company used to have mortars, but they had run out of ammunition long ago. Now they had only one automatic rifle with maybe fifty bullets. The rest were old rifles left over from the revolution.

Bagio's small company operated along the line between Sipirok and Sidempuan. They might cause a bit of bother now and then for army convoys on the road winding around the foothills, and sporadic gunfire at least showed that the war was still going on. But it was increasingly clear that the PRRI soldiers were not going to win this war. Every day their movement was more constrained. Tondi had become part of them. They had to join the attack or retreat further into the hills.

The central army soldiers in the area were from West Java, the Siliwangi Division, and some said there were also Command troops who were renowned for their battle expertise. There were also a few Dutch officers who supported Indonesia's independence. They taught war strategy. This is why Bagio's company's attacks were met with such fierce retaliation. It was truly an uneven battle. Bagio's men would have to scatter, and it took them a few days to regroup. What kind of war was this?

The logistics supply from central command had long since ceased. Who even knew where they were? Bagio's soldiers had to fend for themselves. Now they were on the outskirts of Pargautan. The road below felt closer from here. Not only could you see the public transport joining the army convoys, you could hear the roar of their engines. It looked as though conditions around here were improving. There were many more buses and trucks on the road, but always with army convoys. Rebel attacks were fewer. Bagio's men had to be careful with their sparse ammunition.

It was unclear how long this guerrilla war would go on. Bagio himself did not know what to do other than make sure his men were not all killed. A raggle-taggle company in the forest on the slopes of Mount Lubukraya, every now and then collecting rice from the locals. But often the locals had nothing to give. The soldiers were now more isolated than ever, in a poor area where people relied on rain for their rice harvest. Locals and soldiers were as hungry as each other. Tondi's horse from Sarulla had long since been sacrificed to the stomachs of the soldiers.

Whenever they made camp, Tondi would share a shelter with Masrul. It would be totally quiet, because Masrul did not like to talk. Tondi had never in his life spent time with anyone so quiet. Usually, he was with men who loved to talk, especially about politics. Like Bagio. Chatting with Bagio reminded Tondi of the men at the rice-wine stalls back where he came from. His lessons in Indonesian history took place when they were hiding in the forest, and Tondi found Bagio's classes quite different to the history lessons he had at school.

'I really admired Sukarno at the start,' Bagio said. 'When I was young, I used to listen to my teacher when he told us stories about Sukarno fighting the Dutch. But now, I think Sukarno was good only when he confronted the Dutch politically.'

Then would follow the story of Sukarno's defence when he was on trial at the Dutch colonial court. About his extraordinary speech that roused people to fight against the Dutch.

'During the revolution,' Bagio continued, 'when Sukarno was arrested, he probably thought he was going to be tried and could give another rousing speech.'

It was true that Sukarno's stature was because of his oratory. Many of his speeches were inspirational in the fight against colonial rule. He could rouse people to fight against foreign colonialism. But as for the military fight, he could not manage it. That was why he could never understand the suffering of the soldiers fighting against the Dutch.

Vice President Hatta was just the same. He was the one who issued the decision to rationalize the republican army, which meant that fighters who did not meet certain conditions were stood down. And who made these conditions? Army leaders who had received Dutch military training. Clearly, many of the soldiers who fought for independence could not meet these 'conditions'.

Bagio fired a ball of spit, almost hitting Tondi sitting across from him.

'I ask you, how could we have met those "conditions"? Fighting for independence had nothing to do with education. Most of us had no school certificate. And as for health, how could you be healthy when you had to live in the forest, scavenging for food? Take Masrul. He has tuberculosis now. Not like the soldiers who fought with the Dutch, eating canned meat and cheese, drinking milk. Of course, they were strong. But what about their morals, eh? Killing their fellow countrymen. Our men were decommissioned. Fired, just like that. They became beggars. I did better. I was among the healthy ones. But I had no school certificate because I hadn't gone to a government school. So they lowered my army rank. Yes, that's the way this republic thanked its fighters!'

Tondi merely nodded as Bagio went on and on. He sort of understood that his father had graduated from a Dutch school, had been trained during the Japanese occupation for their volunteer army, become an officer, and during the war for independence had been made colonel. Maybe he was a general by now. Tondi did not let these thoughts of his father last long. He shuddered to think that people might find out he was the son of Pardomutua, a loyal follower of Sukarno.

'And you, Tondi. How much schooling did you have?' Bagio asked.

'I got to second class of high school and stopped,' Tondi said softly. Whenever he thought of school, he felt depressed. He remembered his mother. But he warded it off, changing the subject.

'How many of your men used to be in the army?' he asked.

'All of them,' Bagio said. 'That's why they're old. I knew all of them from the independence fight. Some were still in the army, but most had stopped. Some were small traders in the market, some were brokers in Medan, car mechanics, construction workers. I asked them to join up and fight. And now, look! We don't know who we're fighting, and we don't know who we're defending. If we want some direction from our superiors, we don't even know where to go.'

Bagio sighed deeply and looked around him. He had called his men a company, but really they were just a few men living in a few huts with walls of coconut palm and roofs of dried grass. When it rained, it leaked and soaked the earthen floors. There was no food in the forest. They used to get rice from local people, but now poverty was wringing the locals dry. Their daily diet was maize or cassava. This area was hilly and covered in coarse cogon grass, which the locals used for their roofs. There was not a tin roof to be seen, a sure sign of poverty. How could you expect support from them? Bagio's men might be safe here because there was no road into the area, but that was also why it was poor and neglected. Like his men.

Their clothes were rags. Their shoes gaped like lizards' mouths. Tondi was lucky to share a shelter with Masrul. He went over to keep him company in front of their shack and took off his shirt. Masrul had borrowed a needle from a local and started to patch the shirt. The army-issue material was fit only for rags, but Masrul managed to patch it with bits of other old clothes.

Masrul was clever at sewing. Tondi watched, impressed. He had never sewed in his life. Masrul finished and handed over the shirt with a smile, his eyes beaming with pride in his handiwork. Tondi accepted with his eyes beaming gratitude. It was a meeting of eyes.

Tondi put on his newly patched shirt. Masrul still said not a word, but took Tondi's shoes and began to sew them using a large needle used for gunnysacks. It was not really a needle but more like a nail about ten centimetres long with one end flattened and pierced for thread. Masrul's hand moved the needle swiftly into the shoe, pulling the thread made from ramie fibre, binding the holes. Tondi observed Masrul's skill with needle and thread. Every now and then he glanced at Masrul whose face showed how much he was enjoying his work, licking his lips while checking the progress of his knots. Masrul continued working until dusk.

The sun had already set when the sewing was done. The shoes were ready. The two walked to the spring outside the village as dark fell. They bathed close to each other under the water spout. Their touching skin created warmth. Masrul only came up to Tondi's chest. How small and fragile he is, Tondi thought. He scrubbed Masrul's back.

Night covered the moonless dark. It was the cold of dry season. The wind pierced the bamboo walls. As usual, they slept on the earth floor lined with grass covered with cloth. The cold came through the walls, came up from the earth, and the only way to fight it was to combine body warmth. Tondi hugged Masrul from behind. Masrul, who had been shivering with cold, warmed up.

Was Tondi dreaming when he felt he was hugging Habibah? The body he embraced writhed. Ah, Habibah. He held the body tight. He stretched in his dream. In the dark of night, Tondi felt he had crossed into warmth, as though he had gushed all his strength into the body in his embrace.

The two awoke with the birdsong. They looked at each other. Tondi was confused. Masrul smiled. He stood and went outside.

In the shafts of sunlight piercing the holes in the walls, Tondi looked thoughtfully at the young man's back. Habibah had taught him parts of the body to explore. She had first taught him how a female body roused male passion. And now, here was Masrul, the husband, giving him an intimacy he had never imagined. A husband and wife had given him the quelling of passion, for the fire that flared in his young body.

And there in that little shack on the slopes of Lubukraya, Tondi and Masrul became extremely close. Tondi's young body was the source of warmth that gave strength to Masrul. After embracing this man, Tondi stopped dreaming of Habibah. Because day after day, Tondi loved this man, with a feeling like when he longed for Habibah. Can both a husband and wife become a man's lover?

* * *

Bagio's soldiers had spent months here, completely cut off. Hiding with no knowledge of how long it would go on. Tondi was the youngest in the group, and only he and Bagio had not been ill. Some of the others had malaria, and when they had an attack, they would rattle like old trucks. At night, the noise of coughing would go from hut to hut. It was a company of invalids. What kind of war was this?

They were blind to the state of the war. Earlier, Bagio's group had a single radio to use for contacting the battalion, but it had been destroyed by mortar fire back in Sipirok. Not only the radio died, but the radio operators too.

Orphan troops. Poor. Without food. Men having to survive in leaky shacks behind Mount Lubukraya. Perhaps they could keep going with what remained of their revolutionary spirit, but the uncertainty of their position in battle was depressing. They could not carry out any intelligence operations because the central army had the area so tightly under its control. One section had got some news a few months ago from a Medan newspaper. But it was all from the central army, about how they had cleansed the regions of rebels. If you believed that newspaper, then this entire area was now under central army control and all the rebels were totally wiped out. But Bagio's company was still here, so there had to be others elsewhere. After all, those army convoys were still passing through. If the rebels had all gone, why did the national army need to be here in such numbers?

Tondi remembered when his previous commander had sent him on a mission to accompany members of the communication team organize a radio. If he could get a radio transmitter again now, then maybe this would help Bagio's company. At least they would not be like baby chicks without a hen. Even better if they could get some money to buy food, because they clearly couldn't hope for anything from the locals.

'I know a bus operator in Sidempuan,' Tondi exclaimed. He had no idea why he suddenly remembered this.

'What?' Bagio slapped his knee and jumped up. He held Tondi's shoulders. 'Are you thinking what I'm thinking?' he said.

It was Tondi's turn to be flabbergasted.

'How would I know what you're thinking?' Tondi said.

'I think you're thinking what I'm thinking,' Bagio repeated.

'Meaning?'

'Well, I also know a few people in Sidempuan. I know they'd want to give us support. That's what you mean too, isn't it?' Bagio said eagerly.

'Yes.'

'Right. Let's plan a mission.'

Bagio went out and called the man he called his platoon commander. And so it was that a decision was made for the mission. Commander Bagio wrote letters for his contacts who he thought could be approached for support. Back in the days when he was in the military police, he had done a tour of duty in the town, and there were a number of people from whom he could call in favours. It was normal for the police or the army, whose salaries were low, to seek out civilians who were having problems with the law. They were targets for extortion. But if they had good relations with the military police, they felt safe. This law of the jungle was the normal state of things in the young republic. The local police and soldiers respected Bagio back then, as sergeant major in the military police and because he was not part of the army extortion racket. Now, however, would any trace of his charisma remain?

There were to be five in the mission. They would go down the mountain during the next full moon so there would be no need for torches. Three of them would wait outside the town, and only they would carry weapons. The other two would find the contacts in Sidempuan. Masrul and Tondi would enter the town without weapons. It was agreed that they were familiar with the situation and knew people to contact. If anyone from the central army stopped them, they were to say they were civilians. They would probably get away with it because neither of them looked like a soldier. One was a green youth, the other a thin sickly man. Those two, Tondi and Masrul, would be tied to one another forever; it seemed that the spirit from the spirit kingdom had known this.

Chapter 14

Five men slashed their way through the undergrowth, descending the hill. They took short cuts made by the locals, sneaking through forests and fields. The view below was unobstructed, and a bus was crawling along the road. As Tondi slashed his way down the steep path he imagined he was sitting in that bus. How nice it would be. But it was impossible. The central army often had blockades and checked the passengers' papers.

Forget the bus. The group was approaching a village beside the road leading into Sidempuan. After shaking hands, they split up. Three of them remained near a shady salak plantation. In times past, this village was the source of basketloads of fruit bound for markets in the towns, even as far as Medan. But nobody tended this large plantation during the war. The owners rarely came. What was the point? There was no way to transport the harvest. So the fruit was left to rot, and the air was full of the pungent smell of fermentation.

Now it was just Tondi and Masrul. They had to be extremely careful choosing the way as the path through the plantation had not been used for a long time. The moonlight only dimly penetrated the canopy of trees. Momentary bursts of moonlight revealed traces of the old path. The leaf cover on the ground was decayed and rustled with every step. Left and right the spiky salak fronds threatened their legs. And they were wearing only sandals made of old car tyres. No way could they wear their army boots. At last, they came out of the plantation.

They cut through some dry fields. Each was carrying on his back a basket filled with chillies, tomatoes and cucumber that the locals had given them. Until the group split up, they had taken turns carrying the goods. The baskets of vegetables were a disguise if they were stopped by an army check. They would pretend they were farmers carrying their produce.

The moonlight struck the leaves, and the path looked like a snake curving in the hills. There was no need for a torch. Below, you could see the tin roofs of the houses gleaming in the moonlight. The roofs were rusty brown, but some still had patches of silver. Masrul walked furtively as he carried his basket, as though following his own shadow on the earth. Tondi checked the path in the distance now and then. They crushed crickets hiding under the grass underfoot. There was no sound of insects. They both kept silent. Only Masrul's breathing broke the stillness.

Masrul was thinking about his family. Four small children. Three of them like evenly spaced peas in a pod, born two years apart, all girls. Then a gap of five years to the fourth child. Was it a girl? Who knows? He had not received any news. Maybe Habibah could only have girls. Or maybe he only fathered girls. Four little mouths to feed. How could his wife cope? He was not really familiar with the town of Sidempuan. As a newcomer, he had had to do the best he could. Before he left, he had given his wife all the money he received when signing up. Everyone had been given three months' salary, according to their rank. He had asked Habibah to take the children back to East Sumatra. Had she gone? But whether or not she was in Sidempuan, things must be hard for her. Yes, Habibah's struggle was the hardest, not his in the forest, because in fact there had hardly been any fighting. All he and the others did was protect themselves from army attacks. His wife, however, had to struggle for food every single day. Was she coping? Masrul tried to soothe his shallow breathing. His asthma had returned.

He stopped walking. Tondi did not know the thoughts that so burdened his friend as he walked, but it was as though he could hear the confusion in Masrul's head. The actual sound was the sighs of bushes brushed by their legs. Tondi was wondering whether he would meet Habibah in the town. How would he face her, with her husband there too? Would he be as awkward as he was that night at the bus stop a few years ago?

But the situation now was completely different. Masrul was also his lover. Could his longing for Habibah exist? By loving Masrul, was he betraying Habibah? By longing for Habibah, was he hurting Masrul? His confused thoughts went round and round.

Masrul put down the basket he was carrying, then squatted to control his coughing. Tondi helped him to stand and led him over to a log. Masrul sat, still trying to control his coughing. He was gasping for breath. Tondi rubbed his back.

'I can't go on, Tondi,' gasping for breath between coughs.

'That's fine. We'll rest for a while,' Tondi replied.

'But it'll be dawn soon.'

Tondi looked over to the east. He could see the sky clearly. The moon was turning pale, a sign that dawn was near. In the distance he could see a line of flames like a winding yellow snake. It was the torches of people walking in single file.

'In that case, you wait here. It'll be quicker for me to sneak into town.'

'You're all right going alone?'

'Sure.'

'I want to ask a favour. If you have a chance, would you see how my family is?' Masrul said softly.

Tondi's eyes met Masrul's tired gaze full of hope. He nodded. Masrul continued.

'When I was living there, our house was in the area of Padangmatinggi,' he said. He described the house. Near the primary school. One of a row of bamboo-walled houses, the fifth door in the row. The house at the edge on the right.

'Right, Uda. You wait here,' Tondi said. He rearranged the basket he was carrying. Masrul's basket had sprawled on the ground. Masrul shifted his sitting position, wrapping his sarong around him against the biting cold. His endless cough was interspersed with breathing that sounded like the whistle of a steam train.

Tondi walked quickly down the hill. At the foot of the hill was a village road leading to a hanging bridge over the river that crossed the town of Sidempuan. Far below, he could just make out huge stones. For a moment or two he looked across at the end of the bridge, trying to calculate the distance. About thirty metres. Quiet. The bridge was a relic from Dutch times, about one and a half metres wide, its path made of planks, stretching from one bank to the other, and suspended from steel cables as thick as a baby's outstretched arm. He crossed. The bridge swayed with his every step. The basket on his back added to the weight of his tread. He walked quickly so that with every sway of the bridge he could cross five planks.

He arrived at the other side. Behind him the bridge rocked, its cables creaking. He was at the edge of town now. The electricity seemed to be off, or if it was on, the light was dim. This would be because of electricity rationing. It was usual for the electricity to be switched off for different areas in turn. In front of some of the houses tiny oil lamps had been set, their glass funnels black with soot. Tondi walked on under the trees at the side of the road.

As he approached the town centre, he came across the line of people carrying torches. They were farmers taking their produce to market. He joined the group.

'Horas,' he greeted.

'Horas,' came the chorus in reply. But no one stopped. It was not possible to stop when balancing such weight on the shoulders. You could only hear the sound of their sighs of exhaustion. They walked fast, carrying cassava and other vegetables. One carried five huge bunches of bananas. Tondi took his place among those at the end of the line.

They arrived at the market in the centre of the town. The wide square in front of the market was still empty. Back in the days of peace, this square used to be full of trucks waiting to unload. Now it was quiet. It looked as though trading had stopped during the fighting.

Tondi separated from the group. He studied the buildings across from the market. It was a row of connected, two-storeyed wooden buildings set along the road. The shops were on the ground floor, and the owners lived above. This was the only busy part of the town. There was a general store, a Padang restaurant, a coffee stall owned by a Chinese, a photo studio, a dentist and the place Tondi was looking for, the inter-city bus office. The office was squeezed between the coffee stall and the Padang restaurant, which were both there to serve the bus passengers.

But the bus office was closed. So were the Padang restaurant and the coffee stall. Before all the upheaval, these three places were constantly busy, day and night. At night, to save electricity, pressure lamps would light the area. The intercity buses would arrive one after another, especially late at night. They would rest before going on in the morning to Bukittinggi or Pekanbaru. The town had long been a stopover for the inter-city trade. Now everything was quiet.

The bus-office owner did not live there. Tondi did not know where his house was. The rooms in the floor above the office were rented out, usually to bus passengers who were travelling on to Bukittinggi in the morning. You could hear their footsteps above on the wooden floor as they walked down the corridor outside the rooms. It was rare for anyone else to stay there. Visitors from the town would stay with their relatives, and government workers on official business had a government mess.

Where now were the pressure lamps outside the Padang restaurant? Where were the piles of plates in the window, piled high with food? Where was the food cart selling satay in front of the restaurant? The spiced beef gave off such fragrance as it grilled over the charcoal. The sauce was so spicy, it would sting your tongue. And the coffee stall owned by the Chinese man? That used to be Tondi's favourite place, where he would meet all the other bus conductors. Where were they now? Bangun, the Karo man, who was

so brilliant at chess. Pardede, the loudmouth, who would brag that
he was a close friend of some timber merchant in Medan. And the
others who would sit around the big, round, marble-topped table,
slippery and shiny. The chairs were wooden with high backs, brown
and unpainted. Sitting at that coffee stall he would be enveloped
in cigarette smoke and the aroma floating from the coffee in cloth
filters bubbling away in huge tins on a fire that never went out.
And snacks: sticky rice cake layered green, red and white; soft,
steamed cupcakes; steamed banana sweets; toast with custard-apple
jam; Chinese steamed buns. All exuding a perfume of vanilla.

It felt like only yesterday. Now it was quiet and dark, but to
Tondi it was as though those smells were right under his nose. And
now he suddenly remembered that all he had eaten since yesterday
was some cucumber.

Tondi went into the market. He settled his basket near the
gate and sat near an old woman setting out her wares on the floor.
While waiting, he drew his sarong around him like a blanket and
nodded off.

The sun slowly rose from behind the roof of the shops across the
road. The market began to get busy. But the shops remained quiet.
Shop traders are not like farmers who have to sell their produce.
Shop traders are wealthier and can open their shops whenever they
choose. Farmers have to come as early as possible and return home
only when officials come and close the market.

At last, the bus office opened. Soon after, a bus arrived, without
passengers, and parked. Who knows what route that bus was on?
The bus exhaust filled the cold morning. Tondi went over to find
the bus-company owner, an older man of the Harahap marga. In his
working days, Tondi used to address him as amangboru, according
to their marga relations.

He probably had no idea that Tondi had joined the rebellion,
because he greeted him, speaking in the south Batak dialect:

'*Bah, leleng ma ho inda tarida, Tondi. Marganti karejo do ho?* Hey,
I haven't seen you for ages, Tondi. Have you changed your job?'

'I'd like to chat about something,' Tondi replied, using the
same dialect.

'Sure, come in.' Harahap led the way into his office. He called for one of his staff to get some coffee and breakfast from the stall next door. He waited as Tondi arranged his stiff back in the chair. The refreshments arrived. Before the coffee was poured from the pot, the aroma filled the room, together with hot sticky-rice and durian custard. Oh, this was truly a tempting feast after a night staving off hunger. Tondi spoke as he ate:

'I'm here to ask for help, Amangboru.'

'No problem. If I can, sure I'll help.'

Tondi told him the whole story.

'Ah, that can be arranged,' Harahap said. 'I support the struggle. I'll get the stuff you need.'

'I need to meet someone in the army.'

'What? Are you mad?'

'I'm sure you remember Bagio who used to work here in the military police.'

'Sure, I remember him. A good man.'

'He's my commander now. He said there's one of his former staff who can be trusted.'

'Well, that's different. I'll get one of my staff to take you by bicycle.'

Tondi rode pillion on the bicycle to the army repair workshop. That was where the person he had to meet worked. A man, Bagio's age, with the rank of corporal who had been under Bagio's command during the independence war. Now his work was managing the mechanics who repaired army transport vehicles.

'Sure. I'll get it ready,' the corporal said after reading Bagio's letter. 'I'll bring it later this afternoon. Where should we meet?'

'I'll wait by the market gate,' Tondi said.

Without saying any more, the corporal went into the workshop. Tondi hurried off to find a few other people. There was the Chinese owner of a medicine shop, who, without a word, immediately handed over some medicines. So it was with the Chinese dentist and a trader who had a warehouse and gave some money. Bagio's letter was pure gold.

The sun kept rising higher in the sky. It was getting hot.

'Do you know where Padangmatinggi is?' Tondi asked the young man pedalling the bicycle.

He nodded.

'Let's go there,' Tondi said.

Tondi took over the pedalling, and the young man showed the way. They went up and down through alleyways. Sidempuan is hilly, so the roads are not flat. The name Padangmatinggi means 'high ground', so it took a lot of energy to cycle there.

Wooden houses were in rows left and right. They came to a woven bamboo house, connected to the ones next door. And Tondi's heart beat fast. Not because of the weight of the bicycle, but because he remembered Habibah. Was it longing, confusion, worry, or all of them suspended in the cavity in his chest?

One of the houses had whitewashed walls. A guava tree in the front. Was this the one?

Tondi stopped. He handed the bicycle to the boy to hold. He knocked on the door. Silence. He knocked again. The sound on the wooden door knocked in his chest. There was no answer.

The door of the house next door opened. A middle-aged woman poked her head out.

'Who are you looking for?' she asked, speaking southern Batak dialect. She came out of the house.

'I'm looking for the family of Masrul who lived here,' Tondi replied speaking Indonesian and putting on a Deli Malay accent.

'Oh, what a pity. Habibah left here with her children a while ago now,' the woman replied switching to Indonesian with a Mandailing accent.

'Where?'

'She said she was going back to Deli.'

'Oh,' Tondi said, sadly.

'Are you family?'

'Yes, family. How long is it since she left?'

'A long time. Not long after her husband left.'

'Oh, I see.'

'Since she left, no one has rented the house. What with all the fighting, no one's coming to Sidempuan. A house falls into disrepair if it's empty. If you know anyone who wants to rent . . .'

Clearly the woman wanted to keep chatting, but Tondi cut her off. He said goodbye and left. He could not bear the weight of sadness and anxiety and carried this burden with him as he pedalled the bicycle. So, he thought, actually he was weighed with the desire to see Habibah's face. It was not sadness and anxiety. It was longing. But how would he deal with this feeling when her husband was hoping for him to visit his children? His visit was not for Habibah. He had to find out how the children were doing, especially the youngest. Masrul often talked about this one. Tondi was eager to see the baby, too.

Going downhill, the bicycle sped. In the midday heat, the town seemed dead. There was virtually no traffic, just a few horse carts coming in the opposite direction, the horses plodding slowly up the hill. The sound of the horse hooves hitting the pot-holed road mingled with the squeak of the wheels and jingling of the horses' metal decorations.

With the rush of the wind, Tondi's tight knot of feelings loosened. If Habibah had taken the children back to Lubuk Paham, at least they were in a safe place with family. Habibah's family would not let the children go hungry, as might have happened had she stayed here. He looked around. The houses on both sides were mostly wooden, built on piles, with big yards. A few had mango trees in flower. Yellow blossoms dangled from the green leaves, like a bride's adornment. Along the roadside, rows of magnolia trees gave shade. The sun was fierce, but the breeze blew softly between the trees and the fences, carrying the smell of horse manure mixed with magnolia. The bicycle squashed layers of the yellow flowers under its wheels as it sped along.

Yes, at least they were somewhere safe, far from the fighting. Every time that thought passed through his mind, his relief grew. He imagined Habibah and the children far from Sidempuan.

He convinced himself that they were safe. At Lubuk Pakam, a small town on the way to Medan, surrounded by large plantations and untouched by the conflicts.

He had lunch with Harahap, who had ordered food from the Padang restaurant. It was truly luxurious after months of eating only wild cassava and whatever meat they could find. Before him were all kinds of curries: chicken, beef and goat, and a fat, fried egg. The spices seemed to penetrate from his nose right to the tip of his head. The food was a balm to his homesickness. It had been so long. He ate so heartily that he was freed of the thoughts of Habibah and the children. Sweat ran down his face, neck and back.

In the late afternoon, he said goodbye to Harahap and went to the market. He sat among the sellers packing up their wares. He watched the square outside. The army corporal approached, riding a bicycle. He was in uniform. On the back of the bicycle was a cloth package about the size of a pillow. Tondi waited for a few moments, making sure the corporal had not been followed. The corporal leaned his bicycle against the market gate, untied the parcel, sat down, rolled a cigarette and struck a match a few times until it finally lit. He savoured his cigarette. All as Tondi watched.

When the traders started to leave the market, Tondi joined them. He approached the corporal.

'Here it is. Take it,' the corporal said. He indicated with just a nod of his head the parcel wrapped in sacking.

'Thank you,' Tondi said. 'And this is for you,' he said handing over his basket. 'Some vegetables.'

'Thank you,' the corporal replied, putting the basket on the back of his bicycle. Without turning, he called, 'Give my best wishes to Bagio.'

'I will,' Tondi replied.

After the corporal had gone, Tondi picked up the parcel. It was heavy, about twenty kilograms. He knew the contents, so he carried it on his back carefully.

Tondi walked together with the traders leaving the market. Some rode horse carts, but most walked. In the middle of them,

Tondi felt hidden. The chances of the army checking this group of farmers were slim. But if there was a check, Tondi would not be able to escape. No farmer would ever be carrying an army radio. That was what was inside, together with a crank dynamo for electricity. The corporal had fixed the radio and it was ready to use. He hoped the corporal's repairs held true. If this radio did not work well, then the whole mission would have been a waste of time. There was no choice. Tondi had to carry the package. Bagio's company needed this equipment to communicate with headquarters and the other scattered troops. They needed information. If the others still had radios, that is.

He reached the hill without any trouble. The sun was setting. From afar he could see Masrul's silouhette, saying his prayers. Without making a sound, Tondi took out a packet of rice with mixed meat and vegetables and watched him praying on the mat of leaves. He waited a long time for the prayers to finish. Probably Masrul was praying for the safety of his wife and children.

The information about Habibah gave Masrul some relief. At least he was no longer filled with anxiety thinking of them. They left the hill. Masrul's steps were lighter and more energetic. He was imagining his family safe at Lubuk Pakam, or perhaps it was because he had eaten the rice with beef curry, goat stew and boiled egg that Tondi had brought him.

Tondi and Masrul met up with the others, and they returned together to their base. Full of hope, the soldiers gathered around the radio as it was being set up, like children waiting for a long-awaited toy to be assembled. Someone fixed an antenna to the top of a coconut palm and the wire was connected to the radio. Someone else cranked the dynamo, and the electricity began to charge. The radio light went on. The radio started. There was faint sound. Bagio turned the knob searching for frequencies, full of hope. But what the radio picked up was not from their headquarters, but communication between the central army troops.

When they tuned the radio to short wave, they picked up Indonesia's national radio RRI, Radio Malaya and 'The Voice of Free Indonesia'. It was not clear where that radio station was, but it obviously supported the rebellion. Whenever the announcer mentioned the central army, he would add 'Sukarno's dogs'. The broadcast said that the PRRI forces were still carrying out attacks against the central army in many areas. It called Sukarno a dictator and described his ministers as actors on some popular stage dressed up in military costumes. It is true that Sukarno had given high military rank to members of his cabinet.

They kept turning the knob searching for the PRRI army frequency, until the people turning the crank for the dynamo gave up. There was no signal. But they had at least discovered that there were still PRRI troops, even though the only way to work out where they were was from the central army's communications, and these were usually in code. Bagio understood some of it. It was clear that the PRRI fighters were scattered and increasingly isolated. The central army now had posts in almost every town, and they were moving rapidly into the interior. The communication between them revealed their progress hunting down the rebels. The code language was all about hunting pigs. That's what the PRRI fighters were considered now. And it was clear that the PRRI was on the run. So what were the broadcasts of 'The Voice of Free Indonesia' all about? Just empty hope. Fake.

The national radio broadcast the news that in many areas the PRRI had surrendered, and its fighters were coming down from the hills. But could you trust this news? General Nasution distributed pamphlets dropped from planes urging fighters in the forest to surrender and promising that the government would give them amnesty, but the focus of that news was Sulawesi. No rebels in the Tapanuli area of Sumatra had surrendered. The radio only said that many had been arrested, which was something different. But how long could this go on? Whenever he stopped listening to the radio, Bagio was lost in thought.

To Tondi, it was not the news on the radio that bothered him as much as a trembling that often struck him unawares. It was the memory of his grandfather. The image of Ompu Silangit would awaken him. He saw the old man sitting as he was when he left him, staring. What did this mean?

When would this rebellion end? From day to day, it was just endless waiting. The mood of war could no longer inspire enthusiasm. Was war really the way to change destiny? Tondi had little hope of that. It turned out the path he had taken was not like the one his father took. War had brought him glory. But Tondi was stuck here in these hills, wearing patched clothes, sandals made of old tyres, and spending his time running from one hill to the next looking for places to hide.

What kind of war was this? Was it his longing for his grandfather that made the old man visit him in his dreams? The deeper his sleep, the clearer was the image of his grandfather ordering him to come home. Home? That meant surrender. He could not tell the others about his recurring dream. Were they too being visited in their dreams by loved ones telling them to come home? Dreams calling out in the cold nights in the hills.

Was it the assaults by the elite national Siliwangi troops that had erased his fighting spirit? He didn't think so. This call home had started a few weeks ago. He felt his grandfather waking him. While still deep in sleep, he saw Ompu Silangit standing with his arms folded in front of him. Not speaking. Making no sound. Then he would vanish like smoke as Tondi woke. Was his grandfather visiting him because Tondi had not thought of him all this time? During his journey through the forest, he had been thinking only of his mother back in her food stall in Siantar. Who was helping her with the firewood there now?

Now, Tondi thought, here he was, with no honour to carry home to his mother. He could not break free of the bitter fate his father had passed on to him. The road he had travelled had brought him to a dead end. Not to any clear path. It was the wrong road. He harboured revenge towards his father, and yet he had followed his footsteps. It was true. They were a lineage of warriors. They had war in their blood. But this kind of war? Do you gain glory only through battle?

As the assaults on the slopes of Lubukraya became more sustained, Bagio's men had to keep moving. Probably the central army was trying to clean up the whole Tapanuli area as quickly as possible. Even though they were being chased by the elite Siliwangi troops, Bagio's men were better off than they had been because now they at least had money to buy food. Tondi and Masrul's duty was to go down to the market to buy rice, coffee, salted fish, salt and sugar. Tondi was given the task of carrying a sack of rice on his back up the hill. It was not just because he was the strongest, but Bagio also thought that his open and cheerful face would attract sympathy from the market sellers. Masrul, too, with his thin body and pitiful face. He was one of a kind. The other soldiers looked more aggressive and made the locals suspicious, not to mention the army. Putting on airs as a rebel. What a laugh! Bagio had to laugh at himself and his men.

On this particular day, Tondi and Masrul went down to Pargarutan, a small town between Sidempuan and Sipirok. Until now, they had only dared go as far as the foot of the hills. This time, their mission was not only to buy supplies, but also to find out what was really going on. They left at dusk so they could arrive at dawn. Only a pale moon lit the way as they scrambled through the undergrowth.

They were now on the path leading towards the town. It led to a road that ran between rows of connected bamboo houses. Quiet. They walked on. It was more like a big village than a town. The houses in rows that doubled as stalls were only about fifty metres long. A few other houses were scattered in the fields.

The sun was peeping over the hill. It was still quiet. Not a single person was walking towards the market. Maybe they had made a mistake and it was not market day.

The prayer call came from the mosque. Tondi gave a sign. Masrul nodded. They turned in the direction of the mosque. Water was trickling from a spout for ablutions. Tondi washed his face and then sat outside huddled in his sarong.

Masrul was inside the mosque performing his morning prayers. He was taking a long time about it. Tondi was used to this. Masrul liked to pray while waiting for the horizon to appear in the dawn light. Tondi waited, sleepy. Maybe he actually dozed off. He did not know for how long. He thought he saw his grandfather come out of the mosque and walk towards him. He woke up with his grandfather touching his shoulder, as he used to do when he was a boy. He was standing directly in front of him.

'*Nunga sae*,' the old man said. 'It's enough.'

Tondi was startled, and not fully awake. Then Ompu Silangit melted into the mist. For a few moments, Tondi looked around, perplexed, hoping to find him. But the mosque yard was deserted.

The pink of dawn lit the earth. Masrul had finished his prayers, but the food stalls were still closed. Tondi and Masrul sat on the steps of the mosque. Usually, when Tondi's ompung visited him in his dreams, the old man never spoke. This time he had said just one short phrase, 'it's enough'. Must it be ended now?

Footsteps approached. Three army men and a civilian. Someone in the mosque earlier must have reported their presence.

'Oh no. We're done for,' Masrul said. His body was shaking as he moved close to Tondi.

They stood up.

'Where are you from?' one of the army men asked.

'Aekgodang,' Tondi replied with an arbitrary name.

'Destination?'

'Sidempuan. We're waiting for the bus.'

'Papers?'

This was it. How could Masrul and Tondi have travel documents issued by the government? In that area, every passenger had to have an identity card and travel documents.

They were searched. They only had money. It was taken. They were escorted to headquarters. What bad luck, like dogs bumping into dog catchers. It turned out a central army company was based in this small town. It looked as though it was a large company of maybe four platoons, one with heavy weaponry. So this was the company that often fired in the direction of Bagio's troops on the Lubukraya slopes.

Tondi and Masrul were separated. Tondi was left with his hands tied behind his back until afternoon. The army was using a primary school as its base. This meant the children could not attend school. Or perhaps the school was closed because there were no teachers to teach them. On the wall there were still maps of Indonesia and some other drawings of landscapes, probably done by the school children. The desks and seats were a single unit, and there were inkwells in the desks, with ink that had long since dried. The teacher's desk and chair were falling apart. The walls of the school were made of woven bamboo with big holes here and there. It was certainly not a place fit for a prison. The walls would fall as soon as you looked at them. But there were guards outside.

The door opened. A soldier brought some boiled cassava and water in a tin mug. He untied Tondi's hands. Without saying a word, he went out.

Tondi took a sip. It was cold, weak tea. He could hear Masrul coughing in the classroom next door. They had been caught. Well, there was nothing to regret about that. He was only worried about Bagio and the others waiting back in the forest.

A sergeant came in and sat carefully in the teacher's chair. He rocked the chair for a moment, testing it. As soon as he was satisfied, he leaned back and gestured to Tondi to approach. He prepared his writing materials. Tondi studied him and saw that he was middle-aged.

Casually, the sergeant said:

'You're PRRI, aren't you?'

Tondi did not reply. From his accent, Tondi concluded he was Javanese.

The soldier looked up sharply.

'Come on. Just admit it,' he said. His Javanese accent was even more pronounced.

Tondi still did not react.

'Your name?'

Tondi said his name. Three times, spelling it out one syllable at a time so the soldier could write it down. Then came questions about his place and date of birth, his schooling and his address.

Tondi answered these personal questions according to his situation before he joined the rebellion. After that, he felt there was no more need for evasion. He and Masrul had already thought through the possibility of having to explain their involvement with PRRI. They had agreed they would never mention Bagio's troops and their hideout. So, during questioning, he mentioned only Aekgodang, a place to the east and far from Lubukraya, and gave a different name as his commander.

His answers did not convince his interrogator in the least. But the sergeant did not have much time. He had to go and join an operation, leaving Tondi alone in the room. No one paid him any attention other than preventing him from leaving the room, including going to the room next door. A soldier guarded the door. Tondi spent the days lying on the floor. Every now and then someone brought him some rice and dried fish, but more often cassava and boiled banana. Maybe the central army also does not get adequate supplies, Tondi thought.

On the fifth day, his interrogation resumed at night. Probably Masrul too. Shortly after the questioning started, Tondi could hear sounds next door. Masrul was barking. His coughing would not stop. Then there was a sound like choking. Or maybe he had vomited? The soldier questioning him yelled for someone to get the medical officer.

The sergeant questioning Tondi left his desk and went next door. Tondi could hear movement and the sound of hurried footsteps. The sergeant returned.

'Your friend is seriously ill, isn't he?' he asked.

'What happened?' Tondi asked.

'He passed out. Vomited blood. Tomorrow we'll take him to Sidempuan. He should be in hospital.'

The sergeant was from one of the Siliwangi battalions. His name was Sukarjo. He came from East Java and had been with the Siliwangi troops since the revolution, based in West Java. As he interrogated Tondi, he tried to get more details about the numbers, location and weapons of Tondi's group. But it seemed that he was not too concerned about extracting precise information. It looked as though the central army was just biding time, waiting for the end of the PRRI resistance. The sergeant spent most of the time chatting. He brought a thermos of hot coffee. The coffee aroma and warmth in Tondi's tin mug filtered through his whole body.

'Tomorrow the military police from Sidempuan are coming. You'll be their prisoner,' Sergeant Sukarjo said. 'Do you have any family in Sidempuan?'

'No.'

'It can be a problem if you don't have any family to visit you. Funding for the military police is limited because they're not a fighting force.'

But the military police did not arrive. No one knew when he would be taken to Sidempuan. After all, as far as the military police was concerned, Tondi was not an important prisoner. So he spent his days inside the classroom with the holes in the walls and was left alone. In the beginning, Masrul's coughing as he gasped for breath provided some comfort, letting him know that Masrul was still there. Now he found out that Masrul was in hospital in Sidempuan. Tondi hoped that he would also be moved there soon, even though he could not imagine what the military police prison would be like. Every now and then he would have the urge to escape. But what would be the point? Over in the hills his troops were being bombarded, hunted like animals and some were probably already captured. After all, his grandfather had said 'nunga saé'. That's enough. What else was there?

Recently, he had felt freer. The door to his room was no longer locked, and he was free to go in and out as he pleased. Often, he went over and joined the soldiers on guard. The ones from West Java were either Javanese or Sundanese. Most were middle-aged. Only one or two were young. They were all friendly. Maybe that's what people from there are like. From chatting with them, he found out that some of these soldiers had joined the 'long march' during the revolution, from West Java to Central Java.

As they became more friendly, Tondi helped out with the cooking and joined them to eat. It was simple food. He also helped the driver with the transport, washing the vehicles and also with mechanical repairs. His bus-conductor experience was useful now. He only returned to his classroom cell at night.

Because of his skill at motor mechanics, Tondi got to know the company commander. One morning, the commander's vehicle, an old Willys jeep from revolution days, would not start. The engine coughed but would not turn over. The commander, Captain Sunarya, was in a hurry to go to Sidempuan. He cursed the jeep; junk left by the Dutch! Even when the Dutch had the damn thing, it wouldn't go. It had been discarded American WW II junk even then.

Tondi helped the driver check the engine. He was familiar with the carburettor and ignition because most of the engines in the old buses were also American models. The carburettors had to be finely tuned, and only someone familiar with them could do it. The engines were all on their last legs, and the fuel could be anything: petrol, diesel or even kerosene. Drivers had to be able to fiddle with the engine to accommodate that. If the engine wouldn't start, it had to be a spare-part issue.

Tondi signalled to the driver. He turned the ignition and the engine roared into life. Tondi closed the bonnet.

'Hey you, get in! You're coming with us in case it breaks down again on the road like it did the other day,' Captain Sunarya said.

The driver, a corporal, could only give a weak smile. It wasn't his fault. After all, he wasn't from the transport section. He was a battle soldier who happened to be able to drive. Of course, there were no requirements for soldiers to fix vehicles when they broke down. Especially old jeeps. He kept looking straight ahead. Poker faced.

Tondi was confused. The army escort tapped the seat indicating for him to sit in the back beside him. He got in. There were four of them in the jeep. This was the first time Tondi had ridden in any vehicle since the days he travelled the Medan-Bukittinggi bus route. All he could see was the back of Captain Sunarya's clean neck.

Like most Sundanese, Captain Sunarya had light skin. He was middle aged, probably the same age as Bagio. Like Bagio, he had been part of the revolution when they were fighting side by side against the Dutch, but now here they were fighting each other. Tondi looked at the soldier driving. Everyone was silent. Tondi understood that if a commander was present, no one spoke. The only noise was the engine.

'What did you do before you went to the jungle?' Captain Sunarya asked without turning his head. Tondi realized the question was for him.

'I was a bus conductor,' he said.

'Ah, that makes sense. Where are you from?'

'Siantar.'

'Can you drive?'

'Yes.'

The driver was speeding to make up for the time lost getting the car to start. The jeep jumped in the potholes. The asphalt on the road had long gone. The shock absorbers had probably not been changed since the day the jeep left the factory. They functioned no better than old springs on a horse cart. The petrol from the carburettor gave off sharp fumes which would give most people a headache, but which Tondi inhaled with deep pleasure. It was an aroma he had not enjoyed for a long time.

Sadly, from Pargarutan to Sidempuan was not far. Tondi did not have long to enjoy the atmosphere he had craved for so long. The jeep entered the army base. Captain Sunarya entered the office. Tondi joined the soldiers who waited under the shade of a tree. Sitting lazily in the breeze, he thought of Masrul and wondered how his health was. He could not possibly visit him. So he let that thought go and turned his attention to Habibah and the children. Why did he think of her? Then he thought of his mother.

A while back, he had written a letter to his mother. The guard had kindly bought him a postage stamp and put the letter in the post. Now, every day, Tondi had something to wait for. A reply from his mother.

No letter came for a long time. Until now, the only thing he had awaited was the arrival of the military police who were going to move him to a new prison in Sidempuan. But that had not happened.

Then, one day a soldier called him:

'Tondi, there's a letter for you.'

This was the first time in his life that Tondi had ever received a letter. He sat beside the soldier. His heart beat faster. A letter from Inang. He ripped the envelope open. His mother's writing was neat. Short. Like a telegram. But it made his heart stop for an instant. Just an instant. Then his blood rushed. His ompung, Ompu Silangit, had died a few months ago. Could that have been the first time he appeared to Tondi between sleep and waking?

Strange. Tondi did not feel sad. It was like receiving news that his grandfather had just moved to another village. He felt that he would never separate from him. His ompung would often visit him. What was there to worry about? He folded the letter carefully and put it in his shirt pocket.

After accompanying Captain Sunarya on that trip, Tondi's position changed. He no longer had to await the military police. Captain Sunarya ordered Tondi to drive the jeep. The previous driver returned to battle duties.

But there were virtually no more battle duties, anyway. Tondi mainly drove Captain Sunarya to Sipirok or Sidempuan for meetings at command headquarters. The war was about to end, it seemed. The news was that the head of PRRI in this area, Colonel Simbolon, had written to the army chief of staff in Jakarta about a ceasefire. Negotiations followed about surrender. Was this what Ompu Silangit had meant when he said *nunga sae*? Or did he mean that he himself had completed his life journey on this earth and was returning to the banua ginjang, the world above? Tondi did not wish his grandfather to return to the banua ginjang, because there he would be one with the gods and never return to this earthly world. He wanted his grandfather to continue to be by his side, to give him strength as he went through life. He did not know the path to take.

* * *

Tondi was stranded in Sidempuan, not as PRRI, but as private aide to Captain Sunarya. He searched for Masrul at the military police base but did not find him. He discovered that Masrul had never been arrested. After being released from hospital, the military police ordered him to go. Maybe they thought that holding someone so sick would just be trouble. Or then again, maybe among the military police there was a friend of his from the revolution days. Who knew where Masrul was now? Tondi had no time to search for information. He spent his days driving Captain Sunarya around. He almost never stopped. The only spare time he had was when he was waiting for the captain on his visits to the bases.

The war had ended. Colonel Simbolon surrendered at Balige. Ah, no need for the term 'surrender'. Even the central government avoided the use of that term. On 12 August 1961, in a military ceremony held on Singamangaraja Square in Balige, the PRRI troops officially declared an end to their opposition to the government. Wearing military uniform, they stood in neat lines on the square. Those who had previously been in the national army wore their old national army uniforms and insignia showing their troop affiliation and rank. Those who had never been in the national army wore just the uniform. Colonel Simbolon reported that his troops in Tapanuli had come down from the hills. As he gave his report, he was wearing his central army uniform and insignia.

The PRRI soldiers then greeted any national army soldiers they knew. The embraced each other and some shed tears. The government gave amnesty to all the PRRI followers.

So it was that the war ended for Tondi. He watched the ceremony from afar, from the sidelines of the square. He had driven Major Sunarya there to attend the ceremony. Yes, Captain Sunarya had been promoted. On his shoulder was one star on a black background: major. A gift from this war. The Siliwangi regiment was going to return to its headquarters in West Java.

The war was over. Dust rose in clouds from the vehicles as they crowded the edge of the square. A wave of hot steam beat down from the sky and pushed up from the earth. Biting pain gripped Tondi's chest. His eyes stung. Maybe it was the dust, or maybe he was holding back tears. Ah, the war was over and he had nothing to show for it. He was still a nobody. He used to be a bus conductor, and now he was just a driver for some soldier.

Balige was a small town and had never seen as many vehicles as today. Apart from the vehicles of the high-ranking military who had come from Jakarta, there were also the families of the PRRI men, who had come to collect them. The stifling midday heat and all the dust made it difficult to breathe.

The ceremony was over. Everyone was talking. It sounded like bees in Tondi's ears. It all felt so distant. He felt nothing at all: no sadness, no joy, nothing. All those past years seemed to vanish just like that.

Major Sunarya sat in the jeep. Tondi was ready in position behind the steering wheel. There was no need to start the engine, as they could not move forward. Vehicles crowded the road. The roar of engines mixed with the sound of people calling each other, or shrieks of joy.

'How about we go by your grandfather's village,' Sunarya said. Over the past few months, the two had shared many stories. Tondi knew Sunarya's life story, and Sunarya had got to know about Tondi's origins. Tondi's stories about life in the village on the edge of the lake made Sunarya want to visit the house on the slope of the hill. There was only one thing Tondi never talked about. His father.

Whenever Sunarya asked about him, Tondi would reply, 'He's not here.' This could mean that his father had gone, or was dead, or had disappeared. What was clear was that Tondi did not want to talk about him. Sunarya understood, and never broached the subject.

Gradually, the traffic eased. The jeep slowly left Balige. There was no need to rush. Sunarya wanted to enjoy the breeze off the lake. The earth might be barren, but the lake breeze was still sweet.

They arrived at the foot of the hill. The huge boulder, as large as a buffalo, under the tree was still standing there, undisturbed.

Strangely he felt neither sadness nor joy. They climbed the hill. There was none of that outpouring of happiness he used to feel when he came home for the school holidays. Who was caring for his grandfather's house? It was empty. The door was shut. But the yard was clean.

They went beneath the banyan tree. This is where his ompung and ompunguru lay. Just two heaps of earth. Sunarya muttered away, reading the Al-Fatihah Quranic verse. Tondi glanced for a moment.

A middle-aged man came running towards them up the hill. He must be from the village and had seen the jeep arrive. The house on the hill never had visitors.

He looked at the two men engrossed at Ompu Silangit's grave. Tondi looked at him, then called:

'Lae Luhut?'

The man was startled.

'It's me, Tondi. It's been a long time since I was here,' Tondi said, speaking in Batak.

'Oh, it's you Tondi. Look how tall you are now!' he said.

Tondi introduced Major Sunarya.

'Let's go inside the house to talk. I'll open the door,' Luhut continued, switching to Indonesian because he realized Sunarya was not Batak.

They went inside. Nothing had changed. Except the floor was bare. Luhut quickly unrolled the mats to cover the floor.

'Your *ito* and I have been looking after your grandfather's house,' Luhut said. He used the term ito, for aunt, to refer to his wife. It is a Batak custom to avoid referring to your own family in terms of yourself, but to find a kinship term for the person you are addressing.

Soon his wife arrived. After greeting Tondi, she went to the kitchen to prepare something to drink.

Sunarya got to know more about Tondi's family. Ompu Silangit had died not long before the end of the PRRI war.

'Ompu Silangit was a true man of spiritual powers right to the end,' Luhut said.

Luhut went on, 'A week before he died, Ompu Silangit sent for me. Your ito had been cleaning the house and cooking for him. Lasmia used to do that before or after school. But now she is at high school in Siantar.

'Ompu Silangit asked me to meet a few people who lived in Laguboti, Balige, Siborong-borong and some other places. I had to give them a message to pass on. Ompu Silangit had treated some of them when they were sick, and some had come to him to study Batak custom. Ompu Silangit now asked them to come to his house the next Friday morning.

'On that morning, I did not go to the fields as I usually do. Your ito and I went to the house together. When we opened the door, we saw Ompu Silangit lying on the floor beside the wall where he usually sleeps. But unusually, he was still asleep, even though the sun had reached the river. And unusually, he was covered with ulos cloth.

'I went up to him and pulled back the ulos cloth that was covering him, including his head.

'Lord be praised! Ompu Langit had gone. He was lying neatly. He wore a clean headscarf and new, white clothing.

'I covered him with the ulos cloth again and said to your ito, Ompu has gone. Your ito wailed, and then all the invited people began to arrive.

'Lord be praised!' Luhut said again. 'Who will carry on our ompu's Batak knowledge?'

Luhut was a Christian, and the Batak knowledge he was talking about was something the Dutch missionaries said had to be wiped out.

The house was quiet. You could hear the bees buzzing in the walls.

'Who will care for Ompu's pustaha?' Luhut asked, as though talking to himself.

Luhut was still observing Tondi's face. How he has changed, he thought. The last time they met he was just a teenager. Now he was an adult man. With his build and height, his reddish face and the slightly greenish shadow on his cheeks where he had shaved, he looked every part the warrior, the ulubalang, just like his grandfather. He knew only a little about Tondi from Lasmia, about how he had joined the PRRI. But now here he was with an officer from the central army, who, judging from the emblem on the shoulder of his shirt, was from the Siliwangi troops.

They left the house. Tondi entrusted the care of the house to Luhut, including the contents. The only things of value in the house were the pustaha in the big wooden chest.

As they went down the hill, Tondi felt that his ompung was watching him. He did not feel separated from him. He recalled that the time his ompung had first visited him was the time of his death. Meaning, his ompung could visit him any time at all.

PART FIVE

AMANG

Chapter 15

Four months had passed since the war ended with the ceremony at Balige. The Siliwangi troops gradually returned to West Java. Only a few were left to safeguard security, including Major Sunarya's company which remained in Sidempuan because there were still a few PRRI followers around who had not yet laid down arms.

Tondi was still Major Sunarya's personal driver. He cared for that jeep as though it was ancient treasure. It never broke down. With his flattering ways with the platoon mechanics in Sidempuan, he always managed to get priority to use their equipment and take the spare parts he needed. What's more, the army connection who secretly gave him the field radio was still working in the workshop, and he had been promoted to sergeant. Whenever they met, they would talk about their secret.

This secret brought them close, and they would often go to coffee stalls to chat. When he had spare time, Tondi would go to the workshop and help repair the military vehicles. He got to know all kinds of vehicles there, including old WWII tanks. He could study motor mechanics without having to attend technical school.

He had travelled from Sidempuan to Medan a few times now with no problems. The jeep would fly down the hills and up the slopes on the winding road between Sibolga and Taruntung. You would never know that this was the same old wreck as before.

This time they stopped in Siantar at a Chinese-run coffee stall. The main road was lined with shops and there were many coffee stalls. The aroma of toasted bread with custard-apple jam filled the air. That was the only food this stall sold. In front, there was a barrow selling fried noodles. Tondi enjoyed the clashing sound the wok made as the cook stirred the noodles, and the smell of garlic that filled his nose, making him sneeze.

Throngs of people went back and forth. Most of the people who lived in this area were Chinese. The buildings lining the streets were two storeyed, the ground floor for business and the upstairs was where the owners lived. The Chinese would pray at the temple in Pane. Tondi remembered it from his junior high-school days, because he would often go there with his classmates after school. There would be fruit and cakes left out as offerings. The Chinese children would never dare to touch them because they were offerings for spirits of the ancestors. Tondi's group would pretend to play in the yard, waiting for the temple guard not to notice. Then they would grab the fruit and cakes and run away, like magic. Of course, the guard knew what these kids were up to, and would give them a chance while still appearing to keep guard. Ah, that childhood time. Where were his playmates now?

For the umpteenth time, Tondi read the letter from his mother. She had written in the Batak language, but using roman script.

Your mother has received your letter. This reply is very late. Your letter was addressed to your mother in Siantar, but she has been the last four months in Riau. Thankfully, a helpful person in Siantar forwarded by post the letter you sent to your mother there.

Your Ompung has died. Mother was still in Siantar when that happened. Now both your grandparents are no more. Mother feels there is no longer a need for her to stay in Siantar. She has gone to Riau to open a business there together with someone.

Every time Tondi read the letter, he felt confused. Should he go and search for his mother in Riau? She had given an address in Pekanbaru.

A waiter clearing the table interrupted his musing. He and Sunarya explored the town, first looking at the place where Tondi and his mother used to live, and then visiting the house of his old platoon commander, Pardapdap's house. Tondi wanted to meet Pardapdap's widow, but a neighbour said the old lady had left their rented house. She thought she was now living with her youngest child in Takengon. Tondi wondered whether they would ever visit Pardapdap's grave. He had been shot in battle and it was said he was buried near Batangtoru, a small town between Sibolga and Sidempuan.

Sunarya was enjoying the sights of the town, while Tondi, driving the jeep, was retracing his youth. The sides of the streets were planted with mahogany and tamarind trees giving shade. The centre of town was neat, with attractive Dutch architecture. It was a well laid-out town. They travelled along the road with the hospital where Tondi's mother had once worked, before pulling up at a coffee stall. Tondi did not recognize a single person there. He really was a foreigner now. As foreign as Sunarya.

'Our company's going home,' Sunarya said. 'Looks like there's more fighting coming up.'

Tondi raised his head.

'President Sukarno's given the command to attack Irian,' Sunarya went on.

Tondi had heard something about this on the national radio. It was going to be launched early in 1962 under the command of Major General Suharto. It was called Operation Trikora, and its mission was to take Irian back from the Dutch.

'What are you going to do, Tondi?'

Tondi merely shook his head.

'What about going back to school? I'll pay.'

'Ah, I'm past twenty now. If I went back to school, I'd have to return to second class of high school. People my age are at university,' Tondi said flatly.

'So what? I finished my junior high school during the Japanese time. Then my school was closed, and I went back to school after the revolution, in 1950. I was already thirty. I only got my high school certificate a year ago. So I was past forty-one when I had my final exams.'

'What's the point of the certificate? You were already an officer.'

'I was hoping I could get into SSKAD,' Sunarya said.

'What's that?'

'Army staff and command school. If you don't go there, you'll never become colonel, let alone general.'

'I see.' Tondi nodded, respectfully.

Would Sunarya's wish come true? His use was as a raider on the front line. Back home in the barracks, he would surely get depressed again because he could not join the elite games. People said that just to get into army command school you had to have high connections at headquarters, but he had not been around to press the flesh, let alone press a few bribes. He had been lieutenant during the revolution. His promotion was blocked. So he had made his own future. Since independence, his rank had been raised only once. Once in ten years. For him, the operation in Tapanuli had been good, for he was promoted to major.

Tondi felt there was nothing more to keep him in this town, so he went with Major Sunarya to Belawan. The Siliwangi troops were leaving for Java on a private cargo ship the navy had commandeered during the regional rebellions. The jeep was loaded on to the ship. It was the first vehicle Sunarya had ever owned, and he was hoping the government would not seize it now.

Sunarya took Tondi with him, back to Cimahi in West Java, to his troop headquarters where he lived in an officers' mess. The mess was a relic from the Dutch army during the colonial time.

Tondi became part of Sunarya's family. Sunarya's wife, a Javanese woman, was friendly. There were three sons: two at junior high school, and one at senior high school. The house was small, just two bedrooms and one living room. Tondi and the three boys preferred to sleep sprawled on the floor in the living room. Tondi spent his days looking after the jeep, cleaning the house and yard and driving Major Sunarya to the headquarters in Bandung.

'Tomorrow I want you to go to the motor repair shop owned by that Chinese man,' Sunarya said to him one afternoon. 'I want to change the colour of our jeep,' he said.

Tondi looked at him incredulously. Why change the colour? The paint should just be touched up in regulation military green.

'Then we'll go and sort out the documentation so it can officially be privately owned.'

Tondi understood. All this time the jeep had had no papers. Sunarya had privately commandeered it.

It is at this point that Tondi's next life journey began. He waited as the jeep was dismantled. The engine was removed, the cylinder heads polished and restored. The steering, which used to be on the left, was changed to right-hand drive. The body was cleaned of rust, patched, polished and then painted bright red. This was not a colour Sunarya had chosen. Tondi remembered the red Sibualbuali buses.

The skills Tondi had learned when helping out at the Siliwangi division transport workshop in Tapanuli and the good relations he had built with army mechanics were now useful when he needed to ask for spare parts. Muffler, lights, springs and shock absorbers were located in the regiment's warehouses and brought to the workshop. The most valuable find was the canvas to replace the jeep's roof that was full of holes. You could say that he was using state property, inventorized items belonging to the army. But the thought that this might be corruption did not cross Tondi's mind.

Tondi worked for days at the repair shop. This was where government vehicles were sent, and also military vehicles that could not be repaired at the regiment workshop. Tondi even slept there, together with the mechanics from out of town. He did not see Sunarya's family for almost a full month.

All eyes of the Sunarya family gazed in amazement when the jeep entered the yard. The Willys jeep was now a shining bright red. But the number plate was still the army issue from Sumatra.

'How did you do it?' Sunarya asked, somewhat hesitatingly. He did not recall having to pay.

'Credit of course . . .' Tondi said, grinning. 'We only have to pay for the painting job. And even that can be whenever we want.'

'But how?' Sunarya was still dumbfounded.

'Well, I helped out with repairs. I fixed a lot of vehicles. If you converted my time into money, then the repair shop would owe me. The owner was lucky to get such skilled labour for free,' Tondi chuckled.

Sunarya's sons crowded around, touching the smooth new paint. This was the family's first car.

A few days later Sunarya asked Tondi to go to Bandung to meet a police officer in the West Java police headquarters. There, he received ownership papers and a private number plate. So simple. Whether this was because of 1960s-style easy administration or because of Sunarya's magic power, Tondi did not care. What was important was that he became close to the police inspector there, a Batak named Habinsaran.

Back in the Dutch time, Habinsaran had attended the prestigious Dutch middle-high-school in Bandung. He was able to attend the school because he was the son of a district head in Tapanuli. However, when the Dutch capitulated and the Japanese occupied Indonesia, the school was closed. The Japanese opened another junior high school called the Koto Chu Gakko, but Habinsaran was not interested. He also ignored his father's calls to return home. He made the most of the confusion of the Japanese occupation. Everything was rationed, and the Japanese government organized the distribution of goods using a quota system via the village authorities. Early in the Japanese occupation, Habinsaran studied Japanese, and his language skills helped him obtain ration cards that he sold to villagers who had missed out. So it was that as the situation of the locals worsened, Habinsaran's pockets fattened. He had a good life in Bandung.

During the revolution, he joined as a soldier, even though his fighting skills were mediocre. His military training under the Japanese had never progressed beyond learning how to march.

However, because he could speak Japanese, he had been given security duties and tasked with gathering information and passing it on to the commander of the Japanese army in Bandung. This information-gathering skill proved extremely useful later during the fight for independence.

Habinsaran had managed to ignore his father's call to return home when the Japanese occupation began, but he could not avoid it after the war when his father came to get him. Even though he was now an army officer, it was as though his father was dragging him back home. He was to be married to his cousin. That was the end of his free bachelor army days. As a Batak man, there was absolutely nothing he could do about it. His wife was the daughter of his uncle on his mother's side. If he played up, his wife would complain to her aunt, Habinsaran's mother. No man would dare to attract his mother's ire.

That was Habinsaran's story and how he ended up stranded as a police chief in Bandung. He invited Tondi to accompany him to a favourite spot for Batak food, a stall near the airport. They sold palm wine. The stall owner added a fermenting agent that was sent from North Sumatra, the bark of a tree, which made the palm wine taste just as it did there. It was a taste every Batak craved.

Batak people away from home always seek out compatriots and Batak food. This stall was such a meeting place. Habinsaran had sent an order ahead for some special dishes, like fish marinated in lime juice. There were other more common dishes like a minced meat cooked with blood or whey; buffalo milk curd that looked like tofu; and a fish curry spiced with a special prickly-leaved herb called andaliman that grows wild only in Batak territory.

Everyone ate and drank in the noisy stall until they ran with sweat. A few young men were singing and playing the guitar, Batak songs of course. Everyone knew Inspector Habinsaran. Tondi realized that he was a protector of the young Batak thugs at the bus and train stations. They all addressed him not as inspector, but using close Batak kinship terms, like amangboru, tulang and even amangtua.

As for Tondi, he had already worked out that Habinsaran's marga had no direct ties with his own. Habinsaran's wife, however, came from the same marga as Tondi. This was advantageous to Tondi, because it meant that Habinsaran had to treat him with the same respect as he would treat his father-in-law. Because of their relative ages, however, they addressed each other as equals with the term '*lae*', or brother-in-law.

How complicated the Batak system is, Tondi thought. Habinsaran is much older, but we are treating each other as equals, even though actually Habinsaran should defer to me. Habinsaran still showed awareness of that deference by inviting Tondi to eat first. Tondi returned the respect by speaking politely and accepting Habinsaran's mark of respect to him.

'So you joined the PRRI,' Habinsaran said rather loudly. This was after Tondi finished his story of how he got to know Major Sunarya.

'If I'd been stationed in Medan back then, I probably would have joined them too,' he went on, 'but I ended up fighting with Sunarya,' Habinsaran roared with laughter.

Tondi gave a polite complicit smile.

'Hey, Lae, I want to tell you a story. I used to be in the same division as Sunarya. Yes, I was in the Siliwangi Division during the fight for independence. We were both lieutenants. He was a platoon commander. I was in section one battalion. You probably know that section one means intelligence. I've never been in a battle. Not like Sunarya. He's a battle man. He and I were really close during the guerrilla fighting. Especially when our division was in East Java, wiping out the communist rebellion in Madiun,' Habinsaran said.

Tondi was unnerved for a moment.

'If I think about that time, I can't sleep at night. There were piles of bodies. The communists killed civil servants and villagers who didn't join the rebellion. Then we were ordered to kill any communists who were caught. There was no legal process because the communists had not respected the law themselves. All our operations were carried out based on intelligence. Sunarya and his men acted on the intelligence I gave them. They arrested people and handed them over to the soldiers there.' Habinsaran wiped his face, as though wiping the image from his eyes.

'But were you sure, Lae, that those people really had done wrong?' Tondi asked.

'Well, I got my information only through asking people about communists they knew. I had no time to check whether what they said was true or not. We had to move fast. So those people died because of what their neighbours or friends said. But yes, you could say that it was because of my report. But that's how it was. That's war.'

Habinsaran went quiet for a while. He stared at the alcohol in his glass, then drank it down slowly. Tondi observed his face. He wondered if all the lines at the corner of his eyes were the products of war. He was probably the same age as Sunarya, yet he looked older.

'After I returned to Bandung in 1950, the opportunity arose to join the police, so I moved to the police right away. Fighting battles was not for me anyway. Nor was being in army intelligence. My experiences in Madiun really haunted me. I had to witness every execution. They were lined up, their hands tied behind their backs, and then shot as they stood beside the mass grave. Some civilians also did the executions. The local army soldiers ordered them to be executioners. They had to behead the people rounded up and accused of being communists. I saw those heads roll on the earth. Some didn't die immediately. Heads with bulging eyes. Headless bodies writhing on the ground. The executioner kicking them into the hole. Then the hole filled with earth. Done. I ask you, what kind of war was that, Lae?'

Tondi made no comment. Habinsaran raised his glass, downed the alcohol with big gulps, and burped.

'I thought that by joining the police I would not have to write reports that would be used as evidence to shoot people. Or the only reason for shooting would be because they were armed. Anyone arrested would have to be handed over to the judicial authorities and undergo proper trial. Not the police making decisions about who is a criminal or not. Death sentences should be made by judges.'

Tondi merely nodded to show sympathy. Habinsaran wiped the alcohol froth from his lips and went on.

'When I joined the police, I was given the rank of assistant inspector. So actually, my rank went down. Sunarya stayed in the army. Now he's a major. I'm just inspector, which is equivalent to lieutenant in the army. So I've been promoted only once, bringing my rank back to what it was during the independence war.' Habinsaran laughed. His gloom had lifted.

It seemed that the path in war Sunarya had taken was better than Habinsaran's. Sunarya benefited from the PRRI rebellion, getting a promotion from it. Habinsaran, though, was still stuck in Bandung. Stuck? Well, maybe not. He was creating his own path, expecting nothing from his superiors or from police intrigues.

Chapter 16

If a turning point in Tondi's life had been working at the Chinese-owned mechanic's repair shop in Cimahi and the trip to Bandung where he met Habinsaran, for Sunarya it was in 1961, with the preparations for the attack on West Irian. A special army corps was formed. On their way home from base, Tondi was driving the jeep as usual, but Sunarya's face was dark. When they arrived home, he called out to his wife who was preparing lunch.

'We'll eat later. Come and join us.'

They all sat together in the living room.

'I've been pulled from the force,' Sunarya said.

'What do you mean?' his wife asked.

'I've been moved to Jakarta to do office work. Pulled from active duty.'

'What did you do wrong?' his wife asked, her voice hoarse.

For indeed, to a soldier used to battle, being called in to a desk job was the same as punishment. Major Sunarya was probably considered too old to lead troops. Since his return from operations in Tapanuli with his rank of major, he had become deputy commander of the battalion. Before he had a chance to enjoy being commander, he was now being made staff at army headquarters.

For someone who had spent decades in the field, this was a painful move. It was difficult to even imagine working behind a desk organizing army recruitment, promotions and so forth.

'Maybe I should just ask for early retirement,' Sunarya said.

'And then what would you do? The children are still at school,' his wife replied.

'But I'm not cut out for administrative work. Since returning from the last operation, even having to check the battalion's administration makes me dizzy. And the command they're going to form is supposed to be made up of two divisions. How many thousand men would I have to manage!'

'But you'll not be alone. You'll have staff,' his wife said.

'Maybe you should just try it out,' Tondi said. 'Your wife and children can stay here. I'll go with you to Jakarta. That way you'll still have your personal driver . . .' Tondi chuckled.

'I've heard that because this is a new office, there's no staff housing available. They have to find their own accommodation,' Sunarya said.

'Well then, Tondi should go with you,' his wife said. 'We're used to looking after ourselves. And Jakarta is close. I'm pleased, actually. It's time for you to relax a bit.'

'That's right,' Tondi said. 'I heard on the radio that they're preparing troops to parachute into Irian. It's still jungle there.'

'But I am a battle soldier,' Sunarya said.

'You may be a battle soldier, but your bones are old,' his wife teased.

Sunarya made a face.

'I've got an idea,' Tondi said.

'Yes?'

'Let's make a transport business in Jakarta,' Tondi said.

'What do you mean?'

'Well, from talking to Inspector Habinsaran I found out that in Jakarta there are lots of vehicles that are abandoned wrecks. Their owners do not repair them, and they're free for the taking. Repairs probably cost too much, or the owners can't be bothered sorting out the registration papers. From restoring the jeep, I learnt that if you stay with the vehicle during the repairs, you can save a lot of money. I can ask the owner of the repair place in Cimahi if he knows anyone in Jakarta with a repair place we could use. Then we can arrange the papers. Habinsaran must have connections at police headquarters in Jakarta.'

'That's a great idea, Tondi,' Sunarya's wife said, turning to address her husband. 'Tondi's right. We need our own business on the side. Your salary is barely enough, and things will be worse when the boys are at high school.'

'If we don't have our transport business, then . . . well, we might have to be like Habinsaran,' Tondi said with a chuckle.

'What's his business?'

'He collects protection money from thugs in Bandung.'

'Now stop that, Tondi. As if my husband would protect thugs,' Sunarya's wife interjected.

'Yes . . . but if he wanted to, if could be great. Look at Habinsaran. He has a brand-new car,' Tondi said.

'No, stop that now. Only legal things,' she said.

'But the business I'm thinking of is not totally clean. Actually, people still legally own the vehicles we'd take.'

'Yes, but they're like discarded junk.'

'We'd have to borrow capital from Habinsaran to repair them. When I was chatting with him, I got the impression he has heaps of money.'

'No loans. Invite him in as a partner,' Sunarya's wife said.

'Ha. But maybe his money's not clean,' Tondi teased.

She looked up, startled. Tondi laughed.

'Don't worry. I'm sure it's clean,' Tondi said. 'It's protection, not extortion. How could anyone get work at the bus or train station without some backing? He just helps the kids who are being extorted by the terminal staff.'

Sunarya had been quiet as he followed the conversation between his wife and Tondi. It seemed his wife had a head for business. He had not been aware that all this time she had been supporting the

household economy with her own small business. Left for months
at a time when he was away on military operations, how could his
salary possibly cover the costs for their children? She had been
selling batik to shops in Cimahi. She would bring the batik from
Yogyakarta and Solo. Her younger sister who lived in Yogyakarta
would do the buying and send it by train to Bandung. Sunarya's wife
would go from Cimahi to Bandung railway station to collect it. She
was resourceful at running the household.

'I haven't seen Habinsaran and his wife for a long time,' she said.
'Let's invite them over, Tondi.'

* * *

For a fighting man like Major Sunarya, working in an office in
Jakarta was not easy. Every morning he had to go to the army
headquarters. First, he would attend the obligatory roll call, then
he inspected the troops being prepared for West Irian, and his day
would end with another roll call. He was used to the roll calls but
sitting for hours at a desk made his head spin. He did not know how
long he could stand it.

But he did not have to wait long. Habinsaran would often come
over in the late afternoon. It took only two hours for his shiny sedan
to travel from Bandung to Jakarta. Then, together with Tondi, the
three of them would plan their transport business. This really was a
great choice. There was no proper public transport. People would
ride becaks for short distances, but to travel further they had to wait
for the city buses. There were only the government buses, and they
were few and far between. As a result, people with private cars would
take paying passengers who would pay whatever they could. This
provided their owners with extra income. Their cars were like taxis.

No doubt about it, Inspector Habinsaran was brilliant at
business. The protection business, that is. Whether or not he was
as skilful as a policeman combatting crime, Tondi did not know.
Habinsaran knew people everywhere. Even the pimps at the Planet
Senen prostitution complex knew him, although this was outside

his area of jurisdiction. It was clear he had many friends in police headquarters in Jakarta, and many army friends from his earlier days in the army. Friends were not free, of course. Habinsaran would often help them out financially, and they repaid him with loyalty. Including, needless to say, passing on information about where there were unregistered wrecked cars. Usually the result of crashes.

Habinsaran's rank might be only inspector, but he was able to revive a few casualty cars. He asked Tondi to bring two cars from Bandung. One was a Holden from Australia, and the other a Dodge from America. So now he seemed to own three cars. Unbelievable! Even his boss at police headquarters was not that rich. Tondi found drivers who could operate the cars as taxis.

Those two cars were the initial capital for their business. After two months in Jakarta and hanging around with people at the repair shop, Tondi had no difficulty finding drivers. Now he understood why Habinsaran was paying for the rented house where Sunarya lived in Kalibata. It was a big house with a large yard where he could park the cars. Every day, Sunarya would travel along the road in front of the military heroes' cemetery.

'If you think about all the medals I've received, especially the guerrilla medal, then I should have a plot in there,' he joked with Tondi.

'Does Habinsaran have a guerrilla medal?'

'Oh, for sure. We fought together during the revolution.'

'But he also has a place in the heroes' cemetery,' Tondi teased.

Sunarya always complained about his work at army headquarters, but he enjoyed being with Habinsaran and Tondi. These two Batak men complemented each other so well, and they were always jolly, smart, and good at solving problems. Habinsaran used his connections in the police, while Tondi looked after field logistics, especially ferrying money to the people Habinsaran had asked for services. Sunarya had never imagined that the little notes he wrote asking for favours would have such magic power. A scrap of army headquarters notepaper allowed Tondi to use army tow-trucks to bring the wrecked cars to the workshop. Only the army had completely equipped workshops. Tondi had restored three cars already.

Habinsaran was not cut out to be in the army. He seemed to know where his talents lay. But they did not lie in the police either. So where was the right place for him?

The three were eating lunch together at a restaurant near Kemayoran airport. The spicy Deli Medan food made them sweat. They devoured the goat stew with pineapple. Outside, heat was shimmering on the tarmac and parking lot.

'I've told Lae Tondi here that Jakarta is going to change fast. Believe me, Narya, we've got to get serious about our business,' Habinsaran said to Sunarya.

'Just look. They've almost finished building the new sports stadium. The Hotel Indonesia too. Our first international hotel. There'll be lots of foreigners soon,' he said.

Tondi was enjoying his meal. He had often heard Habinsaran talking like this. Whether Jakarta was changing or not was not his business. He only cared about repairing the cars. Sunarya merely nodded. He was a quiet man.

'You stay on in the army, that's just fine,' Habinsaran said, 'we'll organize things so that you can get a promotion. Money will do it. I know you don't have the education and won't get the rank you want unless you fight in Irian. As for me, I'm not thinking of a career in the police.'

This conversation was a side issue as they discussed setting up their business as a legal entity. So it was that their business was officially established and named Four Friends. Because Habinsaran and Sunarya were government officers, they could not sit on the board. They decided that Mrs Sunarya would be the director, and Mrs Habinsaran the commissioner. Habinsaran's wife would remain living in Bandung because she had no ongoing work with the business, but Sunarya's family would move to Jakarta. The house in Kalibata would now not only be a place to live, but also the business office.

* * *

Jakarta stretched in the cool of the morning, sighed in the heat of the day, and lazed at night. Its inhabitants had to fight for public transport daily. Only on holidays did the competition disappear and the city quieten. Only one or two motorized vehicles passed. Not many people owned cars or motor bikes, because cars were imported. Sukarno's economic policy was to limit imports because of a lack of foreign exchange. People were feeling the pinch of the economic situation. The government felt it too. The long period of fighting regional rebellions followed by the preparations for freeing West Irian from Dutch colonial rule had scoured the state coffers.

Habinsaran's skill at seeing opportunities was proven. In 1962, President Sukarno opened the Hotel Indonesia. Now, those with money had a new place to go. Indonesia's skyscraper hotel had a nightclub where Jakarta's elite liked to dance.

Tondi was engrossed in the world he loved. Sitting around fixing cars at the workshop. He already had seven cars in operation. Two were kept at Banteng Square in the middle of the city, to be used by businessmen who had to visit government offices. These were rented by the hour. The other five were kept at the airport, or at Hotel Indonesia. The fee for their use was determined by the distance travelled and set by negotiation in advance. Tondi had to keep a check on this part of the business, so that he could report to Mrs Sunarya who took the money from the drivers.

And Habinsaran was right yet again, because Mrs Sunarya did indeed have an amazing head for business. She had only attended school to the first class of junior high school during the Japanese occupation. Whether she had studied bookkeeping there, or whether she was self-taught, she was scrupulous with figures. After just three months, they employed two administrative staff.

The taxi rental business was not a simple matter. The drivers had to return every night. When required, Tondi had to use an iron fist. One driver did not return with a car for days. Tondi went after him. He sniffed around all the places where drivers of rented cars went. Finally, someone gave him information that the driver had run off with the car to Sumatra. That was not difficult to trace. Tondi found out the driver's home village from the information on his identity card when he hired the car. Like a sniffer dog, Tondi hunted him down. He first telephoned Habinsaran by placing a long-distance call. He had to shout down the bad line.

'I'm in Bakauheni, Lae. Who can I ask for help in the police around here?'

Bakauheni was a harbour town in south Lampung, where the ferries crossed between Sumatra and Java. Tondi was driving alone from Jakarta.

'I'll find out and call you back,' Habinsaran replied. It did not take long. Tondi was able to meet a police officer in Tanjung Karang.

Tondi's Holden car now had a police escort. Four of them. Two policemen in plain clothes, and two in uniform. Tondi drove to Panjang where he had been told the car had been taken. Maybe the driver wanted to show off in his village. But he wasn't there. As the driver was unemployed, he must have hired out the car. The police escort knew where hire cars waited for customers. It was not difficult to find the driver leisurely drinking coffee at a stall with his friends. His face went as pale as paper when he saw Tondi. His knees shook.

Tondi took him by the collar and dragged him outside the stall. The friends couldn't do a thing. One of the policemen drove the stolen car. Earlier, Tondi had secretly slipped the officer in charge some money for the services of his men. He had then been only too happy to write travel orders for two of them to go to Jakarta. One to drive the stolen car, one to accompany Tondi and the captured driver.

They drove directly back to Jakarta and arrived at midday. Tondi and the two policemen took the driver to the repair workshop. This was where cars were usually checked before being returned to base, and any repairs done.

'You wait here. If I come back and you've gone, I'll search you out even if you hide in a rat hole,' Tondi said. The driver was shaking. Tondi's eyes glistened as cold as ice.

Tondi and the two policemen left. They found a small hotel in Senen and ordered three rooms.

'Take a shower,' Tondi said at the door. 'Then we'll go and get a good meal.'

The two policemen gave a wide grin. Tondi chuckled as he closed the door.

They went to a Chinese restaurant for lunch. Dishes of food covered the entire table. While eating, Tondi got some interesting stories. The police in Tanjung Karang often carried out raids in the hotels where prostitutes plied their trade. Most of them were brought there from Java by their pimps. This was also the case in Palembang, so the women were taken long distances.

'What does a woman cost over there?' Tondi asked.

One of the policemen mentioned a sum depending on whether it was by the hour or the whole night.

'It depends on the hotel. If the woman is good looking, or it is a high-class hotel, the tariff is higher. I once met a beautiful woman, like a film star, but her fee was low. Probably because of the bed in the hotel.'

The two policemen laughed uproariously. Tondi chuckled.

'How would you like to sample what we've got in Jakarta?' Tondi asked. This stifled their laughter. They grinned.

When they got back to the hotel, there were four women waiting in the lobby. One middle-aged and three young. The older woman was dressed in the traditional way, with a *kebaya* blouse and a batik wrap-around skirt. The young women were dressed modishly like film stars. They all went to the hotel restaurant and had coffee. The two policemen kept glancing sideways, swallowing excitedly.

'How come there's four of you? I only ordered three,' Tondi said.

'I brought them here. I'm their madam,' the older woman said.

Tondi looked at her as she sat across from him. She was aged anywhere between thirty-five and forty. A woman in her prime. The front of her kebaya showed off her cleavage and golden skin. She was tall, and her kebaya and batik revealed every curve of her body.

'Are you on offer too?' Tondi asked.

She looked momentarily embarrassed.

'Have you chosen?' Tondi asked the two policemen.

They gave him a thumbs up. Then each went off with the woman of his choice. There were two women remaining.

'Well, I brought the girls here, I'm off now,' the madam said, getting up to leave.

'No need for you to go,' Tondi said.

The madam and young woman exchanged glances. Confused.

'Come on,' Tondi said. The two women went with him. Giggling.

'Two against one. We can do it,' madam whispered to her young charge. She was a veteran, already seasoned in the battlefield of love.

In the room was a big bed. The young woman began to remove her clothes. But Tondi was more interested in the madam. She took off her blouse slowly, undoing the safety pins with fingers moving like a palace dancer. Then she unfastened the long sash wound around her waist. She gave the end of it to Tondi to hold and then turned her body until the sash unravelled. Now she untucked the end of her batik wraparound skirt, and with Tondi holding it she turned until it fell to the floor, and she stood naked. The batik rustled as it fell and gave off an aroma of sandalwood. The young woman was already naked and embraced Tondi. But he could not take his eyes off the madam.

Her body was as finely toned as a horse, her muscles gleaming. Her hair, which had been tied up in a bun, was flowing loose down her back. The jet black of her hair contrasting with her golden skin drew Tondi like a magnet. Her hair exuded perfume.

And the threesome body-wrestling began. Tondi had never been in a threesome before. But he was like a young bull on fire. Like a volcano about to erupt. Like a storm assailing a mountain, shaking the trees. The women wrestled in response to every one of the man's moves. Each woman in turn, until they were panting and the sheet was damp with sweat. The pillows scattered and fell to the floor, kicked by the women in their excitement. The young woman was the first to sleep. Then the madam collapsed with exhaustion.

'I give up,' she said, 'I've never had it like this before, Mas,' she said, embracing Tondi and using the Javanese familiar term to address a man.

'Really?' was all Tondi said. He was making a plan.

'Where do your girls come from?' he asked.

'Various places. But most are from Cirebon, which is where I come from. West Java, mostly. All over, especially if there's a bad harvest, then many come to Jakarta.'

'I see.'

'Next time just come directly to me, Mas. No need to go through the hotel,' she said.

'Sure.'

They were quiet for a few moments. Tondi stroked her.

'Again, Mas?' she said seductively.

'No, that's enough.'

'That's good. I'm not up for another time myself,' she said, wiping the sweat off Tondi's neck.

'Where do you live?' Tondi asked her, switching his term of address to the familiar pronoun.

'I rent a house in Bukit Duri, together with the girls.'

Tondi sat up. Madam did too.

'I've got an idea,' Tondi said. 'I often need escorts for people who help my business. What do you think if I rent a house for you and your girls? I can contact you if I need to.'

'That'd be great . . .' she said.

Madam's name was Siti Rohana, but people usually called her Mami Ana.

'And I'd like to be your own special one,' she said.

'Sure, we can do that. Like before, would you like that?' Tondi said.

'Very much. I got really excited when you were with Neneng,' she said, nestling up against Tondi's chest.

'Right then, let's make a deal. You can keep finding customers for your girls. But your girls must be top class. I will also find a doctor for regular check-ups. My clients are not just anyone. I can help out if you need to find girls from out of town. My driver can take you.'

'That'd be terrific, Mas,' she said.

Tondi stayed at the hotel until evening. He left the two policemen there in their rooms. They were exhausted and in deep sleep.

That day would turn out to be the start of Tondi pioneering a new business. He would not involve Sunarya or Mrs Sunarya in his new sideline.

He went back to the repair workshop. The drivers had gathered there. The firm now employed fifteen drivers, driving ten cars in shifts.

The driver who had been brought back from Sumatra had not budged from his place the whole day.

Tondi sat across from him for a few moments. Some of the other drivers were sitting on a wooden bench, and others were sitting inside a car with the doors open.

'Tell me, what has Mrs Sunarya not given you, eh?' Tondi said, his voice calm. 'Show me another boss who gives you conditions like our firm. You get some of the takings, and food money whether there are customers or not. So what's missing? Oh, I see, you want your own car. Do you think it's that easy to own a car? I had to sleep in the workshop for days to build that car.'

Very slowly, Tondi got up and approached the driver. Suddenly, seemingly with no preparation, he raised his left fist and punched him. It was not a heavy punch, but the driver was thrown back and rolled on the floor.

'Get up!' Tondi said calmly. 'Sit!'

The driver slowly got up and sat, rubbing his red, swollen cheek. Tondi looked at the other drivers.

'You. All of you. Come and hit him until he falls on the floor, one by one. You, start.'

One of the drivers came forward. He copied Tondi's punch. But the driver did not fall.

'Again!' Tondi said.

The driver punched again. But the target still huddled on his chair.

'Until he falls!' Tondi shouted.

The driver hit again with similar results until finally, when he hit as hard as he could, the target fell.

The other drivers also punched as hard as they could. Some kicked. It was getting late. They wanted to go home, so they left the driver sprawled on the workshop floor, covered in piss, his face bloody, his body smeared with old oil. There was a stink of ammonia and urine. The driver was left there and the workshop locked from outside.

Night had enveloped Jakarta. That was a management lesson Tondi-style. He never knew how to give lectures about the need for honesty and loyalty in business. He fists gave the lessons. For all the drivers.

He used the same management method with any pimps causing Mami Ana trouble. The city was on the move with the wheels of Four Friends taxis, while beneath the surface there was secret lovemaking and the sweat of bodies hunting pleasure. So Jakarta got to know Tondi as the manager of a transport business, but in its underbelly he went it alone. Both hard worlds, requiring iron fists.

Chapter 17

Month passed into month as Tondi pursued his two worlds. When he was at the office of the transport company, he was the model young man carrying out his duties in an orderly and diligent way. Particularly when Mrs Sunarya was around. There, he was still Tondi, the sincere young man she had always known. She would never imagine that he also lived in a completely different world. Even more so Mrs Habinsaran, who would come from Bandung to visit the office now and then. She did not know that Tondi had operations that were much more violent than anything her husband was up to. In his official police role, Habinsaran was merely a protector to some Batak thugs at the bus and train station, whereas Tondi was directly managing a group of youths who were filling Jakarta with violence.

He got to know the youths at the workshop, the bus terminal, and the transport stops. Most of them were Batak or from Ambon. He drew them in by offering more regular work than just making it on their own. His activities involved rich people. He found female escorts who were taken to various hotels. If the young men taking them there were dressed well, the women were safer. Safety was important. Hotel security would not treat them badly.

Then there was debt collection. This turned out to be a real business opportunity. Many businesses were reluctant to use legal processes to collect debt. Some said that to reclaim a debt of 2000 rupiah, you had to fork out 3000 by the time you paid the police, the judge and the court. Better to spend 500 without as much mucking around.

This business operated in two ways, the right hand of generosity, the left hand of iron. Tondi thought nothing of giving rewards to his staff who worked well. Not just money, but perhaps entertainment with Mami Ani's girls. Sleeping with a woman usually only for elite use was an extraordinary bonus.

On the other hand, Tondi was strict. He knew how to give orders to his staff. Batak youth were sent to the right places, as were the Ambonese. When they confronted their clients, speaking their own regional languages, things went more smoothly. But if demands got nowhere, Tondi felt no compunction about stepping in himself if necessary.

And so it went. Who would have believed that at just twenty-five, he had assets worth tens of millions of rupiah at a time when a house cost about 5 million. All in just two years. His business with Mami Ani had expanded, and they now had hundreds of girls working for them and living in three houses he had bought. Mami Ani's loyalty was further ensured at their appointments in bed. The young steer was not only generous with money, but he gave her energy and made her feel young. Her face was always bright. Indeed, satisfaction in bed is what everyone craves. So what else did she need except to be loyal to this young man?

One day, Tondi met Mrs Sunarya.

'Tomorrow I'm going to Medan. I'll be there for a few days,' he said.

'This is very sudden. Has anything happened?'

'No. I just want to see some friends. I suddenly thought of them,' Tondi said.

'Sure.'

Yes, it was sudden. He had been lying lazily beside Mami Ana when, like a lightning flash, the image of Habibah had appeared before him. Then Masrul. What was happening with them?

Since then, he had not been able to get the image of them out of his head. Tondi believed in his intuition. Something bad must be happening. He was never troubled with any images of his mother, and so he trusted that she was well in Pekanbaru. He had no urge to see her.

He departed from Kemayoran airport and flew to Medan. Usually only high-ranking officials would fly. It was a new Garuda aircraft which meant it was a direct flight and did not have stopovers, as in the past.

Medan. He was not sure how it would have changed. As he came out of the terminal, taxi drivers came rushing up to him, but he deliberately chose an older driver who stood apart from the group.

'I want to hire the car. How much per hour?' Tondi asked.

The driver mentioned a sum. Tondi did not bargain, just nodded. They went to the car in the parking lot. Tondi sat in front.

'We're going to Lubuk Paham. But let's eat first,' he said. The driver nodded.

The car sped on, the windows open, wind in the car. The sun was beginning to set. Although there were not many cars on the road, drivers would not give way. There were no traffic lights at the crossroads, and the traffic was jammed. Strangely, on the open road the drivers from Medan were courteous and would give way to oncoming traffic. In the city, however, they were like maniacs. There was a cacophony of car horns.

Tondi did not have the exact address. He remembered only a few details that had been mentioned in passing. The house he was looking for was in the Perbuangan area, near a plantation office. That office would surely be a large, imposing building. So the search was for a small house nearby.

After going past a few streets, entering one alleyway after another and asking left and right, finally someone pointed out Masrul and Habibah's house. The car stopped in the alleyway. There was nowhere to pull to the side.

Tondi got out and walked towards the house.

A woman looked, squinting against the setting sun. Orange light from behind revealed Tondi's silhouette. The woman tried to work out who it was. She bit her sweet pale lip. Her mouth began muttering. If Tondi could hear, she was murmuring:

'God, God, God, are my eyes deceiving me?' she rubbed her eyes to sharpen her gaze. Still, she was not sure. They had only met once, and that was in the dark of night on a bus journey to Padang Sidempuan. But she had felt that young man's face in the dark. This man here looked much more adult, but the line of his face had not changed. And she remembered vividly his whispered voice.

Was this really him? How could it be?

They gazed at each other for what seemed an incalculable time. Tondi came closer. He found a woman weak and pale.

'Kak Habibah . . .' he greeted her. That voice. The vibration of that voice struck her eardrums.

She fell. Tondi caught her by the shoulders. A slim body. Thin. Soft as a wilting banana leaf. She sobbed.

'Where's Uda Masrul?'

'Inside,' she replied, her crying exploding into wails.

Supporting her by the shoulders, Tondi led her inside the house. Not fit to be called a house. Just one room in a row of houses.

Masrul was lying on a wooden-frame bed. He was covered with a faded piece of chequered cloth, full of holes. Tondi remembered his small body. But now he was just like an empty sack.

'Uda Masrul,' Tondi took Masrul's hand from under the cloth.

Masrul slowly opened his eyes.

'Is that you, Tondi?' Then he closed his eyes again. 'Ah that dream again . . .'

'This is not a dream, Uda,' Tondi said. He massaged the fingers that were as thin as chicken feet.

Masrul opened his eyes again. A sense of feeling came into his fingers.

'You're here, Tondi?'

'Yes, I'm here.'

Masrul closed his eyes again. Tears flowed down the creases of his hollow face.

Seeing the state of the room, Tondi understood at once why Masrul was lying here, and not in hospital. He kept on massaging Masrul's fingers.

Suddenly there was a banging on the door.

'Hey, you. Where's your debt payment?' a man yelled.

Habibah jumped to her feet to meet the two men at the door.

'I'm sorry, we can't pay yet,' she replied, trembling.

'Don't give us that!' The voice of one man. There were two of them. The other one just looked around like a vulture examining the tiny room.

'This has gone on too long. Do you know how much interest you've got to pay now?' One of the men opened a tall ledger commonly used by loan sharks.

'Yes, yes, yes, we will pay as soon as my husband can work again,' Habibah's voice stuck in her throat.

Tondi got up slowly.

'What's going on here?' he asked.

The two loan sharks, faced with a young man, tall, broad-shouldered, square-jawed, with the look of a legendary Batak warrior, backed off.

'This, this . . .'

'Do you think it's right to bang on the door? There's an invalid here,' Tondi said calmly.

'But, but, but . . .'

Tondi's fist flew. His target had no time to duck. Somehow, Tondi managed to get them both. They could only hold their hot cheeks. They stumbled backwards out of the room.

Tondi followed them. In what was left of the twilight, the two men could see they were faced with a figure with a reddish face, pitch black hair and a threatening gleam in his eye. He was very tall. They only came up to his shoulders.

'How much do they owe?' Tondi demanded.

One of them opened the book, then stuttered out a figure.

'Right. I'll pay it.'

Tondi pulled out some money.

'Done. Don't you ever bother them again. Give me that book.'

Tondi tore out the page. The instant he flung the ledger back to the two men, they took off.

Without a word, Tondi picked Masrul up and carried him to the car. Habibah was beside them, together with a boy aged about seven or eight.

The driver knew the way to the plantation hospital.

'I'll cover the costs whatever they are. Here's the deposit,' Tondi said before the receptionist at the hospital had a chance to say a word. He pulled out rolls of 1000-rupiah notes, the largest denomination, and put them on the receptionist's desk.

'Yes, yes. Please complete the form,' she said.

The receptionist felt intimidated by the gleam in Tondi's eyes. His protruding forehead and deep-set eyes gave his gaze a particularly piercing look. His forehead and eyes were also what Habibah remembered so well. She glanced at him sideways, but seeing the way he was caring for Masrul made her reproach herself. And she turned her gaze to her son standing beside her.

Masrul was taken by stretcher to the ward. He did not let go of Tondi's hand until they arrived at the ward door.

Slowly, Tondi sat down on the long bench in the veranda outside the ward. Habibah and her son sat beside him, all without speaking, the silence broken only by the sound of hurrying footsteps passing by them.

'Thank you, Tondi,' Habibah then said.

'It's nothing,' Tondi replied. 'I should've looked for you both earlier.'

'Uda Masrul often talks about you. I don't know how long you were together, but you're the only one he ever talks about. I don't know why he misses you so much, but it's more than his family. He never talks about his family.'

Tondi was jolted back to his senses.

'Is this your son? Where are the other children?' he asked.

Habibah nodded. Her feet were scraping the floor tiles.

'This is the youngest?'

Habibah nodded.

'And the others?'

'In different places. Staying with family. I don't know how they are.'

'If I remember correctly, they're all girls?'

'Yes, this is the only boy,' Habibah's voice quavered. She stroked the boy's head. Then she took out a coin from her bag and handed it to him.

'Here, go and get yourself something to eat,' she said.

Tondi realized the situation. He pulled some notes from his pocket and gave them to the boy. The boy's eyes shone as he saw the money. He had probably never in his life touched a note worth as much as this. Or perhaps he was thinking of all the food he could buy. He was definitely hungry. He gave the coin back to his mother and ran off down the corridor.

Habibah took a deep breath and leaned back on the bench.

'He's my only son. His name is Tando,' she said, her voice quavering even more, almost gasping. 'He was born when I was in Sidempuan. Uda Masrul was away with the PRRI. He loves him dearly. A relative offered to adopt him, but Masrul wouldn't think of it. "Even if I have to die in poverty, I'll never give that boy to anyone else." That's what he often says.'

Tears were flowing down her pale cheeks. Her lips were trembling, as though they wanted to say something more, but the words were stuck in her throat. Her chest heaved. Her brow furrowed as she tried to hold back her sobs, her bowed head rocking with the effort. Holding back tears seemed to be causing her more pain.

'But Uda Masrul often said that he wanted you to care for the boy,' Habibah said, unaware that she was grasping his arm now, 'even though he did not know where you were.' Then her sobs burst through.

'Hush now,' Tondi said, 'don't be sad. We'll look after Uda Masrul until he is well again. Then we'll organize things so that all of you can have a better life.'

Her grasp of Tondi tightened; her flowing tears like an electrical charge entering Tondi's body.

'Tondi, why are you so kind to Uda Masrul? And why does he miss you so much?'

'I don't know, Kak Habibah. We got to know each other towards the end of the PRRI war. It wasn't for long, but for some reason I felt I had to protect him. I loved him. I don't have any family, so I think of him as my family. Probably more than family.'

And memories of their rocking in the depths of Tapanuli flashed to his mind. Those cold nights. Embracing each other in the search for warmth in the midst of the thick blanket of mist of Lubukraya mountain. The intimacy between bodies that bonded feeling. The touch of skin that spread love into every pore. Male bodies united as one, does this also establish loyalty? Can the life spirit, the tondi, also unite with another? Is that why he could sense the suffering of this man even though they were thousands of kilometres apart?

'Do you ever think of me, Tondi?' the question suddenly jolted him. It jolted not only Tondi, but also seemed to pounce on Habibah herself. She felt embarrassed. At this very moment when her husband was lying in hospital, how could she even say such a thing?

She let go her grip and dropped her hand. Tondi reached for her hand. Her palm was rough, from days of working as a laundress. She became more embarrassed and tried to withdraw her hand. Tondi held her hand fast in his.

She broke out in sobs again. This time she nestled into Tondi's chest, as though trying to hide there. Sobs still racked her body and the recesses of Tondi's heart.

Ah, this woman had experienced only bitterness in her life. Tondi looked down at her head resting on his chest, at her hair covered in her veil, and memories of that bus journey in the night flooded back. His youth had then found its haven in the body of this woman. His first time. His youth broke for this woman. And then again and again throughout the night, as though he was charged with an electric current, or maybe because he knew the short time he

had. The first woman Tondi had known and who had touched his
body. Was that a wedding night?

Tondi raised her face. It was wet with tears. There were fine
lines at the corner of her eyes. But her oval face, her deeply set eyes,
her thick eyebrows, her long eyelashes, her sensuous lips; none of
that had changed. Only that sharp look in her eyes had gone, leaving
just a dim light. She reminded Tondi of an Indian film star.

Tondi used his finger to wipe the tears off her face. She bit his
finger gently, using his finger to quell her crying so it would not
escape her mouth. Tondi left his finger in her grip. Time passed.
They were silent. Both jumped when the boy appeared and said:

'Ma?'

Habibah let go. She moved away from Tondi and wiped the
tears from her face.

'Did you have something to eat, son? Was it good?' Habibah
tousled her son's hair. She looked at Tondi's face, then at her son.

So it was that Tondi arranged for Masrul to get the best
treatment. Yet it seemed it was not the hospital treatment that cured
him. Meeting Tondi was the strongest cure. Their clenched hands
made him strong. And the promise that he would return for him and
bring them all to Jakarta. That was the most effective medicine of all.

Tondi left some money for Habibah to pay the hospital. Enough
to pay their debts and for her to fetch her other children from her
relatives as soon as Masrul was out of hospital.

Tondi would come back and bring them all to Jakarta. He would
find a house. Masrul would work for Tondi.

Chapter 18

This latest war turned out to be not as big as the others. The liberation of West Irian did not involve open warfare, even though there had been preparations for large-scale assault by sea and air. During the operation, the Mandala Command based in Sulawesi dropped small numbers of troops into Irian.

The confrontation with the Dutch in Irian called Operation Trikora was launched in December 1961. It ended in August 1962 after negotiations, facilitated by the United States, were held between Indonesia and Holland. During the operation, Major Sunarya was often sent to Makassar to supervise logistics and personnel. He would stay there for weeks at a time and rarely returned home to Jakarta. Things calmed down when, in 1963, the United Nations finally handed the government of West Irian to Indonesia.

Major Sunarya had thought that the end of this conflict would give him leisure time. He did return home to Jakarta. The transport business was going well. If he were so inclined, he now had enough to give some 'facilitation money' to his superiors at headquarters to enable him to go to the army staff and command school. But it turned out that he was busy back at work. Or perhaps he was too honest. Tondi often heard him chatting with Habinsaran:

'If my superiors cannot see for themselves that I'm a good candidate for command school, then so be it. Why give bribes?'

'But these are the times,' Habinsaran would say. 'You're still stuck in the revolution days when everyone was fighting without personal ambition. Just look around you at headquarters. They're all living well. No one can manage on salary alone.'

'My life journey will stop with major,' Sunarya replied calmly. 'That's enough for me. My family is healthy, my kids can go to school. That's enough.'

Habinsaran did not push further. Especially because the political situation in Jakarta was heating up. Almost every day, there were public meetings and mass gatherings. There were posters and banners all over town, most of them posted by nationalist or leftist organizations who gave enthusiastic support to President Sukarno's speeches. Quotes from the speeches would appear on posters, banners and scrawled on walls everywhere: 'Live or Die, support Bung Karno!'

Now the enemy was not the Dutch, but the country next door. President Sukarno opposed the formation of Malaysia, which was a collection of federated Malay kingdoms on the Malay Peninsula, together with the British colonies of Sabah and Sarawak in Borneo. Bung Karno's speeches incited the people of Indonesia to fight the British and Malaysia. Indonesians were angry with Malaysia. In September 1963, there were anti-Indonesia demonstrations in Kuala Lumpur and an attack on the Indonesian Embassy. People there tore up photos of President Sukarno and removed Indonesia's state emblem, which they carried to Prime Minister Tunku Abdul Rahman and asked him to trample on it. Indonesia's newspapers published photos of it from the foreign press.

Anger flared in Indonesia at this act of humiliation. Mass organizations took turns to hold demonstrations, which always ended with burning effigies of Tunku Abdul Rahman. The climax came in May 1964 when President Sukarno declared war on

Malaysia with the operation called 'Crush Malaysia'. Once again, army headquarters was busy preparing troops.

All this activity in Jakarta was good for the Four Friends business. Now it not only had its taxis, but also three buses for hire. Habinsaran, with his government connections, had managed to get a quota of the Robur buses imported from Eastern Europe. They ran on diesel and were smaller than the city's existing buses, so they could get into smaller streets and travel wider routes.

Jakarta was filled with the noise of loud speakers on the buses hired by the demonstrators. They would drive around the city after a mass meeting at the stadium. Tondi did not care about their causes. What was important to him was that they paid the bus hire.

Sunarya was preoccupied with his daily work at army headquarters. With all the preparations for the Malaysia operation, he rarely came home. Whenever Habinsaran came to Jakarta, Sunarya had no time to meet him. In the past they would make a lunch appointment and talk over business plans, which they would then tell their wives. Now this was impossible. Forget about the three of them going out to eat. Even getting take-away food to eat together at home was a rare occurrence. So Habinsaran would eat with Tondi, just the two of them. They would go to a Sumatran or Chinese restaurant together.

Habinsaran opened a newspaper someone had left on the table. Tondi never read newspapers.

'Now this general here I find rather odd,' Habinsaran said, pointing at a photo. Tondi leaned over and looked at the newspaper. There was an army man with one gold star on his shoulder. Tondi's heart sent a rush of cold blood through his body. But he controlled himself.

'What's so strange, Lae?' Tondi asked, feigning nonchalance.

'I don't know him. From his name you can tell he's Batak but he doesn't use his marga name. That's odd.'

'So what? I don't use my marga name either,' Tondi said.

'Yes, but I know your marga. What's more, you mix with other Batak. We all know each other's marga and how to relate.'

Habinsaran scrutinized the photo in the newspaper again.

'This man has never participated in any gathering of Batak people in Jakarta. Look at me. I have to come all the way from Bandung, but I always try to attend any gathering. Especially a funeral or a wedding.'

Tondi kept his gaze fixed on the food on the table. He took some *dadih*, the tofu-like buffalo-milk squares. They were so soft they just flowed down your throat.

'And it's not just that,' Habinsaran went on. 'It's also never been clear to me where he works and what his position is. Whenever there is a ceremony with President Sukarno he's always there, even though he's not an adjutant or a member of Cakrabirawa, the palace guard.'

'How do you know that, Lae?' Tondi asked.

'Well, Cakrabirawa have a special uniform. They're always neat, as though they're off to a reception. I must ask Sunarya about him one of these days. He knows all the army personnel close to Sukarno.'

'And if you find out, then what? Do you want to ask him to invest in our business,' Tondi joked.

'Ah, come on. I'm just curious. Surprised, that's all, that there's someone in the army at the rank of Brigadier General who's often in the newspaper and talks politics non-stop. What's the army doing attending general meetings of workers unions,' Habinsaran said.

They began to eat. While eating, Tondi read the newspaper. That general had given a speech at a general meeting of some mass organization, and he was quoted in the newspaper: 'The importance of "retooling" in state institutions, particularly in the army.'

Whatever 'retooling' meant. He had never heard of it. So he asked Habinsaran.

'Well, it's a kind of cleansing in an organization,' Habinsaran replied.

'What does "cleansing" mean?'

'Cleaning the place up. Firing people.'

'So what's new about that?'

'Well, "retooling" used to be the word for getting rid of staff who were corrupt. Now it's for anti-revolutionaries.'

'Anti-revolutionaries?'

'If you don't support Sukarno, you're fired.'

'Support how?'

'Doing whatever he wants, of course. Right now, for instance, it's "Crush Malaysia". You have to support it. But what has Malaysia got to do with us? If the nation of Malaysia is formed, why would that be so bad for us? Or if it is not, why would that be good? Our economy is a total mess. Meanwhile Sukarno is busy giving speeches. His followers support him no matter what.'

Tondi chewed his food slowly. Unusually for him, he had no appetite. He didn't even crunch the fish head cooked in a spicy tomato sauce.

'Oh, by the way, Lae,' Habinsaran said, 'if our business has cash earnings, don't hold on to it too long. Buy things we need for the vehicles. It's better to store materials than money. If necessary, buy gold and keep it in the safe, or exchange rupiah for American dollars.

Tondi looked up, surprised.

'Lae, you really need to read the papers. You should know the changes going on. Like right now, the value of the rupiah will continue to fall. Something you buy today for 1000 rupiah is going to cost you 1500 in a few days' time. That's what we call inflation.'

Tondi nodded absent-mindedly.

'I know, the papers are boring,' Habinsaran went on. 'Just look, page one is all quotes from speeches. But in the inside pages there's sometimes news about the rise in price of some spare part, or information about the dollar exchange rate.'

Tondi was silent. His eyes stared in the direction of the paper. That person in the photo was disturbing him. A man so close yet at such a distance with no path of connection. It dragged him to an image of his mother. How was his mother over there in Pekanbaru?

It said in the newspaper that Brigadier General Pardomutua attended a meeting of the workers union that was linked to the Indonesian communist party. The workers union had made a unanimous declaration that it stood behind the great leader of the revolution, Bung Karno, and its members were prepared to volunteer for the Crush Malaysia campaign. Then followed the speech, blah, blah, blah. Tondi did not want to read it.

He had no tie to Pardomutua, let alone to the Crush Malaysia campaign. All his thoughts were for his mother. He missed her. Sadly, the food stall was quiet. It was at moments like these that he wanted to hear some of the old Batak favourites the buskers always sang.

When he finished eating, he and Habinsaran parted. Habinsaran went back to Bandung, and Tondi to the house that was the centre of his business enterprise. It was quiet. There was only the servant. Tondi rarely went there, and only if there was a problem and he had to meet his staff. He lived elsewhere, or he would sleep at Mami Ani's place. Most often he would go to the office of the Four Friends, because running a fleet of taxis and buses was less complicated. He always had to be ready to help Mrs Sunarya.

Masrul and his family lived in a separate section of the house. Tondi had given him work helping out with accounts. His emaciated body had filled out, but his thin face still showed lines of suffering. Masrul was diligent at his work, recording the income of Mami Ana's business, and collecting debts. Tondi trusted him completely.

When Masrul heard the sound of the car entering the yard, he rose from where he had been sitting at the desk in the office, studying a thick ledger. He went to the door and greeted Tondi. Habibah looked over and saw Tondi disappear into the house.

'How're things, Uda?' Tondi asked.

'Everything's fine.'

'Have you eaten?'

'Yes.'

'And the children, all well I hope?

'Alhamdulillah, yes they're all well,'

'Glad to hear it.'

The servant brought them some hot coffee. Sidikalang, Tondi's favourite.

Leaning back in the chair, Tondi looked out at the yard. He could see Habibah in the window, stock-still, and could hear the sound of teenage laughter within.

Whenever Tondi thought of his mother, his heart melted. Strangely, when he thought of her, he also thought of Habibah and her children. Maybe because he had no brothers and sisters, the sound of children cheered him. Masrul and Habibah's four children, three girls and a boy. The girls were teenagers now.

Tondi sniffed his steaming coffee, then slurped it.

'Why don't we all go out for a drive, you, Habibah and the kids,' he said.

Masrul jolted in surprise.

'Great. The children wanted to go out,' he said.

'Let's go to Pasar Baru. Go and get them all,' Tondi said. Masrul went at once, and Tondi could hear the kids shrieking when they were told.

Pasar Baru was the largest shopping complex in Jakarta. Most of the shops sold clothes, including imported clothing. Masrul came back to Tondi.

'Why aren't you getting ready too?' Tondi asked.

'Why don't you just take Habibah and the kids? Seven in a car is enough. It'll be too squashed if I come too,' Masrul said.

'You can sit on each other's knees,' Tondi laughed.

'No, it's fine. I've still got some work to do.'

Habibah and the children lined up beside the car. Three girls aged seventeen, fifteen and thirteen, and a boy.

'Fine, then,' Tondi said as he went to the car.

'Mak can sit in front, and you kids in the back,' Tondi said, using the children's term for their mother to refer to Habibah.

Habibah's face flushed. She felt uneasy sitting in front, like a young girl going out on a date. But she came to her senses when the kids started fooling around behind her, and one of them accidentally knocked her head.

Tondi and Habibah walked along the footpath and went into one of the shops.

'Choose whatever you want,' Tondi said.

'Really, anything?' the eldest girl asked.

'Shhh,' her mother said.

'Yes, anything. You go and choose for yourselves,' Tondi said. The four children ran off looking at the shop window displays.

Now Habibah was left standing awkwardly beside this man. She only came up to his shoulder. He was so tall. Not like when they were on the Sibualbuali bus. He was not this tall back then.

She bit her lip, trying to quell the uneasy feeling in her chest. Standing so near was making her heart beat fast. She turned to look at the things around her.

'Kak Habibah, please choose anything you need,' Tondi said.

'Thank you, but I'm fine,' Habibah said, nervously.

'Well, I'll just have to choose something for you then,' Tondi said and walked off.

Habibah stood alone as the store bustled around her. No, he doesn't remember that night on the bus, she said to herself. He's here not because of me, but because of his closeness with Masrul. Why does this feeling taunt me so? How is it possible that just one night can remain so vivid forever in your memory? Is it because I think of him whenever I look at my son? These questions kept going round and round her head. And when I met him back then, I was nearly thirty and he was only sixteen or seventeen. Why do I keep thinking of him?

Habibah was lost in thought as she gripped the side of the window display. She did not hear the shop attendant speaking to her.

Tondi paid for all the shopping.

'This is for you, Kak Habibah,' Tondi said as he handed her the package.

'What is it?' Habibah asked.

'Clothes. But I don't know if you'll like them,' Tondi said, chuckling.

It was getting late. Tondi took them all to eat grilled fish at the beach. The children's bright faces calmed Habibah's unease. Especially her son. He was hugging a shoe box and a toy. His dark, black eyes shone whenever he looked at Tondi.

Tondi deposited that joy back at their house, with the children busily opening their parcels.

As he was driving, questions kept coming into his mind. When he had seen that photo of his father Pardomutua in the newspaper, he had felt a surge of anger. But why should he be angry? After all, he did not have to have any connection with him. It was just that seeing that photo made him think of his mother. His inang, whom his father had left. And strangely, when he thought of his mother, Habibah came into his head. That long night bus trip, but it felt so fleeting. Habibah, slim and rosy faced, especially after a few sips of that toddy from the Chinese man's stall in Siantar. Was it the warmth of that sweet toddy that had made her forget her husband, and turn him into a man?

It was the image of Habibah under the batik cover on the bus, Tondi thought, that made him speed to Mami Ana's house. He felt as though he was in a whirlpool, swirling from the memory of his mother, to the urge to see Habibah's face, and now here he was ending up with Mami Ana. Habibah was his friend's wife; well, not just a friend, but his lover. So he tried to get rid of the images by gushing them away, surprising Mami Ana with the force of his eruption.

Tondi's longing for his mother was not only because of his father's photo in the newspaper. He always trusted his instincts. There must be something going on. So he booked a flight to Padang, then chartered a car to Pekanbaru. It was a British car, a Land Rover. He had no idea how the owner had managed to buy a car like this.

It was not difficult to find his mother's address in Pekanbaru. He went to the market and looked around for someone who spoke with a Batak accent. From her he found out where his mother would probably be. She seemed to be well known among Batak people in Pekanbaru.

He stood in front of the house for a few minutes, looking at the old woman before him. Inang. Wisps of white hair framed her face. At the same moment, she fixed her gaze on him. Her heart leapt to her mouth. That man standing there. It was as if Pardomutua had reappeared from all those decades ago. Tall, sturdy, square-jawed, with sharp eyes.

'Inang,' Tondi said.

'*Ho doi*, Tondi?' she replied, speaking in Batak. 'Is that you, Tondi?'

'Yes, Mother,' Tondi replied.

It had been nine years. She sobbed as her son embraced her. The sound of sobbing brought a young woman out of the house.

'What's the matter?' she asked, stopping in her tracks. Then they all entered the house.

All these years, his mother had carried on her trading business. She bought things like clothing, perfume and imported watches from Singapore. The business brought a good profit because such goods were scarce. The government strictly controlled imports because of the foreign exchange problem. The wealthy elite, however, wanted luxury goods.

'Oh, this is Lasmia. Maybe you've forgotten her, Tondi. She's Luhut's daughter. She's keeping me company here.'

Tondi nodded. He just wanted to know how his mother's life had been. He looked around. The living room was large. There was an expensive sofa, a large radio and a record turntable on top of a sideboard. It looked as though she was doing well.

'But now trade has stopped. Everything from Singapore is banned. Anything sent is confiscated at the dock. You can be sure the army sells it there.'

The whole coast of Sumatra was under close surveillance. The army was everywhere. Confrontation with Malaysia had put an end to all activity with Singapore and the Malay Peninsula.

'So I'm opening a shop,' she went on.

'Inang, don't you think it would be better to move to Jakarta?' Tondi asked.

'Now what would I do there? I like it here. Lasmia is at school here—her last year of senior high-school. She should have finished school by now, but she had to stop junior high-school for a while because her father could not pay. When I heard about that, I asked her to come here. When she finishes school, I'll send her to university in Medan. And to think I could not afford to pay for your schooling, Tondi.'

'Don't think about that, Inang. Even though I didn't finish high school, the important thing is that I could work,' Tondi replied. He knew that his mother was deliberately changing the topic. She did not want to hear the name Jakarta, because it would bring memories of her husband leaving her.

'Where are you working now, Tondi?' she asked.

Tondi looked at Lasmia as she prepared drinks and cakes on the table and then took some to the driver who was sitting outside on the veranda.

'Transport business, Inang,' he replied. He gave her a summary of what he thought was important. His time was limited. He had only wanted to check on his mother, but seeing the situation, he felt that all was well.

'What kind of shop, Inang?' he asked.

'A clothing shop. Nothing big.'

'Do you need any extra capital?'

'What for? We have enough. I have four staff working for me. Lasmia helps with the accounts.'

Tondi and the driver slept the night at his mother's house. So it hadn't been his mother's problems pulling him back after all. What was it then?

Early the next morning, the car left Pekanbaru and headed towards Bangkinang and on to Pasir Pangarayan. This Land Rover was amazing. It ran so smoothly and flew like the wind.

They went on the road towards South Tapanuli. Tondi had not been in these parts during the PRRI time. Where was he headed now?

In Sidempuan they looked for the place to stay owned by the man of the Harahap marga. So many years had passed. The old bus station was still there.

This was a trip down memory lane, but Tondi had no chance to relax. The owner of the guesthouse was not at home. A worker said he had gone away to attend a ceremony of his marga. There was no one to chat to except the driver, and he had already gone off to his room to sleep.

They left in the morning, heading for Sipirok, then cut across the hills towards Sarulla. He remembered the path at the edge of the mountain, and a coffee plantation.

Longgom. Where are you now? The Land Rover engine roared as they climbed the dirt road.

He found Sibalok and his wife. The old couple was astounded, eyes starting out of their heads, their mouths agape.

'Is it you, Tondi,' Sibalok said, approaching.

'Yes, Amang,' Tondi said.

The old man took Tondi by the hand and drew him into the house.

'Make some coffee, make some coffee,' he said to his wife.

The old woman blew on the embers in the hearth using a bamboo tube.

Tondi looked around. Sibalok took a deep breath and sighed.

'She's gone,' he said.

Tondi was shaken.

'After her husband died three years ago, she said she wanted to leave. I asked her, where to? She said anywhere. She'd die if she stayed here. "I do not want my child to die here," she said.'

'Child?'

Their eyes met briefly.

'Yes, she gave birth to a boy,' the old man said, mumbling.

'Where is the boy?'

'She took him with her.'

Now Tondi took a deep breath, inhaling the cold mountain air. He was calculating.

'So would the child be about six now?' he asked hesitantly.

'That's right,' Sibalok said slowly. He was scratching the floor with the stem of his pipe.

'Where can I find them?'

The old man shrugged his shoulders. An expression of desperation.

So this whole journey had been pointless. Tondi felt desperate too. This meant that the magnet that had drawn him here was that young woman's suffering, the young woman who had been the beauty of her village but married off to her relative and plunged into deep sadness. Her wedding night should have been one of happiness, but her husband had been affected by black magic and gone mad. For years she had a husband in name only.

She had found happiness under a full moon, a wedding night enveloped in the passion of a young man at war.

'What's the boy called?'

'Tarsingot.'

'What?'

'Yes, Longgom called him Tarsingot.'

Tarsingot, a Batak word for memory, especially a deep memory in the heart.

Tondi felt a stab in his chest. He did not dare raise his eyes to meet those of the two old people all alone now in the coffee plantation, far from their village, far from their daughter.

When he left, the old woman took Tondi by the hand and said to him in the local dialect:

'I will pray for you daily at each of the five prayer times, for your health and safety, just as I pray for Longgom.'

Tears flowed down her wrinkled cheeks.

Tondi remembered his mother had held his hand like this when he said goodbye to her in Pekanbaru, and had said the same thing, but for her Christian prayers.

'My prayers are for you whenever I go to church, Tondi.'

And if his grandfather Ompu Silangit were still alive, he would say the same. His prayers to the *Debata di Banua Ginjang*, the Lord of the World Above, would surely be heard and answered.

Chapter 19

Tondi had fought one battle after another to control the jungle of Jakarta. He had given the transport firm his best. He thought of Sunarya and his wife as his parents, and family was his life. The firm had bought the rented house at Kalibata. The yard of the house was not large enough for all the taxis, so they purchased land to use for parking.

Tondi had a new habit now. He read newspapers. He still did not like reading about general X or official Y and what they said. None of that was of any use to him running the business. How could loyalty to the revolution be of use in finding spare parts? And anyway, his experience wandering in the forest during the rebellion, and especially those daily speeches from his commander, Bagio, had given him a negative opinion of Sukarno.

For the Crush Malaysia campaign, Sukarno had given a speech:

'Pray for me. I am about to leave for the battlefield as a patriot and as a bullet of the nation that refuses to have its self-respect trampled upon. Yell, yell to every corner of the land, that we will unite to fight this insult, we will take our revenge, and we will show that we still have strong teeth and bones and still have self-respect. Come on, crush . . . crush Malaysia!'

Blah-blah-blah. Just words. Tondi didn't even know what 'crush' meant. But he did remember his commander Bagio saying, 'During the war for independence, Sukarno said he was going to lead a guerrilla war. Oh yeah? The minute the Dutch entered Yogya, he surrendered!'

'But at school we were taught that the Dutch army arrested him.' Tondi had countered.

'Surrender, or let yourself be arrested. To us in the army it was the same thing. Point is, he didn't fight!' Bagio had snarled. 'We were arrested only when we were surrounded and had run out of bullets.'

Tondi remembered this conversation vividly because Bagio had sprayed him with spit in the fury of his reply.

'If Sukarno had really wanted to lead a guerrilla war, he had an opportunity to get out of Yogya. General Sudirman, sick as he was, managed to get out and then lead guerrilla attacks.'

Speeches are meant for the people, to fire them up. Not Tondi. He scanned the newspapers looking for information about car prices. He discovered there were people close to the president who got special approval to establish car-assembly lines, locally assembling imported models that could then be sold cheaper than fully imported cars. It was time to upgrade the taxis, but it was unclear when these newer model cars would go on the market.

He did, however, find the information Habinsaran wanted. There was news about his father's position. It turned out that Pardomutua was in charge of a number of state enterprises that were formerly Dutch owned but had been nationalized. As manager of a state enterprise, he did not have to wear army uniform, with medals and emblems. That is why Habinsaran had been confused.

The state enterprises Pardomutua managed were huge. This explained why his name was often in the newspapers, not because of the enterprises he directed, but because of his attendance at meetings organized by mass organizations. These were huge meetings, held in stadiums. There was never any news about whether the enterprises he managed actually earned any profit. The newspaper coverage only quoted his speeches exhorting the workers to make sacrifices for their country.

The way Tondi saw it, workers and staff should not have to make sacrifices. Quite the opposite. Bosses should give them large salaries and even bonuses. Many of his workers had families now, and children attending school. His own experience having to leave school because his mother could not afford it had left an indelible impression on him. He wanted the people around him to be secure in their lives. He once heard a lecture about Islam on the radio: pay your workers before their sweat dries. Even though he was not Muslim, he appreciated that teaching. The most important thing was that your staff worked honestly. Masrul paid the workers weekly.

Even though Tondi did not follow his grandfather's ways, he too lived simply. He was never extravagant. His business with Mami Ana provided women for the nightclubs in Jakarta, but Tondi himself never set foot in them. He didn't drink alcohol, or if he did it was only rice wine as part of socializing with Batak friends. Back in his bus-conductor days, he did drink *samsu*, a sweet toddy to warm the body.

Tondi had just finished a meeting with his staff, and the room at the front of the house that he used for an office was empty. There were empty coffee cups and full ashtrays on the table. The servant brought in some fresh coffee for him. Masrul cleared the table and returned to the kitchen.

Tondi was stretched out on the sofa resting. Masrul sat beside him. He understood Tondi's tiredness. The long journey from Sumatra a few days earlier had left him exhausted.

He massaged Tondi's shoulders.

'How long will you wait, Tondi?' he asked.

'What are you talking about?'

'Marriage. When are you going to get married?'

'Not even thinking about it,' Tondi replied.

Masrul continued to massage Tondi's shoulders, then moved to his back.

'I want to say something, but please don't get mad, Tondi,' Masrul said softly.

'Why should I get mad? What is it?'

'Well, it's like this,' Masrul cleared his throat, 'it has to do with Habibah and me.'

Tondi sat up at once. 'Listen here. If you do anything to hurt Habibah, I will get mad.'

He turned to look at Masrul directly. Masrul bowed his head.

'I love Habibah,' he said, shakily.

'So what's wrong, then?'

Masrul stopped his massaging and leaned back. There were a few moments of silence.

'I've not been able to act as her husband for a long time. This started before I left to join the PRRI, I think. I knew she was hurt. I was hurting her,' Masrul's voice was halting.

Tondi was flabbergasted. He looked at the man sitting beside him, lost for words.

'I'm deeply grateful to Habibah for her loyalty. She has raised our children in the most difficult circumstances. I've never been with another woman. Only Habibah. She's like a friend to me, or a sister. But I no longer have feelings of a husband towards her.'

'How come?'

'When I was in the forest, especially when we were together, I felt that I found my true self. In our hardship in the forest back then, I felt joy. When you and I were together, I found extraordinary pleasure, not at all comparable to my experience with Habibah.'

Masrul's voice, now virtually a whisper, continued, 'It's like this, Tondi. When we were together in the forest I felt like my true self.'

Tondi was speechless, and uncomfortable.

'We cannot possibly have that again,' Masrul said. 'I understand that you were dragged into the situation back then. I know that was not your real self. And all I want right now is to care for my children. Also, to make Habibah happy, even though I know I cannot be her husband.'

Tondi did not move.

'I don't want Habibah to suffer. I know she is faithful. She would never have another man,' Masrul said.

Tondi focused hard on sipping his coffee.

'I would like her to be with you, Tondi,' Masrul suddenly blurted out, making Tondi jump.

'What nonsense you're talking, Uda,' Tondi's voice rose in pitch.

Masrul took Tondi's hand.

'I love her,' Masrul said. 'I don't want her to suffer. She's still young. She still needs it.'

Tondi shook his head. Then he stood up.

'You're talking rubbish, Masrul. Stop it. Stop all this!'

Tondi stepped outside and went to his car. He went directly home, not to Mami Ana. This time he had no magma to erupt, just tangled and blocked thoughts.

Masrul watched him go. Ah, if only he knew the conversation he had had just a few days ago, he thought. That night after the shopping trip, the conversation full of tears he had with Habibah.

* * *

They had been lying side by side on the big bed. Masrul's health had continued to improve since his treatment at the plantation hospital in Lubuk Pakam. But still he did not touch Habibah. When he first returned from fighting in the hills and was so ill, she had understood. But now they had spent months in Jakarta and he was still cold towards her. She herself was on fire, especially after seeing Tondi. That evening she and Tondi had walked side by side. In the car, his masculine smell seemed to assault her, and the memory of their night journey with the smell of diesel and the rocking bus had made her blood rush, and her body seem to burst with fluid.

So that night, she tried to get some warmth from Masrul, but there was no reaction. Finally, he said, weakly, 'I just can't do it, Bibah. I can't do it any more.'

Habibah was stunned.

'I feel like you. I'm attracted to men, Bibah.'

'What?' she was shocked.

'I still love you,' Masrul said. 'I don't know why I'm like this. During the war I became a soldier. Why? I suppose I wanted to prove myself as a man. When I married you, I thought I could be a man. I tried very hard to get rid of my feelings of attraction to men.

Habibah was silent.

'Now I must be honest with you. I don't want to hurt you. You're the person closest to me. I love our children. I want to be together with you and raise them together.'

Tears welled in Masrul's eyes, blurring his vision. Habibah took his hand. And she too let her tears fall. Masrul embraced her. They embraced each other. Then Masrul whispered, 'My feelings tell me that you're attracted to Tondi.'

Habibah jerked back, letting go of her embrace, but Masrul kept holding her tight.

'I have feelings like a woman, Bibah. I can sense your feelings.'

Habibah was sobbing in his embrace.

'I'd accept your being with Tondi, Bibah.'

'No, no, no,' Habibah's voice came in choking sobs.

'Only him, Bibah. No one else. I don't want you to play around. You're still the mother of my children. But I want you to enjoy life.'

They both cried. Embraced. Like sisters.

So, when Tondi's car left the house, Masrul went at once to Habibah.

'Have a shower. I'm taking you over to his house,' he said.

Habibah was bewildered and stood awkwardly. Masrul took her to the bathroom and undressed her. Habibah stood naked, her golden skin glowing under the light. Masrul took the dipper and poured the cool water over her, stroking her body until she was completely wet. He shampooed her long black hair. Then he soaped her carefully, every inch of her body.

He wrapped her in a towel and took her to the room. Habibah dried her hair. Masrul opened her closet and picked out some clothes for her. He chose her new clothes, the ones Tondi had bought a few days ago.

With his slim fingers, Masrul applied lipstick to his wife's lips.
He put some pink rouge on her cheeks to brighten her pale face. A little
eyeshadow. He dressed her long hair in a bun. Lastly, he dabbed some
perfume at the nape of her neck, behind her ears and on her breasts.

Habibah looked like a bride. Masrul was pleased with his work.
They stepped out of the house together. The children were playing
in the yard.

'Where are you going?' one of them asked. They others just
stared in amazement.

'Just going out for a bit,' Masrul said.

'But Mama's all dressed up,' the oldest daughter said. And she
was right. They looked so different. Habibah like a bride, and Masrul
in his ordinary old clothes, wearing shorts.

Habibah felt shy.

There was a car in the yard, the one usually used for business.
Right now, though, no one was chasing up payments. Masrul drove,
taking Habibah to Tondi's house. When they got there, he did not
drive the car into the yard.

'You go in,' Masrul said.

Habibah shook her head. She started to cry.

'Don't cry. You'll ruin your make up.'

Habibah still did not budge.

'I already told Tondi that you're coming.'

'Is that true? Did you really?'

Masrul nodded furiously, to convince her.

'What did he say?' Habibah asked.

'Don't worry. I've talked to him,' Masrul said, opening Habibah's
door and nudging her on.

Slowly, Habibah got out. Masrul shut the car door and drove off,
leaving her in front of the gate.

Habibah stood stiffly. The afternoon breeze was swirling dust
from the road. The breeze caught her headscarf. She stepped slowly
towards the door. She was too hesitant to knock, but how long could
she stand on the veranda? Finally, she knocked, the knocking was in
time with the beating of her wild heart.

The door opened. The figure of that man stood in front of her. She fixed her gaze straight, and it came up to his chest.

'Oh, Kak Habibah. Where's Uda Masrul?' Tondi looked around, perplexed. It was only her.

Habibah was confused. She could see the surprise in his eyes. She wanted to turn back. In a split second, Tondi understood what was going on. So this is what Masrul had meant.

He could see anxiety, confusion, embarrassment and acquiescence in her eyes. So he took her by the hand and drew her into the house.

Habibah shivered. It felt like an ice current was creeping down her back. She almost collapsed. Half pushing her, Tondi carried her into the room. He wanted to put her at ease. He gently kissed her cheek. A fragrance of perfume came from her body.

Tondi tried to calm her. He took off her headscarf and her long hair fell down her back. He whispered, 'I've missed you, Habibah.'

She trembled. Tondi had said her name. Just like that, with no 'Kak' before it. Then he undressed her. She trembled even more. When Tondi stroked her skin, it tickled. And even though he was only embracing her, her body felt ready to boil. She had never shuddered like this. And it was just a touch. Only an embrace. But she climaxed. Had Masrul's stroking and soaping of her body helped warm her blood? Or was it because of her pent-up longing over the last nine years?

The evening breeze parted the trees on the roadside and entered the room through the shutters. Habibah felt like she was flying, caught up in a dream. But it was real. The body in her embrace was muscular. When he moved inside her, his muscles went taut like a drawn bow. Then he let the hot arrows fly.

Now, lying on his chest, she said in a quiet sigh: 'Tando, the boy, he's your son Tondi.'

There, she had let it out. She had finally said it. Tondi was startled but kept calm and stroked Habibah's face.

'You're not surprised, Tondi?'

'No. I actually hoped that he was mine, Habibah.'

Habibah trembled again. Then she embraced Tondi tightly as though she wanted to unite her body with his.

'Does Uda Masrul know?' Tondi asked, his voice husky.

'Of course he knows. Tando looks just like you. And even before he went off to join the PRRI, we never had relations as husband and wife. But he just could not imagine it, because as far as he knew, you and I had not been together. How could it have happened? He saw Tando's birth as a miracle. He loves that boy, even more than the other children.'

So from then on, Habibah lived in a world she never imagined. By day she had a husband who was like a sister to her and who helped look after the children. At another place, a man she had always desired was now like the husband brought to her by Batak gods of old.

* * *

Wheels kept spinning on the city roads. Jakarta was noisy. The spirit of war was heating up. Newspapers were full of battles with the British army. Tondi watched television broadcasts. On the small black-and-white screen, he saw President Sukarno giving speeches at Senayan stadium. Full of passion and gestures. Every now and then he would raise his commando baton. The stadium was ringed with flags and banners. Flags fluttered, but on television they were all black and white.

The speeches did not interest Tondi. He just liked to look at the spectacle of all the noisy people in the stadium. And Bung Karno's style. Sometimes his face would fill the television screen. Sometimes there would be shots of the important people on the podium, near Bung Karno giving his speech. There were generals lined up. And yes, there was Pardomutua. He looked proud sitting there in his uniform with medals on his chest. Even with his sunglasses, Tondi could recognize him on the screen.

Tondi's daily travel involved going from the business office to the vehicle base. There were more and more taxis and buses to manage now, and drivers to be supervised. His debt-collecting business had also grown and was more complicated. Because of the declining economy, many businesspeople with debts left town and they had to be chased up.

Every now and then he would visit Mami Ana, but she was busier these days, too. The network she supervised now included almost every large hotel in Jakarta.

One day, when Tondi was visiting her, Mami Ani told him something she had heard.

'There's a Batak girl in the prostitution complex. Codot has forced her to work. She's pretty. She shouldn't be working there.'

This was a serious matter. Mami Ana's girls came from all over Java, from east to west. Maybe there were indeed Batak girls working in Jakarta, but not for Mami Ana. And working for that thug, Codot. Thugs working as pimps were the lowest of the low.

Tondi wanted to investigate. Even though he was relatively young, he was respected in Batak circles in Jakarta. A Batak should never work in a prostitution complex. He asked one of Mami Ana's staff to go and find Codot. Tondi got a straight story from him.

'A month ago, the market at Blok A burnt down.'

'Yes, I remember seeing it in the newspaper,' Tondi said.

'Well, this girl was helping out her relative there. Their kiosk burned down and they were in debt. They couldn't pay up. So that's what happened.'

'They're not actually in the complex yet?'

'No.'

'Now you listen here, Codot. I'm a Batak,' Tondi said. 'I will never allow any Batak to work as a whore in any complex around here. Got it? I'll pay their debts.'

Codot was happy to hear this and sent one of his staff to go and get the girl. Money changed hands.

Tondi did not see the woman standing in the doorway. She stood there for a while looking at the man who had called for her. She had been told that she had a client. But there was something about those eyes.

Tondi raised his head. He recognized that sharp gaze.

'Longgom!' he exclaimed. The word seemed almost to slap her. She recoiled.

Tondi stood and quickly took Longgom by the hand. She followed like a wilted banana leaf. He led her to the car, opened the door and pushed her in.

All this time she was silent. It was as though her senses had shut down. Tondi started the car.

Wheels turn. A journey in a whirlpool. He had gone all the way to Sarulla in Sumatra looking for her, and here she was all along in Jakarta, at Codot's place.

Tondi stopped the car at a restaurant. He had still said not a thing. He half-dragged, half-carried her inside to sit down. Then he ordered drinks. He looked at her carefully.

Longgom's head was bowed, but her blood was rushing, making her feel faint. This is the man I have been chasing in my dreams for years. This is the man I was hoping to meet, to introduce to my child before I die. Words were spinning inside her head.

Ah, this young woman with the calm face. The woman with light-brown skin, thick eyebrows, fine nose, holding layers of sadness. Tondi took her hand.

'Where have you been all this time?' he asked. 'I looked for you.' Still she was silent. Did not move. Did not cry. Solid.

'Where is your son?' Tondi asked. Longgom raised her head and looked directly at him.

'Do you want to meet him?' she asked.

'Yes, I do. I've already met your parents back at Sarulla.'

'You met them? Amang and Inang, are they well?'

Tondi nodded. Longgom now took Tondi's hand. There were tears in her eyes. The two looked at each other. That said it all.

Tondi took Longgom to her home in the southern part of Jakarta. The car could not enter the narrow alleyway. They had to walk. The clay surface was muddy.

They came to a bamboo-thatch house. Longgom lived there in a tiny, crowded space with a family of distant relatives. She had got to know them when on the boat to Jakarta. They were of the same marga. The only thing she had to take to Jakarta was her determination.

This was the first time Tondi met the boy. He remembered his name. Tarsingot. And, by the gods! He looked just like Tando, Habibah's boy. They are my sons. My sons. My blood runs in their bodies. Some of my spirit, my tondi, is in them.

Tondi arranged for Longgom to have a better life. That very day he sent one of his staff to find a shop for sale. She had to have a shop. Wheels turned, and now the person she had been working for, began working for her. At least for the time being, until she could have a kiosk again when the market was rebuilt.

Tondi spent the next few days helping organize the shop. It reminded him of his mother who was opening a clothing shop in Pekanbaru. The clothing business was not new to Longgom, either. The kiosk where she had been working had also sold clothes.

When Tondi was around, Longgom felt protected. He was actually younger than her. When they had first met, she had been twenty-six, and he only eighteen. But how much more adult he was now. How mature he was. Everyone he met seemed in awe of him. Even the tough types who worked for him seemed docile.

God must have sent him to me, and to Tarsingot, she thought. But she was also grateful to the world most people shunned. The world of Codot who peddled women's bodies. Without him, how would she ever have met Tondi in this huge city?

And yes, she was grateful to the quiet of the coffee plantation at the foot of the mountain and to the spirit of her late husband. Whether or not they had been husband and wife, they had been close, and he was still her cousin. When he had died, she had been sure she would meet Tondi, the father of her son. Maybe this was the belief of a crazy person, which is what her mother had said. Her father, though, did not dispel her conviction.

Now she wanted to pursue her life with Tarsingot. She wanted education. She wanted to achieve the best before one day returning to Sarulla.

That night, Tondi stayed in the new house where she had moved. In the evening, they had walked around Pasar Baru and then eaten at Pecenongan.

Tarsingot was tired. When they returned home, he went straight to sleep. Longgom put some water on to boil. Why was it taking so long? She could feel her pulse throbbing all through her body, and every now and then her face felt flushed. Would her second wedding night be tonight? The clink of cups jolted her back to reality, and she served the coffee. Her luminous eyes watched the man in front of her.

'I miss the coffee plantation,' Tondi said.

Longgom seized her chance. She took Tondi by the hand and pulled him to the room, hastily locking the door. She undressed him, hurriedly. Hurriedly. If in the plantation she had initially resisted letting herself go, now she was the one on the attack. She was like a pawing doe on heat. She pounced on Tondi and wound around him like a mythical dragon chasing the moon.

This is the husband the war brought to me. This is the Batak ulubalang the heavens sent. She sighed. This is the body I must melt into my skin. Embrace so tight it almost stops all breath. Breathing became an endless kiss.

The aroma of their untouched coffee filled the living room.

In the plantation, she had had only leaves and hard earth for a mattress. Here on the bed, there were sheets that were soft and slippery on the skin.

In the morning, her hair wet from the shower, Longgom prepared breakfast. Her brown face shone. She licked her red lips a few times after tasting the coffee she had made for Tondi.

As he left the house, Tondi was surprised to find that the city felt strange. Quiet. Virtually no traffic. What was going on?

He drove to the office. All was quiet. Not like usual. There was only the night watchman who had not returned home because his shift replacement had not yet arrived.

Inside, Mrs Sunarya was on the phone. She signalled for Tondi to sit down. Soon after, she put down the phone and, as she came towards Tondi, said:

'Something important happened early this morning.'

'What?'

'It's still unclear. Sunarya just called. There's information that some generals were kidnapped.'

'That's serious. Who?'

'Important people.'

Tondi imagined that if Pardomutua had been kidnapped it would surely be for ransom money. Like in the films. He headed those big government enterprises. He must be rich.

And that early morning was an important turning point for Indonesia. Sukarno fell. Suharto rose. That morning was 1 October 1965.

Chapter 20

Jakarta, 1966. Now wheels were not just turning, but crazily spinning. Destinies upturned. Only a few months ago there had been mass gatherings praising President Sukarno. Now the current was moving in the opposite direction. Demonstrations attacking him. Calls for him to be tried. Where had all these accusers been before? They seemed to suddenly appear out of nowhere. Before, it had felt as though everyone in Jakarta supported the revolution and Sukarno: 'Live or die we support Bung Karno.' The mass gatherings were huge. Everyone was passionate about volunteering for the Crush Malaysia campaign. Now, all had changed.

To Tondi, the clamour of the Sukarno supporters back then was no different to the clamour now of those attacking him. Buses transported the supporters, group after group. Whereas previously they went to the stadium, now they went to the State Palace. No problem. Wherever they wanted to go was fine by him as long as they paid the bus hire.

Sometimes Tondi got the urge to know how his father was faring. Pardomutua was a supporter of the great leader of the revolution, Bung Karno. He never appeared in the newspapers any more. Where was he? But then Tondi's busy days made him forget him. Recently he had been in frequent contact with his mother in Pekanbaru. She now had a telephone installed in her shop and in her house, and could call Tondi whenever she felt like it. When the phone rang late at night Tondi would think it was something important, but it was only his mother.

'I just wanted to hear your voice,' she would say. This made Tondi laugh, especially because she would speak Indonesian to him with a Riau-Malay accent. And he would be relieved. They would chat about this and that, especially about Batak people in Jakarta, and particularly anyone from Siantar. His mother would usually know them, and they her. But the one person they never talked about was Pardomutua. To her, he no longer existed. And yet, wasn't Tondi's existence proof that he had once meant something to her? But that is how it was. Tondi did not want to think about him too much.

One day Tondi invited Masrul and his family to Puncak, in the hills outside of Jakarta, where he owned a bungalow. Tondi went on ahead with Longgom and her son. A few days earlier he had spoken to both Habibah and Longgom. Separately. He had told Habibah about Tarsingot, and had told Longgom that he wanted her to meet Tando. As usual when he had something important to say, he had done this when lying beside each one, stroking her hair.

When Masrul and his family arrived, Masrul took the three girls off for a walk to buy some fruit and vegetables from the roadside stalls. Longgom and Tarsingot were playing in the garden. Habibah approached, and she and Longgom looked at each other. Each knew about the other. They shook hands. Then, Habibah holding Tando's hand, and Longgom Tarsingot's, they entered the bungalow.

Tondi was sitting inside, watching them. The two boys looked just like brothers. They all sat on the sofa. For a few moments everyone looked at each other. Even the two boys. The two mothers looked at the boys. This was the first time they had all seen one another.

These two women were the mothers of his sons. But Tondi was no polygamist. They were not his wives, nor was he their second husband. Tando was Masrul's son. Tarsingot was Sibalatuk's. It was not marriage that made him like a father to these boys, but his feeling and belief that they were indeed the fruit of his loins.

The strength of his feeling for the boys drove his love for their mothers. Yes, it had started as lust, but now with the children, his feeling for the women had deepened to love. And if his love provided the basis for their happiness, then he would bestow it freely.

'Tando, Ingot, why don't you go outside and play,' Tondi said.

The two boys ran outside, hand in hand.

Tondi looked at the two women, one by one. They were both in their prime. One had golden skin the colour of *langsat* fruit, the other had light brown skin like *sawo*. They both had eyes that shone with brightness, fine noses, thin lips and well-formed chins. How lucky he was to be a man beside them, he thought.

'Habibah, Longgom, this is not about us,' Tondi said. Tondi was no longer addressing either of them as 'Kak'. He used their names directly, which made them feel close. 'This is about our children,' he went on. His using the word 'our' also gave them a warm feeling.

'I love you both. I am grateful that you bore all the costs of giving birth and have raised the boys in difficult circumstances. I will love you all forever.'

There were tears. The two women wiped their eyes. The tears were not of sadness, but soothing emotion that went deep into the heart.

'Habibah, I have already talked to Uda Masrul. I am going to adopt Tando. Tarsingot too.'

Habibah was stunned. Longgom briefly took her hand. Then the two women fell on Tondi, pressing their faces on each side of his neck.

Tondi arranged for the adoption, and the two boys officially became his sons. The way he saw it, adoption was not just a matter of status recognized by the state, but it was fulfilment of his own longing to become an amang, a father to his sons.

* * *

The situation in Jakarta was increasingly confused, and the pressure on President Sukarno grew. Demonstrations spread to all the major cities. Some of Sukarno's supporters in the regions organized counter demonstrations. Indonesia was on the threshold of civil war. Finally, President Sukarno issued a letter officially ordering General Suharto to manage security and social order. And how General Suharto exploited that order! Sukarno became his chief target. Was Sukarno really the source of all the political chaos? That's what the newspapers said. Whether true or false, only Suharto knew. There followed a political process to erode Sukarno's power and strengthen General Suharto's, until finally Sukarno was stranded at his home in house arrest. An old man, sick and lonely.

None of this political chaos involved Tondi. He continued to lead his life like water flowing in a river. Water flowing freely to the sea, not heeding any slippages on banks left or right, nor fallen trees or rolling rocks. As long as nothing obstructed his flow, Tondi did not care. But if anything got in the way of his business, he would step in with his iron fists.

When people started to be arrested, this did not affect him. Some were imprisoned. Some were killed. The kidnapping and murder of the generals had led to revenge, with the arrest and murder of hundreds of thousands of people. This was political contest, not war, but it brought death.

Still, politics did not touch Tondi. He was busy arranging a trip to Batak country. He had sent ahead someone he knew, a Batak elder who lived in Jakarta, and asked him to make preparations. Tondi had given him money to buy a few buffalo and other requirements.

In due course, the family group flew to Medan and then drove to Ompu Silangit's village. Tondi was taking his two sons to visit the graves of his grandparents.

'I want both of you to pray now, in whatever way your mothers have taught you,' Tondi said. 'These are the graves of my grandfather and grandmother. They are your great-grandfather and great-grandmother. You must call your great-grandfather "amang" and your great-grandmother "inang". This is the Batak way, because your father's grandparents are once again called father and mother by your generation.'

Tondi held a ceremonial horja to mark his sons' acceptance into their marga. The feast was an offering to the ten generations of ancestors gone before. Tondi wanted his ancestors to accept his two sons as part of their marga. The last time there had been a horja here was at the burial of his grandfather, and before that, at the burial of his grandmother. There were buffalo slaughtered, and the village, especially the followers of the ancient Batak religion, had borne all the costs.

The Batak gondang drums played. Guests performed the traditional tortor dance to honour Tondi and the ancestors who they believed were present to give their blessing. It is no easy thing to enter a marga. It is not for just anyone. The continuation of marga can happen only through biological descent and legal marriage. People might not know of the biological tie of Tondi with the two boys. Legally, they were the sons of Masrul and Sibalatuk, and were only Tondi's adopted sons. However, now with this ceremony, the two would become fully his sons, according to Batak tradition, and would therefore enter his marga. Tondi hoped that his ancestors of ten generations would know that the boys were his sons, and that he felt and believed them to be the fruit of his loins.

Habibah was deeply moved by the feast. The moment her son was officially accepted into the marga, she felt as though she was truly Tondi's wife. She loved him even more. *He is the father of my son. How is it possible for me to obtain such a blessing from that single night of passion?* Her body heated when she thought of it.

To Longgom, this ceremonial feast was nothing new. There were many feasts like this where she came from in Sipirok. But secretly she did feel released from the tie that tethered her to her cousin and husband, Sibalatuk. Her child who came from the seed of another man now shared his marga, as he would with a true father. *And he is my husband under the sky and the moon that witnessed our union in the coffee plantation.*

After the ceremony was over, Tondi took the mothers and their boys out sightseeing. They went to Sitongging, Samosir and Pusuk Buhit. Lake Toba was like paradise. Its blue surface reflected the clouds. Mountain ridges ringed the lake. They spent days driving around and completely forgot the world outside. The two women felt as though it was a honeymoon. Tondi was more focused on showing the boys places and telling them stories. It made him happy. And it made the women happy to see him so close to his sons.

Tondi then took them to Sarulla. To the interior, following village tracks, climbing the lonely hills. Tarsingot had to meet the old couple in the coffee plantation. Longgom met her parents with sobs and embraces. The old woman looked at Tondi, and said something straight from her heart:

'I will always pray for you all.'

It was time to return to Jakarta, but before they left, the boys had to pay a last visit to the grave of Ompu Silangit. A car was parked at the foot of the hill.

A man was kneeling near the grave. At the sound of Tondi and the boys' footsteps, he turned. His eyes collided with Tondi's. Dull, lifeless eyes. Red eyes, moist with tears. He wiped them when he saw Tondi.

Brigadier General Pardomutua. But no uniform in sight.

Tondi looked away and made a sign for Tando and Tarsingot to pray. They approached the grave. Tando, whose mother was Malay, and Tarsingot, whose mother was Batak, said the Al-Fatihah verse together as loud as they could. Then they went to Tondi's grandmother's grave and did the same thing. This is the way they had been taught to pray.

Pardomutua watched, amazed. Tondi paid him no heed. He did not care whether the Debata di Banua Ginjang would hear this Islamic prayer. To him, it was no different to the Christian prayers his mother used to say. He was sure that the gods that Ompu Silangit had worshipped would hear all prayers.

They left, without speaking. Not a word. Only the sound of the Al-Fatihah had broken the silence. They left the man there in front of Ompu Silangit's grave. What did he want? He might be Ompu Silangit's son, but why was he there alone?

Tondi straightened his shoulders and got into his car waiting at the foot of the hill. They returned to Jakarta.

* * *

Habinsaran greeted Tondi at the office. 'Well, Lae, that was a long visit home,' he said. Tondi just laughed.

'So where are we going to eat?' This was their standard greeting. One of them would say it, and sometimes they would say it simultaneously.

'Seeing you're just back from the homeland, you won't be homesick for Batak food,' Habinsaran said.

'Right. A Deli restaurant then,' Tondi said.

On the way in the car, Habinsaran said, 'So, Lae, you must've read that Brigadier General Pardomutua has been arrested.'

'No, I hadn't heard.'

'He was arrested when boarding the plane in Medan, about to return to Jakarta.'

'Oh, really,' Tondi said, keeping his voice flat.

'Who knows what he was doing in Medan. They were searching for him here. They had asked us at police headquarters to help.'

'What has he done?'

'There were many reasons for his arrest. He's always been close to the communists. And they say he was corrupt.'

'Sounds bad. Communist and corrupt too,' Tondi said.

'Well, as for him being a communist, that's not certain. Could've just been a way to get close to Sukarno. A lot of important people did that. Now I see some of those former Sukarno supporters helping the students demonstrate against him. Even those in the army who supported Sukarno aren't necessarily communist. But as for his being corrupt, well that story's been going around for a while. Did you ever see his house at Kebayoran? Like a palace . . .'

It seemed that Habinsaran's curiosity about Pardomutua had led him to obtain a whole cache of information. Pardomutua was Batak.

His wife was Javanese, from an aristocratic family in Solo. His wife was Muslim. He had become Muslim.

'As for whether or not he was circumcised before he married, I don't have that information,' Habinsaran said. Tondi roared with laughter.

'And?'

'Well, when he was heading those state enterprises, it seems he siphoned off funds for political purposes,' Habinsaran went on. 'Funded huge meetings of mass organizations. Circumcising a bit off the top for himself too, of course. He had this flash house with a swimming pool. Jakarta has problems with clean water, and he had a pool! Now, you could understand a goldfish pond. Delicious cooked in spicy tomato sauce. And he had a fancy car. A Cadillac, like Sukarno's. And in Solo, another house, a mini palace. Three kids, all girls. When the eldest got married, he held the reception at the Hotel Indonesia. Sukarno came as a guest. Then a second reception in Solo. People said he was trying to outdo royalty. I don't know if that was true or not. I've never been to a royal reception in Solo. But what is true is that it cost hundreds of millions of rupiah.'

'Your information is really complete, Lae,' Tondi said.

'Of course. I'm in intelligence,' Habinsaran said as they got out of the car.

'Will he be tried?'

'I don't think so.'

'Pretty cosy for him, then,' Tondi said.

'Cosy, you say? Suharto will definitely detain him without trial. He could be killed like other communists. The worst thing is that they will seize all his possessions. I heard that army intelligence has already gathered information about his assets. That'll be hard for him, especially for his kids who are used to the good life.'

They ate. The sun outside was hot. Heat hovered on the asphalt, making ripples of heat haze. The fan in the restaurant was circulating air, but it was not enough to cool bodies hot from eating curry.

So that's how it is, Tondi thought. Strange, the way destiny is determined by the gods. Tondi had met him. Probably

Pardomutua had been confused about how to face the situation encircling him. But he was wrong to go to the grave to ask for Ompu Silangit's protection. Ompu Silangit was a master of Batak knowledge, but how can the dead protect someone guilty of corruption? You might be able to summon spirits, but not to protect those who have done wrong. Spirits come only to give guidance. To show the way.

That scene from years ago flashed into his mind. When his grandmother had died and Pardomutua arrived, an important person who the local officials treated with respect. It seemed that this kind of respect was what he craved. His eyes had glazed over when Tondi had handed him the sacred staff, the Tunggul Panaluan. Ompu Silangit had asked Tondi to hand it to him, the staff essential for traditional ceremonies. Pardomutua had taken it and then had casually just put it on the floor. He clearly did not know its importance. Then his adjutant, a soldier, had carried it to their car. The scene was clearly mapped on Tondi's eyes, but blurred because of the tears. He had cried when people at the funeral had asked Pardomutua to take his son to Jakarta. Tondi had refused. Even though he was still a child, he knew that his father was relieved when he refused. His son would just be a nuisance there.

When Ompu Silangit died, Pardomutua did not come. People in the village said that he could not get there because of the PRRI rebellion. But maybe it was because Ompu Silangit was a datu bolon, and therefore there would be a huge feast attended by all the followers of the Batak religion. Pardomutua was an important figure in Jakarta and known as being Muslim. He would not want to be seen attending such a gathering. His visit would certainly be reported in the papers. What would people in Jakarta say when they found out that he was the son of a Batak traditional priest? His reputation would be ruined.

Oh yes, the respect that came from his rank and wealth were extremely important to Pardomutua. Was that why he had left his wife? Tondi thought of his mother. All she ever got from that man was suffering.

Oh, Ompung, Grandfather, your son was no son to you. I, your grandson, will not desert you. But how can I possibly follow you?

When he had lived with his grandfather, Ompu Silangit had never taught him about the ancient Batak religion, only how to read the old manuscripts in Batak script with their mantra for summoning good spirits and repelling bad ones. His grandfather had always said that only those with a clean heart could use the mantra. Was his father's heart clean, Tondi wondered, as he stood beside Ompu Silangit's grave?

Habinsaran had said Pardomutua was being held in Salemba jail. That was where communists and fanatic Sukarno supporters were detained. And sure enough, as Habinsaran had said, Pardomutua's assets were seized, including gold in bank deposits. His family had been evicted from their luxury house. Habinsaran did not know where they had gone.

Lieutenant Colonel Untung and his subordinates had kidnapped and killed some generals. That entire operation lasted only a few hours in the early morning of 1 October 1965. But the consequences were lasting, not only on the families of those murdered generals, but on hundreds of thousands of others. Including Pardomutua, a soldier and loyal follower of Sukarno who had once been respected in Batak lands.

* * *

Years passed. Communists were imprisoned, and for some of them, this probably saved their lives. Those who were not imprisoned were either in graves or their corpses had been thrown into rivers or down ravines. The army under Suharto annihilated people considered to be communist. Many never thought they were communist. How could they be, when the leftist mass organizations had been targeting them? Pardomutua, whose life had been so extravagant, was accused of being a city-devil, a capitalist-bureaucrat who had diverted funds to workers' organizations. He escaped being a direct target as a communist.

Well, Tondi thought, let Pardomutua cry over his fate there in Salemba prison. Maybe in his narrow cell he would visit his tondi, his spirit that gives him life. As a Batak and the son of Ompu Silangit, Suharto should not crush him. If his spirit were strong, no power could crush him. He might be Ompu Silangit's flesh and blood, but had he absorbed his beauty of behaviour and strength of spirit? In Jakarta he had enjoyed superficial respect, thinking rank and wealth to be strength in life. But they are nothing more than tilled fields or trodden earth. As you till, so shall you reap. As you tread the earth, so shall you find your path. Rotten and greedy or healthy and noble are life choices. If Pardomutua had thought that respect gained from power and wealth would last forever, he was wrong. Power and wealth are never eternal.

Tondi was used to being solitary. On certain nights he had no need of company. He wanted solitude. Although he had been baptized Christian as a child, since becoming adult he had never gone to church. He had never liked church hymns. He did not like noise. But he was also not a follower of the ancient Batak religion, because he did not know its rituals. He just liked times of solitude. He enjoyed silence, when he felt he could be in dialogue with his tondi.

At such times, that recurring scene would come to mind, the moment he handed over the Tunggul Panaluan. Where was that sacred staff? If his father had treasured this heirloom, would he be in the predicament he was in now? As a Batak, he ought to have known the value of this staff used to connect to the gods. He would not have lived an extravagant life. He would not have been involved in corruption. Then there was that other recurring scene, when his father knelt beside Ompu Silangit's grave. Why did he go all the way to the grave when he had the Tunggul Panaluan that could have connected him with Ompu Silangit's spirit?

Tondi was anxious. His grandfather had begun visiting him in his sleep.

'You must not reject your father,' his grandfather would say.

'But he rejected me, his own son! He rejected his own father and his own mother! What kind of a man is that?' Tondi would reply.

But his grandfather would only look at him, eyes open wide, and then vanish. Tondi would wake up.

And again.

'He did not recognize his own son, did not recognize his father. What kind of Batak is that?'

'But you have his blood. You have his marga, through him,' Tondi's ompung would say softly. Tondi wanted to reply, but he could never hold that image long enough before it disappeared.

Tondi was confused. The climax came when not his grandfather, but his grandmother appeared and said to him, speaking in Batak:

'Manang beha pe, pahompukku do i, itomu do i. Despite all, they are also my grandchildren, they are your sisters.'

This no longer concerned Pardomutua.

Tondi awoke, agitated. In the stillness and solitude of the quiet house, surged a flood of deep sobbing that he could not restrain. The gentle face of his grandmother. She who had fed him as a child, spooning food into his mouth even as he was getting ready for school. She who had walked with him every day to the foot of the hill. She who had waited there again when school ended. Oh, ompungboru! If she was also visiting him, why was he being so resistant?

He went to see Sunarya who had now been promoted to lieutenant colonel. His office was still at army headquarters.

'So you mean to say that General Pardomutua is your father? I would never have guessed,' Sunarya said after Tondi explained.

'Yes. That's how it is. When he had his position, we had no contact. I never met him, not even once.'

'So he didn't know you had joined the PRRI?'

'No. We never met.'

'You don't need to worry about him. He'll be released soon,' Sunarya said.

'It's not about him. I don't care how long he's in prison.'

'What is it then?'

'It's his family.'

'I don't know anything about his family, Tondi,' Sunarya said, reverting to his heavy Sundanese accent.

'So what can I do?' Tondi asked.

'Well, I can give you a letter for the head of Salemba prison. You can go there and ask whether Pardomutua has any family visitors. How's that?'

'Oh yes, that's a good idea.'

When Tondi next met Habinsaran, he also told him about his tie to Pardomutua.

'If I'd known, I could've put aside some of his assets for you, Lae,' Habinsaran said.

'Cut it out. That's not what I meant,' Tondi said.

'But according to the law, you, as his son, are entitled to some inheritance.'

'According to the law, a son must also pay off his father's debts when his father dies. Isn't that right? And tell me who wants that?' Tondi replied.

'Well, Suharto's gang have gobbled up all those assets anyway. There's nothing left for you,' Habinsaran said.

'Stop worrying about assets. I'm only worried about his children. They're my father's daughters, my sisters, my ito.'

'Yes, that's true, Lae. And if their fate is the same as the family of other detainees, then your marga, yours and theirs that is, is broken.

* * *

Pardomutua's family was in a bad way. The eldest daughter was divorced. Even in their misery, there had still been more to come. The daughter's husband had divorced her on the grounds that he did not want anything to do with communists. He was an official in a government department. He had been proud enough when President Sukarno had come to his wedding reception. Now he got rid of his wife. Everyone shunned the family.

Mami Ana passed Tondi some information about a daughter of some former big shot who was working as an entertainer in a nightclub. A young divorcee. Evidently, she had to work there to support her younger sisters. Tondi immediately sought out the address of the family.

As Sunarya had suggested, there had been family visiting Pardomutua in jail, and had filled in the visitors' register. Tondi eventually found the address. They were living in the Bukit Duri area. Tondi knew it well. It was a poor area where he had found Longgom. Houses crowded together in tiny alleyways not big enough for a car to enter.

It was a small house down an alleyway. The bottom half of the house was brick, the top half wooden planks. He was invited into the tiny living room. The floors were rough tiles. The wooden walls had been painted white, but parts were eaten away. The house was stuffy, the ceilings low. The cramped quarters meant there was virtually no ventilation in the house.

A mother with her three daughters. The mother still had the look of a Solonese upper-class woman about her. She was wearing a casual dress that flattered her slim body. But her face was worn and sad. The three daughters were all simply dressed, but their natural beauty shone through.

Tondinihuta introduced himself, but the women and girls were suspicious. They sat on rattan chairs, some of which were coming apart. Plastic flowers in a vase. There were only enough chairs for four, so one of the girls sat on the arm of her mother's chair. She had to take care, because the chair was unstable.

'Father never mentioned he had a son,' the mother said. The three girls studied Tondi's face.

'He does look like Papa, Ma,' one of them said.

'Well, he had no need to say that he had a son,' Tondi said. He felt bitterness on his tongue when he said it.

'So why do you feel the need to meet us now? We have nothing at all,' the mother said, her voice sticking in her throat.

'I want to know something. My father took a long, carved staff from the village. Is it still here?'

'Father had it for only a short time. He gave it to someone. I don't know who. We don't know,' the mother said.

Tondi felt his heart being sliced to pieces. His ompung's face flashed before him. He was dumbstruck for a few moments. The mother's voice jolted him:

'Is that the only reason you're here?'

Tondi was unnerved.

'Yes. Well, I also got a feeling I should check how you all are.'

'What for?'

'I heard that one of your girls is working in a night club.'

All four looked down. One started to cry.

'Why have you come here to humiliate us like this?' asked the mother, her voice quavering. 'Our family is destroyed. We've reached the absolute bottom. Why hurt us like this?'

'I didn't mean to,' Tondi said.

One of girls stood.

'Yes. I'm a nightclub hostess. So what? What does this have to do with you, mister, that you can insult the Pardomutua family?' she demanded, her voice rising.

'No, no, that's not it,' Tondi said.

'So?' The girl sat down again and put her face in her hands, hiding her tears.

The other three glared at Tondi. Finally, he spoke slowly, 'According to Batak custom, you girls are my ito, my sisters. I know you have never been to Batak territory. But we all share the same grandfather, we have the same ompung. He died. His son, your father, does not want to use his marga. But as a Batak he has a marga, as do you. You and I are of the same marga.'

Quiet for a few moments. The girls and their mother looked at him, without blinking.

'If you wish, you can attach the marga to your name. You are *boru* in our marga. If you marry, I can represent your father. I have the responsibility to support you, to care for you. That is how it is in Batak custom.'

Moments went by. No one spoke.

'As your brother, I cannot let you have a bad life,' Tondi said.

Still the four remained silent. The room was still. Only the noise of the neighbours outside penetrated the walls.

'I want to help you. You do not need to tell your father. I just do not want you working in a nightclub. I will cover the costs of your schooling. I will help with whatever you need.'

The four were speechless.

'You do not need to tell your father,' Tondi stressed again. 'I don't want that. I don't want to meet him. I'm helping you not because you are my father's daughters, but because you are my grandfather's granddaughters.'

'But . . . why?' asked the mother.

Tondi looked at her long and hard. He saw the dull light in her eyes and the lines at the corners of her eyes. A woman raised in luxury, now living in poverty in Jakarta.

Tondi did not know exactly what they had experienced. He had heard from Habinsaran that many wives of people accused of being communist had been sexually abused by their husbands' interrogators. They took advantage of the situation to abuse them, on the pretext of calling them in for more information. Had this mother and her daughters suffered such humiliation? So many peoples' lives had been destroyed since Suharto took power. Who knows how many mothers had to hide their shame? If your heart was fragile, your life would be destroyed.

Tondi thought of his own mother. She was rock solid. Her face would set, and she would hit back at anyone who bothered her. She had not collapsed when her husband left her. She had become like granite. Women everywhere take on a burden when their husbands leave them. Fragile or solid, it's all the same. Women should not suffer like this. Tondi could feel his chest tightening.

'But why . . . ?' the mother asked again.

Tondi answered sharply.

'I just told you. The three girls are my grandfather's granddaughters. They are my ito!'

That was it. No more than that. He did not want them to hear any tremble of sadness in his voice. How could he explain that his ompung often visited him? That was all too complicated.

Tondi left some money. He found a house for the four of them. From then on, he sent Masrul to visit and take them money regularly.

He did not want to meet Pardomutua. To him that man had gone, swallowed by the past. One generation had to be declared lost. The only thing he wanted was to share love, with his sons, with his family, in this journey of life.

List of main characters

(Compiled by the translator)

Fictional characters

Tondinihuta, Tondi: Tondi's full name is Tondi ni huta, or spirit of the huta. The word *tondi* refers to one's life spirit, but every person has more than one tondi (see glossary). Born in 1940 during Dutch colonial rule, Tondi spends much of his childhood living with his grandparents. He is the main storyteller.

Ompu Silangit: The grandfather of Tondinihuta and father of Pardomutua. Ompu Silangit's childhood name was Rajabondar. He fought in the Batak War (1878–1907) alongside the Batak king Singamangaraja XII (d. 1907) and was imprisoned by the Dutch after that war. At the birth of his first son, Silangit, he became known as Amani Silangit (father of Silangit). After the Batak War, he was given the honorific title Ompu, and became known as Ompu

313

Silangit (*ompu* can mean honorary elder or grandfather). Later, when he became a grandfather to Tondinihuta, his earlier name had stuck, so he was not then called Ompung Tondinihuta as should have been the case.

Silangit: The first-born son of Ompu Silangit, whose mother died when he was a young child and when his father was away fighting the Dutch. As a young adult, Silangit leaves his father and cuts ties with his family and marga.

Pardomutua: The second-born son of Ompu Silangit (by Ompu Silangit's second wife) and father of Tondinihuta. Husband of Halia. At the time of his marriage (late Dutch-colonial time), he is working as a clerk at a Dutch rubber plantation. Pardomutua joins the Indonesian volunteer army established by the Japanese during their occupation of Indonesia (1942–1945). He deserts his wife and baby son (Tondi) and moves to Jakarta where he has another family. He later holds high rank in Indonesia's national army and is close to President Sukarno.

Halia: Tondi's mother, also known as Ina ni si Tondi, mother of Tondi. Wife of Pardomutua, who she marries at sixteen during the late Dutch-colonial time and goes with him to a Dutch rubber plantation near Siantar, where her son Tondi is born. When the Japanese arrive, she and her baby son stay with her in-laws (Ompu Silangit and his wife). Later, when Indonesia is newly independent and her husband has left her, she returns to Siantar where she works for a while in a government hospital kitchen before opening a fried-banana stall.

Ompungboru: Ompu Silangit's second wife. Mother of Pardomutua. Grandmother of Tondi. She comes from the village where Ompu Silangit was sent by the Dutch after the Batak War and given land as a form of house arrest.

Lasmia: A young girl/woman from Ompu Silangit's village who helps out in his house. She later accompanies Tondi's mother in Pekanbaru. Lasmia's father, Luhut, is related to Ompu Silangit's wife.

Habibah: A Deli Malay woman (Malay from the Sumatran east coast) who Tondi meets when working as bus conductor. Wife of Masrul. Mother of four children, including the boy Tando.

Masrul: Husband of Habibah. Soldier in the PRRI rebellion who becomes Tondi's closest companion.

Ompu Bulung: Strange old man Tondi meets during his trek in the forest who takes him to meet inhabitants of the spirit world.

Longgom: Woman Tondi meets during his trek in the forest, when he stays with her father-in-law Sibalok, mother-in-law, and husband Sibalatuk. She is mother of the boy, Tarsingot.

Bagio: Former freedom fighter and former sergeant major in military police. Now commander of a company of rebel soldiers fighting in the PRRI rebellion against the central government, which Tondi joins when he emerges from his forest trek.

Pardapdap: Soldier, former freedom fighter, and Tondi's neighbour in Siantar who deserts the military police to join Colonel Simbolon. He encourages Tondi to join the rebels and becomes Tondi's platoon commander.

Doctor Herman: Dutch doctor who, during the colonial time, lived and worked in North Sumatra. During the Japanese occupation, he and his wife are interned, and at the end of the war they return to Holland. After the death of his wife, Doctor Herman returns to newly independent Indonesia and works at the government hospital in Siantar where he meets Halia.

Sunarya: Former freedom fighter, an army captain (later major) from West Java (Sunda) who is part of the national army fighting the rebels in North Sumatra. He arrests Tondi, who becomes his driver. After the rebels surrender, Tondi accompanies him to Java. Sunarya and his wife become Tondi's transport business partners. Sunarya later works at the army headquarters in Jakarta.

Habinsaran: A Batak police inspector at the West Java command in Bandung. Formerly an intelligence gatherer for the Japanese, then involved in intelligence for the Indonesian army, before joining the police. Runs a protection racket for Batak thugs in Bandung, has links to Jakarta underworld, and becomes Tondi's business partner.

Tando: The son of Habibah, fathered by Tondi

Tarsingot: The son of Longgom, fathered by Tondi

Mami Ana: Madam of prostitutes working in Jakarta who Tondi sets up to run a call-girl service.

Historical characters

Singamangaraja XII (also Si Singamangaraja; Sisingamangaraja): (1849–1907). 'Si' is an honorific. The last Batak priest king who led a long war against the Dutch (1898–1907) and was killed in a clash with Dutch troops on 17 June 1907.

President Sukarno (1901–1970) also referred to as 'Bung Karno': Nationalist and revolutionary who became Indonesia's first president (1945–1967) and together with (vice president) Moh. Hatta, declared Indonesia's independence on 17 August 1945. After a coup and counter-coup in 1965, he was out-manoeuvred by General Suharto, and died under house arrest in 1970.

General Nasution (1918–2000): Army general, a Batak born to a Muslim family in North Sumatra. Became army chief of staff. Fiercely anti-communist and a powerful political figure.

Colonel Simbolon (1916–2000): Commanding officer of first military region and regional regimental commander (East Sumatra) headquartered in Medan who, frustrated with the national government's rejection of demands for more regional autonomy, usurped civil government, and on 22 December 1956 announced a military takeover in North Sumatra. On 27 December he was overthrown by officers loyal to the national government. Simbolon fled to Tapanuli and led the insurgency.

Lieutenant Colonel Ahmad Husein (1925–1998): Renowned freedom fighter, regimental commander in Padang, Central Sumatra, and leader of the Dewan Banteng or Buffalo Council (one of the army councils established in 1956). Leader of central command of the insurgency.

General (later President) **Suharto** (1921–2008): Army general who took control after the coup and counter-coup of 1965, and became Indonesia's second President in 1967.

Timeline of historical events

(Compiled by the translator)

Paderi/Padri War (1803–37)
War in west Sumatra. The 'padri' were Muslim clerics who wanted to impose Sharia law and purge local culture of beliefs and practices considered un-Islamic. The Padri attacked the southern Batak lands in the 1820s–30s, bringing terrible destruction and forcing survivors (the Mandailing and Angkola) to become Muslim.

Batak War (1878–1907)
War of Batak peoples against encroaching Dutch colonization, led by the last Batak priest-king, Si Singamangaraja XII, who was killed in battle on 17 June 1907.

Aceh War (1873–1903)
Armed conflict between the Sultanate of Aceh and the colonizing Dutch, which ended Aceh's independence. While the Aceh sultan and other leaders submitted in 1903, fighting in the highlands continued until 1912.

Japanese Occupation (1942–1945)
The Japanese occupied the Dutch East Indies (later Indonesia) during World War II from March 1942 until September 1945. Those Dutch who remained in the country were interned.

Indonesian Proclamation of Independence
On **17 August 1945**, after news of the Japanese surrender in WWII (on 15 August 1945) had been confirmed, president-to-be Sukarno and vice president-to-be Hatta proclaimed Indonesia an independent republic.

Indonesia's fight for independence; also called **the Revolution (August 1945–December 1949)**
Indonesian freedom fighters fought against the returning Dutch who wanted to reclaim their former colony. At the same time, Indonesian negotiators continued the diplomatic fight for a settlement.

Transfer of Sovereignty
On **27 December 1949**, the territory of the Netherlands East Indies was transferred to the Indonesian government after four and a half years of fighting and negotiation. However, the Dutch retained West Papua (West Irian) as their colony.

Military manoeuvres in Sumatra, (1956–1957)
In December 1956, regimental commanders of Central Sumatra, North Sumatra (Colonel Simbolon) and South Sumatra took over civilian government, formed army councils and began introducing autonomy measures. On **27 December 1956** local officers in Medan overthrew Colonel Simbolon, a Toba Batak, who withdrew to the Toba Highland stronghold of Tapanuli. President Sukarno and Army Chief-of-Staff Nasution persuaded other Karo Batak (and Malay) officers to move against them. In **September–October 1957**, Simbolon and the other military dissidents formulated demands to the central government, which were rejected.

PRRI (*Pemerintah Revolusioner Republik Indonesia*: **Revolutionary Government of the Republic of Indonesia) (1958–1961)**
Name of the rebel government proclaimed on **15 February 1958** in Sumatra, with its headquarters in Bukittinggi, in opposition to the central government of Indonesia. Two days later, a separate rebel movement in Sulawesi, known as Permesta, pledged allegiance with the PRRI. The PRRI rebels officially surrendered on **12 August 1961**.

West Papua/ West Irian campaign (1961–1962)
After the transfer of sovereignty in 1949, the Dutch retained West Papua. In 1957, the UN failed to pass a resolution for the Dutch to negotiate a settlement with Indonesia on the issue. In December 1961, President Sukarno launched the military operation 'Operation Trikora' for the Liberation of West Irian. A ceasefire between the Netherlands and Indonesia was signed in August 1962, and the territory was formally ceded to Indonesia on 1 May 1963.

'Konfrontasi' anti-Malaysia campaign (1963–1966)
President Sukarno announced the campaign of 'Confrontation' on 27 July 1963 in opposition to the creation of the Federation of Malaysia, which became official in September 1963. The campaign involved armed incursions, bomb attacks and other destabilizing activities in the states included in the Malaysian Federation.

1965 Coup and counter-coup
On the night of 30 September–1 October 1965, a battalion of the palace guard and others abducted and murdered six generals and one aide in Jakarta and announced the '30 September movement' to protect Sukarno from an alleged planned coup by CIA-leaning generals. An immediate counter-coup took place, and General Suharto took control. The coup was blamed on the communists, and a long and brutal purge of communists, alleged communists and left-leaning Sukarno loyalists ensued.

1966 transfer of power to Suharto

On 11 March 1966, President Sukarno signed an order giving General Suharto authority to take measures 'deemed necessary' to restore order. This effectively transferred power to General Suharto who was made Indonesia's acting President in March 1967. President Sukarno remained under house arrest until his death in June 1970.

Glossary

(All words are Batak unless noted otherwise)

Adat   (Malay, Indonesian, Batak) customary law

Amang   Father. The word can also be used as a term of
                    endearment to a boy, as 'son'

Amani   Father of X. Once a man becomes a father, he is
                    known by the name of his firstborn child, whether
                    male or female (e.g. Amani Langit is Father
                    of Langit)

Amangboru   Uncle, specifically the uncle married to one's
                    father's sister (one's *inangboru*)

Amangtua   Uncle, specifically the older brother of one's
                    father, either literally or treated as such

Amanguda   Uncle, specifically the younger brother of
                    one's father

Anakboru   The marga that receives a bride from the bride-giving marga or hula-hula. Anakboru also means male 'in-law'

Banua Ginjang The world above. Heaven

Batak   Term used to designate the ethnic groups residing in Batak territory, who associate themselves with the genealogy of *Si Raja Batak* and the marga tied to kinship custom. Batak are subdivided into 6 subgroups based on language, namely (1) Karo (2) Pakpak and Dairi (3) Simalungun (4) Toba (5) Angkola and Sipirok and (6) Mandailing

Begu   Spirits of the dead who are still in the world and have not yet moved on to the world above. Every begu was once a *tondi*. Good begu protect their descendants and live in sacred places like trees, springs or hills. Malevolent begu can be employed for black magic. A *begu siar* can enter someone in trance

Bius   A ritual community comprising several huta, led by a *raja bius*, and having its own weekly market. The bius holds an annual 'cleansing ceremony' to offer thanks to the *Debata Mulajadi na Bolon* and *Debata di Banua Ginjang*

Boru Tulang see Tulang.

Datu   healer, spiritual healer

Datu bolon man of great spiritual powers

Debata di Banua Ginjang	Lord of the World Above
Debata Mulajadi na Bolon	Supreme Source of All Life
Gondang	Traditional Batak drum in many different sizes
Horja	Ceremonial feast
Hula-hula	The bride-giving marga (term used by Toba Batak)
Huta	A village or group of villages established by one marga branch. Its inhabitants include the huta founders (*raja ni huta*), their in-laws (*anak boru*), and newcomers. Spiritually, the huta is the place of residence that unites the children and grandchildren of a community. A group of huta forms a *bius*
Iboto, Ito	Sibling of different sex. A term used between different sex siblings of the same father; a brother to his sisters, a sister to her brothers. The term is also used more widely to those beyond one's immediate family, but still of the same marga
Inang, Ina	Mother. The term is also used as endearment for daughter or daughter-in-law. When a woman has a child, she is known as Mother of X, *Ina ni X*, whether that child is male or female
Inangboru	Aunt, specifically the sister of one's father; also a term of address used by a woman to her mother-in-law

Inangtua   Aunt, specifically the wife of one's *amangtua*

Kak   Malay/Indonesian non-gender-specific term of
                      address, literally '*kakak*', older sibling

Lae   brother-in-law; technically, a term for a man who
                      has married a woman from the other man's marga.
                      A term of address between men of relatively
                      same status

Mas   Javanese term of address for man; brother

Marga   Often translated into English as 'clan', marga is a
                      genealogical term referring to the descendants of
                      Si Raja Batak, who comprise the original group
                      and its branches. All Batak have a marga name
                      that marks which lineage they are from

Ompu   Respectful term of address for elder. Also
                      Grandfather. *Ompu ni* X is grandfather of X

Ompung   Grandfather (on either father's or mother's side).
                      The term can also be used in endearment, as
                      daompung, to address a grandchild (either gender)

Ompungboru   Grandmother (on either father's or mother's side)

Parbaringin   Priest of the old Batak religion

Parmalim   Follower of the Batak Religion known as *Ugamo
                      Malim*, the ancient religion that predated the
                      coming of Christianity and Islam to the area.
                      Followers worship the gods *Debata di Banua
                      Ginjang* and *Debata Mulajadi na Bolon*, and
                      respect the ancestors as founders of the marga.

Raja Si Singamangaraja is the supreme leader of
the Batak religion. Ceremonies are led by *raja bius*

Pustaha

Manuscripts usually written in the Batak
language and script on sheaves of bamboo or
bark, containing traditional teachings on healing,
medicine, prediction and mantras

Raja Bius

The male leader of a group of huta, known as a bius.
A bius is a ceremonial unit, and the *raja bius* has
the authority to lead traditional ceremonies.

**Raja Si
Singamangaraja**

The Batak king and leader of the Batak religion
known as Parmalim. The Batak kingship
descended for twelve generations and ended
with the death of Raja Singamangaraja XII.
The 'Si' before the name is an honorific.
(His Majesty, King Singamangaraja). Sometimes,
the name is written as Sisingamangaraja.

Ruma Bolon

The northern Batak traditional house. It is a large
wooden house raised on columns. The thatched
rumbia-leaf roof is curved in shape, inspired by
the back of a buffalo

Si Raja Batak

The Batak Adam. The legendary first Batak
priest-king who is the ancestor and source of all
the Batak marga

Tondi

Translated into English as 'spirit' or 'soul', the
Batak word *tondi* has a wider meaning as 'force' or
'life-energy'. In old Batak belief, every person has
three tondi: the *tondi sigonggoman* which is the
living spirit that stays with one's being; the *tondi
sijunjung* which is outside of one's being and is

one's protective guardian, and the *tondi sanggapati* which exists in one's placenta. The tondi within and outside of a person are able to communicate. If one is in a state of purity, one can connect with one's other tondi and ask for strength and protection.

Tortor Traditional Batak dance, which historically was used in rituals associated with spirits, danced by women and accompanied by traditional drums (gondang).

Tulang Uncle, specifically a brother of one's mother, but used more generally for male relative on one's mother's side. Also, a term of address of son-in-law to his father-in-law, or a term of greeting from members of the bride-receiving marga towards male members of the bride-giving marga. The daughter of one's tulang is called *boru tulang*. The wife of one's tulang is called *Nantulang*

Uda Term in Minang language to address older brother or older male

Ugamo Malim The traditional Batak religion. See Parmalim, above

Ulos A woven cloth used in traditional ceremonies. The cloth has three colours, white, red and black signifying the upper, central and lower worlds. The symbolic meaning is the giving of the bride-giving marga (*hula-hula*) to their *anak boru* or in-law marga

Ulubalang Warrior. Defender of the king, royal guard